LYRIC

KINGDOM OF FAIRYTALES
SEASON TWELVE

You all know the story of your favorite fairytale, but did you ever wonder what happened after the fairytale ending? Well we know. Not all afters end up happily, sometimes the real adventure starts much later...

Following famous fairytale characters, eighteen years after their happily ever after, the Kingdom of Fairytales offers an edge of the seat thrill ride in an all new and sensational way to read.

Lighting-fast reads you won't be able to put down

Fantasy has never been so epic!

QUEEN OF SKIES

4TH NOVEMBER

The leaf shone, catching the light on its way to the forest floor. I spotted it from several yards away and watched it drift, skating from side to side, reluctant to fall. My heart skipped, and I ran to it before its slow descent was complete. Swiping the large, ballooned leaf from the air, I shifted the satchel at my waist and slipped out a small pouch half-filled with pixie dust.

The dust clinging to the leaf was minuscule, but it added to my modest store. The leaves and the trees of Skyla, in fact, the entire island, needed to be coated in the stuff to remain afloat. I just needed a sprinkle of magic, a mere dash. Coupled with enough faith, the magical dust would keep me afloat as well. That, in turn, enabled me to fly. How long it lasted depended on how much I used. The faith part was no problem. As my best friend Whisper said, I had faith for days.

Dropping the leaf, and closing my pouch, I plucked my knife from the sheath around my thigh, tossed it in the air, and caught the handle on its way down. The perfectly balanced blade sang through the wind when I threw it across the forest into a knot on a far tree.

I grinned when I heard the melody of the discussion of a group of fairies as they conversed with their language of chimes. Following the melody, I plodded on. The job of collecting the dust continued. It was repeated until it grew dull. I had forgotten which way I'd come from, where I wanted to go, and what I wanted to do. Being half-lost was perhaps the only thrilling part of the entire episode because I had the security of knowing I was never fully lost. I could always climb a tree and see my way or ask a pixie to point me in the right direction.

Dozens and dozens, dare I say *hundreds*, of vacant floating islands surrounded Skyla's mainland, most only accessible by using dust to fly to them. Some were large enough to get lost on and others, small enough to hold only a single pixie oak. I spent my days exploring the islands, tossing my knife, and collecting dust. Since I was utterly forbidden to leave Skyla, it was all I could do to stay sane.

With a sigh, I threw my knife nowhere in particular. It skimmed between trees, and my heart leaped as it fled from my sight. A sudden bout of panic overwhelmed me. Peter had given me that knife. I'd had it since I was a child. He'd trained me with it.

I pounded over dead leaves, my moccasined feet finding the hard ground and never slipping. Desperate for a glimpse of the glittering blue of the sapphire-encrusted hilt, my gaze roamed the greens and browns of the forest. Light winked off the gems at a distance, and I drew a deep breath, ease rushing through me.

"That's enough excitement for the day, Lyric," I mumbled to myself, approaching the spot where my blade had landed true. "You'll give yourself a heart attack."

Before I clasped my knife, I noticed the barest sliver of a silver string dangling from it—pixie floss. There was no way I could have known it was there unless I was this close. Pulling my knife free, I lifted the sheer, thin thread dangling from somewhere above me that had been tied off just below where my knife had struck.

The sun lit the canopy as I peered up, trying to find the rest of the string. Pixies zipped from place to place, little more than cheery blips. But their distraction was hardly the reason I couldn't locate the floss's origin. It was too fine. I needed to be up there.

Exhaling, I slipped the long blade of my knife back into its sheath on my thigh. Then I lifted myself up into the tree, shimmying out onto a branch and holding myself steady with the trunk. My ears rang with the pixies' voices as they crowded me, each with something to say, some red-faced and upset I had entered the vicinity of their homes.

"Easy," I said. "I'm a friend of Peter's."

Their eyes went wide for a moment, then they gasped and cooed, delving into my blazing orange hair like it was some telltale sign. I had no idea how every pixie I'd ever met knew Peter. But that was consistently the case, no matter how far I went from the mainland and Aire, the capital City of Skyla. Maybe the legend of his adventures had spread to even the pixies he'd never met.

Of everyone on Skyla—maybe in all the kingdoms—he was the only person who could speak with the pixies in their language. However, I thought it was somehow more likely he knew every pixie personally. I wouldn't put the impossible past him.

"Can you help me?" I asked, figuring they weren't going to settle any time soon.

A pixie with brilliant pink hair stopped in front of my face and tilted her head. Her brows were pinched, and her eyes guarded, and she watched me intently. Pixies didn't share their dust with just anyone, and that was what most humans wanted from them.

"There's some pixie floss tied down there. I think I cut it by mistake. Do you know anything about it?" Hurriedly, I added, "If I've broken something, I want to fix it before I continue exploring."

Pixies, though temperamental and vibrant in every emotion, were generally very polite creatures.

The pink-haired one eased, smiled, and chimed something. The stir around me and in my hair settled a moment to gather replies. When the conversation stopped, she waved me on, out across the branch, and through the tree canopy.

I followed, struggling to keep up as the branch narrowed and bent beneath my weight. Looking back, the pixie zipped over, showering me in dust. My heart lightened with the rare but familiar touch of fresh magic skating over my skin. The feel of the branch disappeared. Nothing but air to hold me now.

My elation didn't appear to amuse the pixie, and she rolled her eyes before holding up a finger, chiding me, and likely instructing me on how little dust she'd provided, how short a time I'd be able to fly, and how I should follow her quickly. She'd led me just two trees over when the lightness slipped away, lowering me onto a branch.

She pointed down, and I followed the direction of her motion. There, lying across a branch, was a limp thread trailing farther into the distance. My eyes widened. "So it isn't yours? The pixies, I mean?"

Her head shook.

I peered at the thread, the taste of adventure on the tip of my tongue. "Thank you."

Nodding, she grinned and zipped away.

By now, the information that I was related to Peter had swept the entire island, so as I made my way over the branches, following the thread wherever it would lead, pixies dove past me, ogled my hair, gazed at my brown eyes, and laughed. I offered smiles, sighing to think what they must make of me. True, Peter had raised me—as weird as that seemed the older I got and the younger he stayed—but no blood connected us despite the resemblance.

Abandoned as a baby, I'd been told a woman had given me to him as a good luck charm for Skyla. Earlier in my life, I had wanted to know everything about the woman who may have been my mother, but Peter could only scratch his head, peer at the ceiling, and nod that she was beautiful, definitely beautiful. Even that detail had faded from his memory now. The one thing connected to my delivery that he hadn't forgotten was the fact I was Skyla's good luck charm. And that curse had followed me eighteen years, forbidding me from seeing the world with my best friend, Whisper.

An ember of sadness swelled in my chest, burning. I lived for Peter's stories of when he left on adventures. I lived for moments like this when I followed what was likely a discarded trail of thread through the treetops and told myself it was some huge mystery I had to solve.

Afternoon crept by overhead, and I winced. This was useless. I'd be better off heading back to the mainland and helping Tiger Lily with the shop. Prying my gaze from the branch before me, I looked straight ahead.

Everything in me stilled, consumed with a bursting excitement. Nestled a single tree away, was an elegant house with a sloping, dark roof and several feet of a wrap-around porch. It sat amidst the quiet canopy, no pixies troubling it.

My mouth remained agape. I had never come across a home anywhere but in Aire and the three residential bridged islands connected to it. Hell, I had never seen a house in the trees before. The trees were sacredly the pixies' home. Sometimes they didn't mind if you visited. If they liked you well enough, you could stick around for quite a while, but I couldn't so much as pluck leaves or shake off fresh dust without disrupting their lives enough to warrant shrill complaints and an onslaught of attacks.

Balancing across the branch I was on, I hopped off onto the porch of the treehouse. The sturdy wood didn't so much as creak with my weight. Glass windows framed the door; broad, slitted blinds obscured the interior. Nosily, I squinted through the barest cracks, but I couldn't make out much of anything other than shadows.

I knocked. I waited. No one appeared.

And yet, it was in perfectly kept condition. Someone lived here, so I couldn't just barge in. Biting my lip, I turned, following the pixie floss the rest of the way to whatever it was tied to. It connected to a rope ladder that spilled out of a square hole in the porch.

"Oops," I whispered. I thought perhaps I had ruined

a cleverly concealed trail to a secret hide-away. My lip chewing transformed into guilty gnawing. Whoever was out here didn't want to be found. Like. At all.

Ashamed, I had to apologize.

Plopping my ass down and dangling my legs out of the hole, I settled in for a late lunch. Eating the two pheasant sandwiches and pear I'd brought with me in my satchel stretched out for a good thirty minutes, but still, no one appeared.

I lay back against the porch, staring at the upside-down wooden house, wondering what secrets it held. Discovering hidden alcoves or giant, gnarled climbing trees were one thing, but to stumble upon something another human had made? That really was an adventure just waiting to be peeled apart.

My fingers skimmed over the sheath at my thigh. People who didn't want to be found had things to hide. Would they be dangerous? Maybe a long-lost pirate from the stories surrounding Peter's favorite trophy—a massive ship dubbed the Jolly Roger. As the story went, he'd flown it up from the sea and landed it on a small island near the mainland after defeating a most fearsome of captains.

"Ah, but none are as fearsome a captain as I, right, Lyric?" I could picture his bright brown eyes and wicked grin as I murmured his words. I ate those moments up, those moments when he'd drag me into his stories as if I had been there, fighting beside him. He'd plop a pirate hat on my head, tip it down, then get serious. Something Peter rarely got to enjoy. *It's because of you we defeated those pirates. Skyla's lucky charm.* By the time I had fixed the hat so I could see, he was back to normal, puffing his chest and claiming that he'd only ever share such credit with me. Most times, he could vanquish a thousand foes on his own, he would claim. "Must've been sick that day," I mimicked his exact words, then snorted, picturing him sniff and drift flawlessly into another tale.

Reminiscing and staring at the house led me into an hour of waiting, but my patience wore thin. "What are you doing?" I snapped at the quiet wood's owner. "Having a party somewhere? Hermits aren't supposed to...party."

My heart stopped.

The party. Whisper's birthday party. I promised her I'd meet her and help plan it today. An hour ago. Maybe longer.

A coarse word bubbled out of my throat as I shot upright, dug into my bag for my gloves, then took hold of the ladder. I slid the whole way to the ground, hitting it with a force that rattled my legs.

"Pardon me!" I called up to the trees. The pixies had been absent around the house, but I hoped one would hear me now. "I'm sorry to bother you! Could anyone point me toward Aire?"

The zipping lights paused, a soft buzz surrounding the area, then in unison they directed me right.

"Thank you so much!" The gratitude barely had a chance to escape before I was running, praying to the great airwoman in the skies that Whisper would find it in her heart not to kill me.

Whisper's hide-brown eyes stared at me, anything but the theme of her party on her mind. Her brow quirked. It dropped again. Her pink lips pursed, then eased. She raised a delicate finger to her cheek and tapped the dark skin with the most precise motions I had ever witnessed.

"I said I was painfully and tragically sorry."

"Hmm?" The syllable stretched. "I know. I forgive you, silly. What's an hour anyway, if not enough time to fall in love with a mysterious stranger deep in the woods? Perhaps some lone boy who also takes to adventuring the outer isles. Quiet. Strong. Enchanting in the *best* way." Her hands clasped, a tiny sigh adding to the dreamy glaze her eyes had adopted. It all shattered. "I mean, why else would you have forgotten this, the most important party I shall ever have?"

As she had said for her tenth, thirteenth, and sixteenth in turn. Nineteen was hardly a special number, but at this party was when she and her true love would finally begin their happily ever after—or so she had decided, all on her own.

I offered a bashful smile, her mock guilt trip hiding the deeper knowledge spinning in her head. She knew something had happened that I wasn't telling her. She knew it likely didn't involve some magical romantic fantasy, but she wished it did, if only a little.

"I just lost track of time," I half-lied. My heart pinched when the deeper glimpse of hurt blinked across her face. I normally told her everything. I didn't know why this was special. A mix of the possibility it could be dangerous and the feeling it was my first real adventure? She had had her adventures.

When she was younger before her Vale father had abandoned her and her mother, Tiger Lily, she had visited the nearby country countless times on family vacations I was forbidden from participating in, no matter how much I begged.

This was *my* adventure.

The idea of how selfish that sounded nearly forced me to blurt everything about the pixie floss path and the treehouse, but she gasped, shaking off the sorrow like it had never been.

"A night to remember." Her hands splayed in front of her and parted as she looked off somewhere in the distance, past the ceiling of her house. "Just think of it, Lyly. A starry sky stretching above us. Lantern light accompanying a roaring fire."

My guilt eased, and I smirked, leaning forward and resting my elbows on the table. I settled my head into my palms. "Adam's arms curled around you beneath a tree canopy laced with pixie floss and paper charms."

Her eyes went wide, only a hint of flush upon her dark skin. She shook her head, wild blond curls flailing as she surveyed the quiet house for unwelcome ears. Leaning close, she grinned. "Oh, that is perfect. You know Mom is making me a special dress. This will be *the* moment for him to see me and fall desperately in love."

I snickered. I wasn't sure about all that, but I did like Adam. The shy boy lived alone, tending to the silk moths past the goat farms, gathering and weaving cloth while making sure the populations didn't grow past what our modest country could handle. The tree leaves were what kept us afloat, after all, and silk moth larvae thought they were delicious. Whisper fell the moment she saw him, dozens of pure white wings flitting about his "ethereal form," as she'd relayed. He was her moth prince. And I couldn't be happier for her.

However, last I heard, he was oblivious to her affections, and she was determined he would be the one to confess his undying love first. Like in a fairytale.

"Life's not a fairytale, Whisper," I chided. Her face morphed into distaste, her nose scrunching. I continued, "If you want something to happen, you have to take the first step on the adventure. So here's what you do when he sees you wearing your fancy dress made with silk from his very own swarm—"

"Kaleidoscope," she chirped. "Call them a kaleidoscope. It's the proper term, after all. You know that. I told you."

My eyes rolled, but I obliged. "Fine. When he sees you wearing silk made from his very own *kaleidoscope*, you sashay up to him, flutter your big, beautiful, brown eyes, then lean close and coo, 'You helped make this dress. Why don't you help me take it off?'"

Whisper gasped. "That is wicked. Positively wicked." She hid a smile that claimed she wasn't entirely against the idea behind her hand, but the expression tipped toward impishness. "But do tell me, how many successful romantic engagements have you partaken of?"

I harrumphed. "Using your proper voice now? Why don't you throw a couple more big words into that sentence?" Every crush I'd ever had ended in failure. I was always too insecure or too late or too boyish or too absent-minded or too *something*. It was always something, and I was never enough.

"I'm sorry, Lyly," she breathed before I realized my smile had dropped off the edge of an island. "I didn't mean anything by that."

"I know. I just..." Shrugging, I sighed. "You have to get your moth prince so I can live vicariously through you, all right? For alas, like Peter, I am doomed to a life of adventure, skirting love like the cooties would kill me."

"Heaven praise the airwoman." Whisper patted my cheek. "You are not forever twelve. You'll have your romance. *You are enough.*"

I slipped down until my head could rest in the cradle

of my folded arms. Whisper always knew what to say. "I love you, you know that, right? That's my romance."

"Of course." She chuckled, collapsing against the table as well. "And I will never abandon you."

Her hand held tight to mine, and I squeezed it, completing the dumb mantra we had started shortly after her father had gone. "We will never be apart."

She knew how much I wanted to leave. She was the only one who knew I was collecting dust to do so, and she said—no matter what, be it a lover or family or the whole of Skyla—she was coming with me so I would never have to be alone.

Our friendship was my fairytale when I worried about not being good enough, when I worried that the only special thing about me was a "luckiness" I didn't control and barely believed existed. When I remembered that not even my parents wanted me, she reminded me someone did. Not because I was lucky, just because I was me.

And I needed that reminder a lot.

"And that's when we release the white doves." I laughed. We had been planning Whisper's party for hours, snacking on the grilled cheese sandwiches Tiger Lily had made for us when she came home. I had half of one left.

Whisper shoved my arm, correcting me, "White moths."

Adamant, I shook my head. "No, that'll be at the wedding."

"One party at a time! Besides, we already planned my wedding back when we were seven."

My mind drifted back to the tedious scribbles we'd etched together of the two happiest days of our lives. I don't know where my doodles had found themselves, but I was dead sure Whisper still had hers. "If your wedding doesn't have copious amounts of moths, the plan needs revision."

"You think it's hilarious Adam takes care of moths."

"I think it's priceless his official title in the records is 'Silk Moth Babysitter,' yes."

"I should never have told you that."

My stomach hurt holding in so many giggles. "Oh, no. You definitely did the right thing in sharing such valuable information with me."

She tipped up her chin and peered down her nose. "This is the last time such valuable information will ever cross your ears, madam."

I munched my sandwich. "No, it's not."

"No, it's not." She sighed, her eyes shifting behind me to the window. Her smile fell. "Lyly, I think it might almost be midnight."

"What?" I spun, staring outside. The waning moon gleamed back at me, boasting of hours well past ten. "Peter is going to kill me." Stuffing the rest of my sandwich in my mouth, I pushed out of the chair and looked around for wherever my bag had ended up. Not under the table. The other chairs? No. I frantically ruffled my hair. "Killed by a twelve-year-old, the humiliation!"

Sighing, Whisper stood, holding out my satchel after plucking it off the floor beneath my chair. "You really need to talk to him. You'll be nineteen next month. A ten o'clock curfew is a little...restricting."

I took the bag and scoffed. "Tell me about it. But, I mean, he worries. And it's not like he can wait up for very long."

"The ageless twelve-year-old, defeated by the after dark."

My lips spread. I could hardly count the number of

times Peter had worn me out with all-night expeditions, parties, full moon swims. When I survived till morning, we'd greet the rising sun with a crow. "It's not the after dark. It's the waiting. He's useless for it. Pretty sure it gives him hives."

Whisper laughed, the bubbly sound like a skipping brook. "Okay, fine. Off with you then." She extended her pinky, and I linked mine around it before pressing my forehead against hers in our classic farewell. I didn't know what was with us and our rituals, but the consistency was reassuring.

"I'll probably see you sometime tomorrow, if an enthralling stranger doesn't whisk me away."

"Excuse you." We parted, and she stared me down. "*Especially* if an enthralling stranger whisks you away. I will need the details immediately succeeding said whisking."

"Bearing that in mind, away I go."

She walked me to the door and leaned against the jam as I exited, calling, with no regard for the neighbors, "Love you!"

"Love you too!" I waved, capturing her grin in the moment prior to her shutting the door. She was a light. And as I wandered into the dark, chilled woods—every treetop gleaming silver as dust-coated foliage reflected moonlight—I needed to hold onto her brightness.

On a scale of one to definitely, how likely was Peter to kill me?

Probably one? Hopefully one? Maybe one...

I picked up the pace, locating our secret underground home deep in the woods on a smaller island past Aire's marketplace and the residential island where Whisper lived. Peering around as I'd always been taught, I checked for anyone who may be lurking then ducked into the hollow trunk entrance when I was sure only the whistling wind would know.

Pushing aside the animal fur that separated the entrance from the main room, I girded myself for...a sleeping Peter. All the air left my lungs when I spotted the fiery-haired boy out cold in his chair. Tinkerbell rested on his shoulder, curled up cheerfully.

All tension easing away, I approached and ruffled the orange locks peeking out beneath his hat. He didn't so much as twitch. I whispered, "I'm home safe," then I lifted Tink off his shoulder. She, unlike him, did stir, blinking groggily at me before frowning.

A pissy chime fell sharp on my ears.

"I know I'm late," I replied quietly. "I'm sorry."

The little pixie sighed and pouted. She patted my hand, content to curl back up once I'd set her in her house. Next, I found a blanket Tiger Lily had made for us and wrapped it around Peter. "We're a weird pair, aren't we?" I murmured, listening to the Lost Boys snore in their bedroom. Father, brother, friend, and child all in one and almost never only one at a time. He could be frustrating, as hot-headed as me, but even our countless squabbles hadn't dashed our bond yet.

Daughter of Pan, that's what the pixies call you. Imagine that. I'm a father. His grins seared my mind, always crystal clear in low points when I needed them most. To everyone on the islands, he was our fearless leader. Respected despite his appearance. All knew how ancient he was though none knew how he had come to be so.

"Night, Peter," I murmured, crossing the room to my private quarters. As the only girl in the house, the addition had been made just for me not long ago.

When I had readied myself for bed, I collapsed into

the padded mattress and furs, curling into the silken sheets. Tomorrow, I'd return to the house in the forest. Wait all day if I had to.

Whoever appeared, friend or foe, I'd be ready for them.

5TH NOVEMBER

As per usual, I woke up first. Birdcalls drifted into my room, announcing the start of a clear morning, and I fumbled to turn on the oil lamp by my bed. At night, a light glow illuminated the rooms thanks to large enchanted bulbs that clung to the ceiling, but during the day, the blue-green hue felt dim.

I supposed lack of light was something the treehouse person didn't have to worry about. Living in a treehouse would be so much nicer than living in this root house, but secrecy was a game Peter particularly liked.

My eyes snapped wide open, all sleepiness shaken. *People who didn't want to be found had something to hide.* A dry laugh escaped before I could dwell on that thought. "No, duh. A forever twelve-year-old obviously has, oh, I don't know, a massive secret about eternal life to hide." Thing was, neither Peter nor the Lost Boys remembered the secret about their youth. And at least for Peter, that bothered him. If he didn't remember how it happened, he couldn't know where to start to reverse it.

There are stories about The Boy Who Never Grew Up, Lyric. They're tales of adventure and wonder and so many fun things, but they overlook the fact that on some quiet nights, when the world is passing by at a rapid speed, the boy wants desperately *to grow up, join it.* The memory put a sick taste in my mouth as I got dressed. I don't remember how many years ago he had told me this, and he only told me once, but it vividly broke my heart each time I recalled. I was little, little enough that he appeared big. My eyes were wide, my lips parted in awe. He patted my head, his brown gaze meeting mine, the only difference being that my irises were ringed in gold. The saddest smile I'd ever seen him wear had crossed his face. *That's why, in the end, I forget. I hate endings, so it's better if they never had beginnings, if I pretend they never were.*

Maybe even he didn't get the message he'd put in my mind then, but I heard it all too clearly. In my end, in Tiger Lily's, in Tinkerbell's, we would all be forgotten. Because if he cared about something, if he cared about us, we were too painful to remember, and if he didn't, some adventure would put us from his head all the quicker.

Haunted by dark thoughts on such a cheerful morning, I exited my room with my bag at my side and puffed my cheeks full of air. Crossing the room, I headed for our food storage and sifted through the fresh fruit,

18

nudging aside the less-than-fresh fruit.

A harsh jab in the face made air pour from my mouth, and I whipped toward the offender, holding an apple close to my chest like it could save me.

Peter's frown and extended finger greeted me. "You were home late," he accused. "Tink says so late it was nearly today."

I stared down at him. "I was with Whisper, helping plan her birthday party, and lost track of time."

"Whisper...?" A confused brow rose.

"Whispering Meadow. Tiger Lily's daughter. My best friend." Every time I mentioned her, it seemed I had to go through the same reminder. It hurt to know such huge pieces of my life were forgettable. How long could I hope to last in his mind after I was gone? A day or two?

"Oh, Tiger Lily's kid. Still..."—his arms folded—"if anything happened to you..."

"I know," I snapped. His tone, his posture, his expression, *something* about it all pinched a nerve. "Skyla would be doomed. But don't you think I'm a little too old now to have a curfew? I can take care of myself. I'm going to be nineteen next month and—"

"And I need to make sure you stay safe, for everyone's sake. Try not to act so childish."

I flinched, my nails biting into the apple until juice bled over the fruit. "*Childish? Me?* Have you looked in the mirror lately, Peter? Not even. Have you seen your bedroom? It looks like a tornado of slingshots and dress-up exploded in there! And when was the last time you bathed properly? If someone isn't reminding you, do you even change your socks? I know you don't. Don't you dare accuse *me* of being childish."

"Lyric!" he complained, his voice pitching. His feet left the ground as he hovered at my height. Despite

Tinkerbell still being in her house, Peter always had pixie dust clinging to him—another telltale sign he hadn't bathed properly for a while. "I'm looking out for you and everyone on these islands!"

I shoved the apple in my bag. "I'm just saying, I'm an adult. I shouldn't have to report back to a preteen when I come home a little late. Honest to the great airwoman, Peter, I can't even tell you what others my age spend their nights doing."

His face reddened, apparently less oblivious than I thought. His voice was softer when he spoke again. "I have to keep you safe. I have to know you're safe each day, especially right now."

"And yet when you go off on adventures all over the world, it's good enough to leave me with Tiger Lily, who—for your information—doesn't give me a curfew at all. Is it so much to ask for at least the freedom I can have while trapped here?"

He ran his fingers back through his hair, paused, and looked behind him. His usual green hat rested on the floor, so he skipped over to it and snatched it up.

I took the moment to head toward the exit.

"Where are you going?"

"None of your business."

"It is." He planted his hands on his hips. "What's gotten into you?"

"Nothing." I clenched my bag strap. "Nothing you'd understand anyway. I'm just growing up. That's all."

Silence thickened the air, and it was heavy with everything I hated to feel. When he spoke again, the words were steady, sad. "Which island are you exploring today? I need to know in case something happens and I need to find you."

I pushed aside the furs that covered the exit.

Swallowing everything but stubbornness, I mumbled, "I can take care of myself," then I left.

Guilt. Bitter guilt coated me like a layer of cement. It weighed down my actions as I trudged through the bustling market, perusing stalls and greeting acquaintances. I couldn't risk heading back to the treehouse island now. If Peter followed me there in the name of making sure he knew where I was and that I was okay, he'd learn my secret, and if he thought the same thing I did—that someone dangerous possibly lived there—he'd forbid me from discovering the mystery on my own.

He might not forbid my being a part of it. In fact, I was nearly certain he, the Lost Boys, and I would all stake it out and play games in the area until glorious battle or interrogation commenced. But *this was my adventure*. Sidestepping an oncoming rush of people, I ducked beneath the shade of a covered booth and mumbled a curse beneath my breath.

I was being selfish again. Just hurting Whisper wasn't enough for me. Oh no. I had to stab the kid in the back who had taken responsibility for me since my abandonment.

"Lyric?" Tiger Lily's voice yanked my attention from my thoughts. The woman sat in the center of her booth—and how had I missed that this was her booth? Concern rippled through her brown eyes, her dark hair pulled over her shoulder in a single thick braid. "Is everything all right?" Before I could reply, she patted the ground beside her.

My whole body sagged, the cement cracking off as I went to her and plopped down on her hand-woven rug. "I had a fight with Peter."

She hummed, wrapping me in her arms. Her cool

brown skin sapped everything negative away like magic. Unlike Peter, Tiger Lily remembered when I was a baby and told me stories about how I grew up. Peter, being—well—Peter, didn't know how to care for an infant. I would have starved had Tiger Lily not discovered my existence and had only just given birth to Whisper. Like sisters, we breastfed beside one another. The woman was the closest thing I had to a mother.

"Can you talk to him?" I asked. "He doesn't understand that I'm growing up."

"I imagine he does but rather doesn't want to admit it." Tiger Lily cupped my chin and looked into my eyes. The depths there made me swallow, and I remembered she had been an orphan beside Peter when she was his apparent age, and her parents died at the hands of pirates. They were close. They fought together. She grew up. "There are a lot of things Peter doesn't admit to himself because they hurt, and he's too young to understand hurt. Ancient, fearless, clever, respected above any here as our leader, and yet so very young. We must protect him while he thinks he's protecting us."

Tears burned in my eyes, so I looked away, swallowing a lump in my throat that threatened to choke me. "I'm sorry, Tiger Lily."

Her head shook. "If you believe you've said something to warrant an apology, it isn't me who needs to hear it. Peter is stubborn, but he isn't unreasonable. He dwells. And he cares."

I knew that. I knew that because staring at Peter was like staring at the person I wanted to be; we were so alike and so different all at once. Taking a deep breath, I wiped my eyes and stood. "Thanks."

She nodded, smiling as I left.

Exiting into the crowd, I turned myself toward home, fully intent on making peace and making him see reason, but a cloaked figure caught my eye. Shifting on the sidelines, a broad, concealed man strode toward me, passing with uncomfortable speed. My gaze tracked him, and my brow furrowed.

A chill of unease skittered down my spine, whispering on the wind, so I touched the sapphire hilt of my knife and followed him at a distance. He never paused. Could this be the person who lived in the treehouse? No. That island rested past my home, and no bridge connected to it; it was rare that an adult could fly, and we were headed in the opposite direction.

He tore from the crowds, entering the trees, and—he was heading toward the bridge that led to the Jolly Roger. My stomach jumped as I picked up the pace so I wouldn't lose him in the woods. The second my foot hit a dry twig, it was over.

His head whipped toward me, a shadowed sneer just visible beneath his hood. Then, he ran.

I gave chase. "Stop right there!" I yelled. "Who are you?" But conversation was not the stranger's strong suit. My feet pounded against sparse twigs and dead leaves until we broke out onto the bridge that connected to Peter's trophy island. The Jolly Roger sat just out of sight beyond the circle of gleaming trees that kept the small island afloat.

My hand closed around my dagger, but I didn't want to kill him. I wasn't even sure I could find the stomach to send my blade into his thigh. "Get a grip, Lyric," I spat at myself. I had been raised on Peter's tales of gore. But the price of his youth and the people he'd forgotten also grew like a weed in my skull.

Killing people meant they never came back. Dead

people *did not come back*. And unlike Peter, I wouldn't forget. How could I deem myself worthy of taking a life when I didn't even know if I took it justly or not? For all I knew, I was chasing an innocent recluse.

I screamed when we broke out of the trees and into view of the pirate ship, more from frustration than anything else. The man looked back in the same instant I plunged my hand into my satchel and grabbed my apple. My aim held true, and the fruit careened into his forehead, splitting apart. His body tumbled to the ground.

I jumped him. Cramming my feet against his elbows and sitting on his chest, I finally gained the guts to pull my knife free and press it against his neck. I yanked off his hood just as he was coming to. "Who—"

My heart stopped.

Golden teeth pulled in a rancid smile leered at me. The man's stubbled face and oily hair screamed pirate. Or at least he displayed everything I thought a pirate would from Tiger Lily's and Peter's stories.

"W-who are you?" I stammered, wondering if I should draw blood to make a point I wasn't playing any games.

The man's eyes slithered over my body until I felt violated in the worst ways until being this close made me want to dry heave. Something popped in his mouth, and my body tensed. Foam bubbled from his lips, sputtering as he laughed. I scrambled off him, terrified. The foam and sputtering grew worse, his laughter descending into chokes. But they weren't half as horrible as the silence, the stillness, that followed.

The pirate was dead.

Dead.

There was a pirate on Skyla. And he was dead.

Blood hammered in my ears, clouding all rational

thought until I wasn't sure what was worse. I only knew one thing as I skidded back and turned to run. Peter had to know about this.

Now.

"PETER!" I practically fell through the entrance, batting aside the fur covering the main room. Panting, I scanned the Lost Boys, catching Peter's raised brow at the head of the table.

Was it already lunchtime?

That didn't matter. "Peter," I repeated, relieved, still scared, and panicked.

He picked some burnt meat off his plate, and I knew they'd been cooking without supervision again. He did that when he was mad; that is, he pretended to be a capable adult. "What is it?" he asked.

"You a'ight?" Slightly asked.

My head could only shake. "Peter, there was a pirate in the market." He went deathly still. "I think... I think..." Bile rose, but I forced my words out. "I think I killed him, Peter. On the trophy island, in front of the Jolly Roger. He started to foam at the mouth before I knew it, and—"

Peter slammed his hands against the table, startling Tinkerbell as he stood. More than a little anger painted his expression, and I actually shrunk back from the boy. "That's nothing to joke about, Lyric. I know we had an argument this morning, but you don't have to make up stories to prove you can take care of yourself. That's the opposite of maturity." Worry and anger mixed and melded in his eyes.

Everything in me felt run through with an arrow. "I'm not making it up. Peter—"

His eyes hardened.

Tootles's small voice interjected. "You know what

the pirates did to us, Lyric."

"I—"

The boys' heads turned away from me, their eyes looking from one to the next. Only Peter's livid gaze clung to my skin. His blaze of anger sparked my own.

"You don't believe me. How can you not believe me!" My fists clenched. "I've never lied to you before!"

"You've never grown up before either!" His shout hung in the air. Even Tinkerbell looked between us, her lips parted. She rose, fluttering in front of him and shaking her head, but he swatted her away. "Adults are lying, sniveling, dangerous things. They only think about themselves, which isn't the best, but I understand. However, the minute they play others to get what they want is the minute they stop being a friend of mine."

My eyes stung. Water dripped down my cheek when I blinked. "Fine," I said, my voice shaking. "Don't believe me and quit being my friend." I forced my legs to move me toward my room, stopping just before I crossed the threshold. "I wish I had a real father. A real father would trust me. Instead, I'm stuck with an insipid child like you."

"Lyric..."

I didn't wait for him to continue. I all but slammed the door and collapsed into bed, crying myself to sleep. Like an adult.

Groggy, I awoke with an urgent need to relieve myself. The flowers on my ceiling glowed over my room, their calming shade doing little to hide the memories that hit me the moment I sat up. Peter hated me now.

Deflated, I wiped my cheeks. Disgusting, crusted tears clung around my eyes, and worse still, I wanted to continue crying. I wanted to scream and scream until my weird little family would curl up around me and make all the dumb things better. Did Peter think I wanted to grow up? Did he think I liked not knowing what I was doing with myself? Did he think I enjoyed the thought of leaving him behind, of attempting to find my own way in this scary, unknown world?

Everything I wanted—adventures, knowledge, purpose—were all his fault. The damn twelve-year-old was all I aspired to be. But my wings had been clipped, trapping me here where nothing happened, where I made adventures out of treehouses and got yelled at when I thought I'd finally found something important.

Or maybe I'd just made things worse. If I hadn't been there, that man would have lived. Peter could have found him, and he would have known what to do better. He could have information about what the pirate was doing here, how the pirate had even gotten here. Now he had nothing to go on, and because he thought I was lying, he wouldn't even think to look for anything else.

Bracing myself, I grabbed my satchel, sniffed, and peeked out my door. The quiet main room looked back at me, not even Tinkerbell glowing asleep in her house. No snores. No whispers.

I slipped out of my room and into the mild evening on my way to the outhouse. Where was everyone? Thoughts of being abandoned now that I was an adult scathed the edges of my mind, and it took all my power to keep my breaths steady. Something like this wouldn't make Peter abandon me, right? I was still Skyla's good luck charm, wasn't I?

I still had purpose. *Didn't I?*

Gasping, I finished up in the outhouse as quickly as I could, washing my hands in the river faster than I normally did. My feet pounded against the soft earth, set on fleeing to Whisper. She could reassure me. If nothing else, she would tell me I was enough for her, that we'd always be friends, that—

Peter.

His orange hair shone in the distance, moonlight reflecting off the pixie dust dousing it. I stopped beside the entrance to our home, my throat tight. A tear trickled down my cheek as he approached.

Lost in thought, he didn't look up until he was just a few steps away, then he stopped. "Lyric..." The wind caught my name, pulled it away. "Why are you still crying?"

I scrubbed my cheek against my shoulder, but more tears followed. "I thought... Well, no one was here. I just..." My lip trembled, and I leaned my head back to try and stop the tears.

"Head off to bed, men. We'll talk later."

The Lost Boys hesitated before slipping past us and entering the secret entrance to our home.

When it was just us, Peter sighed, scratching the back of his head. "I'm sorry I yelled at you. You just know that..." He floated toward me, his arms crossed at first, then limp at his sides. "I don't have to tell you what you understand. I'm sorry for yelling. I'm sorry for what I said. You are my friend, Lyric. More than that. Things are just a little odd right now. Something is changing in the air, and I don't like it."

Water blurred my vision, but I numbly recognized Tinkerbell's tiny hands against my cheek, pushing droplets away and soaking herself as she tried to dry my tears. She hugged my face when she realized I just couldn't stop crying. "I'm sorry," I blubbered.

"And about your curfew," he began.

I started to shake my head but didn't want to throw

Tinkerbell, so I stopped and whispered, "I don't care about that anymore."

He bumped my shoulder, floating beside me. "Sure, you do. Just maybe not right in this moment when all you can focus on is leaking, like a little girl." Plucking Tinkerbell off my face by her wings, he plopped her into his pocket to dry off, then he removed his hat and used it to dry my tears. "You're smart. We've raised you smart enough to handle yourself. So what if you come back a little late now and again? As long as I know you're safe and sound when the second star sets. Okay?"

"I'm sorry for what I said about a real father."

He shrugged, reclining midair. "You didn't mean it."

Though smiling, I could feel the hurt swirling in his eyes. It stabbed me through the gut. "I could never mean it." I swallowed. "Never." I looked up at the star-spattered sky, and a lightness swelled in my chest. Shifting my satchel around, I pulled my pan flute out. "Can we play in the tree tonight?" It had been so long since we'd played together, watched the stars, and joked about how we ruled the world. The tree was where he'd taught me to play; hell, it was where we'd made my pan flute.

Peter looked at the oak that hid our home beneath it. Massive, it stretched above all the other trees in the area and plateaued near the top, creating a flatbed large enough to stretch out on. When he looked back at me, I knew the answer before he spoke. "I need to talk to the boys tonight, and it's getting late, but you're welcome to stay out for as long as you want. Try...try not to go too far tonight though. Please."

"Is something wrong?" The pirate flashed through my mind, and I paled. "Did you...?"

He shook his head. "Wrong? Of course not. What

6TH NOVEMBER

Less than gracefully, I snorted upright, blinking at my surroundings. When had I fallen asleep? My pan flute rested at my side, unharmed, so I brushed it off and glanced through the silver-dusted leaves and branches at the sky to gather the time.

Before I could judge the position of the stars, a humanoid streak flew past them. My breath caught. Fumbling in my bag, I ripped out a homemade spyglass and positioned it at my eye. Sure enough, in the distant sky, a person soared toward Skyla. Was it Peter? But, no, it seemed larger than Peter.

Heart racing, I stood, measuring the person's trajectory. If they kept straight, they'd land on treehouse island. I watched them for several seconds. They continued straight.

I couldn't afford to lose them.

Torn between only just making up with Peter and going against his wishes again, I kept my distressed grunts and grumbles to a minimum as I snagged my pouch of pixie dust from my bag, sprinkled as much as I dared to lose on my head, and whipped out of the tree.

I couldn't lose the person. Even if I didn't wait to confront them until I told Peter, I had to find out if they were another pirate. If they were connected to that house. Gaze narrowed, I darted through the air after them. My dust ran out before I made it all the way, but the second I touched down on that island, I set my hand at my knife and ran toward the treehouse.

All my life, Peter had told me I was the charm protecting Skyla. Maybe this was the moment when I'd actually put work into that title, when my physical efforts would be Skyla's protection.

Close now, I slowed, hiding behind trees and pushing forward, careful to watch my step. When I was certain the house was hidden in the branches just before me, I pressed my back against a large trunk and pulled my blade free. I surveyed everything in front of me first, then to either side. Finding nothing, I glued my gaze to the small clearing beyond the trunk and before the hidden treehouse.

My heart beat erratically, the rhythm a mixture of flying, running, and waiting. What if they found me? They could fly. Like Peter. I'd never seen anyone else fly as high as that. Pixie dust could be fickle, and if you ran out at that height, only a bitter end awaited unless a pixie caught you. I knew. I'd flown so high a number of times, and the pixies were *never* happy when they had to catch me.

Leaves rustled above.

I stopped breathing.

A boy dropped through the canopy, pulling up at the last second and landing with his back toward me. Muscular arms reached up toward a thick braid of chocolate brown hair. Strong hands pulled the tie free, then his fingers slipped through the starlight-spattered locks. His whole body glimmered in the dappled moonlight.

My mouth opened, tongue going dry.

Murmured, deep, enticing words I couldn't make out sliced through the chirping night. Was he talking to something? A ball of silver light flitted before him, and my eyes bulged. A pixie?

Only Peter... But here this boy—nearly my age if not older—stood, drenched in pixie dust and talking with one *just like Peter*. Who was he? I had to know. I just had to.

I nearly stepped out from behind the tree when his head nodded toward the ladder, and his low murmur continued.

Every blooming curse I knew dredged through my mind. *The. Ladder.*

Darting back to my hiding place, I dropped my knife and missed dodging a stick when I dodged the blade. The loudest *snap* I'd ever heard broke the woods.

The boy's back tightened, tension filling him. I didn't move. My hands clamped against my mouth.

He glanced over his shoulder, a smoldering gaze of mixed greens and browns finding me, widening. Sensual, full lips parted, and his head cocked.

I backstepped, a chorus of curses continuing confidently inside my skull. My foot hit another stick, and the world mocked me as that *crack* echoed. I closed my eyes to wallow in dark embarrassment alone.

"Hello," he said, loud enough for me to hear. "To whom do I owe the pleasure of such a late and unexpected visit?"

My eyes opened, and fear coursed through me. His face had darkened, his eyes pinned on the blade by my feet.

"That's a pirate's knife," he said. He didn't touch the sheath at his waist, but his hand hovered near it. "Who are you?"

All kindness sucked from his melodic voice, my mind shook free of entrancement. I held up my hands. "Lyric. Daughter of Pan." I don't know why I said that, but I glanced at the male pixie, hoping he'd come to my aid like most did. He settled on the boy's shoulder, saying nothing. I inhaled, continuing, "What do you know about pirates?" I looked him over again. He wore a loose linen shirt and dark trousers. The style wasn't unlike most of Skyla's clothes, though his hair was longer than most male residents kept theirs. He didn't look like a pirate. At least, not like the pirate I'd seen yesterday.

"What do I know about pirates? Nothing." He tapped his dagger's hilt, and I realized he had more than one, maybe four or five, on his belt. "But blades are a different story."

My breath hitched when he strode forward, eating the ground between us. He bent in front of me, plucked my knife from the ground, and flipped it to blade-side between his fingers, offering.

"How do you come by a pirate's knife?" he whispered.

My eyes flicked between him and the pixie on his shoulder. The tiny creature's stare was nearly as severe as his. I clasped the handle, meeting resistance. Quickly, I snatched it from him.

His chin tilted up, and he looked at me with half-lidded eyes.

"My father gave it to me," I answered, sheathing it, but keeping my hand near.

The boy's arms folded. "Was your father a pirate?"

Did they not know of Peter Pan? I sterned my expression. "No. He killed them."

Finally, the pixie chimed, the hushed words said so softly I almost believed I should be able to understand them.

The boy shrugged his free shoulder and turned on his heel. "Skye says you're safe—what was it?—Lyric? Like a song lyric?"

"My father—" It was so weird calling Peter that. He was always Peter to me. "—named me after the words because we call the wind music and those who fly through its song lyrics."

"You fly then?"

"I'm sorry. Who are you?" My thumb touched the sapphire hilt of my knife as my brows lowered. Peter had trained me in one-on-one combat, not that I'd practiced it for a while. I could hit a mark halfway across a forest, but I'd grown rusty in everything else involving a blade. Even cutting vegetables if I were being honest, but I didn't have to be quite that honest with him.

"Bay."

"*Bay?*"

A satirical smile turned up one corner of his lips. "I'm sorry. I don't have a poetic story to accompany my name. It's just *Bay.*"

"Do you live here, just *Bay?*"

"Have you been snooping around my house, Wind Song?"

My cheeks heated, but I frowned. "Not intentionally.

There was a freak accident involving a bit of cut pixie floss when I was wandering the forest."

"Was there now?" He lifted off the ground. "Well, thank you for stopping by. Please don't come back. Cheers."

"Hold on right there. Just a minute, sir."

He turned in the air, even his pixie raising a brow at me.

Swallowing, I blurted every thought in my head, "I saw you fly in. Where did you come from? Why are you out here living secretly in the woods? How in the name of the airwoman do you have a pixie with you?"

He stared at me for several moments. "Do you have any other questions, or would you prefer I write you an autobiography of my personal life? In your nosiness, I hope you haven't disorganized my house. Everything was alphabetized."

I glowered at him, and he was lucky I wasn't holding my knife anymore, or it may have shaved off a bit of his hair. "Oh, I'm sorry. Are there actually things in your house? With an attitude that large, I'm surprised you fit at all."

He leaned forward, looking down at me with his arms set akimbo. That dark hair slid over his shoulders like silk. "Cheeky. My apologies. I'm not used to guests grilling me in the middle of the night about every detail of my livelihood." He flipped upside down, and it was becoming the slightest bit clear how a pixie had attached itself to him.

Pixies adored children. Adults lost whatever special thing it was that allowed them to bond and communicate. I don't remember ever having been able to hear their words, but Whisper swore she had, and she missed it. The childish, arrogant person before me was nothing less than a suave Peter, playing a game by toying with me.

My eyes closed briefly because I did *not* just think he was suave.

"What was that first question again?" he prompted, his gaze drifting away. "Oh, wait. I don't want to answer the first one. How about the second one, then? Why I'm living secretly in the woods. That's an easy one." The cheeriness fell away. "I don't like company. Good eve." He floated up onto his porch and yanked the ladder through the hole, closing off the entrance.

I stared up through the trees, barely making out the house's foundation even when a soft yellow light blinked on.

"You're an ass!" I snapped after several minutes of gaping.

"Am I?" he called back. "I'm not the one shouting at someone's house while a hundred pixies are trying to sleep nearby."

He had a point. And it made me want to punch him. Growling, I surveyed the area, found a knotted tree with a good starting hold, and pulled myself up into the bows. Careful to be precise when I entered the treetops, I led myself to his porch and hopped down. The blinds were still closed, but light gleamed through the cracks.

Before I could knock, his door flew open. He stared at me, looked at the bundle of ladder beside my feet, then narrowed his eyes, perhaps, looking for dust. "How did you—"

"You're an ass," I whispered.

His head reeled back, and he blinked, then an odd smile twisted his lips. He leaned against the door jam. "All right, Wind Song. All right. Well played, I'll give you that."

I mockingly held an invisible gown and curtsied.

"But I'm really not this interesting. Just a hermit with a pixie. We can't be that rare. Would you *please*, very politely, go away now?"

"No," I said simply. "It's not normal for people to have pixies and fly in from the stars. You're hiding something, and I need to find out what."

"Is that your job?"

"Well, it certainly isn't Silk Moth Babysitter's..."

He chuckled, the sound deep and smooth like roasted chestnuts. "I swear, if that's a thing..."

"I'll never tell." My eyes drifted over his shoulder to the one-room abode. Tidy yet lived-in, it boasted the same essence I'd gotten from the exterior, except it was filled with incredible things. Books. Papers. Trinkets of all kinds that I'd never seen before. A huge map covered the far wall. My eyes widened.

He glanced over his own shoulder and quirked a brow. "What? Have you never seen a bachelor pad before?"

"Can I look at your map?" The words left my mouth breathless, and I met his gaze.

His lips pinched, but he surprised me. "Sure."

The boy stepped aside, and I forgot that he was a stranger as I entered the enclosed space. His pixie sat off in the corner on a full-sized cot, watching me, but I paid him little mind. My hand stretched toward the intricate etchings, each detail impeccably placed. "You made this?"

"...yeah." He stood beside me, close enough that I could feel heat near my back.

"It's Skyla." I faced him.

His eyes drifted to the calligraphy title, boasting *Skyla*. "How'd you guess?"

"Don't make me hit you."

"You'd hit a man in his own home while he was just minding his business and trying to get to bed?" He placed an offended hand against his heart, playing up a wounded expression.

I elbowed him in the side, remembered he wasn't a friend, then cleared my throat, sidestepping to put distance between us. "I definitely would."

He rubbed his ribs. "A wonder why I don't regularly entertain company."

I looked at the wall above his cot. Another untitled map splayed there, this one dotted with notes. "Where's that?" I asked, approaching it.

"That's elsewhere," he mumbled. "I'm sorry. How rude of me. Would you like a tour?"

"Yep." I grinned. He wasn't exactly frowning, so I looked closer at the map, skimming over the notes

Sirens aren't nixies. Nixies aren't mermaids. Don't be in Skull Rock after dark.

Excitement bubbled in my chest, and I whirled on him. "Tell me your secrets."

"What in the world is wrong with you?"

"Many, many things, Star Boy. Secrets now. Therapy later."

He laughed, and it was full. Shaking his head, he patted my hair. "Calm down. It's late. Scratch that, it is very, very early, and I haven't slept yet."

"It really sounds like you're inviting me back. Are you inviting me back?"

"Regrettably." He smirked. "But only because you've flattered me by ogling my maps." He folded his arms. "Here's the deal: tomorrow night bring an offering of good grace—food, I mean food—and tell no one where I live. I'll tell you some stories, then you can go away, a satiated little monster."

"How do I know you aren't planning to get me alone and jump me?"

He raised a brow, extending his arms to the room.

I glanced at the space in which we were alone and pressed my lips together. "Fair point. How do I know you aren't going to fly off somewhere before I come back, then?"

He scratched his chin. "I suppose you don't. You'll just have to have a little faith and trust when I say I'm sticking around till the tenth."

I held up a pinky. He looked at it, blanking. "You aren't serious."

"Am." I wiggled my pinky.

Sighing, he linked his finger with mine. "If you bring cheese tomorrow, I might forgive you for this."

"Do you mind if it's goat?" I pulled my hand away, trying not to take offense when he wiped his on his shirt.

"I won't be picky."

"Great." I led myself to the door. "Tomorrow then."

"Later today, really."

"Promise you'll be here?" I set my hand on the doorknob.

He shrugged, but it was as good an answer as any. "You said you knew how to fly? Do you need some dust to get back home?"

Skye chirped, the sound a clear protest, so I shook my head. "I always keep a bit on me. As long as I don't fall out of the tree, I should be fine."

"A pity if that did happen." His smirk stretched into a wicked grin.

I rolled my eyes and lowered the rope ladder. Despite his words, he watched me until I made it safely down.

Floating just over his porch like a silver ghost in the moonlight, he continued watching until I was out of sight.

My tired mind wandered while I helped Whisper set up the small island grove for her party tomorrow. I had managed a short nap after meeting Bay, but past that, my head refused to quiet down. Questions and mysteries swirled.

When I'd spotted him, he was little more than a shooting star, heading straight down to his home. He hadn't come in from the horizon. He had come from the sky.

A sigh filtered past my lips.

"Okay!" Whisper stopped passing me the next lantern to string in the trees beside our party location on the edge of the island. I looked down from my perch and quirked a brow. She set her arms akimbo. "What is up with you? You don't sigh wistfully. I sigh wistfully. You're a million miles away, and we know you aren't allowed that much traveling time." A grin brightened her soft brown cheeks. "Tell me everything."

"What?" I cleared my throat. "What are you talking about? Everything about what?"

"Let's start with the dark circles under your eyes. Did you sleep at all last night? Or...were you *involved* in something else?" She finally relinquished the lantern and reached for the next while I threaded it in a hammock of glimmering pixie floss. In the late sunlight, the threads gleamed.

"I slept." *Some.*

"You're hiding something." Her lips pulled in a pout. Gaze averting, she handed me the next lantern. "Is it a boy?"

Feigning coolness, I replied, "Not everything is a boy."

41

I feared the heat rising to my cheeks gave me away.

"Definitely a boy." Her sage nod accompanied a wistful sigh, and she was rightfully the queen of those. What was I thinking in allowing myself to encroach upon her domain? Her long lashes fluttered. "Oh, please tell me something about him."

"There's nothing to tell." Trying to change the subject, I asked, "Do you think I could have some of your mom's goat cheese?"

"Lyly, it's my birthday." The serious undertone to her words almost hid the childish notion. "You shouldn't lie to me on my birthday."

The sick, guilty feeling in my gut boiled, but I had promised to tell no one about him. Or rather. I'd promised to tell no one where he lived. Hopping out of the tree, I grinned. "If there is someone worth mentioning, he'd be my date to your party tomorrow night."

Whisper's eyes bulged, and she clasped my hands. "Yes, this is absolutely true." Before I could get another word in, she squealed. "This is the best gift ever. We'll have to have a joint wedding."

"Oh, so if we are renovating the plans, we must include as many moths as possible, right?"

"You have to stop being so jealous that Adam is a moth prince."

I snickered. "A most regal prince of moths indeed."

She nodded, pressing the last lantern into my hand. "Quite."

"Where are you going?" Peter stopped me before I'd made it far from home. Half a foot off the ground, he hovered, arms folded and brow quirked. Beside him, Tinkerbell flitted, her stance much the same as his.

I diminished my groan and faced his steady brown stare. The white moon sent cool light over us, accentuating the chill in the air. "Out." I moistened my lips. "I'll be back before morning."

His expression hardened. "Are you going far?"

"Not too far." Nowhere in Skyla was particularly far.

He scrutinized me several moments, my stomach tight with worry he'd stop me, but then he sighed. "Okay. You have your knife?"

I brushed the sheath at my thigh, though I doubted it would do me much good if I didn't have the guts to use the blade. "Yeah. Always."

"Be back by morning." Jabbing a finger toward me, he jutted out his chin and narrowed his eyes.

I nodded, trying not to show my elation when he ducked back into the hollow trunk and disappeared down into our home. Breath held, I waited and watched for any sign he might be coming back, but nothing moved.

Turning on my heel, I held my bag close and darted toward Bay's island, only using a smidge of dust each time I needed to cross an un-bridged divide. When a shadowed form entered my vision just before reaching his house, I skidded to a stop. Crouched, the figure seemed to be toiling in the bushes, a silver ball of light sending a soft glow over a defined profile.

All the air in my lungs escaped in a gentle breath.

"Evening, Wind Song," Bay greeted, not bothering to look up.

I noticed the slight curve of his lips deepen, so I smiled to match. "I come bearing bribery."

"Bribery?" He settled back on his haunches, finally gracing me with a look. "Let's see if it's acceptable then."

Skye peered at me, judgment in his tiny eyes when I approached and lifted the flap of my satchel, revealing half a loaf of soft bread, a ball of gooey cheese, and a handful of berries not unlike the ones he had gathered in a basket at his side.

He peeled back the cheesecloth and sniffed the white mound. "It's fresh."

"The goats breed year-round here since the weather is always so temperate." An icy breeze swept through my long hair to spite my words, and my skin prickled in response.

His wry smile set a flurry of butterflies loose in my stomach. I ignored them the best I could.

"Have you ever had blackberry tea?" he asked.

I shook my head.

He plucked the basket off the ground and rose into the air. "A pity. You're missing out."

"Your bad manners can't sway me as long as you tell me your secrets." I followed him when he drifted toward his home, popping berries into his mouth as he went.

"A shame I have no secrets to tell." Before I could protest, he added, "I do, however, have a few stories you might like." He tossed me a berry before soaring into the treetops.

Moments later, the rope ladder dropped before me. Minutes later, we were seated in the center of his house, the floor strewn with dozens of things I'd never seen before. He showed me a real telescope and a golden sextant with elaborate designs. He told me about the mermaids of Atlantis, a genuine scale scintillating between his fingers.

We talked and ate and did, in fact, drink some blackberry tea until, quickly and without my notice, the night slipped into the next day.

7TH NOVEMBER

Bay paused, his knife glinting in the oil lamp light as he twirled it into a sheath on his belt and lowered his hands from the dramatic rendition he was acting out. An odd grin tugged on the corner of his lips. "Close your mouth, Wind Song. Surviving a bear is hardly the highlight of tonight's multi-story event."

"It's not just a bear. You've got sirens after you too." Lying on my stomach, I propped my head in my hands and crossed my ankles.

He twisted, tossing a glance over his shoulder. His eyes widened into massive circles like he had just spotted the winged creatures through the make-believe foliage. "I forgot about them." A muffled curse whispered into the suddenly tense air. Then he pulled his knife again, blocking an invisible blow. His body careened back, narrowly missing the bookshelf as he crashed into the floor. "Don't you dare even try to bewitch me," he struggled to say, clamping a hand above his knife like he was covering the woman's mouth.

Skye's chirping laughter broke the heavy moment, and I glanced at the pixie as he rocked and kicked his legs.

The scene fell away, and Bay deadpanned, floating back to his feet. "You ruined it, Skye."

Chiming responded.

"That is exactly what happened, thank you very much." Bay's eyes rolled in light of Skye's next response. "I did not forget the bear. I fought him off with my third arm, obviously."

"You are significantly less of an ass tonight," I said, flashing him a grin.

He floated into a cross-legged position on the floor. "A miracle the change in a man's character when he's not sleep deprived."

"Uh huh."

He reached over me, snagging a piece of bread from my satchel. "Food helps too."

My cheeks heated. "You still haven't told me where you came from last night, Star Boy."

"I haven't?" He fell back, the piece of bread hanging out of his mouth. "Oops."

"Please?"

"I told you, I have no secrets for you to pry out of me. Just stories, with a side of sarcasm."

I rolled my eyes. "An unnecessary side, really."

"You appreciate it." He swallowed the bread and shot up. "You already know where I came from. The stars.

I'm a fallen angel. A little bird just out of my egg."

My brows knitted. "Am I supposed to know what that means?"

He shrugged.

"Do you even know what that means?"

Another shrug. "Should I? Seems entirely unimportant."

Skye flitted over to my bag and ripped a handful of cheese out before plopping onto Bay's head. Bay looked up, trying to see the little creature, then his gaze dropped to me, all childishness gone in an instant. His lips spread in an alluring smirk. "It's your turn, Wind Song."

"What?"

"Tell me a story about one of your adventures."

My heart sank, and I pulled myself up off the floor, hugging my legs close to my chest. "I've never actually left Skyla, so I don't have any adventures to tell."

He scoffed. "You mean to say you know how to scale the pixie oaks, but you've never stumbled upon anything more interesting than my house?"

Casting off the empty sensation filling my stomach, I leaned toward him. "Why, yes. That is exactly what I'm saying. Why do you ask? Should I have?"

"Secrets fill these islands, more than you'd expect. At least, I'm half-certain."

Excitement burbled to the surface. "Show me."

His head shook. "Sadly—for you—that's not how it works. You have to find them yourself, or they have no meaning."

I pouted. "I suppose begging wouldn't do me much good?"

"You know they say that only the innocent and heartless can fly, and I fly better than the best of them."

"Heartlessness. What a thing to be proud of," I grumbled, but I knew that wasn't the real reason we could fly. It wasn't innocence or happy thoughts or youth. It was belief. Belief that you could never abandon. The second you doubted whether or not you could fly was the second you never would be able to again, or so the story went.

I hadn't realized silence encompassed us until he released a breath, murmuring, "I hope the thoughts streaming behind your eyes are a story you'd like to tell me."

"Sorry to disappoint."

"I find it very difficult to believe someone who carries a pirate's knife at her hip has nothing interesting to share." He lifted his cup and swirled the tea, pausing before taking a sip. "Unless you're dressing for the life you want, not the one you have. Are you scared to leave, or are you unable to?"

"That's none of your business." I swallowed the bitterness resting on my tongue and sifted through my bag to find any stray berries. Their sweetness mellowed my unease.

"The last five hours have been none of your business, and yet, I hate to inform you, this is what conversation and getting to know someone looks like."

I frowned. "You've kept your secrets. I won't lie and say I don't have any of my own, but I'm also not going to share them."

His eyes sparkled, the lamplight sending a shimmer across his tan skin. "Can you really fly?"

"Yeah, of course. How else would I get to this remote island?"

"Then why haven't you left Skyla?"

My mouth fell open, and I smacked him. "You tricked

me."

"You are violent." But he laughed and fell back again, knocking Skye out of his hair. The little pixie took the tumble in stride, to my surprise floating to sit on my shoulder with his cheese. "Interesting," Bay said, linking his arms under his head. "I guess he's warmed up to you."

"Most pixies are comfortable around me because they know Peter."

"Are you sure that's why?" He kept his gaze on the ceiling.

I blinked. "Yes, of course."

"Hm."

"What?"

"Nothing." His expression turned pensive, hazel eyes drifting toward the unnamed map. "I've enjoyed this." His lips quirked. "Despite your nosiness, rudeness, and violence, it hasn't been horrible."

"That's one hell of a compliment," I noted dryly.

"Yeah."

Calm saturated the air, and I breathed it in, looking out the window. The still-dark sky hinted at the coming dawn, all too soon lightening with gentle blues. "I have to go soon," I murmured.

"Why?" The soft edge to his deep voice sent a chill racing down my spine.

"Because." When the second star moon set, Peter expected me home.

"Why?" he repeated in the same enticing manner.

I scoffed. "How old are you?"

"Not sure." His eyes closed, and I took a moment to trace the shape of his jaw, the downturn of his mouth, the long, still lashes framing his eyes.

The quietest chime met my ear, and I glanced at

Skye to find the most mature expression I'd ever seen on a pixie before. He winked, floating off my shoulder with the last bit of his cheese to settle onto the cot. My cheeks heated, and I pressed my lips together.

Gathering my courage, I said, "Tomorrow night at dusk, my friend is having a birthday party on one of the smaller islands near the mainland."

"Hmm?" He didn't shift.

"Would you like to go? With me?"

"Yeah," he answered. My chest fluttered with the word, unprepared for an added, "It's a date."

Air caught in my throat. His half-lidded gaze fell on me when I didn't reply, then the least childish smile spread across his face. He nodded toward the Skyla map. "Which island?"

I pried my eyes off him to find the location and pointed it out.

"Okay. I'll see you then." His eyes reclosed. Skye chirped, and Bay chuckled. "All right. All right. Would you be so kind as to leave the bread and cheese?"

I looked at the pixie's broad grin and rolled my eyes. "How could I say no to that face?" Lifting the food out of my bag, I set it beside Skye, who spun into the air above my head. Dust showered over me, and my feet were off the ground in an instant.

"Well, what do you know. You really are a lyric in the wind." Unmoved, Bay lit a fire in my chest with nothing but the intense gleam in his eyes. I took a deep breath, attempting to quell the flurries, but they didn't dare settle.

I wasn't a romantic. I wasn't Whisper. I didn't have the confidence she did when it came to love and being loved. But I had enjoyed talking to him tonight. He carried so much adventure and mystery and allure. I wanted to pick him apart for his secrets and then dig deeper, finding what he hid within his soul.

I also wanted to destroy the twinges of pain that came with the knowledge he only stayed till the tenth before disappearing and stealing the magnetism that drew me in.

My toes curled in my moccasins, and I floated over Bay on my way to the door. "I told you I could."

"I did doubt it just a little." His body lifted into the air, pausing upside down and a couple feet off the ground.

I opened his door and smirked. "Because you're an ass."

Arms folded and head shaking, he mumbled, "Good eve, Wind Song."

"Sleep well, Star Boy." Before I stared at his crooked smile for too long, I flew out into the night.

Flying home was far easier than walking, and I made great time, running out of dust just before hitting the last bit of trek through the woods. A mixture of feelings coalesced within me as I collapsed into my bed, ready to sleep away all the hours between now and Whisper's party.

I hardly knew what to do with the wistful sensations. Part of me liked them. Another part was afraid. Too many risks filled the cracks, and I had no way to know how to bridge them.

So I closed my eyes and tried to set aside my crush before it could morph into something far, far more dangerous and unknown and...sweet.

8TH NOVEMBER

The grove was alive with motion and brightness, even in the dusk. Pixie floss gleamed silver and gold, thanks to the moonlight and lantern light. Delicious scents wafted off the snack table, and music filled the air.

I stood by one snack table now, glancing at the bridge leading to the mainland every few seconds in between watching Whisper greet her other friends and accept gifts. Her smile never faltered, but even she was hyper-focused on the bridge in anticipation of her moth prince's arrival.

"He better come," she said once she had fulfilled her duty as hostess and conceded to stand beside me. Leaning over the snack table, she snatched a cracker and popped it in her mouth.

"I'm sure the dear babysitter is just settling his charge into bed and will be here shortly."

Her eyes went wide. "Of course, *Adam* will be here. He wouldn't pass up all of this for anything." She twirled, her short, silk dress lifting teasingly higher as the gauzy layers caught the wind. "I mean to say *your* boy better come. Or I, without any trace of knowledge about him, will hunt him down and deliver his entrails to his parents on a silver platter."

Did Bay have parents? It hadn't really come up. Maybe we were both orphans? My cheeks heated at that thought, and shame made me look away from Whisper. I shouldn't hope for anyone to have lived with the same fears and complications of having been unwanted.

"What's the matter, chickie?" Whisper's concerned face poked in front of mine. Her delicate brows drew above pinched lips. "If he's not here shortly, he's unworthy. That simple." She glanced at the bridge again and huffed, folding her arms. "That will, indeed, go for both of us."

"It doesn't matter if he comes or not." The words felt heavy in my mouth. "It doesn't." Come the tenth of the month, he'd be gone, and I knew I had no right to think of it like abandonment, but he would be leaving me behind, and it was hard to see it in any other way.

A few more vibrantly dressed partygoers crossed the bridge, and Whisper sighed, fluffing her blond curls. "Pardon me, dearest. I'm afraid my subjects require my attention." Without another moment's notice, she darted through the center of the grove where people talked, swaying to the band, and pounced, hugging those who had just arrived.

Elaborate motions accompanied her conversation, and my stomach rocked, reminding me of Bay's vivid recollections just the night before. I wasn't like that. Them. Insecurity kept me wrapped in a thread that threatened to break at any moment. Doubts and fears clouded my head, suggesting I wasn't good enough or I wouldn't be. It was only a matter of time before everyone I held onto disappeared.

Maybe it would be best if he didn't come. If I didn't grow attached to someone else, someone I knew was scheduled to leave me.

"What's wrong, Wind Song?" The quiet, deep voice yanked me from every negative thought, and I whirled, facing Bay. He smiled, his skin absent of dust save the very top of his head, where some glittered, already fading.

"You came." I stared.

"I said I would."

"Yes, but..." Flushed, I dropped my gaze to our feet. I was worried he had been polite and hadn't wanted to waste any more time on me.

He curled a finger beneath my chin, bumping my attention back up to his face. "Dusk isn't a particularly precise time. If I'm late, that's my excuse."

A smile pulled on my lips. "Well? What do you think? I helped set up."

He gave the party a once-over that consisted of a half-second scrutiny before skimming his eyes over me for far longer. Clinging where my dress did, his gaze sampled and tasted and teased, then flicked away. He shoved his hands in his pockets, looking up at the sky. "It's very nice." His smile eased into a smirk. "The green compliments your hair."

I forced myself to hold onto dignity even though my hair wasn't the only thing that was red right now. "I never took you for a flirt."

"Really?" He shifted his stance. "You're either oblivious, or I'm bad at it then."

"Must be difficult to see underneath the assiness."

"Under the sassiness? I suppose so. It is my primary characteristic, the sass. Hard to see anything else beyond it, really."

I laughed, elbowing him, not for the first time. Keeping his hands in his pockets, he returned the shove awkwardly. A beat passed where he cleared his throat, and I gasped. "Could you be nervous?"

"What?"

"You're nervous, aren't you?"

His look turned incredulous, saying without so many words, "How dare you suggest such a thing, madam?" but his body language confirmed my suspicions.

"You're tense," I added.

He ruffled his hair, fingers catching in his braid and pulling it loose. Releasing a breath, he confessed, "You've found me out. I don't normally do things like this. Rather, I've *never* done something like this before."

"You've never gone to a party before?" With how frequent parties were on Skyla, I was justifiably shocked.

"I've never gone to a party with a girl before."

And now I was justifiably flattered. And he was considerably darker in the cheeks. My grin spread. "How old are you?"

"I'm…really not sure."

I looked him over from his brown hair down his muscular frame to his bare feet. "You look twenty. You act ten."

"Has anyone ever told you that you have a way with words, specifically to destroy self-esteem?"

"I don't believe it's come up, no."

We exchanged smiles, and I fought against the

twinge of pain in my chest. After he left, when would he visit again? If he traveled the world, there was so much more to do out there than worry about seeing Skyla, or me.

Before I could gather enough courage to ask about his plans, a shrill gasp pulled both our attentions to Whisper. A hand before her mouth, she didn't bother concealing the way her eyes danced up and down, and up and down over Bay. "Oh. My. Yes." She blindly reached for my arm, touching my shoulder. "Yes." Brightening, she stepped forward, palm outstretched. "It's so nice to meet you. My name's Whispering Meadow, and I'm Lyric's best, dare I say, only friend."

Bay took her fingers, pressing a kiss to her knuckles, and I thought she would die right there. "Charmed to meet you. I'm just Bay."

I held myself back from a laugh.

"*Bay*. That's such a perfectly romantic name." Whisper sighed, her eyes going dreamy. As though she'd just remembered, she tossed a glance toward the bridge, then harrumphed. Spite edged her melodic voice when she mumbled, "How kind of you to be on time."

"So, I *was* on time." Bay's eyes stuck on me, his smile impish. "Lyric made me feel as though I was late. Maybe she was just overly anticipating my arrival."

"Was she now?" Whisper's voice pitched. Her lashes fluttered, the look in her eyes nothing short of manic. "How absolutely thrilling."

I glared at them both, attempting to stab them with my eyes. They hardly noticed.

"Well, if it doesn't work out between you two...I may just be available." She winked, and my heart stopped at the implication.

"I'm afraid I only go for redheads." Bay shrugged

a shoulder, appearing casual, but some tension had filtered back into his body, and he pocketed his hands again.

I chewed my cheek, hoping Whisper would catch on. "We're not really..."

When my voice fizzled out, Bay interjected, "At least, not yet, anyway."

My eyes widened, and I wasn't sure if all the breath had escaped my chest or if I was holding it hostage.

He added, "Anything could happen." Dipping toward my ear, he whispered, "Unless, of course, you only consider me a ten-year-old."

Whisper cupped her hands over her mouth when Bay straightened, innocently watching dark clouds slip by the moon. Breathlessly, she said, "I like this. I like this a lot. You're perfect." She clasped his arm, forcefully prying his hand from his pocket so she could hold it. "Get married to my bestie and have a dozen sass-castic babies. I need them in my life."

He snickered. "Are you up for a dozen, Wind Song?"

"I think I should leave now." My heart was pounding. Despite him taking everything as calmly as anyone could, their teasing hit too close to hope for me. I liked the idea of him sticking around and making something more out of this, but that wasn't what he had planned, and I certainly wasn't going to bend any of his plans in a matter of days.

"'Wind Song'?" Whisper's grin rounded her cheeks. "We already have pet names? Can I just say I'm in love with both of you?"

To avoid her burning gaze, I glanced across the grove and released a pent-up breath; salvation had come to me at last. "Is that Adam?"

All joking died when Whisper whirled, spotting the

dark-haired boy across the way. "How's my hair? Is my dress wrinkled, like, anywhere?" She stretched out her fingers, examining her nails, then shot me a pleading expression. "Am I wearing too much makeup?"

My eyes rolled. "You're a queen, Whisper. Go snag your prince."

She looked at Bay. "Male perspective?"

"If he likes you, it won't be because of how you look, but, no, you're not too shabby."

Whisper glowed. Snatching my pinky in hers, she pressed her forehead to mine, then said, "Keep him." In the next instant, she and her frothy dress were off like a streak.

I sighed, relaxing up until the moment I remembered I had to deal with the aftermath of her conversation with Bay. Peeking at him, I caught a lazy smirk and knew there would be no escaping. I had to ride out the waves she had caused.

"She's...something else." He passed me, perusing the snack table. "I can see why she's your best—pardon—only friend." Plucking a mini tart off a plate, he stuck it inside his vest.

Ignoring his words completely, I asked, "Skye came with you?"

"Of course. He's my best—pardon—only friend."

"And you're hiding him." That wasn't a question. "You knew it wasn't normal to talk with a pixie even though you acted like it was a few days ago."

"Or I could not have known until your reaction and be playing off it now so I don't stand out."

"I find that unlikely."

He popped another tart into his own mouth and twisted toward me on his heel. "Well, I can't control your thoughts, so have fun with them." He nodded toward the tree line behind me. "Let's sit over there where it's a bit more private."

I looked at the outskirts of the party where pixie floss threaded every tree, and dangling lanterns illuminated every shadow surrounding it. Before I replied, Bay strode past me and reclined against one of the oaks, relaxing for the first time since he'd arrived.

Skye snuck out of his pocket, joining the other pixies in the canopy, and Bay watched them, half a smile on his face.

Even without pixie dust covering every inch of his skin, he glowed, at one with the illuminated forest scene. When he patted the ground beside him, a piece of my heart lightened. I nearly glided to him and may have flown had any dust been on my skin. Sitting beside him, my back against the rough bark, I wondered if I fit just as perfectly in the picture or if I marred it. Attempting to relax as well as he had, I pulled off my satchel and set it beside me.

"You look very nice." His soft words barely reached above the music, but after them, everything except his presence muffled, dropping away.

"So do you." I pushed my hair over my ear. "Did you take a bath or something?"

"Did I smell that bad before?"

My head whipped toward him. "I didn't mean—"

His playful grin stopped my words. "I know. Now look who's tense."

Folding my hands in my lap, I fooled with the simple green dress I wore. "Maybe we're both ten-year-olds."

He leaned close, his voice little more than a secretive purr. "You mean to say you've never been to a party with a boy before either?"

I mimicked the same secretive tone. "Nope." Setting

the teasing aside, I sighed. Starlight bathed us, every twinkling light familiar and new all at once. "I spend most of my time exploring the islands, looking for adventures, but none ever come up. At least, not until meeting you."

"I'm an adventure, then?" He chuckled.

In complete seriousness, I murmured, "I think so. But I'm worried I won't get to be a part of it."

Tentative silence burdened with laughter and music and voices filled the space between us, keeping us so far from each other.

"Why can't you leave?"

I swallowed. Saying I wasn't allowed to felt so childish, and I didn't want to appear childish to him. The only real, logical attachment I had to him was the fact that he lived the life I longed for. Still, I wanted, needed, his approval. "I'm duty-bound to Skyla," I said instead. "I'm protecting it. Somehow."

Bay's brows knitted, but he didn't press the issue. Pulling a leg up to his chest, he rested an elbow on it and rubbed his lips with his thumb. "It's exhausting, what we do because of duty."

"Yeah..." My eyes drifted up, finding Whisper among everyone, and a laugh escaped me. "Well, I suppose they live happily ever after."

At the other side of the island, right on the edge where any wrong move would mean plummeting into the ocean, Whisper and Adam stood locked together. Her foot kicked up behind her, his lips on hers, their hands in one another's hair. Even from so far away, nothing but bliss shone off them. I smiled, anticipating all the details after the lights had gone out, and the party had slipped into silence.

My heart tripped, my gaze dropping to my hand.

Beside it, just brushing, was Bay's. He continued staring ahead like he hadn't moved closer, but his quirked lips gave him away entirely. Mischief and innocence radiated in his expression.

I told myself not to take it seriously and wracked my brain for another topic, something to say. "Are you really leaving in two days?" The second the words left me, my eyes closed, and I bit my tongue.

"I am." His hand didn't move. His gaze didn't redirect. Only sorrow tinted his smile, and I knew somewhere deep within me. I had nothing to do with it.

"Will you be back?" I confined myself to the shameful questions, deciding if I'd started down this path, I may as well not back out.

"I always come back. But I never know when." Now, he looked at me, and we were far closer than we'd been before. I could pick out golden flecks dancing in his hazel eyes. They were soft, and maybe it was a trick of the light, but they were beautiful. His lips parted to say something, but a shriek sliced through me.

My heart stopped cold. A wash of ice chilled me to the bone.

I'd know that voice anywhere.

Jumping to my feet, I zoned in on Whisper in the moment after a man crashed into her, sending them both over the edge toward an unforgiving sea.

From this height, she would die.

She would die.

She would die.

My legs moved on their own, force slamming through my joints. Sheer terror closed my throat, blocking all my breath. I couldn't see anything but the panic in her eyes as she'd fallen. I couldn't hear anything but her shriek, on replay. I plowed through everyone, caring less if they all fell than if she did.

Without thought or pause, I dove after her.

Wind whipped my hair, her dress. The man who had pushed her was nowhere in sight. She kept her body flat to the wind, slowing her descent, but not enough.

"Lyric!" she screamed. Her eyes searched me, and I realized moments after her brown skin went ashy that I didn't have my satchel; I didn't have any dust.

"It's okay!" I yelled, knowing it wasn't, but hoping it might be. I had fallen countless times before. I trusted the pixies would catch me—if they knew, if they made it in time. Air burned my eyes, tears dashed away before they could roll down my cheeks. "We will never be apart." I caught up to her, touching her hand. She gripped my fingers, her tears slapping against my face.

Her smile shook as we both stretched our bodies to give us as much time as we could garner. Near my ear, nearly lost to the roaring wind, she murmured, "I wish we were apart now, Lyly. I'm so sorry."

I held her. The churning waters below were dark and formless, depthless, a pool of ink streaming closer with every lost moment. Everything in my head was a blur. I had never been afraid of falling; I had always been afraid of losing my best—and only—friend.

Now, I may not need to be afraid of either ever again.

Closing my eyes, I embraced whatever fate held.

"Fly, you idiot!" Bay's voice screamed, and Whisper was wrenched from my arms. A hand gripped my clothes, yanking my body up. *"Fly!"*

A glimmer of dust surrounded me, and I screeched to a stop, suspended in the air. My heart panicked, jerked from accepting death to understanding it wouldn't come today. I looked at Bay, who held Whisper over his shoulder and searched the water. "There," he said, darting for a dark spot.

I looked at Skye, who chirped and beckoned me after. I followed Bay to an outcropping of an island and rushed to Whisper's side when he dumped her in the sand. "Hey!" I growled. "Be careful!"

"Yes, you're welcome." His face was hard as stone, no care in his expression. He scanned the waves, his lip curled, then he lifted off the ground and zipped into the dark.

Whisper held a hand at her head, blinking after Bay and Skye. "He...has a pixie with him?"

"Are you okay?" I clasped her hand, unable to care less what Bay was up to.

Her lashes fluttered, and a waterfall of tears streamed down her cheeks. Her chest rose and fell in horrid, uneven motions, and her beautiful, dainty face contorted. "N-no. We almost died. W-what... W-who..." She was such an ugly crier, always feeling every emotion completely. "I want my moth prince," she blubbered.

My heart still thudded irregularly, but we were okay. We were okay. I had to remember that if I was going to keep my sanity. Dropping my forehead to hers, I took deep breaths and forced myself to get a grip. Who had shoved her and jumped off the edge themselves? And why?

"No trace." Bay interrupted my thoughts, and I looked up. He emerged from the water, shaking out his hair. Waves crashed behind him, and Skye circled his head, dousing him anew in dust before sitting on his shoulder. "Did you see him clearly at all, Whispering Meadow?"

She sniffled. "What?"

"The man. Did you see at all what he looked like?"

Whisper's head began to shake, her lip quivering,

but she stopped. "There was a flash of light, and he was gone. But the light reflected on something gold for a split second. Maybe an earring?"

Bay's jaw clenched. "Was it large and hooped?"

Dumbly, Whisper nodded.

"Pirate," Bay growled, cramming his fingers into his hair. His braid came loose, and Skye caught the tie before the lapping tide could snatch it away. Pacing, Bay inhaled and exhaled deeply; then he stopped. "Okay. You both need to get back home. I don't think you can fly, but we can both manage to carry you." He pointed at Whisper, and my eyes widened.

"Of course, she—"

"I can't."

My heart stopped again. "What?"

Shame tainted her tear-streaked cheeks, her wobbly smile pleading. "I'm sorry, Lyly... I haven't been able to since...since Papa left. I don't like to think about it, and I didn't know how to tell you."

"But we were—" My words came out breathless before I cut them short and swallowed. That was a topic for later. We needed to get home safe and figure out why there had been two pirates in Skyla. Peter had to believe me if all three of us told him. We needed to do something about it before anything else like this happened, or worse.

After all, why were they here? Surely, they weren't visiting to pay their respects to a boy who had killed their kind for sport.

"How do you have a pixie?" Whisper asked, slowly gaining her feet. I helped support her, and after she was stable, she released my hand.

"Doesn't everyone?" Bay brushed her surprise aside, squinting upward. At Skyla.

It hit me then, shoving everything else from my brain.

I wasn't on Skyla. I was in the real world. For the first time in my life, my feet rested on grounded earth. I stood in front of the ocean I always saw from so far above. It rolled, each wave a distinct creature, and I couldn't find words.

"Wind Song, are you still with us?" Bay's voice was more gentle than it had been for the past few minutes.

I focused on him, nodding.

He glanced out at the waves, a hint of a smile lifting his lips. It was small, but it proved no matter how many times he had seen it, he'd never lost the wonder. "It is beautiful." Clapping his hands together, he jerked us from the moment. "Okay, Skye, do your thing."

The pixie dropped Bay's hair tie into his hand and spun over Whisper and I. Even if she couldn't use the magic to fly herself, with our support, being doused in it would make carrying her back up easier.

We each took a side and lifted her through the air to the deserted party location. Lanterns still swayed in the wind, and pixies still darted through the trees, oblivious. But, the piles of food had been abandoned, save for the stray pixie who had decided they belonged to it now.

"Whisper..." The soft voice made my friend tense, and her head whipped up the second her feet touched the ground. Her brown eyes widened, and she yanked her arms free from around our shoulders to scrub her face. Thankfully she hadn't been wearing too much makeup, but it still was clear in her puffy eyes that she had been fiercely crying.

"Adam, what are you—"

The large boy wrapped her in a hug before she could

get her sentence out. Bay and I spared one another a glance when Adam's lip quivered. He bit it, sucking in a breath. "After Lyric jumped, I thought you'd have to be all right."

Whisper laughed shortly, still shaken. "Naturally."

Adam's eyes snapped open on Bay and me, settling on Bay. "But why did you..."

"Faith and trust," Bay mumbled, passing by them, "'Lyly' was missing one last thing, so I brought it to her." He headed for the trees where my satchel lay, useless. I would never take it off again.

Whisper pulled out of Adam's hold and shook her head. "It doesn't matter. What does matter is I'm okay, and you're okay, and everyone is okay. We need to get home now. Only Lyric knows how to get to Peter at this time, and he needs to know what happened immediately."

Adam's brows furrowed. He glanced at me before rustling his dark hair and addressing Whisper. "Yeah ..., okay. May I walk you home?"

Flushing, Whisper looked at me, her wide smile almost erasing the faint streaks smudged over her cheeks. "Are you okay?"

I extended my pinky. "Of course."

"Even with..." She pressed her lips together and linked her finger with mine. When she leaned forward to press our foreheads together, she whispered, "I'm sorry. I meant to tell you, but I couldn't."

I watched her and Adam walk away, ignoring the empty feeling spinning in my chest. Too much was changing at once. If Whisper couldn't fly, our plans of leaving together and seeing the world evaporated. Even though she had said if it came to a choice between Adam and me she'd choose me, I wouldn't want to take her from the happily ever after she had been searching for since we were kids.

My throat tightened. We said we'd never be apart, and now, I knew if ever we were, it would be because I had broken the oath. I would be the one who abandoned her.

Bay dangled my satchel before my face, blocking the view of the bridge where I remained staring despite Whisper and Adam having vanished several minutes ago. He dropped the bag into my hands before elaborating a bow. "May *I* have the pleasure of walking you home?"

I slipped the strap over my head, adjusting the bag at my waist where pixie dust would never be far from my hands again. Then I looked at him. "Nope."

His brow quirked as he straightened. "Why not?"

"My house is like your house, secret. But unlike yours, mine is well-hidden."

"Ouch. After I saved your life too." He glanced over his shoulder where his pixie perused the snack tables with several other of his kind. "I suppose the party is left to the wild things now."

The melody of the night and the chirring of pixies surrounded us. "I guess so."

He rebraided his hair, sighing. "May I walk you back to the mainland, at least?" When his braid was tied, his gaze averted. "And will I see you tomorrow?"

I looked at my moccasins, wanting to say yes.

"I'm not leaving without saying goodbye, even if I have to hunt down your secret house before I go."

I rolled my eyes. "I guess I have no choice, then."

"Not really, no." His smile drifted away, and he looked at the edge of the island. "Skye," he said into the wind, but the pixie heard him, "let's go."

Our walk was silent as we headed through Aire, both

our heads seemingly packed with thoughts. I couldn't tell why seeing the pirate had rattled him so much unless, of course, his talk about knowing blades and not pirates was a lie. Who knew where his adventures had taken him. I still didn't know what country the map above his bed belonged to. I had studied it that night a few days ago, and the image wouldn't soon leave my head. Nothing from these brief days would.

Stopping when we reached the trees on my home island, I toyed with my satchel's flap. "This is my stop."

Bay peered around the area, scouring the treetops for any hint of construction. He'd find nothing of the sort. Huffing, he crossed his arms and examined me as though I'd give away the secret.

I smiled pleasantly and batted my eyelashes.

A sliver of moonlight cascaded through the treetops, catching his eye, and the gleam that followed made my chest tighten and my heart skip a beat. His hand raised, my gaze darting to it, and even in the dim light, I could tell hard work had calloused his fingers. He moved close, catching a flaming lock between his fingers and tucking it behind my ear. The barest touch of his skin sent a shiver careening through me, and... I didn't want to say goodbye. Not tonight. Not tomorrow.

Before my mouth could open and I could beg for something I'd regret, Peter's voice shredded the forest. "LYRIC!"

I jerked back, away from Bay, and faced the boy speeding through the trees. Tinkerbell glared at his side, per usual. Alight with dust in the moonlight, he appeared little more than a will o' the wisp.

"You're okay," he panted, ignoring Bay entirely as he clapped his hands against my cheeks and turned my head this way and that. "You're okay?"

"I'm fine." I swatted him off me. "How'd you hear about what happened?"

"Apparently, Tiger Lily knows where we live." He grumbled; his brows furrowed. "I had no idea."

I'd suspected as much, even though she'd never said anything. Tiger Lily raised me on stories of her and Peter's adventures, stories Peter had long forgotten when she'd aged.

"Some people went to her house and said there had been an accident, and you were involved."

Likely Whisper's other guests had gone straight to her mother. I swallowed. "Did Tiger Lily tell you exactly what had happened?"

"Only that you and I guess one of your friends had fallen." His furrowed brows made me wonder if he'd forgotten the more important detail that someone had shoved 'one of my friends' over the edge before disappearing without a trace.

My mouth opened, but Bay beat me to words. "You never mentioned you had a little brother, Wind Song."

I blinked. Peter blinked. Tinkerbell blinked, turning in Peter's hair to face Bay. Her head tilted so far, she nearly went upside down.

Peter didn't grace him with a glance. "I'm her father. Now, what exactly happened, Lyric?"

"Her *father*?" Concern rippled over Bay's face.

Peter whirled then, floating off the ground to meet Bay's height. "Yes. Who in Skyla are you? What are you doing here?"

Bay's lips parted and closed several times, his eyes flicking between me and my underage parental unit before he managed, "I'm a friend. From the party. I wanted to make sure she got home safe."

Peter scoffed, folding his arms. Long moments

passed, and his lips pursed. "She hasn't mentioned you before. It's always a girl. I know it's always a girl." He looked over his shoulder at me, and I held my breath. Snapping his fingers, he stated, "Tiger Lily's girl. Yeah. It's always Tiger Lily's girl. You're not Tiger Lily's girl."

"No...sir...I'm not."

If the moment weren't entirely insane, I might have laughed at how, well, insane it was.

Bay's gaze narrowed. "You're Peter Pan, then."

Peter stuck his nose in the air. "Who else would I be?"

"How old are you?" Bay's eyes were intent on Peter, and his body retained a stillness that sent chills down my spine. *What did it matter how old Peter was?*

"Why would you expect me to know? I'm older than her and older than you and older than Skyla itself. I obviously have more important things to think about."

"Obviously," Bay murmured, and the dark glint in his eye made me stiffen. When he looked at me, the feeling was gone. "I suppose I'll leave you in your father's capable hands."

"Right."

He raised a hand, turned around, and walked away. When he had disappeared in the foliage, Peter remained glaring after him. "He had dust." The intensity in his voice disappeared when he faced me again. "You have dust."

Tinkerbell chimed, and Peter harrumphed.

"She recognizes who it belongs to, but says I won't remember."

My stomach flipped, but I shoved the comment aside, knowing Peter was nothing if not easy to distract. "It doesn't matter. It's the only reason I'm alive right now. But, Peter, I know you didn't believe me before about the pirate, but Whisper, my friend, Tiger Lily's girl, didn't just fall off the island. Another pirate pushed her, then he disappeared midair."

Peter remained silent, and anger built behind my eyes. He didn't believe me *again*. Skyla was probably under attack, and yet, he didn't believe me. Rubbing his nose, he dropped his gaze. "No, the boys and I... we looked after you told us. Felt bad for making you cry and all... I believe you. But this is very bad." His fists clenched. "We'll figure it out. What have I always told you? We'll figure it out; Peter Pan always does." Determination burned in his eyes, and I knew this was only the beginning.

9TH NOVEMBER

"What?" I stared at Peter, baffled. I couldn't have just heard what I thought I'd heard. "Stay put today."

Okay, maybe I did. I planted my hands on my hips and glared down at him. "Excuse me. I'm not a child. You can't just ground me to my room because you think it might be dangerous outside."

"It *is* dangerous outside. You've come across two pirates in a single week. We don't know why they're here, but I have a hunch it might have something to do with you. This is the most secure place in Skyla, so *stay put.*"

I threw my hands in the air. "Why would it have anything to do with me? I'm inconsequential. I wasn't even born when you fought against the pirates."

Peter's eyes narrowed, searching for something. He clamped his hand against his mouth, then murmured, "Maybe. Maybe not. Just stay here for a day while I figure things out."

"Oh, and I can't help you figure things out?" No, that's not what I wanted to say. Shaking my head, I breathed. "Listen, you don't understand. I'm going to stay out of trouble. This is just the last day I'll get to see my friend before he moves away. I don't know when he'll visit again."

Peter sneered. "I don't trust that kid from last night. Good riddance to him."

Anger sparked. I stomped out of my room toward the exit. "Well, you can't keep me here."

Peter scratched the back of his head. "Chubs."

The hefty boy saluted and planted himself in the exit, blocking it completely. Stomping my foot, I exclaimed, "That's not fair!"

"It's for your own good." Peter actually looked exhausted when he rubbed his eyes. "Listen, I'm sorry this coincides with your friend leaving, but I'd be lost without you, Skyla'd be lost without you."

My heart pinched, and it hurt to swallow. "I'm not magical. I'm not special. I'm not some protective amulet that is keeping Skyla afloat, Peter. I'm just...me. An orphan who was abandoned in the clouds." Holding back my tears, I scanned his face. "But you'll never accept that because you always forget the important things."

"Lyric...I—"

Walking past him, I shut myself in my room, slipping to the floor beside my bed. My legs pulled tight against my chest, I refused to cry. In the past few days, I had cried too much. Nothing came from the tears, but plans boiled from the anger.

I was going to see Bay before he left. I was going to get to the bottom of this mystery.

And I was certain the boy and the mystery were shrouded as one.

I had two books, only two, and I kept them in my satchel along with some food, my telescope, the bag of pixie dust, a pair of gloves, and my pan flute. Though I'd read them countless times before, they were all I had now to pass the time between my argument with Peter and when Chubs inevitably fell asleep in front of the exit.

My ears perked when the soft snores drifted throughout the small home, and I tucked my novel back into my bag. Creeping to my door, I peeked out. Chubs sat in the exit, his face crammed against the wall. His mouth was open, and drool leaked onto his fur clothing. No one else was in view.

I scanned several times before gathering the courage to sprinkle some dust on my head and tiptoe toward him. At the exit, I listened past the snores to make sure no one was returning. When I was certain I could make it out unnoticed, I floated into the air above Chubs and out into the night.

Not wasting any time, I darted for Bay's island, landing on the porch. I brushed back my hair, raised my hand, and watched the door open before I could knock.

"There you are." Bay's gaze ran over me from head to toe. "I thought I'd have to hunt you down. Is everything okay?"

Within, his oil lamp flickered light over strewn papers and curling maps. I recognized the landmarks peeking out as the same ones found on the map above his cot. "Where is that?" I asked, ignoring his question.

He turned, stilling. Running his hand over his hair, he shrugged. "Elsewhere."

"That's where you're going? Why?" I slipped past him and crouched, spreading the curling page flat.

"It's where I have to go." He floated to the ground across from me, catching my hand before I could completely view the next map flat. "Why do you have to be so nosy?"

I stared at him.

Bay's fingers left mine, clenching into a fist. "You aren't here for a casual visit and then a goodbye, are you?"

My head shook. Wordlessly, I dropped my gaze, peeled back the curled edge of the map, and saw the etched visage of a pirate ship. A bleeding red skull marked it. "You knew that pirate," I murmured. "Why are they here? Is it because you are?"

"No. I don't know why they're here." He paused, swallowed, and continued, "I do have a hunch."

Skye appeared out of nowhere, chiming madly at Bay. The little pixie's hands were splayed in objection, but Bay scrubbed a hand over his face. "I know. I know!" Torment darkened his eyes, but he made them meet mine. "She's been hidden away here all her life by Pan. And she might just be the only hope for both us and Skyla."

"What are you talking about?"

Bay kicked up a leg and rested his arm against it, cradling his forehead in his hand. "I know it's not normal to talk with pixies, certainly not at my age. I know most our age can't fly. We both know Pan, probably better than he remembers to know himself.

We have a hunch about why the pirates are here, and we have encountered them...many, many times before. I don't know my age because I'm older than I look and younger than I feel."

"You aren't making any sense."

He laughed, but it was bitter. "No, I suppose I'm not."

"Just tell me plainly why I've seen two pirates in the past few days when I'd never seen any before."

"Two?" His jaw tightened.

Right, he hadn't been here then. "I saw one and chased him to the island where Peter keeps his pirate ship. I pinned him down, but before I could get any answers, he began foaming at the mouth...then he died."

"Appeared to." Bay cursed beneath his breath.

"No, he definitely did. Peter saw him afterward."

"Sure." Bay divided his attention between his thoughts and Skye, completely ignoring me, so I slammed my hand against the floor. He glanced up, and Skye's tinkling words stopped.

"Explain," I growled. "I came here for answers."

Bay lounged back. "And here I thought you enjoyed my company." When my expression didn't crack, he sighed. "Okay. I'm sorry. It's hard to explain the magic the pirates have come into. I learned a long time ago not to trust any of them if they 'died.' Pirates are selfish. They aren't as loyal to their captains as their captains would like to believe. If threatened, they will tell you everything. And they definitely aren't going to kill themselves to keep any secrets."

"So how did he..."

"Short answer? Magic. Long answer? Powerful magic. The kind pirates don't normally have, so I know they are getting help. From where or whom...that's something I haven't been able to solve."

My heart pounded, picking up in tempo. "Why are you fighting the pirates?"

"Fighting them?" He laughed. "I'm not. They simply keep getting in my way. And I think I won't tell you what I'm up to. At least not right now. Maybe if...you came with me, though..."

I froze, down to the blood in my veins. "W-what?"

"Come with me." His smile was carefree, gentle, enticing like we hadn't been talking about villains with powerful magic that were infesting my home. Skye chirped, looking at me too, waiting. When I still didn't respond, couldn't find the words, Bay tapped the map between us. "To elsewhere, to Neverland."

My lips parted, my eyes widening. I felt I'd heard that title before, in the corners of Peter's stories, though, he'd never mentioned it by name. Why? Why did something I'd never known existed feel so familiar?

Bay continued, "If your enemy is the pirates, why not meet them where they are? Shave them off bit by bit before they ever reach Skyla?"

"I can't." My own words surprised me. I wanted nothing more than to go with him, to Neverland, to this magical place that his stories lived and breathed in, but I couldn't. I couldn't leave Peter or Whisper, especially if we were under attack. I had to be here for them. Not because I was some lucky charm. If Whisper were at risk, I could throw a blade. I could fly. Not many on our island could both fight and use the magic of the pixies. "If they are already coming, we'll have to be ready for them. I'll have to fight for my home."

Maybe this was why I had been left here all those years ago.

Bay rubbed his jaw. "Okay. I get it." Skye settled on

his shoulder while he scanned the map. "I don't know when I'll be back. Even if the pirates leave Neverland and you defeat them, it won't guarantee my success."

Those words weighed against my body, but I nodded, lifting the flap to my pack. "Then I guess we have tonight." Bringing out some bread, cheese, and berries, I offered him a weak smile.

He reached forward, moving his face close to mine when he grabbed one ripe, blackberry. "Don't you forget me."

My cheeks heated, but he moved back before he was close enough to feel his breath on my lips. I whispered, "Never."

We talked about silly things, stupid things, stories, fears, dreams. We talked like tomorrow we wouldn't say goodbye. We talked through the night, though I hadn't meant to stay so long. We talked curled together though I'd never meant to end up in his arms.

We talked.

We laughed.

And I, maybe a little bit, right before accidentally falling asleep, cried.

10TH NOVEMBER

Heavy thuds marred my dreams, shaking the foundation of my imagination. The pictures in my head distorted till they burned around the edges. The charred pieces closed in, then popped.

I jolted upright, gasping, and peered at the small room before me. Bay's house. Bay. I must have fallen asleep? Turning my head, I looked at him. He rubbed his face, meeting my eyes before noting our precarious sleeping position—me in his arms—with half a smirk.

I couldn't think on it for more than an instant. Dawn streamed through the windows. Gongs screamed in steady beats, metal clamoring to be heard across all of Skyla.

"What is that airwoman-forsaken noise?" Bay

murmured his voice thick with rest.

The sleepy tenor may have made my cheeks go hot at any other point in time, but my body was awash in ice. "The warning signal."

"What?"

I scrambled to my feet, checked for my bag, and rushed to the door. "I have to go. I have to go now. This could be it. What if the pirates are here?"

Bay's eyes widened. Zipping off the floor and to his cot, he snatched Skye off the blanket and poked the little pixie's cheeks. Skye awoke complaining before he tilted his head to the noise.

"Dust her," he commanded, and Skye dashed into the air toward me without question. Bay added, "It's faster to fly than run."

Glitter ran over my skin, tingling as it fell, and my feet left the wooden planks. "Thank you. Are you coming?"

He shook his head. "If the pirates are here, they can't see me. I can't risk fighting them. I'm sorry...I..."

"I don't understand, but I do." Every loud hammering sound reminded me of all I had to lose, but I flew into Bay's arms, squeezing him tight for as long as I dared. "I'll miss you. Good luck."

Strong, large hands clamped against my back, fingers splayed, leaving a sensation I didn't think I'd ever be able to forget. He whispered, "Good luck to you too."

When I left, I didn't look back. Wind whipped against my cheeks, the warmth biting as I streaked toward the capital. I searched the air and the sea and the ground for any signs of danger. I saw nothing.

A sense of calm nearly took hold. Perhaps Peter had panicked when he checked my room and found me missing? I could find him, get yelled at, and everything would be okay. We would have more time to prepare, and then when the pirates did come, we would be ready.

Changing my focus, I looked for brilliant orange hair.

Instead, I found a crowd of people toward the far end of the mainland, standing just before the path to Whisper's neighborhood.

"No." My throat closed. My heartbeat grew short.

The bridge meant to connect the islands dangled like a broken wing, limp and frayed like it had snapped. The island itself rested in the water far below, cracked. Jagged stone and wood protruded across the surface of collapsed homes. Clumps of dirt drifted in heaps, bobbing with the waves.

Peter rose from the rubble, hovering in front of the crowd. Before he opened his mouth, I slammed into him, clutching his shoulders. His eyes went wide, relief filling them moments later. "You're okay. When we couldn't find you, I thought perhaps—"

"Where is she?" I demanded, clipping his words.

His brows knitted, and his head tilted.

"Where is she!"

"We don't know the damage yet. Bombs went off at the base of each tree some time ago. They woke everyone. The pixies helped whoever could fly, and those who could make it jumped into the ocean." He scratched his head, but I wasn't hearing anything reassuring. Whisper lived in the center of the island. She couldn't fly. He continued, "The boys are helping—"

I pushed him aside and fled toward the fractured land where I'd spent half my life, so much of my childhood. "Whisper!" I screamed. Tears blurred my vision. We had just survived near-death. We had just made it.

"No." I panted. Breath raked in and out of my lungs as I sped from one broken section of land to the next.

"Tiger Lily!" My voice broke. Lips trembling, I hugged myself, whirling and blinking fast. I couldn't miss her because I was crying; I had to clear my eyes. She was fine. She just needed help. I had to find her and help her.

"WHISPER!" I caught sight of her house. The roof was tilted, the walls caved in, and I imagined her trapped inside, bleeding, cold. I couldn't stomach the images that followed, so I dashed forward, scraping my knees when I fell to them on the rough ground. I clawed my way to an opening and peered in through the shadows.

Her perfect new dress lay tattered, halfway beneath a fallen beam and covered in a thick, red liquid. Nothing moved. Waves and people and noise and the incessant gongs filled my ears till my head boiled, but all was silent.

"You said you wouldn't leave me!" I screamed into the hole. "You promised! Every day!"

"Lyric!" Peter pulled me away from the house, turning my head to face him. I couldn't see anything. I couldn't feel anything. I couldn't hear anything. Images of her suffering and trapped and drowning and alone crammed their way into my skull until I was right there with her, suffocating in a dozen different ways.

"Lyric, breathe!" Peter yelled.

And I was. I was breathing. But I was breathing too much, and there was no air.

"Lyric, damn it." I'd never heard him curse before. "C'mon. You're okay. Twins! Get the others! Help me with her. Let's get her somewhere safer." He wrapped his arms around me, and I faintly registered Tinkerbell chiming soothing tones in my ear just before it all went dark.

Whisper smiled at me, but something wasn't right. She wasn't completely clear. Something muffled her laugh, and it was gone too soon. Everything around me got darker and darker, then I could hear other voices.

"We've searched everywhere, Peter." Tootles.

"We've lost a group of people." One twin.

And the other: "Including Tiger Lily..."

There was a pause while I pried my eyes open. Something thick wanted to keep them closed, so I rubbed away a gooey crust and squinted into the dim space.

"Who's Tiger Lily?"

Instantly awake, I jerked upright. Peter stood in the center of our home with his arms folded, each Lost Boy before him. Genuine confusion muddled his expression, and the boys looked at one another.

Slightly saw me first, extending a finger. "Ay, she's up."

That set aside the conversation—for them.

"*Who's Tiger Lily?*" My voice cracked, raw from something—screaming? "What are you talking about?"

Peter stared at me. "Was she a friend of yours?"

I stumbled out of Peter's large chair, dropping the blankets they had covered me with. Focusing on each Lost Boy, I asked, "Did you find Whisper? Is Tiger Lily... really...?"

Sadness pulled their expressions down, then one at a time they murmured, "Tiger Lily? What did she look like?"

"A friend of yours?"

"Everyone is gathered on the mainland. You could go look?"

Their eyes betrayed them, sorrow gleaming in their averted gazes. But when I turned toward Peter, I found nothing of the sort. His brows were lowered with concern, but nothing more.

"Are you okay, Lyric?"

My head shook, and my lips parted dumbly. "It happens that quickly?" I trembled, taking a step back when he took one closer. "How long has it been? A few hours?"

"It's nearly dusk," one Lost Boy offered; I wasn't sure whom. Sound distorted in my head, blurring until I heard the phantom of Whisper's laugh, something I would never hear again.

"What's gotten into you?" Peter rubbed the back of his neck. "We have to make a plan to strike against the pirates who did this."

The pirates who did this. Of course. That's why they had been here. To thin our numbers before their attack. My fists clenched, anger overwhelming the empty feeling residing in my gut. Nails biting flesh, I turned around.

"Lyric?" True bafflement coated Peter's voice. "Where are you going?"

"To check and see if my friend's among the survivors." I knew she wasn't.

"Be back soon so we can plan."

I ignored his words as I climbed outside and opened my satchel. Lifting my pouch of pixie dust, I sprinkled just enough to take me to Bay's house on my head. I would scour his maps and notes until I found my way to Neverland, to the pirates who had done this, then I would make them pay.

My throat closed as I soared through the early night, sped along by a rush of wind. Light hues blanketed the sky still, but two or three stars blinked on in the twilight.

I rubbed my eyes. Tears were getting me nowhere. And yet I couldn't make them stop.

I landed directly on Bay's porch, sniffling, and reached for the door. I had to pull myself together, let anger guide my steps, or I wouldn't have what it took to fight when I found the pirates responsible. But I couldn't shake the urge to scream. How could she be gone? After all we'd been through, I couldn't picture my life without her nearby.

"Wind Song?" Bay's voice drifted through the night, starkly soft compared to the screaming in my head.

I looked behind me, down at him. His eyes widened where he stood on the grass. Moments later, he was hovering in front of me, just beyond the porch rail.

"What...happened?"

"You haven't left yet?" I croaked. He shook his head. I didn't have words. I couldn't find anything to say clearly. "The pirates, they... She's gone, and I..." *I did nothing.* Couldn't do anything. What if I had been there? If I had just been there. A sob caught in my chest as I tunneled my fingers into my hair and gripped the ends until my scalp stung.

"Hey." Bay touched my hand, trying to pull it free. He gave up, awkwardly drawing me toward his chest. "It's okay. Are the pirates still here?"

It wasn't okay! Nothing was okay! I wanted to scream and hit him, but instead, all I could manage was a limp, "No."

"Who's gone?"

My jaw tightened until my teeth ached, but I captured a single breath. "Whisper."

Bay stilled.

Everything unleashed then in a tide. The bombs. The island falling. Tiger Lily and Whisper. How Peter had forgotten in less than a day. How I felt empty and lost and scared. I had to be strong, but I couldn't stop shaking.

She had abandoned me.

I couldn't be sure how long I cried, but it was well over an hour. The night was full by the time I ambled to Bay's side again. He sat on the porch, gazing up at the heavens, having allowed me to mourn in his house for as long as I needed.

"I hope you didn't get snot all over everything in there." He offered me half a smile, but I couldn't return the expression even for his sake.

My skin felt clammy, and everything was numb right down to my toes. How had so much changed in so short a time? Just last week, I was wandering the woods in my usual routine, thinking about exploring the world beyond, thinking about Whisper's birthday party, dreaming about the adventures we would have. Then, we both nearly died. And I found out she couldn't fly. And now she was really gone.

Maybe Peter had been right all along. Maybe I was lucky, but in the same way, he was. No matter what came our way, we continued even when others didn't have that luxury.

"It's nearly time," Bay murmured into my thoughts.

I looked at him. "What do you mean?"

He pointed up through the branches at two gleaming stars. "Do you see the second star on the right?" I did. "That's where we need to fly. To reach Neverland."

I stared at it. "So, Star Boy really came directly from a star." My voice was absent of emotion, but he didn't mind.

"Yup." A tentative pause passed between us where I could feel his eyes on me, looking deeper than I dared to right now. "Are you sure you—"

"Yes." There was no doubt about that—none at all in my mind. If I left, I could avenge Whisper. If I died trying, the only person I left behind now would forget about me in a matter of hours. Maybe if he didn't know I was dead, he'd remember me for a few days.

Maybe the second I disappeared into that dark sky, he'd ask: *Lyric, who?*

That thought soured my tongue, nearly bringing back an onslaught of tears, but there were none left. "I have to go. I don't have anything left to lose, and there's no one really left to lose me."

Bay laughed, standing, and my brows furrowed. He extended a hand to me, Skye just over his shoulder, waiting and watching. "Well, that's not true. I'm still here. And I'll be damned if I lose you. Understood?"

The ghost of what may have been a smile a few days ago lifted my lips as I clasped his hand. Warmth sparked through his fingers, a residue of dust allowing me to float off the porch with him. "I understand," I replied before Skye doused me in dust and hugged my cheek for the barest moment. It was enough to bolster my courage and make me grip Bay's hand tighter.

"Take me to Neverland, Star Boy."

He faced the twinkling sky, the specks of light reflecting in his hazel eyes. His chest filled with breath, determination etched in his expression. His lips barely moved, but I heard him, crystal clear: "Away we go."

And away we went.

Continue the story in Heiress of Stars

HEIRESS OF STARS

11TH NOVEMBER

One moment, the night enveloped us in a pitch-black haze. The next, light bled into my eyes, burning my retinas and making me almost fall out of the sky. I blinked violently against the building tears, certain they came from discomfort and blindness, not from the sensation of my world being ripped away.

A hand caught my arm, stopping me in the air. "Look down," Bay said.

I pulled my attention away from the sky and squinted at a beach. Sunlight hit the golden sand like it was glass, spewing rainbows across shallow shoreline pools. High grass, filtering into dense, menacing woods, waved in a warm breeze. I could make out jagged outlines rising in the distance, but a wash of deep green covered everything as we descended.

My feet touched the ground, and I released a breath. "This is it?" I turned slowly, taking in the never-ending cerulean sea. It stretched into the horizon and then dropped off. I was half-certain it ended where the light no longer could be seen glinting off the water.

"It's beautiful, isn't it?"

I wrung my hands before dropping my arms to my sides and facing the treeline once more. "Freedom has never felt so bittersweet."

"Bittersweet," Bay repeated, "that's a good word for this place. Lovely and lethal. We really should get moving."

Spinning on his heel, he headed toward the darkest shadows in the ominous foliage. My gut tightened, but I followed him. "Do you have a safety guide? Any tips, tricks, or comments you'd like to share that will help me stay alive long enough to find and defeat the pirates?"

"I do hope you have a plan to defeat the pirates. That would be my first tip."

"I'll figure one out once I see what I'm dealing with unless you already know?"

He picked up the pace. "Who? Me? I don't know anything."

I glanced over my shoulder. It took a conscious effort not to freeze on the beach. Out of the water rose a giant, bulbous head, easily ten times my size. Water streamed off the grey flesh in torrents. When I met the creature's single crimson eye, its beak clacked, and a suctioned tentacle lifted out of the foaming waves.

"Okay," Bay said with an edge of panic in the lilt of the word. "Maybe I know one thing. Run!" Snatching my hand, he tore through the grass, yanking me behind him just in time for the Kraken's arm to plunge into the sand at our heels. A divot remained, filling with rainbow-strewn water.

My feet pounded against the sand as it thickened with dirt, and Bay didn't slow when we ducked into the forest. Hundreds of green shades, some lightened by streams of sunlight, and others blackened by shadows, fled past us in a blur. Skye zipped along overhead, disappearing in and out of the branches like he'd done this before, and it hardly bothered him.

"A terrible place to land, really. Truly dreadful. We're lucky to be alive." Bay bounded over a fallen log in a manner that boasted the pixie dust still coating his skin. I tripped over it, stumbled, and only narrowly missed careening into the ground headfirst thanks to his firm hold on my hand.

"Can we—" I gulped air. "—pause for a moment?"

"Not yet."

"Why not?"

Trees cracked behind me on my left, and my organs leaped out of my skin as I jumped, looking back. A tentacle slithered through splinters back to the source like a snake to its nest. My blood curdled, bile rising. Bay merely, and calmly, stated, "Because we're still within reach."

My muscles were tense by the time Bay slowed and glanced behind us. Trees completely obscured the ocean from view, but he appeared to see what he needed to. Exhaling, he released me. "Welcome to Neverland."

Fearlessness painted his face in excitement that didn't fit the situation. A giant squid nearly crushed us five seconds after landing. What lay ahead if this was how it started?

I looked back through the trees, wishing the sickness in my gut would settle. What was I thinking coming here? That I could take on all the pirates by myself?

Was I that naïve?

No, I knew better than that. I ran away. And I wouldn't pretend otherwise. Maybe a part of me thought if I avenged Whisper, the gaping hole in my chest would close, and I'd be able to breathe again.

Blinking back, and forcing away emotions that threatened to consume me, I clenched my fists and faced my guide. "What now? How do I find the pirates?"

"Well, we should probably make our way to one of my hideouts. That's where everything I need will be. And the pirates..." He whipped sweat out of his eyes and pushed his bangs back. "They generally find me."

"Comforting," I mumbled.

He shrugged, slipping his hands into his pockets. "After we get some supplies, I can take you to their nest if you'd like to see what you're dealing with."

Hugging myself, I rubbed my arms and positioned my back away from the ocean. "I don't actually know why you're here. You said you'd tell me if I came with you, but then..." *Things didn't quite go as smoothly as they might have.*

If I didn't focus on the ache in my soul, I could almost trick myself into believing Whisper was at home, waiting for me to make Skyla safe again. She'd run to me when I returned, wrap me in a hug, and hint that more happened between Bay and me than I would be willing to admit.

Damn it. I scrubbed a hand over my face, cursing the burning behind my eyes, throughout my whole head.

"Are you all right?"

"Yes," I snapped. "Just tell me why you're here already."

Bay stared at me in a way that almost made me feel guilty, but it was when he looked away that the sorrow deep in my chest called to the pain etched on his face. "I'm looking for something."

Deliberately, I softened my tone. "What are you looking for?"

"It's hard to explain, and we need to keep moving." He spun on his heel again, pausing before taking a step. Tightening his braid, he met my gaze. "Stay with me and don't wander off. Those are my tips and tricks to maybe surviving Neverland."

"Aren't you being a tad bit presumptuous? I doubt you could save me from that thing back there if we faced it head-on." I didn't have the strength to argue or press the issue, so I kept his pace.

"I'm nothing if not ostentatious, and unless I'm mistaken, I did just save you from *that thing back there*, so unless you fancy a swim, we'll never have to face it head-on."

"*Ostentatious*. Big, showy word for someone who hides in a treehouse, hating company. Are you sure you know what it means?"

He cast me a disapproving grimace. "You clearly do."

"Because I'm perspicacious when it comes to details and words."

"Indubitably."

A tiny smile touched my lips while we crunched through the forest, no path in sight. Skye zipped out of the treetops and settled on Bay's head. The tiny creature glanced at me, hummed something and zipped off again. He returned moments later, chirped something else and then lay down in Bay's hair.

Bay didn't reply, but his eyes peered into the distance, narrowing. "Watch your—"

He didn't finish the line before the ground fell out from under me. Pain exploded in my side, then frigid water submerged my head. I gasped when my mouth bobbed above the surface. The current yanked me back under. Squinting through the murky blackness, I saw nothing. Breaching the surface again, I sucked in another breath, using it to scream, "Bay!" Torrents ripped me downstream, slamming my body against rocks along the way.

Heat bloomed in my skull as I frantically did everything I could to reach air. The river had appeared out of nowhere as if the terrain had moved in the time it took me to take a step. Could that happen? Did that happen here?

Bay's stories had included numerous situations I never thought possible, so there was no telling what I would come to face. With Krakens living in the ocean, what could possibly dwell in inky black rivers that appeared out of forest floors?

I shivered with icy fear, fighting to see through the darkness. If I could just reach the bank... I had to. Rivers, if I wasn't mistaken, led to the ocean, and that thing was probably still waiting for its next meal.

Heart pounding, I fought the current. Stubborn, it thrust me beneath the water again, tumbling me around like a stray stone. I couldn't let it win. Not now. Not before I avenged Whisper and saved Skyla, then— then...

Then I didn't know what, but Whisper would never let me give in or give up. Holding an image of her smile and an echo of her laugh in my mind, I forced my battered and aching body to obey, to drag me one inch at a time to a cleft of dirt overhanging the rushing depths. I dug my nails into it, but the mud gave way. My legs scraped the wall, so I crammed my moccasins into crevices. Burying my hands again, I found sturdy roots and pried myself from the chilling rapids.

Collapsing, I stared up at the blackening tree canopy. Dread spun in my stomach, and I shot upright, feeling for my knife. It was still at my thigh. It was okay. Next, I found my sopping bag. The bread I had on me fell through my fingers in sodden clumps. My books were destroyed. My gloves, spyglass, and pan flute were waterlogged. But, hopefully, they would dry out, and... My heart sank as I lifted the pouch of pixie dust.

It flopped to the side, empty, all its contents lost to the river, annihilated in the water.

My hands shook from cold as I put everything back, and I jumped when the ground beside me slammed closed, the river gone like it had never been. A thin seam that almost looked like a scar in the earth was the only hint I had ever been at the water's mercy.

"Bay?" I called into the woods, tightening my jaw to avoid chattering my teeth. Only bugs and rustling leaves responded. Then, thunder.

The island quaked. A long-fingered bolt of lightning reached down from the sky, grasped Neverland, and rattled it. After the second impact, a downpour of rain burst from the clouds, hitting me like needles.

The force alone made it difficult to stand, but I found my legs and staggered ahead. The trees broke shortly after to display a sky at war and a lone skull carved into the edge of the beach.

Skull Rock.

I knew it as though I'd always known it. Its ominous form seemed branded on my brain. Gaping mouth. Dead, hollow eyes. It offered nothing but an unsettling sensation—and shelter from the stabbing rain and raging sky.

I peered behind me, then at the ocean.

The grey water surged and crashed, blending with the horizon. Could I get that close to it, or would the Kraken come back?

An ear-splitting noise sent me hurtling forward. I whirled on the trees. Eyes bulging, I stared at an ashy trunk, sliced through the middle. Char washed off the wood to pool in the mulch on the ground. Lingering electricity crawled up my spine. The strike couldn't have been more than thirty feet from me.

"May the airwoman protect me from threats of sky and sea." Choking on the prayer, I dashed through the pelting rain into the maws of the cavern rock. Hand on my knife, I awaited glowing eyes, screeching laughter, silent footsteps, shadows, danger, death But only an empty pit with an ascending tunnel at the back stared at me. It couldn't really be safe. Could it?

I remembered a note on Bay's map of Neverland: *Watch out for Skull Rock after dark.*

It was dark—the rain hammered on, a rush of noise that clouded my mind—but it wasn't technically *after* dark. Unless time worked differently here, it had been dawn no less than an hour ago, so maybe it was safe until after dark? Would the rain last that long?

Would I?

My hand left my knife and clamped against my mouth. Shivers wracked my soaked body, every inhale burning down my throat. I was freezing. I was tired. Random patches of my skin stung in the open air; others ached from bruises. Neverland had swallowed me and spit me out minutes after I'd stepped foot on its soil. I wanted to scream, but my throat was too raw, my spirit too exhausted.

"Whisper," I managed through trembling lips, "help me." Those weren't the words I was thinking. She couldn't help me. Not now. The words I was thinking were *it should have been me.*

But it wasn't. So here I stood, alone.

And I had to pull myself together.

Slapping my cheeks, I gasped in a breath and ran over my options. I had to wait out the storm and find Bay, all before dark. Bay appeared to know this world, so even if the storm lasted past dark, I needed to be out of this cave before then in accordance with his notes.

Defeat the pirates.

Save Skyla.

Return...home.

My heart dipped, weighed down by the certainty "home" would never feel that way again. By now, Peter may have forgotten me. Tiger Lily and Whisper were gone. Maybe the Lost Boys would remember me if I made it back quickly, but their memory was little better than Peter's after a certain amount of time.

Overwhelmed, confused, scared, and above all else, cold to the bone, I leaned against the cave wall.

It vibrated. Leaping off, I turned around, and my eyes widened. The grinding sound of stone against stone filled the space as the skull snapped its mouth closed, leaving me in near-perfect darkness. The barest outline of light between the rock's jagged teeth did little to illuminate the space—until fire crackled behind me.

Scared to see what next awaited, I wrapped my fingers around the hilt of my knife, pulled it free, then slowly rotated toward the sizzling pops. Several torches lined the tunnel at the far end of the skull.

I swallowed, my throat dry. My heart thundered, its beats resounding through the tips of my toes. "There's no way I'm going back there," I whispered into the eerie, white noise of rain and thunder.

Stepping back, my moccasins splashed into a puddle. A trickle of light beneath the storm drew my gaze back to the skull's maws, and my stomach tightened. Water spilled in, filling the room at an alarming rate.

Did some cruel god orchestrate this horrific situation? Thrown about from one near demise to the next, I was doing all I could just to keep breathing.

The water reached my ankles, so I closed my eyes briefly, cursed Neverland, and started for the lit tunnel. The path ascended, curling, and I noted several ridges in the walls shaped like arched doorways. I assumed like the skull's mouth, the stone blocking the passages moved, but I didn't know how to make it, so I followed the path until it opened into a chamber.

Piles of straw threaded with silk and down lay before me. Random objects—chests, gold, broken plates, chair legs, mirror glass—sat neglected all around. Lightning crashed across a sky visible through two large holes and a smaller one between them, and...those were the skull's eyes.

This was something's nest.

My only consolation was that the chamber appeared, for the time being,, empty. I started for one of the piles of miscellaneous pieces, hoping the ivory bone I glimpsed wasn't human, but a tittering voice stopped me in my tracks.

"It's dreadful," the voice sighed, sending me hurtling toward the piles of straw. I tucked myself into a corner behind them and held my breath. If I had any luck left in me, the rain would mask my pounding heart.

"So you've said, sister." Three women entered the room. White gowns spilled over their slender bodies, beautifully contrasting with their dark hair and dark skin. But it was their incandescent wings that froze me in place. The pure feathers gleamed, drawing my eyes away from the spindly teeth pouring out of their mouths.

Sirens.

The eldest of them folded her arms, peering outside with a grace that negated her grisliness. "It's so rare we have visitors," the woman murmured.

My heart stopped, but she pivoted to face her sisters instead of looking at me.

"So many at once after so few in so long." The middle siren curled her lips back against her teeth in an appalling grimace. "It can mean nothing good."

"We know this," the eldest returned. "Since long ago."

"Still, it's..." Sorrow touched the woman's features, and she shook her head, glancing at the youngest sister.

Her bright voice was airy and kind despite her horrific maws. "I do love when Bay is back, though. He's terribly fun."

"Occasionally, overmuch." The eldest smiled, her teeth hidden, but the expression still sharp.

"The children say he has come with a girl this time." The youngest held her fingers before her lips. Deadly excitement sparked in her eyes. "Imagine that. Our Bay with a girl."

Icy shoots of fear trickled down my spine, raising all the hair on my flesh. I fought every instinct that screamed at me to run because I had nowhere to go.

"Already?" Both the others' eyes widened.

The eldest's lips parted. "It can't be."

"Oh, it is, though. I'm certain of it. She has hair like a sunset, and her eyes...they're ringed in gold the children say."

The eldest clasped her hands. Distress marred her

face, and she turned toward the storm again. Lightning flashed across her defined cheeks, outlining the barest trace of panic. "We must find them before the worst occurs." Her eyes closed, her teeth clacking. "Come, sisters, the children are hungry. After they're fed, we'll send them to search for our Bay and the girl; we must make sure we are there in time."

Without flourish, the woman ushered the others from the room.

I stayed where I was, staring after them until my legs burned, begging to be stretched. Three sirens were after us, after me, and I was hiding right behind their beds. I squeezed my eyes closed in case it was all a dream, but my wet clothes clung to my skin, making me shiver so completely I knew it couldn't be.

I had to get out of here, even if it meant braving the storm.

Lightning cracked across the sky, drawing my attention to the only clear exits. If I could scale the rock face—or rock forehead—I could make it down the back of the skull and into the woods.

Inching toward an eye socket, I peered outside. Wind whipped rain into my face hard enough to leave welts on my cheeks, but I squinted against the torrents at the ocean. No creatures rose from the depths, but a bed of sharp rocks peeked out of the boiling waves.

Stay here with the sirens or be dashed against the stone.

My head swirled, so I ran my fingers through my wet hair, gripping the strands. Thunder rumbled in the distance like the great airwoman was laughing. I sneered. "You're Skyla's *lucky charm*." I lifted myself onto the ledge, gripping the stone until my nails chipped. "What could possibly go wrong?"

Rain beat into my side as I found a foothold. My moccasin skidded, and I clenched the rock, scraping my palms. One at a time, I pried my shoes off and secured them in my bag before locking my toes on the water-washed stone.

Water soaked everything but my dry mouth as I felt for a handhold, then delivered myself onto the curved forehead. One slow movement after another, I dragged my body above the skull's eye.

Rain stabbed my back; water rushed against me like a river. I narrowed my eyes through the blur. Shaking violently from the cold, I nearly missed grasping solid holds every three movements, but by grace or luck or some other unseen force, I managed to reach the top of the skull's head.

The back of the skull wasn't as sheer. Piles of mossy stones descended like steps into the forest, but I still took my time reaching the ground in the tempest. Out of breath, I faced inland, leaned against a mossy boulder, and put my sopping shoes back on as though protecting my feet mattered much now. Even as the rain carried everything away, I knew my hands and feet bled.

I started ahead at a pitiful limp, daring the world to throw something else at me. I had no idea where I was going, if I'd ever find Bay, the pirates, my way back home, and I hardly cared at this point.

Everything hurt. Neverland hadn't simply swallowed me up and spit me out. It had chewed me up then regurgitated my remains.

Walking for hours in the pouring rain, half-starved was about as glamorous as it sounded. Thankfully, the lightning had died down some time ago, and the downpour had eased, but I still had no way to navigate through the thick woods.

Ambling in circles was exhausting, but Bay had mentioned twice how we needed to keep moving, so I supposed that was the least I could do. Not to mention, I feared if I stopped, the cold would set in beyond repair.

My fingers were stiff, and only memories of Whisper kept me continuing forward. *She wouldn't want you to give up. She wouldn't want you to stop.* If I believed in an afterlife, I would have stopped back at Skull Rock and thrown myself into the ocean, but death accomplished nothing.

She wouldn't want that for you anyway.

"Right," I chattered, "but how exactly am I supposed to continue without her?"

I trudged on, pausing when the rain slowed. Could it really be letting up? I held out a shaking hand, hopeful. I had begun to forget what being dry felt like. Looking up at the sky through the canopy, I watched the dark clouds disperse. A sliver of moon loomed above, offering less light than the rest of the stars. They seemed closer than in Skyla, each twinkling brightly in the pitch expanse.

Had I really walked the entire day away?

As I stood there, staring at the sky, I knew it wasn't as unlikely as it seemed. Everything hurt. I was no stranger to long walks in the woods, or climbing, or getting caught in the rain. But all of it at once, plus running for my life, had strained my muscles and my mind.

No end lay in sight. I didn't know where I was going, how I would get there, or even, really, where I had come from. Glancing behind me, I witnessed nothing but wet trees and brush. Facing forward again, I clenched my teeth. It all looked the same.

My stomach swirled with hunger and unease. Could Neverland have put me in a loop? Could I be walking toward nothing, coming from nothing, ending up nowhere?

"Why do you hate me?" I whispered my throat raw with thirst. Surrounded by water, I hadn't thought to drink any, but I was parched.

Pressing my palms against my eyes, I teetered and shook my head. I had to keep moving. My foot took a step forward, but the world slanted off-kilter. Humming filled my head, the soft noises so calm, so comforting. My lips parted in a yawn that I succumbed to.

I fought to keep my eyes open and took another step. The world doubled, turning vibrant colors. Something was very wrong. Violet melded with emerald, dipping into shades of crimson and tangerine.

My back straightened. The sensation of something crawling on my neck held me steady in place even as everything around me tumbled into insanity. I reached back, plucking a long splinter from my skin.

"What?" I mumbled.

My vision failed. The touch of long fingers skittered down both my arms just before I collapsed in a wet heap on the ground.

12TH NOVEMBER

Movement. That's what woke me. Exhausted to my core, nothing short of being jostled like a sack of potatoes would have done the trick, so that's exactly what I felt like when I came to in someone's arms. Darkness still bathed the forest, washing everything I could see in muted greens and charcoal shadows.

I blinked at a smooth face, hoping to clear my mind, but it lagged, confused and not at all happy to be present right now. The person holding me was running. That was a good deduction. Where was the person going with me? Who was the person?

I squinted through the fog in my head. The face was handsome. His—definitely a his—hair was dark. A short braid hopped up when the person jumped. My senses crashed down on me.

"Bay!"

Bay startled, his hazel eyes going wide. He met my gaze and stared, but he didn't stop moving. "You're awake?"

"Yeah, thanks to you. Think you could handle me a little more violently?" Relief filled my chest, and for the first time in hours, I could breathe again. "Because I don't."

He stayed silent. His eyes shifted from the path before us, to me, and back to the path.

My brows furrowed. "Put me down. I think I can walk." I hoped I could. My muscles were little more than goo at this point, and my bones were mush, but being carried like a princess didn't suit either of us.

"You're covered in bruises," he stated.

"White water rafting without a raft will do that to you."

When he didn't so much as hint at slowing to set me down, I shifted in his hold to peer over his shoulder. "Are we being chased? Where are you going so quickly?"

"Our base."

Our? The relief at seeing him trickled away, one droplet at a time, but my mind cleared more with every shock rattling through his bones to mine. I pursed my lips and narrowed my eyes.

He provided me half a smile, but something about it wasn't right. "What is it, Lyric?"

"Where's Skye?" Bay's clothes were dry, and it wasn't raining anymore. Here, especially here in Neverland with danger around every bend, he would be coated in shimmering dust, but not a single fleck touched his skin.

"Skye's waiting for us at our base."

No way would they be separated at such a distance. "Put me down," I demanded.

"But—"

"Now." I let my fingers drift to the sheath at my thigh. A cold wash of fear ran over me when I found it empty.

The wide-eyed concern painting Bay's face vanished. His hazel eyes flickered between the earth tones and a mustard yellow. He licked his lips. "If you insist."

My heart clenched. Bay hurled me into a tree. The impact cracked against my joints, sending piercing shots of hurt stabbing out through my nerves.

The creature's voice distorted, a mix of Bay's tenor and something entirely repugnant. "Better?" Sapphire caught my eye, and he flipped my blade into the air, catching it precariously. "Little Lyric,"—his form shifted. Sallow skin stretched over thin, protruding bones. Cracked teeth grinned at me, a blood-red tongue tracing each point—"so alone in the world."

I planted my hands beneath me, shoving the damp ground, but my muscles wouldn't cooperate. My arms shook like a baby goat's legs; then my face fell splat into the mud. "What are you?" I choked, turning my body so at least I wouldn't inhale dirt and mold.

"I'm your friend Bay." The creature's form transitioned, Bay's voice lilting in its words. "Or perhaps..." The words softened, turning feminine, and a mass of curly blond hair spilled over small, dark shoulders.

"No—"

She touched the tip of my knife, a coy smile lightening her face. "Perhaps I'm Whis—"

Her mouth went slack, and she tumbled forward, buckling in a heap of sallow skin and gangly limbs. I gasped, panting, starved for air. A long knife protruded from the creature's back. The thing's back. Not

Whisper's. Not... But it felt like I'd witnessed her dying right in front of me. Again. So close, and yet again, I could do nothing to save her.

I scrambled in the mud, finding, at last, a way to pull myself off the ground. Pressing my back against the trunk behind me for support, I stared as a gleaming form dropped out of the trees and yanked the long knife out of the creature's back.

"Are you all right?" Bay asked. He wiped black blood off his blade and secured it before looking at me. I didn't reply. He took a step toward me. My heart thundered in my chest. "You're not exactly easy to track; I hope you haven't gone on any adventures without me." He stopped, and his attention dropped to the sapphire-encrusted hilt of my knife. It lay within the bony fingers of the creature still. Bay plucked it free and cleaned it off on his pant leg, floating over the corpse as if it didn't faze him.

I crushed myself against the trunk. "How do I know you're not...one of those things?"

"I suppose in the same way you knew that thing wasn't me." He flipped my blade, offering it to me exactly how he had when we first met. "It was a young one, that's for sure. Some of them can copy mannerisms, habits, and emulate a person based on recent memories far better than he could." Bay's head tipped down, his gaze darkening. "Also, I'm sure most other changelings know by now not to toy with my form."

I clamped a shaking hand around my knife's handle, met the briefest hint of resistance, then snatched it from him.

Skye flitted out of the trees to sit on Bay's shoulder shortly after I managed to settle my breathing. Concern marred the pixie's tiny brows and, admittedly, seeing him set me somewhat at ease.

"I suppose he was your first hint that something wasn't right." Bay smiled at his companion. "That's one thing you can always count on. If we aren't together, something is terribly wrong."

"Actually,"—I swallowed—"the first hint was you called me Lyric."

His brow quirked. "I haven't called you Lyric before?"

"Never once." Whatever strength kept me upright drained away until I was relying entirely on the trunk behind me to keep from collapsing. I couldn't dwell on this; I had to tell him about the sirens. My lips parted, but I never reached the words.

Bay had one arm at my back and the other at my knees before I knew where to start. He lifted me off the ground, not quite touching it himself. His lips thinned in a teasing smirk. "Goodness. You're lighter than you look. Are you made of air?"

My cheeks flushed. "I can walk."

"Clearly, you can barely stand." He floated up through the branches until the forest was a patch of green below us. "Besides, why walk when you can fly?" He shifted my weight so I could easily lay my head against his chest and murmured, "Rest for a bit, Wind Song. We'll be in a safe place soon, and I'll treat your injuries."

I watched Bay's face, searching for anything that might be another Neverland trick, but he didn't so much as inch forward without my first accepting what he had said. He held my gaze, the depths of his eyes flecked with gold in the starlight, a gentle smile curving full lips. Only when I leaned my head against him and gave in to the darkness did I feel the soft breeze of movement against my skin.

I clung to his heat and that warm breeze, desperate for the image of Whisper crumbling in the woods to burn away. It didn't.

My eyes fluttered open, the space around me completely unfamiliar. Firelight cast shadows on the walls, and I realized they were dirt. Roots stuck out of the ceiling, the spindly fingers interlocking like spider webs.

Skye hummed, and I found Bay hunkered beside the fire, pouring over several maps. He looked up at me, his eyes alight in the glow. Coated in reflective dust, he appeared spectral, and I wondered for a moment when he floated off the ground if I were dreaming.

He touched my cheek, his hand, pleasantly cool. "How are you feeling?"

I assessed the bandages wrapped around my arms and legs. They had been skillfully bound, and I wondered how familiar he was with tending to his own wounds. Shifting in the bed of clover, I winced. "Everything's sore."

"After the trip you took, I'm surprised nothing's broken." He brushed the hair off my cheek, and it felt phenomenally good. I nearly sighed into his touch, but I groaned instead.

"I think sirens are after us," I croaked.

"What?" His hand drew away.

"Sirens," I repeated their sharp faces and angelic forms burned in my mind. "It started to pour after I escaped the river. When lightning crashed too close for comfort, I took shelter in Skull Rock. The mouth closed. It filled with water. I followed a path toward the back to the chamber with the eyes, and..." I felt sick.

"You went inside Skull Rock?" Shock masked Bay's face.

"I didn't have much of a choice, I—"

"You saw a skull-shaped edifice and thought, 'Hmm, that looks like a lovely place. Let me just pop on inside to wait out the storm?'"

"Lightning nearly hit me! It was the best option I could think of after being thrown downstream and nearly drowning half a dozen times. What else would you have expected me to do?"

He deadpanned. "Trace the river seam back so we could have met in the middle."

I bit my tongue on any snarky remark I was brewing. That, the most logical of thoughts, hadn't crossed my mind even briefly.

Bay laughed, shaking his head. "I'm not mad. You're a little worse for wear, but you're all right. We're a little set back, but we haven't been put out beyond repair. You were probably concussed just a bit." His brows crashed down, and he folded his arms, floating near so his face was just before mine. "Actually, you probably *are* concussed just a bit. How old are you? What's your mother's name?"

I frowned at him. "I don't have a mother." And I didn't want to think about what had happened to the closest thing I did have to a mother. Averting my gaze, I focused on the physical aches blooming all over my body to avoid concentrating on the emotional ones bleeding in my chest.

"Everyone has a mother." He sat back down, his legs crossed.

"Well, I never knew mine."

"Oh." The single word stilled the air in the space. Only the crackling fire continued its murmurs. Several heartbeats passed, then Bay cleared his throat, rubbed the back of his neck. "You're probably hungry."

My stomach growled at the mere thought of food. "I

wasn't until you said that."

He chuckled. "It's a good thing I caught a real delicacy while you were asleep then." He dashed toward the fire, and I watched him warily, expecting a rat or a snake.

He returned with neither. I breathed a sigh of relief and forced my aching body to sit up and take the wooden bowl he offered. A leg of meat and a salad of what looked like weeds sat side by side. "What is all this?"

"Rabbit and greens. It's the best we can do out here most of the time."

"It's more than enough." I lifted the meat to my lips and savoured the gamey, perhaps slightly burnt, taste. The juice seasoned the salad, and though both could have used salt and herbs, it seemed a meal fit for royalty.

Before I had to ask, Bay put a cup of water in my hand.

"You're awfully accommodating for the Bay I know. Have you been switched out with one of those things?"

"A changeling? No." He hovered cross-legged above the ground. "Can't fly, them. Not an ounce of belief in any of their yellow bodies."

"Then, about the sirens..." I stared into my cup.

Bay waved a hand, dismissing it. "Don't worry about them."

"But they knew you, me. They know we're both here somehow, and they said something about sending 'the children' out to find us."

"They're nothing new." A wry smile tipped his lips as he glanced at the ceiling. "I know how to handle them by now. Time moves differently for us here. That is to say, it stops. Get it? *Neverland*. Never grow up. I've survived this place for years, and you don't survive long if you

114

don't know how to handle a handful of sirens."

"Is that why you don't know how old you are?"

"Never grow up. Never grow old. Neverland's curse is Neverland's blessing." He exhaled, setting the matter aside. "I charted a path to Pirate Bay. It's a three-day journey, taking into account feasible setbacks. It's been a while since I dared go near there, so I don't know what to expect."

"I do," I noted, finishing my food.

His brows rose. "You do?"

"Pirates."

He rolled his eyes, flopping down beside me on the clover bed. "Ha ha ha."

"You mean, 'har har har.'" I smirked.

"Congratulations." He adjusted his dagger belt, removing some of the larger sheaths and setting them aside. "You've offended every pirate on this island. Let's hope none were within earshot." He took my bowl and set it next to his knives, waiting until I finished my water to do the same with the cup. Afterward, he smiled. "Good eve, Wind Song."

My heart thumped. Seeing him so close, deliberately sleeping next to me, set my mind adrift in a realm of inappropriate thoughts. *Shut up. You're concussed.* My reprimand did little to train the stream of thoughts as I lay back down. I stared at the ceiling, lips pressed together, and tamed my breathing.

Moments passed. Minutes.

"Oh," Bay murmured, "do you have any idea which group of pirates you're looking for? I'd suggest not taking on all of them if you can help it."

"There's more than one?" I replied.

He rolled over to face me and propped his head in his hand. "Of course."

I moistened my lips, trying not to look at his. "You recognized the pirate on Skyla. Don't you know?"

"Maybe."

"Well?"

He traced my face and pulled the tie out of his hair. His braid spilled free over his shoulders before he settled back down beside me, crossing his arms beneath his head. "Hook's Crew."

I froze. "But Hook's dead."

"No?"

"He is. Peter threw him off his ship and flew it to Skyla before I was born." I faced Bay. Our noses were mere inches apart.

He scratched his cheek. "What did I tell you about pirates who appear to have died? Captain James Hook is more cunning than the whole lot of them."

"But how would he have gotten to Neverland? You can't expect me to believe he knows how to fly."

"There's always more than one way to get home." Bay's voice was quiet, his expression solemn. Then he cupped my cheek and smiled through a hidden anguish I couldn't place the origin of. "It's late, Wind Song. Putting all this information on a concussed brain is probably bad for you. We'll talk more in the morning, I'm sure."

Then, without another word, he rolled over and went to sleep.

I crawled through the hollow log out of Bay's underground base. My muscles complained with each movement, and I knew it was going to be a long day. When I reached sunlight, Bay helped me up, and I stretched my aching limbs.

The forest gleamed with colors.

Purples and reds and oranges bloomed beside blues

and pinks and whites, not a single space lacking vibrant hues. "What is this?" I asked, watching an iridescent butterfly as it perused the florals.

"Neverland after a storm." Bay hovered about a foot off the ground, his ankles crossed. He braided his hair and tightened the tie. "This was kind of an impromptu stop. My main base still has the supplies we'll need to move forward, so we have to backtrack a bit. I already accounted for the delay."

"I'll need the time to heal some anyway." I smoothed my finger down a delicate petal. A single dewdrop built and plummeted to the earth. "How worried should I be about another river swallowing me today?"

"I don't think we're passing any more river faults." He fished a map from his bag and scanned it quickly. "Nope. It should be a calm day."

I gripped my satchel's strap, thankful it and all of its salvageable contents had dried out by the fire. "Is that my definition of 'calm' or yours?"

He rolled up his map and stuffed it back in his own bag. "Why would they be different?"

"Well, mine is a 'none of the kids fell off the island today' kind of calm. Yours is a 'I know how to handle sirens if I cross paths with them' kind of calm."

He scoffed. "They'll never find us that quickly."

"How reassuring."

He held out a hand for me. "I think so."

I stared at his fingers when they wiggled.

"Are you coming?" he asked.

Skye sat on his shoulder, staring at me. There was a very distinct challenge on his little face, and I wasn't sure if he was daring me to accept or threatening me to decline. Taking a breath, I slipped my hand into Bay's. The pixie didn't move. Softer than I could catch, he murmured something in Bay's ear.

"Right," Bay grumbled, landing. "At this time, we'd be too visible from the sky. If possible, I'd like for the pirates not to know we're here yet."

Skye nodded, flitting into the air. He swirled around my head several times, then returned to Bay's shoulder.

Bay smiled, his hand not having released mine. "It is good to always be able to fly here, though."

Lifting off the forest floor, I reveled in the sensation of nothing holding me down, and nothing pressing against my bruised legs. It was good to be able to fly anywhere.

We started through the colorful woods, Skye zipping in and out of the treetops as was his habit. Whenever he stopped in with us, he'd douse me in more dust, sit on Bay's head, or flutter along at our sides, then he was off again.

"Where does he go?" I asked sometime during mid-afternoon. The sun streamed through the trees, outlining a trail of dust as it sifted through the air to greet the ground.

"He's visiting the others," Bay replied.

"The others?"

"Other pixies." He held a hand above his eyes and stared up through the canopy. "I suppose you can't see them, because it's not like in Skyla. Pixies here remain well-hidden since there are so many dangers."

"There are pixies here too?"

Bay grinned. "Why would that surprise you?"

"I don't know."

"Truth be told, they were here first." He passed a tree, skimming his fingers over the bark. "There was a time when all of Skyla's islands rested in the sea. But the time before the pixies is an age near forgotten."

I could hardly believe that was true. Thinking about Skyla not floating made my stomach clench. It wasn't right. "Why did they leave here?"

"Why do most people leave their homes?"

I left to protect mine, but once I was done, I'd be returning. Since the pixies had remained in Skyla, they couldn't have left Neverland to protect it. It dawned on me. "Because it isn't safe anymore."

Bay pursed his lips and nodded. "Yep."

"How do you know all of this?" My brows knitted. "You return to Skyla like you live there and have bases here like you're just trying to survive some quest. Yet, you know all of these secrets and seem to be a walking encyclopedia of Neverland's history."

"Are we prying again, Miss Nosy One?"

"Don't be an ass, Star Boy." I wanted to know more about him. Everything else in my life had fallen apart. So—as scary at it seemed to consider—this boy I'd only known a little over a week was the closest friend I had left. And I knew nearly nothing about him.

Perhaps some of the desperation I felt showed on my face because he dropped his smirk and ruffled his hair, tossing flyaway strands out of his eyes. "All right. I suppose it's not a huge secret." He huffed, stepping over a fallen tree and continuing to float over the bushes past the decrepit log. "I was born here."

My eyes bulged; my heartbeat stilted. "What?"

He laughed, but it sounded unnatural. "Sorry. Not born. If I was born here, I'd age here. I was born in Skyla, but I was conceived here and raised between both Skyla and Neverland. Only one group of people like us ever lived out their lives here, and they're gone now. Everyone else you meet—the humans I mean—they're wanderers from other lands. We're all just cheating death, for a little while, or as long as we dare."

All my thoughts blanked with those words. He had been raised in both lands? How had I never met him before? Normal people rarely ever traveled to the outer islands that didn't have bridge walkways. His had been a new island for me, but surely Peter had known about it. Peter, at one point or another, knew everything...it was just a matter that he forgot. Had he allowed Bay to cross between the worlds? Did Peter know about Neverland? If he had once, did he remember it?

Bay poked me in the forehead, ripping me from my spiraling thoughts. "Don't look so shocked. Of course, a magical place like this has some pretty deep history."

"Sure. But you're tied into it." And, somehow, so was Skyla.

Bay flicked his gaze across my face, then turned away. "Someone has to be." His whole demeanor changed in the next moment, those foreboding words forgotten. Pulling away a weeping branch, he displayed a cove with a crystal blue pond. "Here we are."

Water spilled over a sheer rock face directly ahead. The rainbow mist touched my face even at this distance. Lush green grass coated the clearing, tiny flowers springing up all around. Rose vines laced before the tree line, as though they were holding the forest back.

"It's beautiful," I breathed, stepping foot into the space only after Bay landed there and let the willow branches fall back over the entrance like a curtain.

"You can wash off in the falls. I should have an extra set of clothes you can wear." He grabbed my arm, examining his bandage work, then nodded. "I'll redress these too."

"Is this place safe?" It looked as much, but the beach and the forest had seemed that way mere moments before both had tried to kill me.

Bay scanned the cove, secrets and memories spilling into his eyes. "Safe?" he whispered. "It's home." Looking down, he smoothed his fingers across his leather dagger belt and started for the waterfall. "I'll get you that change of clothes."

He slipped through a crevice behind the falls, and I followed, pausing when I saw what lay beyond. A cave space opened up before me, a log cabin sitting on aquamarine stone. Light scintillated through the falls to wash over the house in colored ribbons.

"This is incredible."

Bay smiled at the front door. "Is it?"

We both entered a quaint living space with a sitting area on the left and a food preparation area on the right. Stone counters, wooden utensils, and light cabinets more luxurious than anything I'd ever seen adorned the kitchenette.

Bay crossed between and entered a hallway with two doors, opening the nearest one. I only glimpsed the bedroom briefly, but it felt more like Bay's treehouse than the rest of the cabin. Papers, trinkets, and bookshelves displaying random odds and ends decorated the interior.

He emerged after a few moments with a linen shirt and a pair of trousers, not at all unlike what he was currently wearing. "I think I have some soap in the kitchen."

"Do you live here alone?" My eyes drifted to the untouched door, and I already knew the answer by the drastic differences between the single room treehouse and this place. It had a woman's touch. More than that, it had a family's essence.

So, where was his family?

"Not always," he replied, setting the bundle of clothes in my arms. The expression on his face begged me not to press further, but how could I leave it at that?

"What happened?" I floated over the counter dividing the kitchen from the rest of the room when he started searching through the cabinets under an empty water basin.

"That's none of your business." The words stung even though he'd said them so pleasantly.

I swallowed the bitterness resting on my tongue and held my head high. "I hate to inform you, but this is what a desperately wanting to know someone looks like."

He rose with a bar of soap, approaching. I hovered a foot above him, so he looked up as he took my hand and placed the soap there, wrapping my fingers around the waxy bar. "You're desperate to know me?" he asked, his tone seductive.

"A little." My face heated, and I tried not to think about his lingering touch.

"Why?"

My chest pinched, a lump catching in my throat. If I expected him to answer me honestly, I had to offer him the same courtesy. "Because—" The words were neither easy to think nor say. "—you're the closest thing I have left to call a friend."

The moments passing afterward took ages. He stared at me, every second building in my heart and making it beat faster. It was childish, wasn't it? Of course, it was. I was stupid, desperate, and alone—exactly like the changeling had said.

Before I had the chance to pull away in my own embarrassment, Bay floated up so he was taller than me and wrapped me in a hug. I didn't know what to do, so I clutched the clothing bundle and the soap until I was certain the bar had an imprint of my fingers.

"You're the first human to call me that in years," he murmured, his breath fanning past my ear. The same lonely, desperate tone echoed in his voice.

Dropping the clothes, I threw my arms around him and squeezed, biting back the emotions threatening to choke me. I didn't know how long we stayed like that in one another's arms or who pulled away first; all I knew was that when we met gazes again afterward, his eyes were glassy, and his cheeks were stained with tears.

13TH NOVEMBER

"**I**s this a good idea?" a soft, masculine voice pried open my dream and plucked it apart. I didn't recognize the person's voice, though something about the rise and fall was familiar.

"We don't have much choice. I'm open to other ideas, but if not, we have to try." That was Bay.

I stared straight ahead at the wall from where I lay on the couch in the cabin's sitting room. Bay and someone else were just behind me. Some wooden bowls shifted against one another, and I knew they were in the kitchen.

A long pause stretched before the other person responded, "We don't know if it'll even do any good. Lyric is...well. It's not like Neverland has offered her much kindness so far."

That statement was so true I felt it in my still-healing limbs, but why were Bay and a stranger talking about me?

"What do the other pixies think?"

The person scoffed.

"Well?"

"Yeah, okay, fine. There's *something*, but that doesn't mean it's anything we need. She can't even understand us, despite living with Tink all this time. Children lose their ability to understand; adults don't gain it. It's like flying." The person sighed deeply. "*Faith* and trust, Bay."

"Well, she has enough faith to fly," Bay grumbled, sincerely sounding wounded. "And you've been away from your kind since you were an infant. Maybe there are things you don't know."

"I'm not going to argue with you."

Bay laughed sardonically. "Skye, that is *exactly* what we're doing."

My heart thudded. *Skye?* Their conversation made a world more sense, but at the same time, it didn't. If I was hearing *Skye's* voice, everything they were talking about was invalid. I had to be dreaming. And yet, I was too scared to move and check.

The hushed tones and topic made it clear I hadn't been invited to eavesdrop, and I didn't know what would happen if they realized I was awake.

"I told you I was against this back when you first thought it up. She's only here because she lost her friend, and I think she has a chance against the pirates. But I don't want to see her, or anyone else, get hurt over a speculation." Anger built in Skye's tone. "Enough people have gotten hurt for our family."

"Ah, I see. You like her." Footsteps started away,

drifting toward Bay's bedroom.

Before their voices disappeared behind the door, Skye mumbled, "As if you're one to talk."

When the door opened and closed, I released a breath, gasped in another, and clenched my jaw. *What?* The word screamed in my brain again, *WHAT?* No. No, I was dreaming. I shot upright, ready to pinch myself, but pain ricocheted throughout my limbs at the abrupt movement before I had a chance.

Okay. Not dreaming. At least not anymore. I may have been hallucinating?

A murmur of conversation I couldn't make out continued in Bay's room, and I knew hallucination wasn't right either. So, what was right?

Bay needed me for something dangerous, and Skye was against using me because it might not even work. *What?* I scrubbed my hands over my face, but there were too many holes to fill in, and my mind was still groggy with sleep. Pieces of their conversation, likely important bits, had already faded into the confusion.

I needed air.

My gaze shifted to the front door, and I peered between it and Bay's room. The voices had died down now, leaving nothing but the consistent white noise of the falls. My heart hammered when I stood and tightened the rope belt that held Bay's pants around my waist.

This past day had been nearly as bad an emotional ride as the river was a physical one. What would I do at this point if I couldn't trust Bay? Crossing to the door, I kept that question in my mind, along with the image of his tear-streaked face. If he needed help with something, even something dangerous, didn't he know he could just ask? That's what friends did, helped each other. Even after death, my motivational force was Whisper.

A twinge of soul-crushing pain choked me as I pushed my way out into the cave and slipped past the waterfall. Misty spray washed over my cheeks, cooling them in the gentle night breeze. Right now, I didn't care if being out here was safe; at least I could breathe.

Starlight glimmered off the pond, the moon invisible to my eye. It felt as though I could see for ages, and I wondered if one of those twinkling stars was really Skyla in disguise.

I moved away from the noise of the falls and into the murmur of the evening. Cricket song highlighted the buzz of other insects and hints I couldn't place. A creature zipped across the pond, snatching water as it passed. I squinted, tense, but settled when I realized it was just a pixie.

My eyes widened, everything stilling. The hints beneath the crickets and insects were voices. Soft, lilting voices. All at once, they chimed like bells—as they always had—but now, when I concentrated, I could make out words. Language.

I jerked back when a pixie darted before my eyes. She wore a little leafy skirt and a flower petal for a shirt. Her laughter was distinct. She flitted away, returning with someone else and pointed at me. "I scared her. Try it. It's fun."

Her companion made a twisted face, sticking out his tongue, and I blinked, honestly and truly terrified but for completely different reasons. The male pixie laughed too. "She isn't very fiery. I wonder if she'd run away if I touched her hair. Do you think it burns?"

My lips parted, closed, and parted again. I'm not sure how I managed to stay still when the male pixie shrugged and said, "I'm going to see," before diving into my locks.

Other pixies gathered around me, and I spun when something tugged on my shirt from behind. An elegant pixie with violet hair smirked. "She's wearing Bay's clothes. I do wonder what that means." The sly woman caught several of the others' eyes, and I flushed when they erupted in giggles.

"Bay has never brought anyone here before."

"She smells like something special. Magic?"

"She must be special to him."

Was I? Or was I a means to an end?

They continued, ignorant of my thoughts. "Do you think they're in love?"

"I wonder."

I went deathly still because that reply wasn't a pixie. Pivoting slowly, I found Bay with Skye seated and looking bored on his shoulder. The little pixie met my gaze and averted his eyes.

"What are you doing out here, Wind Song?" Bay asked.

The pixies buzzed, dashing toward him and running through his unbraided hair, tugging on his clothes. A few crawled between his dagger belt and his tunic, laughing when he loosened the strap and gave it to them.

"I, uh..." My gaze followed the handful of pixies who were spinning around with his belt. One tiny creature had managed to pluck a knife out, cover it in dust, and wave it about like a massive sword. "I needed fresh air."

"You look like you've seen a ghost."

Heard one, rather. I nearly blurted everything, but I stopped just in time. If I couldn't trust him, I shouldn't let him know I could understand the pixies. I may need to know what he and Skye are saying without them knowing. Swallowing my words, I settled on a lie I could easily pull off. "I had a nightmare."

"A nightmare?" His smile faded. "About...?"

All I had to do was drop my gaze to the damp, flowering grass at my feet.

"Right," he murmured.

"Is she okay?" a pixie's voice zipped past my ear.

Another gasped. "Bay, she's going to cry."

"Hold her." That turned into a chant. "Hold her! Hold her!"

Bay let loose an exasperated breath, stopping in the middle to address me. "Sorry, that was for them, not you."

"What are they saying?" I asked, peeking at him from under my lashes.

Their voices tripped into giggles.

"That he loves you!"

"He should hug you!"

"Kiss!" That one also turned into a chant, and I hoped Bay didn't connect it to my reddening face.

"Nothing," he grumbled, "important."

"Rude," Skye chimed, smirking.

It took everything within me in that moment to continue feigning ignorance, because this—hearing them, being a part of the secrets and the jokes—was thrilling. Is this what it was always like for Peter? Is this why he always had half a smirk on his face whenever he left the treetops? This was incredible and magical, more real and special than being dubbed "Skyla's lucky charm" could ever manage.

It was inclusive instead of isolating.

Or it would be if I could make sense of what Bay seemed to be planning. For the moment, I was in on their secret, but my own kept me from saying so.

"It's going to be a long day tomorrow." Bay yanked me from my thoughts. "Why don't we head inside and try to get some more sleep?"

I nodded dumbly. Bay skipped off the ground, clasping his dagger belt from the pixies, who complained. Snatching his floating knife out of the air, he returned to the grass before me and smiled.

I wanted to believe in that smile, but then I caught the troubled look on Skye's face and knew I couldn't. Silently, I followed him back inside, bid him goodnight, and suffered through an uneasy rest.

14TH NOVEMBER

Light shimmered in through the window, falling across my eyes. Still exhausted from the night's events, I resisted waking up until I heard a shuffle of paper.

Bay sat in the window seat with his legs kicked up, studying a sheet of parchment. His hand flowed over the page, long strokes, precise. His brows lowered with concentration, and it seemed as though nothing could break him out of the moment. Was he creating a new map?

He glanced up at me, and the spell broke. "Wind Song. Good morn." His eyes dropped to the page before him, then flicked back up. "I hadn't realized you were awake. Did you sleep well?"

No. "Well enough. What are you doing?"

"I was going over today's course." He cleared his throat, shifting the pages against the square of wood that served as a drawing table. "I may have gotten distracted."

Prying myself from the comfort of the couch cushions, I crossed the room and looked over Bay's shoulder. The now-familiar map of Neverland sat in his lap, but the usually vacant ocean in the top left corner held a sketch of a young woman.

Long lashes framed the woman's closed eyes, her mid-length hair spilling over her shoulders in a disarray that boasted rest. My heart dipped into my stomach, unleashing a swarm of butterflies in my gut. "Who's that?" I whispered.

Bay ran his fingers through his free hair, ruffling it as he tilted his head. "I thought I'd done a pretty good job. You really can't tell?"

My voice came out tiny, embarrassed. "Is it me?"

"Phew. That's good. A career as an artist is still attainable for me, then."

"But,"—I took a breath, looking over the delicate shape of the woman's cheeks, the peace, the full lips, the small nose—"she's beautiful."

Bay's brows crashed together, and he pinned me with a perplexed stare. "Yeah?" His lips pinched. "I mean..." He ruffled his hair again, pulling his attention back to the image on the page. "I'm not sure how to respond to that. Would you have preferred I'd drawn you ugly or something?"

When I thought of beauty, I always thought of Whisper. Her dark skin, petite fullness, and coy smiles. Self-consciously, I tugged on my pin-straight hair and knew instinctively it didn't contain the volume Bay had drawn it with.

"For the airwoman's sake." Skye's chirping voice made me blink out of the hypnotic state I'd fallen into. The little pixie settled onto Bay's shoulder, whipping aside strands of Bay's hair, and sighed. "You're hopeless."

"It is a near-perfect likeness, isn't it?" Bay responded, puffing out his chest. Skye rolled his eyes. When Bay popped out of the window seat, he nearly threw Skye off his shoulder. "We should probably get some breakfast, pack our supplies, and head out if we want to expedite our demise at Pirate Bay."

"Wait." I swallowed when he paused and quirked a brow at me. "After we reach this 'Pirate Bay,' then what? What about what you're looking for? Will we find it on the way, or..."

Bay rested his drawing table against his side. For a moment, it looked as if the weight of an island rested on top of him, then it was gone. "I highly doubt we'll find what I'm looking for in the next few days, though I suppose anything is possible. Once I take you to the bay, I'll tell you some of the ropes, then, I suppose we'll part ways. Pirates don't really like anyone, but they really, *really* don't like me, so the quicker I'm in and out, the better." He took a breath, a grimness to his expression that made my heart bleed. "I'm sorry. I can take you there, but I can't help you past that."

"I understand." My chest twisted, uncomfortably tight. Did this mean he had decided against using me for whatever it was? Was I not good enough in the end? Somehow the thought of parting ways hurt more than the idea of not being useful. "Thank you for risking so much already."

He swiped his hair back and released a breath,

turning toward his room. "What are friends for?"

A staleness coated the air, silence consuming the clearing as we stepped into it. After a day and of walking with scrapes and bruises, I had finally begun to heal enough that any aches from our traveling distance seemed minuscule.

Bay hadn't asked anything of me, and as far as I could tell, we were heading in the right direction. Perhaps I had dreamed the conversation from before? Or maybe they'd just decided against whatever they were planning. There was no way to know until we parted ways.

"Neverland weeps," Skye murmured, and I forced myself not to pause at the foreboding tone. I'd never heard a pixie sound so dire before. "We shouldn't have come this way. You can't still be—"

"No, but we've avoided it for too long." Bay turned his head away from me, quieting his words. "Whatever we're missing is here. I'm going to check, with or without help."

"I don't like this." Skye shot off into the trees, and Bay sighed, smiling when I sent him a worried look.

"What's going on?" I asked. "It's..." Tense? Still?

"Silent?" Bay swept his gaze over the clearing. Swiping a hand across his mouth, he released a shaky breath. "Yeah."

The space opened the further we went, and I glanced back at where we had come from. None of the full color that had decorated the forest lingered. Weeds patched the ground. Roughness thickened the dirt, making it appear coarse.

Skye zipped back and hovered in front of Bay's face. "No one's up there. Still. *We should not be here.*"

My heartbeat accelerated, but I forced the building

fear down. "What's wrong?"

Bay looked between us, then shook his head. "Nothing. It's just a bad memory."

Skye's eyes narrowed. They stared at one another for several long moments, and I waited to see who would win. In the end, Bay passed the pixie and continued through the menacing air.

Skye frowned after him, looked at me, then sat on my shoulder and crossed his arms. I watched Bay's back, following slowly. "What is this place?" I whispered, more to Skye than anyone else.

The little pixie merely snapped, "Insufferable," and glared away.

I followed Bay, glad that at least Skye seemed on my side with whatever was happening but concerned that the tiny pixie would be little help if any danger appeared. The farther we went, the less I thought danger would appear. Like Skye had said, Neverland wept. More than that, it mourned. I could feel the ground almost tremble with sobs and had to focus on keeping my feet.

Nothing actually moved, but the sensation rocked my chest, connecting with the ever-present ache of losing Whisper.

That's when I saw them.

Protruding from the ground in great heaps were ivory bones. I froze where I stood, my eyes separating the mounds into individual pieces. There had to be hundreds, each and every femur, tibia, and skull picked clean like they had been resting here for years.

A tiny hand pulled on my hair, and I looked at Skye. His blue eyes stuck on the mountains of bone, sorrow etched deep in the crevices of his gaze. "You don't have to," he whispered with a softness that conveyed he didn't think I understood him.

Gathering my strength, I moved again, walking forward. Sickness laced the back of my tongue, and my stomach clenched. I anticipated a rotting scent to carry on the breeze at any moment, but only the same stale air wheezed in and out of my lungs.

This had happened so long ago now, not even death retained its hold.

"Bay," I called ahead.

The boy stopped where he was, and his chest shuddered with the breath. "Yes?"

"What...what happened here?" I reached his side and found dome-shaped homes slanted before us. Most of the structures had been knocked over or burned. Charred wood crumbled in a permanent state of decay.

"I told you before that a group of people like us used to live here. And that they were gone now." His face remained a solemn mask. "The pirates tricked them into a false sense of security, ambushed them, and slaughtered everyone."

A lump closed off my throat, but I managed a soft, "The pirates?"

"Hook and his crew. Few of the others saw reason to torment the natives like this. They were peaceful, dwelling among themselves, helpful when the situation presented the need." Bay looked at me, and chills ran over my body. Even though his face was young, his eyes bore a tale of an age past appearance, an age weighted with pain. "Culture and history that goes back to the beginning of Neverland died on this soil."

Closing my eyes, I felt that. Suffering and loss seeped through the thin leather of my moccasins, telling a story without words. "Why are we here?" My voice was raw, accusing, and I knew it, but I sided with Skye. *We should not be here.* This place was sacred, and if

138

Neverland was willing to throw me into a river and nearly strike me with lightning for no reason, I didn't want to think about what would happen if I defiled this grave.

Bay nodded toward a stone structure. Large, painted blocks piled into a pyramid that shot into the sky, towering above the broken homes. A single dark entrance had been carved into the monolith. "I need to look in that."

"You *what?*" The monument was no less than a temple built beside hundreds, maybe thousands, of deceased people. "You're not serious." He said nothing. His expression didn't change. "I can't let you do that."

Bay's brow quirked, doubtful. "You can't *let* me?"

What was I saying? For all I knew, this was his culture, and he had every right to visit the temple of his ancestors. Insistent, I bit my lip. "No."

"Well, then. I can't let you stop me." He turned, facing the temple. "Skye, are you coming?"

"No."

"I'll be a few minutes, at the most. Skye says he'll stay with you since you seem a little shaken." Bay lifted off the ground and zipped through the entrance before I could hope to stop him. At best, I threw up my hand, opened my mouth, and stood there like a wounded statue, watching him disappear into the darkness.

Lowering my arm, I sighed, wincing at the bones when I faced them. "I'm not shaken," I murmured to Bay, though I knew he couldn't hear me. And, of course, that wasn't what Skye had said.

"We're both shaken," Skye mumbled.

"I can't believe he's doing this."—I chose my words carefully, pursing my lips—"unless, this is his ancestry."

Skye laughed shortly. "It's really not."

My brows furrowed, but I murmured, "I hope that was a confirmation."

Skye kept quiet then, conveying that it wasn't. Resigned not to push my luck, I didn't say anything else as I found a fallen log in decent shape to sit on. Neverland remained still around me, but the soft breezes rustling the trees sounded like a hundred sobbing voices. It prickled my skin and raised the hair on my arms.

Minutes passed.

My hands grew clammy. The longer Bay was gone, the more I twisted to look at the monolith, hoping he'd materialize out of the shadows. The longer he was gone, the more my hope waned that he would return at all.

"It's been ten minutes, hasn't it?" I whispered.

"It's been nearly thirty." Skye kicked his legs against my shoulder and wrung his hands in his lap. For a pixie, he had to be one of the calmest I'd seen. But since I couldn't understand them until recently, I hadn't made a point of getting to know many personally.

I gnawed my lip, letting out a breath. "I hope he's okay. Should we follow him...?"

Skye went still, his eyes bulging. Darting off my shoulder, he whirled beside me to face the structure. "That *bastard!*"

My mouth fell open. I snapped it shut as quickly as possible, lucky Skye's boiling focus was hyper-set on the temple. The tiny pixie people with bright hair and flower petal clothes *cursed?* Maybe Skye was special— he did spend all his time with Bay after all—but still.

It broke every innocent image I had of the creatures.

And I wasn't completely sure how not to respond to him for a few moments. Blinking out of the shock, I asked, "What is it?" A spike of terror shot through my gut, and I leaped to my feet. "Is Bay okay?"

Skye's nose scrunched in a sneer that made him look part feral dog. "I don't know," he growled. Facing me, he offered the non-verbal response of an infuriated shrug.

"Should we go in after him?" Anything could have happened. Thirty minutes was a long time, and I'd managed to nearly kill myself twice in less.

Skye shook his head, chiming, "No. You stay here." He motioned for me to wait, then zipped toward the entrance.

I jolted after him. "I'm not letting you go in there alone."

Skye froze, shooting me a glare.

I held my ground, planting my hands on my hips. "If something did happen, the last thing we want is for all of us to be separated. If you go alone and don't come back, I'll follow you, but I won't be able to fly. Our best chance is together."

He turned to look at the temple, then he faced me again. A sound I'd never expected to escape a pixie rumbled up his throat as he dredged his hands back through his hair. "Fine," he snapped. "Fine, you're right, and you can't understand me—" Frustrated, he scrubbed a hand down his face. Zipping to me, he nodded.

I nodded back, trying not to dig too much into the anger and concern melded on his face. Was he worried about Bay or mad at him? I didn't have the luxury to ask, so I took a breath and stepped forward, entering the darkness.

It swallowed us whole.

One hand fixed on the wall, I slipped forward and downward, testing the ground before placing my full weight onto any step. No light touched within, the black chasm seeming to stretch on forever. "Bay?" I hissed. My voice echoed against the stone, returning to me in distorted waves. "What was he expecting to find here?"

"Clues, answers, hints. He's desperate. He's looking for anything." Skye's voice drifted from the emptiness.

Answers to what questions? I pursed my lips, straining to pick the pixie's form out of the bleakness. The barest shimmer outlined him, but I couldn't make out his expression.

"This was a bad idea," I muttered. "We should turn around and make a torch or something before going deeper."

"Can't."

I hesitated, nearly asking why not, before shaking myself and remembering to act like I couldn't understand whether or not he'd agreed. Turning, I ran directly into a wall. "What?" I rubbed my nose and squinted, but naturally, I couldn't see the structure. I pressed my palm against the rough obstacle, fear curdling in my throat. "We can't get out."

"Nope."

My breaths shortened, and I halted on the step, scared to go forward unable to move back. It was so *dark.* "Where are you?" I asked, my voice more panicked than I would have liked.

A tiny sigh brushed near my ear, then little hands touched my forehead. The silkiest wisp of hair skimmed my skin as Skye pressed his head against mine. "I'm right here. Calm down. I'm not going to run off on my own, okay?" The soothing words turned harsh. "Unlike some people."

Gathering myself, I inhaled deeply, closed my eyes, and snapped them back open when I found no comfort in the action. There was absolutely no difference whether they were open or shut. "Can you see anything?" I whispered, adding, "Clap once for yes and twice for no.."

He clapped once, and my heart lifted before his voice fell on my ears again. "Well, I can see darkness, but that's hardly encouraging, so one clap for scared Lyric."

For the love of the airwoman, I was trapped in a temple with a sarcastic pixie. Acting like he could see enough to guide us forward would do no good, so I conceded to accept that desperate times called for profane language. "Damn it, Skye. If you can't see, don't pretend you can."

Silence.

I rolled my eyes, glad that at least I could feel his soft breath in front of me, entering and leaving his lungs. "Skye?"

"If you can understand me, clap once for yes and twice for no."

My teeth gritted. Out of spite, I clapped twice.

"Well." He moved, but his voice didn't go far. "Why have you pretended this entire time?"

"I haven't. I really couldn't understand you—or any of the others—last week."

Skye's tone morphed into the kind someone could only manage with folded arms and a look of condescension. "Then why have you pretended since last week?"

"Because," I spat, "Bay lies."

The pixie scoffed, muttering, "He sure does. Or did you actually believe all his stories?"

My cheeks flared red, and I was somewhat glad for the darkness in the moment. Putting that whole situation aside, I steered us back on topic. "That doesn't matter.

What are we supposed to do?"

His wings buzzed in the darkness, flitting away before returning. "There's only one way to go, so let's continue down. There's a wind current in a few steps, so something must lie ahead, another exit. For all we know, Bay came this same way."

Carefully picking my way down the stone slabs, I sucked my finger and held it up. Just as Skye had said, a light breeze meandered from the right.

The more I focused on it, the stronger it became. The ground leveled, and I followed the wind around a corner.

"What does Bay need answers to so badly that he would come in here alone? And why didn't you want to go with him?" The breeze whistled through the hall, growing stronger. I swore I could hear voices laced in it, murmurs and whispers, but when I tried to listen harder, the air rushed against me, whipping my hair and clothes back.

Skye slapped into my chest, clinging to my shirt, and I raised a hand to cover my eyes from the stinging onslaught. "What is this? It's unnatural!"

"A lot of things in Neverland are." Skye braced himself beneath my satchel strap like a belt.

The wind howled, as though in pain, so I yelled over it, "How can we be sure we're even going toward an exit then?"

"Do you have a better idea?"

I backstepped, but the phantom and silent wall blocking us from retreat met my back. There was only the one way to go. "No," I grumbled, pushing ahead. My hair beat against my neck and face, and I winced when the strands slashed at my eyes. "This would be so much easier if you would just *quiet down*!" I sliced my arm through the torrent, and wind wrapped around it like a physical sheet I could pull away, so I did.

Calm filled the tunnel, the gentle breeze returning to little more than an exhale of breath.

"What did you just..." Skye's chest heaved against my own.

I stood still, wondering the same. It couldn't have had anything to do with me. Not really. My brows furrowed when a glow blinked on in the distance. "Is that light?"

"Not sunlight."

I wasn't about to be picky. My pace quickened toward the blue-green hue. The closer I got, the larger the space around us became. The tunnel opened into a circular chamber illuminated by large flowers clinging to the ceiling. "Mirabel." The same flower that lit my room back in Skyla. My eyes searched the familiar petals and colors. "This is in Skyla, too."

"Sk-ye...is that you?" A fragmented voice trailed from one of many tunnels carved into the room before us. Something about it wasn't right.

Before I could say anything, Skye pushed away from me. "Bay."

"It hu-rts," the voice moaned, a breeze rustling from the same tunnel.

"Hold on!" Panic spiked in the pixie's tone.

"Wait!" I threw up my hand, but Skye had already darted into the tunnel. I started after him, colliding with a wall that slammed between us and blocked the path. "Skye!" I yelled, banging against the stone. "Skye, come back! Something isn't right. I don't think that's Bay!"

My nostrils flared, and my fists clenched. Teeth gritted, I rubbed my face. "I cannot keep running into walls," I grumbled, twisting to look at the other tunnels. A stone blocked the one we had come through, unsurprisingly. The rest were as dark and foreboding as everything else in this twisted place.

"Lyly."

Cold air poured from one of the tunnels, carrying a voice. Whisper's voice. My body stiffened against the chill.

"You should not be here," she said.

"I know that," I croaked. "I'm sorry. I never meant—"

"Trusting, innocent Lyly. You cannot trust anyone here." The voice aged, and hints of Tiger Lily melded into it. "Not even yourself."

"Are you a changeling?" I slipped my knife from its sheath on my thigh and brandished the blade. It caught the ghastly light, glinting floral reflections. "Your kind won't toy with me again."

"No." A woman whom I'd never heard before now spoke from the shadows, from the frigid wind. "I am the memory of my brothers and sisters, a wisp of magic manifested to guard our home, a kindred spirit. Come with me."

"But my friends—"

"Will be safe. Time is irrelevant here, but I shan't keep you for long." The woman's voice blended with others, hundreds, thousands, some vaguely familiar, the rest not. "We have been waiting. So long. So long in this timeless place. For the touch of another soul."

I gripped my knife, but the wind wrapped around me, beckoning me forward. "If I can't trust anyone, why should I trust you?"

"I am not anyone." The words came from behind, but only rock stood there. The voices floated on the breeze, coaxing, so I gave in.

There was little else I could do in a dark cave with no clear exit. Alone here now, my only hope of making it out and finding the others was to see where this led me and trust it was safe. *All things happen for a reason,* Tiger Lily had told me after her husband left. Tears had glistened in her eyes then, but she had continued to stare out at the sunset. *We may not know why, the pain may be unbearable, but if we trust ourselves and our hearts, we will find incredible things are born in our darkest moments.*

Peter, how come you don't age? Young, yet, I had looked up to him.

Sadness had crossed his brown eyes, but it lingered only for a second, then he ruffled my hair and grinned. *Maybe so I would have the chance to meet you.*

I couldn't explain a lot of things. I couldn't find reason in losing Whisper, leaving Peter, or following this voice. Still, as my feet continued to hit solid ground and I continued to breathe, I knew I had to keep moving forward. For everyone I still had, and for everyone I didn't.

"You cry," the wind murmured, touching the dampness on my cheeks.

Holding myself firm, I swallowed the lump in my throat. "If you aren't a someone, how can you see me?"

"Yes. And how can I speak?"

I froze. "My mind is playing tricks on me. You said I couldn't trust myself. What if you meant now, in following you?"

"Will you listen to me or not?" it hissed. "Taking what I say to do in part means nothing."

I didn't budge. "Why wouldn't I be able to trust myself then?"

"Because you know not what you are."

"I'm Lyric."

"And who is *Lyric?* The words drifting in the song

of the air? The music on the wind? A charm of good fortune? A girl, a friend, a wanderer, an orphan?" The chill bit at my nose and fingers and ears. "You have always doubted you were anything. Because you knew, deep in your heart, you were nothing worth keeping."

My knife shook in my hand. "That's not true. Maybe—" I spat, "maybe I was abandoned, but the people who took me in, they kept me. And they're extraordinary. If I really am nothing and if I came from nothing special, then that means incredible people still saw something worthwhile in me." *And didn't that make me, just a little, incredible, too?* "I don't need your help. I'm going to trust myself here."

Long, icy fingers caressed my cheeks, and a breath escaped me. "Very well." Whisper's voice. I closed my eyes tight, wishing the wraith had picked anyone else. "We will meet again."

"I said I—" My eyes opened on a room illuminated by fire. Large sconces flickered with heat, painting the stone walls in orange. No tunnels led in or out of the space. I stood in the middle, staring ahead at pictures. Children's pictures.

Drawn into the wall in shades of sky blue and sun yellow and grass green and blood red were images depicting a stream of events. A lightning bolt struck what appeared to be a large rock—an island?—splitting it into dozens of fractured pieces. The pieces fell into the ocean and took root there. I stilled at seeing the next image.

It was a boy. A boy with burning hair, green clothes, and a splash of yellow gleaming near his shoulder. My fingers brushed over the stone. "Peter...?" The chipped paint had been there for years, maybe centuries. I couldn't tell. But I had always speculated Peter had

148

existed for just as long.

The story continued. The boy traveled the islands, unraveling secrets that led him to a spring. At least it looked like a spring. This water, unlike the rest in the images, was a striking shade of gold, and he drank it.

The rest of the pictures were of forts and treehouses and swimming with mermaids and flying with birds. Casual child scribbles. The more I looked, the more seemed to appear, and the longer I tried to focus on any one in particular, the more convoluted they all became. Some of the pictures felt like stories I'd heard before. Others were crusted with time and lost to the ages.

The pictures spun in my head now more than on the walls, and I saw other children with the flame-haired boy. Several others. More that I recognized. A hook chipped them away until I knew each figure's name.

The Lost Boys.

The Lost Boys and Peter.

With that realization, wind appeared out of nowhere, crashing into me and throwing me off my feet. I hit stone. The impact jarred every thought and image, shaking them from my head. Sweat beaded on my brow in the firelight, then froze. Icelets flecked off my cheeks. An eerie voice called to me.

Then silence and darkness swallowed my mind.

"I can't believe you did this. She could have died."

"But, she didn't."

"We don't know that yet."

Someone slapped my cheeks. "Yes. We do," Bay growled. "She's fine."

I took a quivering breath, wondering how "fine" I looked. It felt like I'd been put through a rock grinder and tumbled around with stones twice my size. Unfortunately, I couldn't quite find the strength to open my eyes.

"See? She's breathing."

"I know someone else who's breathing and not at all fine," Skye hissed.

Bay's hand rested on my cheek an instant before drawing away. "That's too far."

"*This* was too far." A light body landed on my shoulder. "I mean it, Bay. No one else suffers for our family. No one."

I had to pry myself awake. Were we still in the cave? Was that sunlight or firelight against my face?

Taking a heaving breath, I cracked open my eyelids and squinted through the trees at the dying sun. Bay sighed over me, smiling. "Hello, Wind Song. Are you back with us?"

Sand coated my tongue. Everything ached. Was I meant to always be in a state of pain here?

"Wa-ter?" I croaked.

Bay's eyes widened. "Water? What about—"

"She wants water, you idiot." Skye darted off my shoulder and dove into Bay's bag, pulling a flask larger than him out when he emerged.

"Right," Bay mumbled, taking the weight from Skye and propping my head so I could drink. The liquid washed down my throat, cooling my chest and lightening the strain on my breath. When I'd had enough, I could almost sit up on my own.

"What...happened?" I remembered the voice in the wind and the pictures. Was either real? Now, looking back and finding myself inexplicably here, a haze covered it all, like I was peering into a dream.

"I'm not sure. We woke up here shortly before you did."

"So does this feeling like death thing wear off fairly

quickly, or am I just special?" Flexing my fingers and toes, I tested whether or not I could move my limbs. Not well, apparently, but some.

"I, uh..." Bay met Skye's glare as the tiny creature hovered defensively before me. "I think you're just special."

"Lovely." I glanced at the space around me, realizing that though it was quiet, the stale air from before had lessened. "Where are we?" A large cylindrical building sat surrounded by blazing orange flowers. Unlike the other homes, this one appeared mostly intact. Yet two gravestones jutted out of the flowers, proving the battle hadn't left even here unscathed.

Bay turned toward the solemn home, and his jaw clenched. Sorrow saturated his gaze, but he wiped the expression clean when he looked back at me. "This is where the former chief lived with his family." Rising, he held a hand out for me, helping me onto my feet. "We should probably take shelter here for the night."

"What?" I snatched my hand out of his, regretting it when the world toppled. He steadied me, nothing but concern in his hazel eyes. I swallowed a shaking breath and forced myself to remain calm, if for no reason other than the headache brewing. "Wouldn't that be disrespectful?"

His attention shifted to the graves. "I don't think they would mind...and I don't think you'd make it to my next shelter. Not right now, anyway. It's probably better if we don't hobble through the night."

"I'm not hobbling."

"You're right," Skye snipped. "You're not even hobbling. Come on. It's fine." He motioned me forward, raising his brows at Bay.

Bay cleared his throat. "He says it's fine also."

I glanced between them. Had I dreamed the pixie finding out I could understand him? Or was he respecting my reasons for not telling Bay in the first place? It didn't matter right now. Protection from the night and possibly a place to sleep took precedence. "Fine." I stared at the doorway, trying to keep my focus off the graves. "If you're sure."

Skye nodded and zipped ahead through the cracked door while Bay eased me forward, one step at a time. "Whatever happened really did a number on you," he said close to my ear. "Do you...remember anything?"

A little too much hope laced his voice as if he knew something had happened, and though it had left me unable to walk, he wanted to know what it was. Shaking my head, I mumbled, "Nothing I can remember. It was dark."

"Right." The frail hope dissipated, planting a seed of guilt in my chest.

He had lied to me more than once—I was half certain he had planned this whole event too; for some reason I couldn't discern. Why should I feel bad about keeping information I didn't understand from him? Glancing at his face, seeing the absence of any gleam in his eye, I figured out why.

He's desperate.

If I hadn't imagined everything with Skye, Bay was just as he'd said—*desperate*. Perhaps the answers or hints or clues he was looking for had poured into my head through those pictures, but until I knew what they meant and the reason he was looking for them, I didn't feel comfortable sharing.

I dropped my attention to the bed of flowers just before the front door. They blazed in the last rays of light, each spotted orange lily bursting with new life in the desolate area. Bobbing in the breeze, they radiated a sense of calm I hadn't felt since...

"Tiger lilies." Bay nudged the door open fully with his foot, meeting my gaze when I looked up.

My throat tightened in on itself, but I managed a whispered, "What?"

He nodded at the patch of flowers. "They're tiger lilies. The chief's wife planted them here to honor their daughter's birth in the time of peace before the slaughter."

Without another word, my gaze still fixed on the brilliant blooms, Bay pulled me inside.

15TH NOVEMBER

As we walked through the deepest part of the forest we had come upon yet, I could hardly keep my attention on the still-dull ache tracing down my limbs. A weight held me to the earth even though dust coated my hair and skin. Bay floated beside me, oblivious.

Could the tiger lilies in front of the chief's house be a coincidence?

The images of Peter plastered against the stone walls of that temple cave made me think otherwise. If Peter had been here, perhaps Tiger Lily had been too. Perhaps, this was even her original home. It all tied together. Hook, enemy of the natives and Peter. Peter, enemy of Hook and friend of most. Tiger Lily, Peter's oldest living friend—as far as I knew.

What if there had been more Lost Boys? What if Hook had vanquished them? What if Peter had saved a chieftain's daughter and escaped to Skyla with the ones he had left?

What if Bay, all this time, knew the truth? What if he had the entire story, the one Peter had long since forgotten, and I suppose Tiger Lily was either too young to remember or chose not to share?

"You're awfully quiet this morning." Bay didn't smile. The solemn tastes from the day before lingered, but more than that, he appeared on edge. A bird streaked overhead with a splitting caw, and the fearless boy who laughed casually in the face of Krakens stiffened, watching the feathered fiend disappear into the distance before daring to relax.

"I guess I don't feel much like talking." The half-lie spilled easily from my lips, exhaustion a dark cloud clinging to me like a tick. I wanted desperately to talk about all the questions and speculations spinning in my head. But I couldn't shake the feeling that what the voice in the wind had said before was the truth. I couldn't trust anything here. Not Bay. Not Skye. Not even myself—seeing as my first instinct was to blurt everything to him and wait for answers I doubted would come. That last bit was hardly new. Since when did I trust myself anyway?

Grief pooled in my veins, making me something pliable and reliant, but there was nothing to rely on— everything I had once relied on was little more than a ghost to haunt me now. I was here for revenge and bloodshed, so no wonder Neverland wasn't making it easy for me. The magical island had seen far too much of both.

Bay rebraided his hair and tightened the tie around the short tail. "Are you reluctant to talk because of yesterday?"

A nerve snapped. "Which part of yesterday? Leading me through piles of bones or tricking me into following you through a sacred temple?"

"I didn't trick you?" His eyes widened with innocence. "I said I had to go. You just happened to follow me."

"You knew I would." I trudged on, pushing aside a low-hanging branch. "Don't act like you didn't have it planned from the start. I just can't figure out why. We both could have *died.*"

Bay landed beside me, his bare feet squishing through damp clumps of leaves, and I caught him glance accusingly at Skye.

I snapped, "No, your pixie didn't mime the truth to me. Maybe I'm just a little smarter than you thought."

"I've never thought you weren't smart." He frowned. "I wouldn't have invited dead weight to come with me to a place as deadly as this. I don't have time to babysit, Wind Song."

Stopping, I whirled on him and placed my hands on my hips. He stopped just short of running into me, and I hovered half an inch taller than him, just like Peter often did to me. "Then, I want the truth. What do you know about Peter and Tiger Lily? How are they connected to this place? Am I?"

His lips parted, then they closed. His eyes drifted toward the ground, then a bird screamed near us, and he jerked. "Shit!" Fear curdled in his eyes as he peered through the thick forest for the offending creature.

"While we're at it, why don't you tell me why birds are scaring you out of your skin today?" I settled back on the ground and folded my arms, forcing my attention to remain steady on him instead of traveling through the trees, looking for danger. He knew this place. If he was scared of something, I would likely be terrified. But I didn't have that luxury right now.

He swiped his bangs back and glared at me. "Fine. You want me to confirm it? Tiger Lily was the chief's daughter. Thanks to Peter, she was the only native who hadn't already left who escaped the slaughter."

My mouth went dry. "So...this all couldn't have happened more than twenty years ago."

"Ninteen." Bay's eyes closed, and he took a deep breath. "It happened about nineteen years ago."

I looked at Bay, seeing the soft lines near his eyes. He looked like a boy, only two years older than I was. But when his hazel gaze fixed on me, I saw wisdom in his eyes. "You... Were you there?" I asked.

A self-degrading smile tipped his lips. "What do you think, Wind Song?"

I didn't know what to think. I didn't have time to respond either. Something white and brown screamed through the trees behind Bay, and Skye shrieked, "Run!"

Our feet pounded against the ground, each thudding step reminding me of the aches and pains I had encountered the day before. My muscles tightened from the strain, each tendon one jarring pull away from snapping.

The trees were packed together like woven threads, impossible to maneuver through quickly by air. So, we continued running, listening to the branches behind us catch wings and flailing limbs. Bay mumbled curses beneath his breath and threw glances in my direction to make sure I kept up. We gained ground for a moment.

Then my foot caught on a fallen log. I careened

into the brush, my flesh shredded on the harsh bark. My ankle burned, and I hissed, clutching it with both hands.

"Wind Song, get up!" Bay gripped my shoulder, yanking me back onto protesting feet. A sharp stab shot through my calf. Sweat poured into my cut and stung. I forgot how to breathe for a moment, then I gasped in air, my eyes watering.

Staring ahead, I met the huge eyes of an owl. The creature's beak split in a deafening trill, and I blurted, "That's not a siren!"

"Nope! It's a harpy!" Bay grabbed my hand and ripped me away from the half-human half-bird abomination. Unlike the sirens who could pass as beautiful and graceful, this creature appeared made of mismatched parts, awkwardly battling through the trees.

"What in the name of the airwoman is a harpy?" I screamed, fighting to keep my legs moving. The surety I would die if I stopped was all the motivation I needed to fight through every rattling step.

"*That* is a harpy." Bay squeezed my hand, tugging me through a narrow gap between two towering spruce trees, and my mouth fell open.

"Is *that* why you've been scared of birds today?"

"I haven't been scared of birds," he protested.

The screeching harpy yowled in pain, and I dared a look back to find its wing trapped on a branch. "So normal people who aren't scared of birds panic whenever one tweets in their vicinity?"

Bay dodged a thorny bush. "Okay, fine. But who likes birds anyway?"

"I do. I mean, I *used* to!"

"We're almost there!" Skye chirped.

"Great." Bay tossed his hair back, peered over his

shoulder at the harpy, and released a breath. "I think we're going to make it."

"What? Make it where?"

"Just trust me."

I was told explicitly not to, and all signs pointed to that being a good idea, but I didn't quite have a choice right now—worse yet, I still wanted to trust him. The forest broke suddenly, displaying a sheer cliff. Bay pulled me over the edge, and we plummeted.

Water spilled from the rock at more than a dozen points, each waterfall distinct as it rushed into snaking streams at the bottom. Mist sprayed my body, soaking me to the skin.

"Hold your breath!" Bay yelled.

No sooner than I'd taken a gasping breath did he plunge us through the falls. Any hope of flying washed off in the downpour, and we rolled in a pile of appendages across a stone floor. I panted once the world stopped spinning.

Bay dragged himself into a seated position and rubbed his neck. "Well, that was eventful."

The rushing water before us muted anything beyond, but I still jumped when a distant caw broke through the full silence. Shivering, I tried adjusting myself to stand, but the scrape on my ankle wasn't having it, so I slumped. "Everything hurts. Again." Out of habit, I felt for my bag—wet, also again, and my knife. It was all still here.

A sharp breath whistled through my nose when Bay grabbed my ankle and stretched out my leg. He examined the purple area then pressed on my heel, watching me for any reaction. Shifting his bag in front of him, he set my foot down. "It's not broken or sprained, thankfully." He pulled out a damp roll of scrap cloth and wrung out what water he could before using it to clean and wrap my cut. "Another bruise for your collection."

I grimaced at his grin and pulled my treated leg close against my chest. "I'm glad it amuses you."

"I've never met someone so attracted to danger before."

Grumbling, I said, "I think it's attracted to me."

"So I have a rival. We might as well stop here for a soggy lunch." Bay fished out some food from his bag, half of it unappetizing, yet my stomach growled in response. He passed me the better pieces of tough bread and a handful of berries. "We aren't far from Pirate Bay now. We'll reach my base tonight, and then it's just a short walk through the meadow come morning."

"Wonderful."

His gaze flicked up, and he watched me for a long moment. "You're welcome to stay in my base for as long as you need to plan your attack."

"I'll scout everything out as soon as possible." Tearing off a piece of bread, I popped it in my mouth and avoided dwelling on the mushy texture. I was almost there. Almost to what was sure to be my demise. The most I could do was attempt to thin the adversary, then hopefully, Skyla would have a better chance.

"Your best chance is probably to light it up," Bay murmured. "I know where the explosives are kept. Gunpowder. Lighting fuel. It might take a bit of strategy, but if you can set the bay on fire, you'll be able to wipe it off Neverland before anyone would notice."

I stared at him, eyes wide. "I thought you couldn't enter in case someone recognized you?"

Popping a berry in his mouth, he shrugged. "Yeah, if someone recognizes me, it's all over, but I guess I've changed my mind about how much I'm willing to help you. If I can help it, I'm not sending you to your death."

I dropped my gaze to the bandage around my ankle. Like the others, it had been wrapped with precision and habit. How many wounds had he suffered in the years he'd spent here? How long had it been just him and Skye looking for something always out of reach? "Thank you," I whispered, and before I realized, I added, "If I survive this, maybe I can help you next."

"You wouldn't want to go home?" Softness blanketed the question because we both knew that's exactly what I wanted, especially right now when everything hurt. It's probably all either of us wanted: *to go home*. He was really asking why I felt I didn't have that option anymore.

I stuffed several berries in my mouth, downed the sweet-bitter flavor, and swallowed. "Peter forgets things. The kinds of things you don't think you can ever forget. It doesn't take long. He's never mourned anything. He just...forgets any reason he might have to be sad."

"You think he's forgotten you."

I nodded. "And with Whisper and Tiger Lily..."

"Right," he said as Skye settled on his shoulder. He looked at the silent creature. "I'm sorry. I didn't mean to... Well..., yeah."

My lips pulled in a twisted grin. "Very smooth, Star Boy."

He met my expression with a pained smile of his own. "I do try, Wind Song. I do try."

We finished our pathetic meal before launching ourselves out of the crevice and catching fresh pixie dust to avoid an untimely collision with the ground. Landing among sparse trees and winding streams, we maintained a slow pace as every step stung or ached or stabbed somewhere new in me.

I planted my focus around me as completely as I could to avoid dwelling on the pain rushing my body in overwhelming tides. The area was beautiful. Color saturated the banks of each stream, hundreds of flowers and butterflies painting everything in a rainbow kaleidoscope. Perfumed scents rose and fell on the wind as it rustled the slender trees, their light branches swaying.

If my head wasn't throbbing, I might have enjoyed it.

"Here we are," Bay stopped, and I looked up from a cluster of yellow buds dancing in the breeze.

A wide span of meadow stretched before us. The streams pooled together in a rushing river that skittered off to one side and plowed toward the ocean that glinted on the horizon. Bobbing atop what blue waves I could see were massive ships, each and every one bearing some form of black or red flag. The ocean I couldn't see was blocked by a town with a variety of square buildings. Some jutted into the sky. Others sat squat near the ground. No two shapes appeared entirely the same. They rested in blocks like a clump of fool's gold.

My nose scrunched when some acrid fume reached me. "What is that?"

"Cheap rum." Bay tilted his head toward the setting sun. "At this time, barrels and barrels of cheap rum."

"It's awful." I covered my mouth to avoid heaving.

Shadows coated Bay's eyes when the sun dipped completely from view, leaving nothing but a faint glow in the sky. "You get used to it," he said, the words dark. Jaw clenched, he sighed. "I suppose we have some work to do tonight. No offense, but you don't look particularly pirate-y." He brushed some crawling flowers off a trap door at the base of several slender trees. Bound together, the trunks hid the secret chamber well from view. "It might be a bit of a mess. It's been a while since I've come here."

I stared into the dim hole and shook my head. "That's all right. I doubt it's worse than what we've already gone through today." *Beside*—I sank into the cool embrace of the earth, my breath catching when I found mirabel decorating the ceiling—*it's practically home.*

"I look like a milkmaid," I grumbled, staring at my reflection in the slim mirror propped against the dirt walls of Bay's hideout. As he'd said, everything was a bit dusty, and we had fought several webs away, but it remained the closest thing to home I'd come across since entering Neverland.

Bay floated behind me, his chin propped in his palm. "Yeah, yeah, you kind of do."

I swiped the rag off my head, freeing my hair, and hovered to avoid putting pressure on my bruised ankle. My orange locks spilled into my eyes, so I blew them away. "Don't other people have orange hair? Surely Peter isn't the only one, and I'm not even blood-related to him, so he absolutely isn't."

"Maybe, but no one here that I remember. It isn't every day Neverland has visitors, so we really need to blend in. It's bad enough I can't do anything about that gold in your eyes." Bay turned toward the chest of attire we were picking apart and dug deeper.

I faced the mirror again, staring at the golden rings around my irises. A phantom brush of wind that couldn't have come from anywhere down here teased the candle resting on a table to my left, and I lowered my brows at it.

"How about this!" Bay wrenched my attention away from the flame and toward the cotton dress in his hand. Some kind of laced and leather contraption rested in

164

his other palm, and he waved it. "It comes with a thing."

I took the tangled mess from him and frowned. "I think this is a corset."

"Try it on."

"Um. No." I returned it to him. "I already have clothes." I gestured at my trousers and leather vest over a white top. "We need to figure out the hair problem." Planking above the trunk midair, I tried to find a better bandana than the one that made me look like I'd come straight from the goat farms. Instead, I found a small woven bag with long needles and a glass jar of ink. "What's this?"

Bay dumped the rejected outfit and peered over my shoulder. "A tattoo kit." Reaching for it, he stopped, and his hand clenched in a fist. "A friend taught me long ago."

I turned the bag over, examining the faded dye coloring the wool. "This looks like something Tiger Lily would make."

"I'd imagine so. Her mother made it."

My heart dropped into my stomach and stuck there. "What?"

"Receiving a mark was a tradition when children came of age. Generally, the mark represented some achievement or title.. Usually, it tied in with the child's name since the native's names tended to change with either of those things. Her father taught me. Her mother made me a set of my own." Scoffing, he ran his fingers through his loose hair. "What were they thinking? I was—what?—maybe ten?" His voice quieted. "Though, I suppose not technically... Anyway, I never really got to use it on anything past animal hide. They said when Tiger Lily came of age, I'd be the one honored to do her mark, but...that didn't happen either."

Running my finger along the spine of a bone needle, I whispered, "What's of age?"

"Sixteen."

Pressing my lips together, I lowered myself onto the rug and sat cross-legged, handing him the set of needles and ink. "Then, I guess we're both a little late."

His brows rose, and he blinked. "What?"

"Tiger Lily was more like a mother to me than anyone. If she was the last of her people and this tradition died with her, without her even knowing, I couldn't bear it. You seem to know what you're talking about, so tell me and show me. Let me keep some of my mother's heritage alive." I kept my eyes fixed on him, and gradually he sat across from me, taking the tools and holding them tight.

"It doesn't go away."

I provided him an annoyed glare. "I do know what a tattoo is."

He wet his lips. "I mean, it's been a while since I learned. Any mistakes won't go away."

"Then don't make any."

He laughed, but I raised my brows, and he quieted. Glancing around the room, he found Skye asleep on a pillow in the corner. "You must have some insane faith in me."

I looked him over, from his tousled waves to his bare feet. Even "seated," he floated slightly above the ground. Sincerity, memories, and honor for a culture he had touched weighted his expression. I took a breath. "Is that a mistake?"

He nodded. "Probably."

And yet right now, it didn't feel like it was. "Will you be honest with me, Bay?"

"If I can." He looked back at me, as though he was

waiting for a question, but I had already asked it, and his reply was about as good as I was going to get.

I held out my arms, unsure what the next step was.

He smiled, shaking his head. "It's going to be a later night than I expected."

16TH NOVEMBER

O vernight, my right arm had gone red around the markings, but the pictures remained clear. Half a dozen tiny feathers floated down my skin like a breeze chased them.

They were perfect, and when I asked why Bay had chosen them over music notes or something relating to "Wind Song,", hed merely shrugged and said he couldn't help it; they were from my wings. *Wings*, I thought, resting at the base of the cluster of trees and staring out at the dozens of butterflies playing by the stream banks. If I had wings like them, where would I go? If I didn't need dust or a friendly pixie near me, if I could be as independent and strong as Whisper, what would I do?

I probably wouldn't have run away to Neverland with a death wish.

Releasing a breath, I glanced back down at my sleeve of feathers, then stretched my hand to the sky. Sunlight poured through my fingers and over the designs.

"It's there for good," Bay said, emerging from the trap door with Skye and stretching in the air. A yawn clung to his mouth, so he covered it with a hand, mumbling through it, "I hope you aren't having regrets. I'd feel terrible if I spent seven hours on something you'd regret."

His expression made me think it wouldn't bother him in the slightest. I dropped my arm back into my lap. "I love it."

"Good." He smirked, fluttering an orange bandana at me. "I found this for your hair. Maybe no one will notice if a bit peeks through."

"Are we leaving now, then?" I tied the cloth around my head, hoping it looked normal enough, and stood.

Leaning forward, Bay provided me a once-over that ended with him tucking an already-straying lock of hair back beneath the cloth. My cheeks heated, but he moved away without reacting. "Almost. What do you think?" Plucking a dark eye mask from his darker coat, he covered half his face, not the half that showcased a carefree grin, though.

"Little too friendly and floaty for a pirate if you ask me."

His smile fell as he planted his feet on the ground. "Good thing you're beat up enough for the both of us if I'm too 'friendly,'" Shaking his hair out, he brushed off his cloak, mumbling something about how Skye shed worse than a cat.

Skye shot me a warning look and an eye roll. I held

in a laugh.

"All right. That's that," he stated, resting his arm on the hilt of his cutlass. His usual dagger belt remained in place, but the cutlass definitely added a much-needed pirate-y flare. "Let's hope we survive this. We've both got things to do afterward."

"I suppose when we get to those things, you'll finally tell me what they are?"

"Surprise is the spice of life." Lifting his coat, he let Skye zip into an inner pocket, then we began walking.

"Are we talking surprise like: 'Surprise! It's your birthday!' or surprise like 'Surprise! A harpy is chasing you through the woods, and the only chance of surviving you have is jumping off a cliff and diving through a waterfall at the exact moment a ledge is hidden behind it'?"

"Closer to the second one, but with sprinkles."

"Lovely." My smile betrayed the subtle anxiety swirling in my chest. I felt lighter today, even with the task looming before me. We had to hunt down Hook and his crew, and wipe them from Neverland before they could ever reach Skyla, yet it was less daunting beside Bay. He may be a liar, and I might not know much about him—he may have even intentionally put me in danger for undisclosed reasons—but he still gathered confidence around him like a living beast.

Beside him, impossible things felt probable. Win or lose, it was all a game, and he'd come out laughing in the end.

"You're a lot like Peter," I murmured.

His nose scrunched, and he stopped short. "What?"

"The way you act, fearlessly and all that. A bit cocky. Easily able to tread my nerves. Never providing enough information—though I'm pretty certain he can't, and you just choose not to." Perhaps pixies only ever clung to a very specific type of person—the most innocent assholes.

Bay deadpanned. "Thank you for comparing me to your father figure slash twelve-year-old somehow-your-guardian person. My pride is not at all wounded, and I am also not at all resentful."

"I don't think it's a bad thing. I've lived my entire life wishing I could be like Peter." A cloud drifted along the horizon, disappearing behind buildings and peeking through the cracks. "He's completely free."

Bay huffed a breath. "He is definitely not. He has all of Skyla to look after."

"Maybe, but he does it effortlessly like he's playing king. And, when he doesn't feel like it, he goes on an adventure, returning with any stories he remembers, making up the ones he doesn't." I frowned.

Bay laughed, but the sound was so bitter as he started walking again. "He has you completely tricked."

"What are you talking about?"

"Peter is anything but free. When he leaves, he's keeping up relations with all the other kingdoms that he has kept Skyla majorly outside of. His adventures are tasks at their cores, tasks that keep Skyla safe from the messes on the ground."

"How would you know?" I spat.

"Because I know Peter. Or rather I knew him, and when I knew him, it was in a time of war. Trust me, that perpetual kid lives in a constant cycle of duty and suffering."

My head shook of its own accord. "I don't want to hear this." My bright mood died, and my chest clenched. I knew Bay lied, it could all be a lie, but—

"Sorry..." Bay scrubbed a hand across his mouth.

"Of course, you wouldn't. I guess the comparison hit a little close to home, is all."

"Is the way you see Peter how you see yourself?" I stilled on the edge of the town. Just a few more yards and we'd have to put any strange talk aside, and I had to know. What duties was he bound to that made him suffer?

"I'll never admit it." The dark air lifted, his hazel eyes gleaming within the mask. "After all, I'm nothing like that brat. Not even a little bit."

"I thought you said you'd be honest with me." Genuine hurt touched my heart, but I bit my cheek and pretended I was angry.

"When I can," he said. "Sometimes, it's too hard. Sometimes, I can't even be honest with myself." Before I could prod him further, he strode the rest of the way into the town, ducking into a dark alley. Hurrying after him was all I could do to keep up.

We kept to the shadows, trailing through alleyways until my head spun with every crooked path. When what seemed like an hour had passed, I caught Bay's coat and hissed, "I thought you knew where we were going?"

"Ah." He glanced back at me, his mask catching a straying streak of sunlight and sheening obsidian. "About that. We passed the storage forty minutes ago. They've changed things."

My mouth gaped. "How long has it been since you were last here?"

"A while, I told you that." His attention shifted to the street in front of us when a sturdy man flew across the alley's exit. A tall woman with golden teeth and brilliant raven hair leaped after him like a snarling cat. "Maybe we should go another way."

"Another way to where?" I asked as Bay backstepped toward me. He stopped in the narrower part of the walkway, his chest nearly pressed against mine. Masterly-crafted stone foundations made up the walls around us, but they were askew in their placement, acting like a funnel, a funnel that had sifted us closer than I would have liked.

"Just elsewhere. We're looking for something, so we need to keep looking, right?" A tinge of annoyance touched his tone, but his gaze remained off me and on the two people who were fighting.

I started to turn my gaze toward them when he caught my face with his hand, firmly shaking his head. A garbled cry mingled with shrieks of triumph, and I didn't need to see what had happened.

"You need to chill," Skye muttered from within Bay's coat, "and I need to breathe. Let's regroup at that place if it's still there."

My brows furrowed, wanting clarification more than translation. "What did he say?"

Bay narrowed his eyes on the mouth of the alley, then snatched my hand, ignoring everything he had just seen. "He says we need a break. I'm hungry. Are you hungry? Let's get some food."

Without an explanation, he pulled me along behind him through the narrow exit and into another— thankfully, wider—alley. We crossed it and two others before spilling out onto a cobblestone road. Here, something like laughter trickled on the breeze, kinder conversations spinning in the air. Bay towed me past a group of young women, and one smiled at me before resuming her conversation. "Are we still in Pirate Bay?" I mused.

"Hush." He squeezed my hand and dragged me up

a gentle incline of stone slabs. His head bobbed from one side to the next, ever alert even though the grimy, dangerous place had changed into something almost peaceful.

I huffed but obliged to remain quiet.

When we crested the hill, a pocket of buildings stood before us, their doors open, letting scents of cooked food waft by. My mouth watered. It had been a week since I'd eaten properly cooked food. Was this safe?

Not to say much on Neverland seemed to be. It was easy enough to die standing still.

I, for one, was willing to take the risk.

We stepped into a building, a wash of scented heat coating my skin. I didn't even care if it came with a layer of grease that made my flesh want to crawl. All I could think about was a warm meal.

"Table for two?" a woman droned from behind an upright barrel, serving as a waiter's stand. She tapped a pen against the sheet of parchment laid across it and regarded us with tired eyes. Her gaze flicked between us a couple times, but no lights went off.

"A private room, actually," Bay responded, his tone mimicking hers, flawlessly bored.

I looked up at him, impressed.

The woman's lips contorted with something like a smile, and she folded her arms atop the barrel, adjusting her weight and pressing a heavy bosom against them. "That's sweet, kid, but probably a little outta your price range. What? You new here? Just wash up on shore?"

Bay's responding sigh was likewise impressive in the you-dare-insult-me area. In a single smooth motion, he reached into his coat and drew out a bag, tossing it before her. It clinked with the weight of many gold coins. "Quite the opposite, dear. Don't bother getting up. I know the way."

Leaving the woman with wide eyes, he snatched my hand again and pulled me through an arrangement of tables in an open room. Each patron appeared consumed in their own food or in their company, too bothered to glance up, so we cleared them without event.

In the back, we traversed a hall. Thick gauze and silk was pulled back from each of several doorways. Bay walked into one room and dropped the curtains as he did. Inside, a round table with a cushioned booth circling it rested on polished wooden floor before two gauze-covered windows. Two sheets of paper I assumed were the menus lay on the table on either side of a half-melted candle. It's firelight flickered, spilling shadows over the walls.

"Is this the lap of luxury?" I whistled when Bay released my hand.

He plopped into one side of the booth, lifted his coat flap, and stared at me, unanswering.

Skye zipped free immediately, darting about the room like a hummingbird. I watched him for a moment, my patience thin. Bay's attitude today had been nothing short of shitty. Dropping into the least graceful curtsy anyone could ever make, I pinned him with a glare. "Sorry, may I speak now, Your Highness? Or would you prefer I remain hushed?"

Lifting a menu, he murmured, "You can speak now."

I flinched. Stomping over to the seat across from him, I plopped against the cushion, forcing myself not to sigh into the plushness. "That wasn't actually a question. What's wrong with you today?"

Skye smacked into my shoulder and clung to the cloth of my shirt. "We're surrounded by a lot of people who want to kill him. He's seen a lot of old faces in one afternoon, and none of them are friendly. Well, anymore."

Bay's eyes narrowed on Skye before he snapped, "Nothing." Flailing a hand at me, he said, "Pick whatever you want to eat. I've got the doubloons to cover it."

Skye squeezed my shirt, so I swallowed my retort, snatched the menu, and repeated, "*Doubloons.*" What a weird-ass word. Scowling at the print, I hardly realized when Skye vanished from sight, and a woman entered the room.

Significantly more cheerful than the lady at the front, she smiled at us, displaying a missing tooth. Her nose hooked at the halfway point, like it had been broken awkwardly once, and I couldn't help but think the freckled brunette didn't seem the fighting type. "Hello! My name's Taffy, and I'll be taking care of you today. Can I help you both to some drinks, and are you ready to order, or should I give you a few minutes?"

"We'll need a few minutes," Bay answered, "but two rum and waters will work to start."

"Two rum and waters, great. Take all the time you need." She shot us another smile before leaving the room.

"Rum?" I sneered, as though Taffy could still hear us beyond the gauze.

"I'll drink yours. You can have the water."

My brows jumped. "So, you're getting drunk now?"

"It's decently watered down. The supply and demand around here is a little out of kilter." He lowered the menu and peered at me over the flickering candle. In that moment, his eyes appeared weary and cruel. "This isn't anything new to me, and I know what I'm doing. A little trust would be nice since I'm risking my neck here."

A bitter taste coated my tongue and contorted my insides until my chest clenched. "I never asked you to, so if you're just going to be one massive asshole, you can get lost, Star Boy. I'll figure this out on my own."

Skye appeared once more, settling on Bay's shoulder this time. *"This is where you apologize, asshole."*

Bay's jaw clenched, and he shifted his gaze back down. Mumbling, he capitulated. "You'd die." Then softer, "I can't let you die."

Skye sighed, sending me a shrug that meant "I tried."

Something was going on. Something more than I could see. That much was clear. But little else was. Taffy returned with our drinks, and the scent of the rum made my nose scrunch. Bay asked for more time, and we were alone again, glaring at our menus like they'd killed our firstborns.

"Why not?" I asked after deciding I wanted a turkey leg and fried onions—I don't think I ever wanted anything more than a turkey leg and fried onions.

Bay didn't look up. "What?"

"Why can't you let me die?" Setting my menu aside, I stared at him.

He didn't provide the same courtesy. "It's not obvious?"

"Not really."

"Sorry," he began, but it wasn't really an apology, "my mistake. I thought we were friends."

The notion may have been sweet had a thick layer of sarcasm not coated each syllable as thickly as the layer of grease on my skin. I snapped, "So?"

His menu hit the table harder than I would have thought possible. He clenched my gaze with his eyes and didn't waver in the hold. "Friends care about friends. You don't let people you care about just die."

His words hit like a knife thrown into my gut. I couldn't breathe for a second, but gasped when I remembered why. That's exactly what I'd done. I clutched a feather painted on my right arm and squeezed till my skin burned.

"*Wake up, idiot,*" Skye hissed from somewhere.

Realization fell over Bay's face, but the damage had been done. I glanced at the gauzy exit and was on my feet. Bay caught my hand before I made it far.

"Let go of me!" I demanded. A breeze rushed from nowhere and squelched the candle, dimming the light in the room to whatever made it through the covered windows. Tears welled in my eyes, blurring his face and that stupid mask that made him someone I didn't know.

"No." He held on tighter, daring to pull my body against his. Heat erupted where flesh met flesh, but I accounted it all to anger. "I'm sorry. You know I didn't... I didn't mean anything by that. I care about you."

"Shut up."

"I don't think I will, Wind Song. I care about you. That's all I meant."

Gauze rustled behind me, and Bay looked up for an instant, his demeanour flicking into something else for a split second. The gauze rustled again, and that character switched back off. Tenderness encompassed his touch as he caressed my cheek with his free hand and dropped his attention back to my eyes.

"I'm going to hit you," I stated, less forcefully than I wanted.

He shrugged, his chest rubbing against mine. "I'd deserve it."

Everything had changed the moment we stepped into this bay, and it was more than the threat presented. I wasn't an idiot. People like Bay and Peter got a high off threats. The challenge was welcome. He'd laughed at the Kraken and grinned when we'd plummeted over the cliff away from the harpy. What was a town full of pirates to him but a maze with consequences? "Are you going to tell me exactly what's wrong with you?"

He plopped his forehead against mine. "I'm an asshole."

"Yeah, besides that."

His eyes went half-lidded, and even so close, he looked away. Before he replied, I knew his answer wouldn't be one at all. "I'm the prince of the assholes."

Closing my eyes, I dwelled on his hold around my wrist a little too heavily. Would I ever get to know him like I wanted? Or was I just another game? He was all I had left, but I wasn't something so precious. I was hardly anything at all. Throat tight, I whispered, "You're the damn king."

He chuckled, "Sadly, no," but wouldn't elaborate.

The sun dipped out of sight, and I sighed, glancing at Bay. He rested against the alley wall, his lips pinched in thought. "Well?" I asked.

"A lot has changed. A lot more than I thought." His mouth opened again, but he shut it before letting anything else escape.

"Do we head back and try again in the morning?" Rambling, singing, and drunken shouts grew with every minute. The darker it got, the lighter the voices, the more violence coiled around the bay.

He stiffened. "I don't know if we'd make it back without suspicion. It's normal for pirates to leave for a time and return, but hardly anyone has a base in the wild. This place, however filthy, is home. If anyone saw us come and go and they see us again in the morning,

180

we may attract the worst kind of attention."

I laughed. "Which would be?"

"Hook's." He stuffed his hands in his coat pockets, balling them into fists. "Here, he's king. Nothing weird happens without going through him. He built his empire here ever since he failed against Pan, and he rules with an iron hand."

"Literally." I smirked, but Bay only shot me a frown.

Sighing, he ran his fingers through his hair and leaned his head back to look at the sky. The navy hue bled out with every moment that passed; with every moment that passed, Bay's mask blended with the shadows until only his hazel eyes caught slips of stray light. "We'll have to get a place here for the night."

"Will that be as simple as getting dinner?"

His eyes closed, disappearing from view into the shadows of his mask. "I've never actually done it before. I'm not sure I even know where to start. Nights tend to be late here, too." He dragged one hand from his pocket and rubbed his mouth. Exhaustion filtered off him in waves. "I hate this place."

My heart sank, and I had to remind myself I never asked him to help me this much. I never asked him to enter this place. If he hadn't already decided to take me this far by the time we landed, all I would have asked for would have been a map. I'd likely have been some strange thing's dinner by my second day, but this was my battle. He had no connection with it. I was just a burden.

"All right." He leaped off the wall, seemingly renewed. Clapping his hands together, he turned those gleaming hazel eyes on me. "We need a place to stay. I don't know about you, but I'm dying for a bed. We just have to skirt our way around the night crowds and figure out where they keep their inns nowadays."

I nodded, and we started out of the alley. We didn't make it far. A dark form dropped from the rooftops, landing before us in a crouch. Before I could determine the barest details of the figure, it had Bay pinned and a cloth against his mouth. He slumped out of the person's smaller grasp and fell like a heap on the stones.

"Who are you?" I reached for my knife. In the instant my attention drifted to Bay, hoping to catch a hint of movement, the being disappeared.

Hands knocked the wind out of me from behind, dredging into my gut. My knife slipped out of my grasp, and I gasped, inhaling a clinical, damp scent saturating a rag. Choking, my knees buckled, and I sagged against a soft body. Definitely, a woman.

In the final moments as my vision vanished and my mind shut off, all I could think about was the murder Bay had witnessed earlier. That woman's shrieking laughter echoed throughout my addled mind, and then there was nothing.

17TH NOVEMBER

I groaned awake, sore in my stomach. It took me several moments to remember what had happened, then I groaned again. Just another average day in Neverland, ending in horrors. Of course, it had been too calm; we needed the excitement of being kidnapped after doing nothing but slinking around all day.

Squinting through the darkness of the room, I tried to get my bearings. The space was empty, save for a flickering lantern several yards away. The floor was dirt, except for scattered rocks. Four pillars supported a structure above us, and Bay and I had been roughly tied to two of them. He was across the room at a diagonal, and his head still lolled to one side.

A jolt of panic shot through me, but in the dim light

coming from the lantern, I could just see enough to know his chest moved.

"You're awake." Skye's voice made me jump, and I jerked my attention to the pixie. His large eyes were wide with worry. "How are you feeling? They gave you both an overdose." He looked at Bay, then back to me. "I've been trying to wake him for hours."

I wasn't doing great. I had the sense I needed to puke, but all I could do was gag. "How long have I been out?"

Skye wrung his hands. "Almost a day?"

"Shit," I blurted, trying to rub my face. Naturally, I couldn't because harsh ropes kept me firm against the wooden pillar. "Where's the woman?"

"No idea." His brows furrowed. "I snuck out when I couldn't hear movement anymore. She's been gone for a couple hours."

"Hopefully, not reporting to Hook," I mumbled. Skye's responding silence was all I needed to confirm that was a real concern. We had to get out of here. What if Hook did know?, Would he have enough honor to face me one-on-one. Even if I died trying, I'd die for Whisper's vengeance and provide enough distraction for Bay to get back to his own mission. "Can you untie me?"

Skye's brows nearly shot clean off his face. "Excuse me? Those ropes are thicker than my body? What do you think?"

"I think I've just been drugged," I snarled. "Give me a break."

Skye folded his arms. "If I had something sharp, I might be able to cut you loose, but they took Bay's knives, and I can't find a way out of here to look for anything else."

"Brilliant." I fought the tight coils wrapped around me to get a full breath, then I let it out slowly. "Okay. Did they take my bag?" Hopefully not. There was nothing of importance in there.

"It's behind your pillar."

My eyes closed. "Thank the airwoman. There's a spyglass that I made in there. If you press on the glass part, it gets loose, and you can pop it out. It's sharp around the edges once it's free."

"Perfect." Skye brightened, zipping behind me. Shuffles ended in a crack that resonated in my soul.

"Did you break it?" I choked. I'd had that thing for years, dreaming of adventures I'd use it on. And I hadn't been alone when I'd made it. I'd been with Whisper. And though the "adventures" we'd used it on were childish, they were every bit as magical to me. If it was broken...

"No," he replied.

The coils of rope loosened, slipping away one by one, and I took a fuller breath, dragging myself back to the moment, the matter at hand. I clutched the feathers on my arm for strength and focused on Bay. "I can't carry him, so he needs to wake up, and—"

Wood thunked. I whirled. Skye vanished from sight.

The woman who had captured us dropped in through a trapdoor on the edge of the room, her gaze pinned on the ground before her. When she looked up, she caught my eye, and I stood frozen in place.

She hissed, "So, you're still here. And free now. Wonderful. I'm not in the mood for games." A cutlass, possibly Bay's, balanced in her hand, and she pointed the blade at me. "Drop your disguise, or I won't think twice about running you through."

At every turn, Neverland toyed with my mind, twisting it until wounds broke open, raw and festering.

I couldn't take it anymore. I was done with these games. I glared. I glared at her small, brown face, her fierce eyes, and disapproving lips. I glared at her limp curls of blond hair. I glared, willing Whisper to fall away into whatever horror was her true form.

"I mean it," she gritted. "Mom said to watch out for scum like you. I know what you are, so you can drop it."

"Likewise," I said, "I'm in a really shitty mood, so do your worst." I opened my arms to her. "I dare you."

She tightened her grip. "Explain him to me." Motioning with the blade, she flicked her gaze to Bay then back to me. "You, you, I get. But he's nothing to me. I met him for what, five minutes? I don't even remember his name at this point."

I dropped my arms. "What?"

Her nose scrunched, so flawlessly Whisper, it hurt. "You imprint upon my recent memories, and I've thought about you a damn lot, Lyly, but not him. In fact, you're a couple of idiots because if you'd really wanted to trick anyone, you'd have been my mom." Her anger heightened to a point I knew I was treading carefully. "I know Hook must employ you bastards, but I suppose only the morons are dumb enough to go into service."

Everything. Everything was perfect. Her tone. Her actions. Whisper stood before me, not her at all—I was certain of that—but whatever held her form had fished her mannerisms out of my head in the time I'd been asleep.

"Speaking of my mom," she growled, "where is she?"

"Dead." The word fell from my lips, leaving me hollow. "She's dead. You're dead. Everything I've called family is gone."

"I know she's not dead," she spat, but her hand shook. "Hook needs her alive or the bait won't work on Peter because he won't remember who she is at all. I'm not an idiot! He could barely remember me at all." Her voice pitched, tears glassing her eyes in the lantern light. "Mom said it was because I was proof of something he hated, proof she had grown up, but still!"

I scoffed, but my throat closed. "He already forgot her. He forgot her in less than a day. Imagine that. Someone he'd known for a lifetime, gone in minutes."

"I said no games!"

"Kill me then!" I shouted. "You'll have to break character to do it! The girl you've stolen from my head has never hurt a single thing. I've watched her spend over an hour catching a moth in her house just to free it. She's vegetarian because it's too sad if animals have to die for her to eat. She once cried because her pet *caterpillar* died." Tears streamed down my cheeks, and I gasped. She'd named the stupid thing Fuzzy, and I'd sat with her while she cried.

Whisper hesitated, watching me with a wary gaze. Her voice was tiny when she spoke again. "That happened over eight years ago."

"Yeah. It did," I bit. "And yet dryocampa rubicunda is forever imprinted on my skull. Would it have killed you to call it a rosy maple moth? Because I don't think so."

Whisper covered her mouth with her free hand. "Lyly?" She swallowed, never releasing the sword. "Unless there's something other than a changeling that can take another's form, that's really you, isn't it?" She wet her lips. "Changelings can reach no further back than a year."

"Cute. I don't believe you, but the new tactic is

endearing. You've had over a day to dig around in my unconscious brain, so who knows what you know."

Someone shifted behind me, then a groan filled the room. Mumbled curse words cut through our conversation. I had hoped that Skye would have Bay untied and at my side to figure this out before I found myself on the business end of a sword.

"Where's his pixie? Changelings don't have pixies." Whisper waved the sword around, then panicked. "Oh my airwoman, did I crush him in his coat?" She started for Bay, and my heart collided with my ribs.

Before I could think, I threw myself between them. "Don't touch him."

She blinked at me momentarily, then her mouth fell open. "No way." Her brows crashed together. "You got a boyfriend a week after you thought I died. I don't know whether to be proud or hurt."

I didn't know how to respond. There was no logical explanation on how she had managed to get here alive if she was really Whisper. None. But she had mentioned her mother, Tiger Lily, was here too. The last princess of Neverland.

There's always more than one way to get home.

"Skye," I snapped, my heart rate accelerating with a hope I knew would kill me if it ended up unfounded, "is that true? Only a year?"

A soft voice settled near me. "Yes, but if you've thought of it at all in this past year..."

"How do I tell, for sure." My words shook while I stared at Whisper. *Please*, thrummed in my head, begging. Desperate. Another cruel trick. A better one than before. A much better one than before. Yet it was stuck inside my skull, giving me hope.

Whisper gasped, lifting the cutlass. I flinched, ready

for all my hope to die with me, but she ran it across her finger, wincing when she shoved her hand at me. "See? Red."

There was a pause between us, then Skye muttered, "I mean. Yeah. That's a way. Changeling blood is black."

"Really?" I trembled. My voice wobbled. Tears filled my eyes and poured down my cheeks.

Before Skye could reply, I threw my arms around Whisper. The cutlass hit the dirt with a soft sound as she laughed and returned my hug. "It hasn't been that long, Lyly. But yikes. Okay. Yeah." She melted against me, her damp cheek against my shoulder. "I missed you too."

"You were dead," I choked on my sobs. "Dead."

"For a minute there, I thought I was. I have so much to tell you. Mom, well, she's kept a huge secret from us. I can't believe it."

"I know." I squeezed her, my laugh a garbled mess. "Did she tell you she was a princess?"

"No." Whisper scoffed. "She knows some magic, though! We're going to have a long talk once everything is back to normal. How in the world are you even here!"

"Is someone going to untie me...?" Bay mumbled. Everything but Whisper had fallen completely away, so much so I didn't remember he was even there until the moment he spoke. Without letting her go, I glanced at him, the goofiest smile on my face. He met it with a bleary cringe. "And tell me what's going on?"

"Whisper's *alive*. Somehow," I chimed. "But alive. And real. And right here."

Just as cheerily, Whisper added, "Also, Hook is alive and going to attack Skyla, using my mother to force Peter to tell him where the Fountain of Youth is."

The silence that followed was as still as death.

THRONE OF FEATHERS

18TH NOVEMBER

"The Fountain of Youth?" I stared at Whisper, my brows drawn. The stillness in the air was something physical, and breaking it didn't ease the tension packed within the cramped space.

"Apparently, it's a spring of ancient magical water that gives eternal life to anyone who finds and drinks from it." Her lips curved. "I think we both know a certain forever-twelve-year-old who more-likely-than-not stumbled upon it a long, long time ago. My goodness, it's like this place fills in every gap and question I've ever had."

The way her smile lit her eyes when she called Peter a "forever-twelve-year-old" made my heart so happy I thought I was going to start crying again. We'd only just pried ourselves away from one another's arms, but

I swore to myself in that moment I wouldn't let my best friend slip through my fingers ever again. We'd figure this out, then we'd find our way home.

"He shouldn't know it exists," Bay snapped, yanking my attention from Whisper. Anger ignited in his blazing eyes. "Hook shouldn't have the faintest clue what he's looking for."

"Well, he does." Whisper twirled an oily curl around her finger, scrunched her nose, and dropped her hand. "Mom and I were unfortunate enough to encounter Hook shortly after coming here. She managed to let me get away...but when he had us both, he monologued for a dreadful amount of time."

Still tied to the pillar, Bay shook his head and growled, "How?"

"Some enchantress or something appeared one day less than a year ago and told him that all hope wasn't lost. He could have everything he wished for if he shared some of it. She set him on the right track, searching for the Fountain, but he's grown frustrated. Now that he has my mom, he's thinking he'll use her to force Peter to tell him where the Fountain is instead of finding the Fountain first and using the magic to get his revenge afterward." Whisper set Bay aside in her thoughts, turning to me again. "Wait a second. You said Peter *forgot* Tiger Lily?" She blinked. "*Wait another second.* How were you talking to that pixie? And how did you get here? I have a hundred questions."

"I have a couple of my own." Frowning, I looked at Bay. "How do you know about this Fountain in the first place?"

Jaw clenched, he stared, and his throat bobbed with a swallow. "Is anyone going to untie me?"

"Maybe, after you answer the question."

His gaze dropped to the dusty ground, his eyes tracing the lines the light from the lantern cast over the dusty floor. "It's what I've been looking for all these years."

I'd already figured that part out. "Why would you want eternal life?"

"I don't." Pain engulfed his expression, but he wiped it away. "Its magic offers more than eternal life, and it's not for me." A shaky breath left his lungs, and he tossed his head back to whip sweaty hair out of his face. "Is this interrogation done now? If Hook really is on his way to Skyla with the intent to force information about the Fountain out of Peter, we need to stop him."

"He's waiting on magical resources so he can reach Skyla. We need to save my mother and find the Fountain before he gets them. If this Fountain has as much power as he seems to think it does, we'll need it." Whisper swiped the cutlass off the ground and sashayed to Bay, slicing his ropes in a single clean motion. She pinned her gaze on me. "Something is very wrong. It's not just in Neverland or Skyla. Mom says the whole world has begun unraveling, and I think it has to do with whatever this enchantress is planning. We have to stop her and Hook wherever we can."

I didn't like the idea of meddling in the affairs of a powerful enchantress, but the facts stood. Tiger Lily needed our help, and Bay, for his own reasons, needed the Fountain of Youth. The cave images from the temple floated to the forefront of my mind. The golden spring. Could it have been a nod to this Fountain? Could there have been a hidden message indicating its location?

"We have a lot to talk about." Bay brushed off his clothes and glared at Skye. "A lot."

"So she understands me. Big deal." Skye settled

on my shoulder, the picture of innocence. Bay only narrowed his eyes.

Taking a step forward, he swayed to the right, and I caught him by the shoulder. He threw a hand to his head. "How much knightworth did you use to knock us out?"

Whisper straightened. "I don't know? Why? Is it..."

"Not deadly, no." He took several deep breaths. "It just clings worse than a hangover."

All things considered, I felt fine. I helped Bay upright, turning my attention toward the trapdoor exit. Laughter bellowed through the cracks, drunken songs lilting in the wind. Where had Whisper brought us? My body went cold, remembering the events just before I'd fallen prey to the knightworth. "Whisper, you have my knife, don't you?"

Shock widened her eyes, and her head shook. "I'm sorry... I don't."

A town crawling with pirates. I knew I had dropped it in that alley, but the chances of it still being there were nill. My fingers absently found their way to the empty sheath on my leg. It was just a knife. Now that Whisper was here, back from the dead, things weren't hopeless anymore. I didn't need to cling to material pieces, even if Peter didn't remember me, and that piece was his. I needed to—

Bay fell over.

I blinked at him, collapsed on the ground, then met Whisper's eyes.

She flushed violently in the dim light, stammering, "I didn't know what I was doing. Mom showed me the knightworth and told me how to use it, but she didn't give many specifics."

"I'm fine," Bay gritted, his arms jutting up like

chicken wings as he pushed against the ground.

I crouched beside him. "Do you need some help?"

His fists clenched into the dirt, but he didn't snap at me. Looking away, he nodded. "I'm going to be dead weight like this."

"If we can help you walk, and you can pretend to be drunk, I have a room at one of the taverns. You can rest some more, and I can sleep tonight." Whisper offered Bay the cutlass, and he stared at it dumbly.

"In this state, I would impale myself on that. Hold onto it. If we run into trouble, I've seen you move and have a feeling it'd be of more use in your hands."

She tensed but nodded. "I'll hang onto your dagger belt until you're feeling better too then."

"Okay, where's his mask?" I asked.

"In your bag." Whisper crossed to the pillar I had been tied to, retrieving my bag and the mask. Seeing me preoccupied with Bay, she slung the bag over her shoulder and offered him the mask. "Why do you need this, though?"

"This whole place isn't exactly fond of me."

Whisper chuckled. "More questions in need of answers, but one step at a time, I suppose."

Bay released a deep breath, sending a dark look towards Skye. The little pixie on my shoulder peered at his nails a long moment before "becoming aware" of Bay's glare. "Oh, I'm sorry. Is it back into the coat time for Skye? You could use your words."

"I'm not in the mood for this, you little imp," he grumbled, and I could tell it was the truth. More of his weight seemed on my body than on his feet. If this was how the oil had affected him, why was I okay?

After Skye zipped into place and we'd turned out the lantern, Whisper guided us up and out into the same alley she had caught us in. I glanced at the dusty ground for my knife, but as suspected, nothing remained. Lifting my head to the dark sky, I focused on the barest sliver of the moon to keep tears from falling, then I set my sights on the matter at hand.

Get to safety. Rescue Tiger Lily. Find the Fountain.

Go home.

"Wow," Whisper breathed beside me in the small bed. Bay had already collapsed in a pile of blankets on the floor of the modest room, but we had been talking for the past hour—about everything. Just a few days apart, yet we had whole books worth of stories to share. "I can't believe this place has been so tied to Skyla from the start."

"Neither can I. Do you think Peter has really forgotten it? All of it?" Noise from the bar downstairs blanketed the pitch-dark room in a murmur, and I wondered if this town ever slept.

"He has. Mom said he hasn't remembered for years, and she stopped visiting her family's graves when Dad left. She hasn't been able to fly since either, and she only knows the magic to take her here, not back." Her voice softened considerably, so much so that I had to strain to hear it above the drone of the tavern background noise. "Why do you think Peter forgets like he does?"

My head shook though I don't think she could see me in the darkness. "He has to. He's lived for so long and done so many things that anything not presently a piece of his life gets shoved out of his head." Bitterly, my mind added *like me*.

"Is that what he's told you?"

"Yeah."

She paused, and I could picture her pinched lips and lowered brows as she murmured, "I wonder if it's true then." Before I could ask what she meant, her hand clasped mine. "I'm still coming to terms with the fact Mom never told me she could do some magic."

A dark splotch on the floor shifted and groaned, settling shortly after. I kept my tone lower than Whisper had when I replied, "How can she anyway? I've only heard of people in Enchantia able to do stuff like that."

"People born here have a chance of coming into it, and she did. Because of everything, she never learned how to use it well, but one of the first things taught is how to get home. When our house began to fall, she grabbed a knife, held me tight, then sliced her arm. We were in the middle of the woods before I knew what was happening."

The blood in her home. That's what it came from.

"Isn't it sad?" Whisper asked while I was still wrapping my mind around what she had said. The only magic I was familiar with was pixie dust, and I never considered that particularly special. It had always been a piece of my life, and my island-locked existence wasn't particularly special. Whisper continued, breaking through my thoughts, "My mom's the last true human native of Neverland. Even my blood is soiled."

Her words weighed against my chest with a suddenness I didn't expect. My free hand clasped my right arm where feathers danced over my skin as a piece of Tiger Lily's history that perhaps one she never learned about or didn't remember. Squeezing Whisper's hand, I picked my words as carefully as I could manage. "Your blood isn't soiled as long as your heart isn't. Neverland is full of people and creatures who call this insane magical place their home, whether they've stopped by or lived here for centuries. A piece of the past might be gone now, but that same piece has a chance to live on in you, in all of Skyla. It's *Never*land. The most precious things are never forgotten here."

She chuckled, the sound light. "You say that like you've lived here for ages."

"I'm pretty sure Neverland hates me, actually."

"It doesn't." Her head turned, a rustle of hair the only indication. "I know that much. You can speak to the pixies, and Mom says they're the embodiment of Neverland's spirit. Everywhere you go always wraps around you, like the air itself is giving you a hug. Just walking into a room, you change the atmosphere." She sighed, and her breath fanned against my cheek like a cooling balm, emphasizing her words. "You've always wanted to explore the world, Lyly. Now we have a chance to change it. To make sure important things aren't forgotten. To make sure more wrongs aren't repeated. Mom seems to believe in destiny, but I believe in us. Right here. Right now. Us."

When she said it like that, I wanted to believe in us too. At the least, I knew I believed in her, and one way or another, all of us would get through this. Together.

We passed around what meager food stores we each had in our bags, from over-salted and burnt meat to berries, to the final crusts of bread. It would suffice for breakfast, and since Bay seemed to be hiding quite a bit of gold in his coat, maybe we could manage another stop for actual food.

I could dream, anyway.

"I'm glad you're feeling better. Sorry about the misunderstanding yesterday." Whisper gnawed on a sliver of tough meat and barely met Bay's gaze. I didn't blame her. He hadn't exactly been the cheeriest person. Airwoman, I missed their carefree banter from the moments when they first met.

200

He blinked out of his thoughts, glanced at her, then at Skye. The pixie sighed and responded to what she'd said. "Don't worry about it. You can't really be too careful here. No lasting damage, and, hey, you're alive, right?" The smile that followed appeared pained more than anything, and I winced.

"O-okay. Well. What's our next step?" I asked. A bird cawed outside the window, and I froze, my eyes widening on the feathered creature before it flapped away. "Right! I forgot to tell you. Sirens are after us, so we have to keep moving. Do you think we've been here too long, or would they not dare to enter the bay?"

"Sirens?" Whisper squeaked. "Why?"

Bay and Skye exchanged a look, then Bay shrugged. "We should be all right. I've never seen them in the bay, at least." He motioned a limp crust at Whisper. "Our first step is finding Tiger Lily. Then I have an idea of where to look next for the Fountain. Sadly, our original plan of blowing Pirate Bay to high heaven is off the table while Tiger Lily is around, and the Fountain takes precedence after we've got her back. My plan is dangerous. More dangerous than anything I could manage alone, but with five of us...we may just be able to manage traveling to the Nixie Cove. It's one place I haven't picked apart for the Fountain, and it's one place that holds innumerable secrets."

"Perfect!" Whisper's eyes flashed with hope and determination. "I don't suppose you'd know where they're keeping my mom? Or if Hook has a new ship? Since we have his old one and all that."

"He doesn't have a new ship." It took just that instant for Bay to simmer back into his own head. Eyes pinned on the floor before us and mouth still moving, he went somewhere else entirely. "He lives further down the beach in no less than a shore-line castle. Every castle has its dungeons. I suppose we'll find her there."

"They wouldn't have hurt her, right?" Whisper's voice cracked, and she ruffled her hair. "Sorry. That's a stupid question. They're pirates. Of course, they've—"

"Probably not."

Whisper's gaze jerked to Bay.

He met her eyes, melancholy in his whole demeanor. "Unless she's fought them. She's no use to them dead or even injured, and she has no information they could want." Bitterness coated each word, each syllable, as something reminiscent of a laugh left his chest. "This isn't her first time meeting Captain James D. Hook. Not her first time being captured by him either. One might say they each have a certain amount of respect for one another by now. The first time he caught her, she was pregnant with you, and one simply does not mess with a pregnant woman. I'm half-certain, she scared his whole crew shitless."

Whisper swallowed. "I'd worry you were just trying to comfort me, but I'm not sure if that's entirely comforting or not."

Bay stood, stretching, and appeared perturbed that his feet remained solid on the floor. "I'm not exactly a comforting person. We should get moving as soon as we can. We woke late, but after last night's noise, I have a feeling the streets are still going to be empty."

"What was with last night?" I asked, rising. "It didn't seem to end. Is that how it is every night?"

"Not since I've been here," Whisper murmured.

Bay looked at both of us, his jaw tight, then turned toward the door, snatching his mask off a table on his way toward it and running his fingers through his loose hair. "It's an anniversary."

202

"Of what?" Whisper tilted her head, questioning me with a glance to see if I knew.

The sick feeling in my gut had its guesses; Bay confirmed them balefully. "Of the slaughter. The day the pirates took Neverland as their own."

"Oh." Whisper's response was the last said as we left the room and slipped out of the silent tavern. Several people lay collapsed on the streets, their hands still wrapped around half-filled mugs of rum. The liquor's putrid scent mixed with other unsavory hints of sweat, blood, and urine, and my nose scrunched, begging for relief.

Thankfully, fresh wind rushed in from the sky, allowing us some peace. It was short-lived.

Whisper gasped, halting beside Bay while we crept through an alley toward Hook's abode. I looked up, and the wind ceased.

I had never seen Hook before, but I didn't need anyone to tell me who stood in the lane before us beside a squat man with a red cap. Swathed in black leather and boasting a feathered hat was the very pirate whose defeat I'd heard stories of throughout my entire life.

Unfocused hatred boiled in his black gaze, like tar. It clung. It stained. I clenched my fists to avoid trembling. The longer I looked, the more uneasy I felt. My mind swam, wondering if I'd seen his face before, maybe in a picture, a painting, an echo of a thought.

Had I seen him in the temple?

Bay's back stiffened, all movement leaving him until I couldn't even tell he was breathing.

I wasn't completely sure if I was either.

"He's already here, Smee." Hook tightened his metal hand and swept his eyes over the space before him. "He's already come for the princess. I can feel it." He inhaled deeply, his nostrils flaring above his combed mustache. "I can smell it."

"I-I thought it was because last night someone found the knife he stole from you."

My gaze dropped to his waist, and sapphire winked in the sunlight. My knife. His hand curled around the jeweled hilt. "Silence, Smee. He's toying with me. Just like always. This time, though, ah yes, this time we'll be one step ahead. He has three days to reveal what I want, or Tiger Lily dies."

"No!"

My head whipped toward Whisper as she dashed from the alley. Bay's hand lunged forward after her, but he yanked it back before it left the shadows. Suspecting I might bolt to her side, he stepped back and held his arm in front of me. Panic pulsed in his eyes while they rapidly moved over the scene.

"I won't let you kill my mother!" Whisper stood before Hook, shaking with rage more than fear. No weapon in hand, she faced him down. He made no move toward her, but my heart remained lodged in my throat.

His hand left the dagger at his waist. "So," he began, calmer than he had been, "you found your way here."

"Where is she?"

"I'm afraid I can't tell you that." A spark ignited on his face, some foul realization coming to life in his mind. "Actually, this is perfect. You want to save your mother? Deliver a message to Pan and have him finally give me what I want, then I will let her go unharmed. My battle is, and always has been, only with him."

"Liar!" she screamed. "Do you even realize how many others you've carved through to get to him? Do you know how much blood is on your hands? How many lives you've taken, how many you've ruined!"

I pressed against Bay's restraining arm, and he cast me a heated glare, daring me to push past him. It would take very little effort. And for Whisper, I'd do it in a heartbeat.

Hook snarled, "You'd do well to watch your tongue, girl." His hand inched back toward his knife, my knife, and I shoved through Bay's meager barrier, snatching a dagger from his belt in a single clean motion as I did.

Heart pounding, I caught Hook's blade with Bay's and shoved it off, staggering back from the force.

The man's eyes bulged, fixing on my hair first, then my eyes. "You," he snapped. "*You!*" He twirled my knife, diving for me with it from one side and plunging his hook at me from the other.

My eyes crashed shut, awaiting the cold sting, but metal sang against metal instead of flesh. Then nothing.

Silence. Silence thickened the air until it was hard to breathe. I peeked hesitantly and found myself shadowed by Bay's form. His cutlass had caught both Hook's metal hand and his knife, sliding them together along the blade until they both sat, almost helplessly, at the guard of the handle. Hook stared, his mouth slack. At his side, Smee looked between them and wrung his hands, anxiety building with every moment.

"Bay," Hook began, an awe in his tone I wouldn't have thought possible. There was something deep in his voice, and though his beady eyes still pulsed with hatred, none of it marred Bay's name, if only for that instant. His black gaze found me, and the moment fled. Hook pulled back, rising tall. "Have you taken the ranks of my enemies, boy?"

"Where's the girl's mother, Hook?" The words grated from Bay's lips, but they came with a dark authority.

My head spun, and I jumped when Whisper's hand

found my back. I couldn't pry my eyes off the pirate before us, but knowing she was there let me breathe easier. How did Bay and Hook know one another? In all of Peter's stories, Hook was a madman. Upon seeing Peter, he would lung in with little thought. Seeing him in person, I knew that wasn't the case. Thoughts pooled in his mind, grinding away with ease, oiled smoothly with hatred and a passion for vengeance.

"She's safe. If Pan—" Hook started.

"Peter's not here," Bay all but growled. "He hasn't been here for years. He doesn't even know what *here* is anymore. *Let it go.*"

"He's fooled you too!" Hook jabbed his dagger forward, but Bay parried it easily. "Why will nobody listen? That child knows more than he ever lets on. It's how he keeps all his secrets for himself. Of all the selfish, insipid fools!"

Hook feinted with his blade and swiped with his hook. I gasped when the silver caught Bay's face, but all it ripped off was his mask. The black scrap of polished and painted wood skidded across the street, collided with a building, and came to rest. Hook stepped back, his chest heaving. Looking Bay over, he lowered his weapon and sneered.

Bay remained on guard, cutlass raised and ready, but neither male moved for several long moments. I wanted to speak up, ask what was going on, demand answers to the hundreds of questions I had streaming through my mind. But a lump of fear still hadn't dislodged itself from my throat, perhaps because Hook continued to pin me with his rotting glare.

"Have you been well?" Hook asked his tone no less harsh than it had been.

I recoiled, looking between them in shock.

"Just peachy." Bay's knuckles went white around his weapon. "I'll ask again, where's the girl's mother? You know how important mothers are to children. How losing one can change a person. Do you really want to make this enemy?"

"Do you speak for yourself or the girl?" With Bay's silence, Hook winced. "You've always had her spirit. I suppose it's no surprise you'd use it against me too."

"I'm not in the mood to chat about old times, old man." Bay's back tightened, but I noticed when he faltered, and his voice wavered with suppressed emotion. "The past between us died; let's not forget who killed it."

Hook didn't waste the opportunity. In the sliver of weakness, he lunged. Metal met metal, but Hook pushed past Bay's block this time, diving directly for me. I jerked back, but he caught me around the waist, clamping my arms to my body. A slice of pain delved into my throat, hot blood washing down my neck, and death gleamed icily before my eyes.

"Don't!" Bay dropped his sword, and it clattered against the cobblestone street. His eyes consumed my vision as fear and adrenaline exploded in my head. Whisper screamed, her hands clawing at Hook's arms. He didn't pay her any mind. He focused entirely on Bay.

Ragged breaths sawed through the boy's chest. "If you kill her, I will never forgive you. I will hunt you down every day and every night until your blood waters the same earth as hers. Then, one by one, I'll peck off each of the minions in this kingdom you've created until nothing remains of you. Nothing. Your name will die in this realm, and I will follow you to the next to make certain it's hell." Anger unlike any I'd ever seen before blazed in Bay's light-colored eyes. It boiled, trapping Hook in place.

Smee dragged Whisper's screaming body off his captain, but her cries fizzled into a void. My life rested in the hands of whatever silent battle went on between Bay and Hook. Bay's single cry to stop had worked when I knew without it, death would have been swift, but Hook hadn't yet pulled the knife from my throat. I pressed my body against his chest, yet with every inhale, my flesh skimmed painfully against the razor-sharp blade.

"Let her go," Bay said, his hand extended, ready to catch me and haul me to safety the second I was free.

"You have no idea what she is," Hook breathed, the stench of his breath unbearable, though the least of my worries. "Does she even know what you are, who you are?"

Bay searched Hook's face, then dropped his gaze to me. I felt helpless and knew how I must look. My hands were numb against Hook's unrelenting hold. My face pale. My shirt, red with the blood slipping down my neck. My eyes, pleading, despite Hook being right. I knew very little about the boy who held the last shred of hope I'd make it out of this alive in his hands.

"You don't need them or Tiger Lily. I know what you're looking for, and I know where it is. All this time, I've been the reason you couldn't find it. If you release them unharmed, now, I'll take you to the Fountain."

Hook laughed bitterly. "You expect me to believe you? I can remove this threat now and have everything else without your help."

"You're right."

I froze, my fingertips going cold, but Bay didn't stop there.

"I don't expect you to believe me. You could have everything else without me if your little plan—which has failed before—works. You could, once again, choose to have everything else without me, without us. Or maybe this time, you could have both for the small price of your revenge." Hook's grip tightened, so Bay's fists clenched. "Hell, fine. Just them. Find and kill Peter later. I don't care. But spare them. *Let her go, Father.*" My ears rang with that word, my mouth dropping open. It echoed on repeat, and I strained to hear his final raw whisper, "Please."

The numb space between Bay's plea and Hook's reply rattled with uncertainty. I hadn't seen Hook before; I'd seen Bay. His son. They looked nearly identical. Heat welled in my head, burning, and Bay wouldn't even look at me anymore.

"I have your word?" Hook asked, his hold already loosening. Bay nodded.

The pirate pulled away his blade and shoved me. I tripped straight into Bay's arms, unsure if I wanted to be there or not as they closed around me, and a trembling breath wracked his body. How could he have kept this from me? What had happened? I was Peter's daughter. He was Hook's son.

And yet, when his arms closed around me, pulling me against his shaking chest, the world fell away. I hadn't just stared down death. I wasn't bleeding at my neck. Panic and adrenaline washed through me until tears stung my eyes. I hit him. He didn't let go.

"How could you?" I choked.

He dragged the bandana off my head and kissed my hair, my temple, my cheek.

I forced myself to glance at him, straight into his eyes. His gaze was tortured, apologetic, and scared.

I slung my arms around him the moment I realized what had just happened, what he had done. For me,

Whisper, and Tiger Lily to make it out of this alive, safe, he had traded himself with a promise I knew he couldn't keep.

"Her too." Bay shifted in my hold, nodding toward Whisper, who remained limply in Smee's grasp. She looked between us and Hook, likely the same questions running through her head.

"You've always been soft, Bay," Hook murmured, motioning for his man to release my friend. "I worried about you in this world."

Bay's hand outstretched and clasped Whisper's to draw her behind him after she was freed. "Because having people you care about more than yourself is dangerous?"

"Because losing people you care about more than yourself is enough to break your soul."

Bay squeezed me. "Maybe that's a sign of true weakness. And I won't say I'm immune to it."

"Both of you will leave the bay." Hook peered at Whisper and I in turn.

Whisper shook, but she pulled away from Bay and me, standing tall. "What about my mother?"

Hook's gaze narrowed, meeting Bay's; then he grumbled, "I'll send her to where the streams meet the river in the Whispering Meadow."

Whisper paled, and my eyes widened. That field separating the bay from the rest of Neverland was what Tiger Lily had named her after?

"I'll make sure of it," Bay added, ignoring the shock on our faces. He pressed his lips against my forehead one last time, then released me from his hold. "Goodbye, Wind Song."

Every muscle in my body tensed.

I couldn't let him do this. We'd find another way. We

could take Hook down.

Wind picked up in the lane, beating against the houses and dusty streets. It whipped my hair into my eyes and muted Hook's voice beyond the sudden tempest. In the center of the whirlwind, Bay, Whisper, and I stood in the eye of the storm.

I didn't pay the wind any mind as I reached for Bay, but his gaze was locked on the skies, then a bitter smile curled his lips. He looked directly at me, cupped my cheek with his warm hand, then whispered something beneath the rush.

"What?" I snatched his hand, jolting when Whisper screamed. The wind hushed. I turned my head and found claws buried in Whisper's skin, her feet dangling off the ground. Spindly teeth barred toward Hook, a siren hissed over her. Three powerful wing flaps and the creature had Whisper above the rooftops. I pulled away from Bay, my fingers slipping out of his grasp, then pain erupted in my shoulder blades.

Talons, sharp and unrelenting, dug into my flesh. I fought the siren's hold, but the woman only buried her claws deeper. Warm blood gushed down my back. My mouth gaped in a silent plea, but as my vision faded, Bay stood still. As spots clouded over my eyes and pain boiled in my back, Hook stepped behind his son and glared up after us.

Bay's grim smile melted into a darker emotion when Hook set his hand on Bay's shoulder. The instant he broke eye contact, the Pirate Bay vanished from my sight.

19TH NOVEMBER

There was no pain. That's all I initially realized when I opened my eyes and stared at a flowering canopy. My mind wrestled with the idea that every ache and sore and cut no longer made its presence known.

I sat up tentatively, certain I'd fainted because talons had dug into my nerves, but no ghosting sensations touched my muscles. Inhaling, I choked and scrambled off the soft grass. "Whisper?"

A grove sat before me, calm and gentle. Hundreds of trees heavy with blooms created a ceiling of leaves that crystal light poured through, but I couldn't so much as find a crack displaying the sky. The grass was so green—the flowers, so vibrant. Iridescence coated the world in a fraudulent manner that made me shiver.

I was alone in the place.

Was this a dream? Turning my head, I scanned the woven trunks that made up the bars of this cage. Delicate twists bound the silver bark together in an impenetrable wall. Or was this a prison?

Frustration coiled around me. I didn't have time for this. Bay was in trouble, and he had a lot of explaining to do. Why hadn't he told me something so important? Then again, how could he have brought something like that up? Our parents, since before we were born, had been sworn enemies. How did one approach a topic like that?

I clenched my fists, turning my gaze inward. At the center of the grove, flowers spilled off a mound like water. They pooled in an unusual shape, their colors contrasting the persistent jewel-green of the grass. Crystal light winked off something in the center, and I narrowed my eyes.

Out of habit, my hand skimmed down my thigh, but only grazed my sheath. *Hook's knife.* My knife. Neverland; Skyla. Peter; Hook. Bay and I. We were, all of us, bound together by something too thick to break.

And that's why, right now, while we were apart, we both had to be okay.

I stopped on the edge of the pond of flowers, and my breath stilted in my chest. A woman lay before me in a glass coffin, her pale skin and brown hair flawless. Beautiful didn't begin to describe her.

Her chest filled with air that poured from her lips, but she didn't move, and I couldn't tell if she were dead or asleep. I'd heard stories of curses that doomed their bearer to a state of eternal rest, yet no darkness clung to this place.

Could it be possible she was here to prolong her life?

My hand reached for her coffin before I knew what was happening. My fingers touched the cool glass, and the chill gripped back, holding firm. Skipping a beat, my heart danced in my chest, leaping up in my throat.

The whole of the dream-like world exploded, falling away as though it were rain.

Mouth open in a gasping cry, I dropped out of my skin completely, something else taking my place in my skull. A wraith's icy touch curled fingers around my consciousness, so soft, but I shook wherever I was with fear.

"My name?" the woman asked peace and laughter in her voice. "It's Wendy."

And then I was no longer me. I was someone else, somewhere else. Memories crashed into my mind that didn't belong to me. They belonged to Wendy...

Chaos ruled this world. No matter where I went, it remained familiar. A breath eased out of my lungs as I kicked the sand along The Vale's shores with my bare feet. Twenty-four years of wandering had brought me here.

To the maddest thing I had ever seen, and I had witnessed the Forge at a distance, eyed all the gears whirring despite the empty, cruel head of the Heartless Queen who ruled there. Nothing compared to islands in the sky.

Like ornaments, they were hung on distant clouds, each of many broken pieces adorned with mist. An ocean of air and water separated me from them, but separation had never stopped my searching before.

Just because I had yet to find my family didn't mean I never would. Just because I had yet to reach those islands didn't mean it was impossible. Even in this crazy, cursed world, nothing was impossible unless you started to believe it was.

So I believed in peace amidst chaos. Kindness alongside cruelty. And magic, above all else.

"Hark, lass," a rough voice called me from my reverie, and I turned to find a man with an unkempt red beard striding toward me from farther down the beach.

"Good morn, sir," I offered, seeing his gaze drift toward the islands as well. "Do you know how to reach them?"

He laughed. "You'd not be the first to peer upon those islands and wonder that. Certainly won't be the last either." Scratching his chin, he sighed, a greedy glint in his eye as he looked across the water at the floating lands. "There's a legend 'bout them. People of The Vale claim one day they fell out of the sky. Before any could reach them, they flew. Then I s'pose only the fae, the birds, and the magic dwellers of Enchantia could touch them if they wanted."

I dropped my gaze to the sand. Enchantia had larger problems to deal with right now. Exploration was a dead hobby embarked upon by few in this age. "I'll find a way, somehow."

The man laughed. "Maybe you would have."

My brows crashed together, but I didn't so much as have time to look up before he covered my mouth with a cloth. Some sickly sweet smell clung to the corners of my mind, and I dropped into a dream.

The world beyond my thoughts rocked. Every dancing fawn and spinning bear in my mind tore into pieces. I gasped awake, but everything remained black. My ankles were wet. Shouts blanketed the tumbling expanse.

"Hello?" I called into the darkness, pulling on restraints. Harsh rope bound my hands and feet to an

upright log.

My ankles were wet? I curled my toes into water that sloshed up my legs and against my dress, plastering it to my thighs.

"Is Smee in the nest?" a voice boomed.

"He was thrown!"

The same crude voice as before yelled, "Someone get up there! We need a way outta this storm, or it'll swallow us whole!"

A storm. A ship.

My mind worked as water bombarded my calves, rising. First, I was bound and blinded. Second, the crew was muffled. I was below deck, likely beside other goods the pirates wished to trade. Third, the chances were good that I was alone.

Whether the ropes had been tied loosely to start or the rocking dampness had made them so, I was able to lean forward and push my wrists against the beam until I wriggled my hands free. When I had, nothing held me upright, and the ship threw my body down against bags of grain.

I wrenched the scrap of fabric off my eyes and squinted at the dim cargo hold. The cramped space was filled with water that poured down an open trapdoor. That was the only way out, and judging by the sounds above, the deck crawled with pirates.

It would only be a matter of time before they were down here passing buckets, so I only had now. Fighting the ropes binding my ankles, I broke free and threw my arms around the post when the ship nearly tipped sideways before slamming back down. Eyes wide, I blinked.

I had never been on a ship during a storm before—much less a pirate ship.

I knew the seas were lawless on this coast, but I hadn't expected to run into any trouble. How was I supposed to get out of this one? My eyes scanned the hold. Broken bags spilling grain and smashed barrels tumbled about. I was lucky none of the splintered pieces had impaled me while I was unconscious, but with the water ever-rising and those crude pieces dancing in the murky depths, I knew I wouldn't continue to be so lucky. I had to brave the storm and get out of here first. Likely none of the crew would be too focused on me if the situation was as dire as it sounded.

Dragging myself toward the ladder leading out, I pried my soaking body out of the death trap it had found itself in and peered above deck. Dozens of booted feet clomped through half a foot of water, fighting with ropes and sails that whipped like loose sheets on a clothing string.

Lightning gleamed across the sky, an electric blue I'd never seen matched before. The thunder that pounded afterward rumbled the whole of the ship.

"What are you doing here?" a panicked voice addressed me. I looked up at the man I'd seen on the beach. His wild eyes were raw with fear. I'd thought his hair and beard unkempt before, but that was nothing to the way they looked now. Water rained off his face and out of his hair, spilling through the tangles.

I didn't know how to reply or if my voice would carry through the wind and waves. My head jerked toward port, and my stomach flipped.

An electric blue wave slammed into the boat, tipping it on its side. I rolled out of the hold and crashed into the rail. The bearded man soared over the edge, a scream on his lips that I couldn't quite hear.

My eyes pinned themselves on the swirling water

beyond the rail. It spun, appearing more like a galaxy of blue and purple and black than an ocean whirlpool. Angry, it seemed determined to eat us all.

Another wave slammed the hull, and a horrid splintering crack filled the air, repeating. Echoing. Yelled commands turned into screams and prayers. Like a child's toy, the massive ship split at the mercy of the water's playing hands.

We went under.

I gasped air whenever it touched my face, but the choking hold of the ocean wouldn't release me or allow me any say in where I went. The whole of my vision spun, yanking me down, down, down. My head submerged. Electricity surrounded me in jolts of blue and green, but I never felt the sting as each shock lit the water.

Water constricted around my lungs, tightening without restraint. Salt burned my eyes, but in the final moments, as darkness crept in, all-consuming, I didn't see death. Not here in this colorful place.

Something brewed here. Something magical. And where magic as bright as this lived, death had no hold.

20TH NOVEMBER

Heat warmed my skin, luring me out of a deep sleep. I coughed gritty powder from my mouth and squinted groggily ahead. Sand. My body lay plastered against sand. Groaning, I took a deep breath of clean air and smiled before closing my eyes again.

I was so tired.

But I was also alive. Where I was didn't matter as much as the fact I simply was. Still. After so many close calls in my adventures, my soul lingered like it had something important to do.

A roaring screech shattered my reverie, igniting a fire in my gut. I rolled onto my back in the same moment a massive tentacle pounded into the sand where I had been. Ten—or even twenty—times my size, a squid loomed over the expanse of ocean stretching endlessly before me. The creature screamed murder, and the apendage rose for another strike.

I covered my face with my arms, peering through the crack between them. Cold terror washed over my skin.

Blinding and dark at once, a man in a whipping black coat streaked in front of me, raised his sword, and cleaved the squid's arm from its body. It soared, wriggling, to land beside me in a fury, then limped until it no longer moved.

The creature's red eye blazed, and the scream it unleashed rattled every grain of sand beneath my back. The man whirled, tossing his sword into his other hand where it hung, grabbed my arm, and pulled me to my feet. "This is not a particularly favorable place for a nap, miss." He grinned, his debonaire smile not at all bemused by the writhing mass of flesh and anger behind him. He tossed it a smirk, then we ran.

As we ran, I realized that had the man not come along, I wouldn't have been able to push my protesting muscles to run. Dull pain traced my bones, making each step echo jolts up and down my spine. We burst through a treeline into a forest, but the man didn't stop there.

Wood cracked and crumbled behind us, and my stomach clenched. The creature's reach went this far?

When at last we slowed to a stop, a troubled screech sounded beyond the trees, then the silence of the woods encompassed us. My savior released my hand, placed his above his eyes to peer at the sky, then snatched my arm and yanked me several feet to the right.

I stumbled, my body complaining, as a chasm split the land. Water rushed through like ink, and I stared dumbly at it before meeting the man's patient smile. "T-thank you," I stammered. Now that the threat appeared for the most part behind us, a flush coated my cheeks. This man was uniquely beautiful.

Dark hair spilled down to his shoulders, caressing his black cloak. An icy blue warmed the gleam in his eyes. The beginnings of a five o'clock shadow touched his strong, square jaw. His lips quirked with humor, like he knew I was staring a little too deeply and he also knew precisely why.

I flicked my gaze down.

"Not a problem, miss," his laughing voice coaxed. "I can't very well leave a lady in dire straights."

My breath caught, but before I could look back up at him, sunlight caught metal. I thought it was his sword at first, then I realized it was a hook. A metal hook. Fashioned in place of a hand. I blinked at it while it winked in the light. "Your...hand's a hook?"

He looked down, his brows rising as though he'd only just noticed. With skill, however, he manoeuvred his sword off the curved metal and into a sheath at his side. "Imagine that. I've gone this long and hadn't the faintest clue."

My cheeks boiled hotter, the river beside us coursing with a rush that didn't hide my embarrassment or the thumping of my heart. "I didn't mean—"

"I know." He slipped the hook into his pocket and continued smiling. It was so disarming, his smile. I didn't know what to do with myself. "As I have just saved your life, would you honor me with the knowledge of your name?"

"My name?" I absently brushed hair behind my ear and realized I was covered in sand. I had to look atrocious. "It's Wendy."

"Wendy?"

I nodded. "I never knew my family, so just Wendy."

"It's a pleasure, Just Wendy."

Butterflies took turns doing flips in my stomach, and no matter how hard I tried, I couldn't get them to settle.

"Most people call me Captain Hook," he said, and the mentioned hook in his pocket shifted. He glanced away. "My name's James, though."

"James," I repeated, finally gathering myself enough to offer him a smile in return. "I can't imagine why they'd call you 'Hook.'"

He chuckled, his chest rumbling with the sound. "One of Neverland's mysteries."

"Neverland?"

Straightening, he leaned back on the heels of his boots. "I suppose you are new here. Generally, only pirates wash up on these shores, even though you don't look quite like a pirate to me."

"I'm not." My brows furrowed. "Are you one?"

He placed his hand against his chest. "Do I not look the part?"

"Look it?" I traced my gaze up all his dark leather, past his cutlass, to his charming face, and pressed my lips together. "Appearances are hardly a good idea to rely on. No, sir, you do not act the part. Unless you wish something of me now that you've saved me?"

"Your name and your thanks have well covered your tab." He watched me as though I were as unusual as he, and I self-consciously brushed off my damp dress. Sand tumbled from it in torrents.

Trying my best to ignore the state of my clothes and skin, and the discomfort that came with both, I asked, "What's your price for information about where I am?"

His head dropped forward, his relaxed smile glimmering with mischief. "Must everything come with a

eyes glanced deeper into the woods. "Maybe
with me, I'll just tell you everything I know."
to me unbelievable stories about the world
into, James led me through the forest until
on a small group of huts. He ended his last
lourish then bid me find shelter in the village
tioning him, for whether I saw it or not, he
and the natives weren't fond of his kind.
I'd see him again, and he said, "Perhaps,"
g my hand and leaving me on the doorstep
His dark coat fluttered through the woods,
view, yet his impression held in my mind,
ther in a way only magic could.

～

Please, sir!" I tugged on my arm and frowned at the two men crowding me against a stone wall. "Let go."

"I dunno, Jack. Whaddaya suppose it is? Ain't seen no bird like her before." The man holding me chuckled, licking his lips and displaying rotting teeth.

I gagged, floating off the ground, but his grip only tightened.

Jack guffawed. "I dunno. I dunno. Ain't never seen one either. Sure pretty, though." Snatching my chin, he pressed cold jewels against my flesh. A shock of fear streaked through me.

Chiming burst from my hair, and my heart dropped into my toes. "No! Stay hidden!"

My pixie friend wouldn't hear of it. He shook his fists and screamed at the men, their wide eyes glinting with greed. One's meaty hand lunged for Skye, so I kicked him in the shin. He howled, though I was certain my poor moccasined toes received the brunt of the action.

Jack yanked on my hair, and I winced. Te
the corners of my eyes. Then the pain died.

He fell, crumpled in a heap at my feet
before the other's throat, and his face went

"You'd do well to release the lady, B
already spoken for."

Tentatively, Barlow's fingers unclasped fro
my wrist, and he stammered, "Cap'n. I didn't
This is your woman?"

"I don't particularly care what you know." J
smacked the flat edge of his sword against the ma
chest. "On your way." He stepped toward me, stoppi
when he nearly stepped onto Jack. "Oh, and take this
mess with you."

Barlow nodded, furiously tugging Jack away. Just
the three of us remained in the quiet lane.

"James," I breathed.

"Wendy." He sheathed his sword and shook his head.
"Is this how we are always destined to meet? With my
blade between you and some ungodly harm?"

I flustered. "Things were going fine. I could have
managed."

"Quite right, I'm sure." He glanced at my pixie when
the tiny creature settled on my shoulder, did a double-
take, then all his charm dropped away. "What in the..."

Triumphant, I smirked. "This is Skye." I only knew so
much because he'd spelled his name out for me when
we first met, but James needn't know that.

"It's a pixie."

"Yes."

His lips parted. "But...only children can..." His brows
furrowed, his gaze falling to my hovering feet. "You can
fly too."

"Yes." I lifted higher off the ground, lighter than air.

226

His eyes snapped closed, and he reached blindly for me. "Heavens, Wendy. No wonder those men were on you like wild pigs. Get down from there before you make me do something ungentlemanly."

I'd never landed so fast. Red as the underbelly of a meadowlark, I gripped my dress and stared up at James in horror.

He sighed, peeking to make sure it was safe to open his eyes again. "You are, by far, the most unusual woman I have ever had the chance to meet."

"Thank you?"

"Why are you in Pirate Bay?"

I looked down the cobblestone street. "Is that what this place is called? I went toward the ships since you said you were a captain and a pirate."

His eyes widened. "You were looking for me?"

Skye chimed, annoyed, and folded his arms. I glanced at him to find him glaring at James. "Yes?"

"Is everything all right with the midget?"

"I don't think he wanted me to come here, but of course, now I know why." I smiled sheepishly. "I'm sorry, Skye. But see? Everything worked out in the end."

Skye's eyes narrowed, and he mumbled something else, but I set his grumbles aside. Pixies were fairly temperamental. Looking back at James, I stilled.

Sorrow thickened his solemn expression as he peered at Skye. Memories danced beyond where I could see, but they clung like briars in an obvious and painful way. Meeting my gaze, he shook the thorny spikes off. "Well, if you've come all this way, I suppose I'm inclined to show you around, the brighter part of town, at least."

Excitement bubbled in my chest. My toes curled off the ground, and I took his hand. "I'd rather see your ship."

"My ship?" His expression contorted into a bewildered half-smile. "You want to see that dreadful, old, smelly thing?"

"Very much."

Almost begrudgingly, but not quite, he tucked my hand into the crook of his arm, sighed, and said, "Very well. You'll have to pardon the men before I yell at them, though. We are not used to such fair guests."

He spoke of his ship with a level of tenderness I'd never seen professed by a man before. Wholly enchanted, I wiled away the day—and many others that later came. Though Skye never seemed thrilled to accompany me, I couldn't keep away from the bay—or James—for long.

～

Metal clattered over the ocean, halting me in the air above Pirate Bay. My eyes widened when I honed in on where the noise came from.

James's ship.

My heart leaped out of my chest, and I dove, a hundred horrible scenarios bombarding my thoughts at once. He was under attack. Injured. Dying. Dead.

Skye rushed out of my hair and tugged on my dress, but I didn't stop until I was near enough to see James's plumed hat.

Disgust and hatred twisted his face into something horrible, worse than I'd ever seen. My lips parted, everything beneath my skin suddenly cold. His sword moved with calculated exactness. He was the one out for the kill.

I shifted my gaze to his opponent, and I didn't have a single moment to think. "What are you doing!" I launched myself into the fray of blades and shouts, standing

228

before the orange-headed child with my arms spread.

James's blade dove for me, screeching to a stop. "Wendy." His voice was breathless with shock as his blade retreated faster than it had come.

"Hullo?" the boy behind me floated to my side, a brow raised. Sweat coated his forehead, but he was at perfect ease. "I didn't think pirates had any friends worth knowing."

A furious chime broke the fabricated calm. All around us, a dozen boys, children, stood facing pirates, blades in hand and wary expressions on their faces. Flitting out of the flying boy's pocket, a pixie reprimanded him, her hands on her hips.

"No, no, I just meant— Well, if you'd let me get a word in, Tink!" He rolled his eyes. "I just meant she can fly."

The pixie turned toward me, eyeing me up and down before sneering away to rest on the boy's shoulder.

"Wendy, what are you doing here?" An icy edge coated James's words, and I'd never heard him speak in that tone before. Times with him were warm, filled with laughter. Now, I was chilled.

"What do you mean? I've visited you a hundred times now! What are you doing fighting all these children?"

He scoffed. Scoffed! My brows dipped low in a frown, but his attitude didn't improve. "They are hardly children, I assure you. Our battle has proceeded for more years than I can count, yet it remains timeless." He sneered, "And he refuses to tell me how."

"How?" I looked between them, incredulous. "You know how! This is Neverland! You told me the day I got here, I wouldn't age anymore."

"No, Wendy…" He simmered for the first time, some harshness leaving his eyes.

"Seems like a bad time." The boy scratched his head,

nodding at his pixie. He floated off the deck while the tiny creature zipped past each of the other children, allowing them to do the same. "Maybe tomorrow will be better, Hook. C'mon, men!" He lifted high, pinning his arms at his sides, and crowed like a rooster. Every boy joined him, and the sound echoed.

The familiar sound echoed.

I'd heard it many times before, and the natives I lived with had told me stories about the child who fought in their name. They called him Peter, sang of him as if he were an ancient force to be reckoned. That was Peter?

When they said child, I thought at least a teenager. He looked no older than twelve.

"Wendy," James growled, and my heart thumped.

I ripped my gaze from the retreating children and found him frowning. Weariness coated his eyes, and his lips were pinched with distaste, but the annoyance in his tone didn't seem as severe now.

"Why were you fighting Peter?" I asked.

"Uhm, Cap'n..."

James whirled, plunging his sword into its sheathe and snatching my hand. "As you were, Smee. Victory will come another day."

Without explanation, he tugged me along behind him into the streets of Pirate Bay. "James, where are we going?"

He didn't reply.

"James?"

Still nothing.

Ripping my hand out of his, I floated away from him and crossed my arms. "Answer me, Hook. Why were you trying to kill that child?"

His back stiffened. He didn't face me. "I'm a pirate, Wendy. I'm not a good man. I'm the furthest from it."

Without looking, he opened his hand, palm up, for me to take. "But I will give you the full truth if you want it. I've tried to avoid it for too long already."

I stared between his hand and his turned back. Automatically, my fingers longed for the embrace of his, but Skye zipped between us, shaking his head.

I ignored him. Maybe I shouldn't have.

"Once, I was a renowned captain, a leader of a marine fleet off Vale's coast. Perhaps you have known a better time than I, but in my days off Neverland, there was nothing but war. War and pain and suffering. I'd wanted to change that ever since the world stole my parents when I was a child. I became the youngest marine general, led countless battles and won, until a mistake to approach Elder under cover of a storm led me to a whirlpool. You know what happens after that." James's hand squeezed my fingers as we plodded through the forest. My heart pounded, partly worried and partly excited. He'd talked so little of his past. I hadn't even known he'd come from the same world I knew. I wanted to know him. I was desperate to find more answers.

He stopped suddenly, before a veil of green and stared at me. "For what it's worth, I am sorry."

"For what?"

Shaking his head, he nodded at Skye. "Before the sun sets, I will likely have many things to apologize to you for, Wendy. But in this moment, I am talking to him."

Arms folded on my shoulder, Skye only glared James's way and dismissed his words.

His eyes closed, and he curled his hook in the vines. Peeling them away, he displayed a land charred and crumbling. Ashes danced in a forlorn wind. Not even bugs chirped here.

"What is—"

His touch left me cold. The world was cold around me. Fire had so clearly destroyed everything, but it was gone now, a horrific memory of another time. "I am not a good man, Wendy. Not even before I became a pirate. I was a tool, a murderer. Hatred has fueled everything in my life. When I first came here, I wanted to go home. Pan," he sneered, "was the only one I had seen come and go as he pleased. I wanted that freedom. But then I noticed he didn't age even when he left. That was a different freedom in itself."

He swiped a hand over his face and couldn't bear to look at me. My nose stung with the phantom residue of burning wood. My eyes stung for other reasons entirely. Before me wasn't the unshakeable man I knew. Torture and regret burdened his eyes.

"The child refused to tell me his secret. I went to him, begging, but he attacked me. He cleaved my hand from my arm, laughed, fed it to a crocodile, and left me to die." He gripped his hook, trembling. Spit flew from his lips. "I had only adapted to the way of a pirate to survive! But he said one as filthy as me didn't deserve freedom from this prison."

"James..." I stepped toward him, but he moved away.

"He's right. I'm a monster. Look around you! I did this! In an effort to smoke out a single child, I set a fire I couldn't control. You've wondered before why your pixie hates me? I murdered his home, probably his family, maybe all his friends." Breath heaved through James as he peered at his hook. A deranged beast glared back in the polished metal. "It's too late for me to stop. I hate Pan, Wendy." His eyes closed, and his arms fell to his sides. "I hate how he laughed. How he ignored my pleas for help. How he's an enigma I can't crack. I hate how the people who took me in fear him. I hate how he's glorified. I hate him. And I hate what I've become due to that hatred."

I never thought I'd see the day James would cry. I never knew a man who smirked at Krakens could. But he shook, and a tear traced down his beautiful face.

"I just wanted to go home. To be free."

Skye didn't protest when I wrapped my arms around him, felt his shaking chest against mine. The pixie lifted off my shoulder, hovering above chaos. The chaos that surrounded us now. The chaos of broken hearts and shattered dreams.

"I've never had a home," I whispered. "I've wandered the war-streaked lands as long as I could walk. Like you, my family was taken from me, but I was spared having to know them before it happened. I've wondered what's worse." Cupping his cheek, I brushed his tears away. I hadn't expected the words to fall from my lips then, but they did. "I love you, James. And I love Neverland, even as strange and terrifying as it can be. I have been able to live peacefully here. The world you've tried to return to is no doubt still marred with suffering, but here...here we have the same freedoms as Peter. Time doesn't bind us."

He swallowed, and his eyes still didn't open. His arms didn't lift to return my embrace. "You would ask me to give up fighting Pan?"

My breath held. "I've seen too much fighting in my life."

"You don't believe me. You've lived among those who sing his praises. You believe I did wrong to him; I deserved what happened; I'm a monster for continuing this war as I have."

He wrenched himself from my arms, and I slapped him. The anger budding on his face died. My hand burned, and I winced. "A war is not forged by one party

233

alone. I blame both of you, and I believe both of you in the wrong, at one point or another." I closed my hand against my chest, tearing up from the sting and something more. "I am, however, asking you to stop. To run away with me, maybe."

His eyes widened, and he blinked dumbly. "What?"

"Run away with me. Away from the natives who sing of the one you hate. Away from the pirates who torment them."

His gaze took me in from my head to my feet. "You said you've lived in peace here."

"Yes?"

"You'd run away from the only home you've ever really known, to be with me?"

My chin raised.

He looked over my shoulder, no doubt at Skye. Whatever he saw made him shift. All the confidence I'd known him to have appeared to waver for the moment. "I can't just run away with an honorable young woman..."

My heart plummeted like an anchor to my heels, and I almost turned away to hide an onslaught of tears that threatened to break free. So this was what rejection felt like? It clogged in my chest and choked the air from my throat.

He dropped to one knee.

I gaped at him.

He took my hand in both his and his hook, realizing only after the fact he'd touched me with it. As long as I'd known him, he'd kept the crude metal away from me. When he began to draw it back, I held on tight. Tenderness entered his gaze, and he sighed. "Just Wendy, may I give you a last name?"

"So wait. Is this a yes to running away with me?" I asked, breathless.

"Is that a yes to my question?"

Red heated my cheeks. "Depends. Am I going to be Wendy Hook?"

He laughed. Surrounded by decay and disaster, laughter filled the air, setting aside that era, making way for the next one. "That doesn't have the best ring to it." Rising, he tucked a stray lock of hair behind my ear. "I was thinking Wendy Darling."

James D. Hook.

"Is that your real…"

"Now you know why I go by 'Hook' in my crowd." He rose and moved close, his breath touching my skin. "It's a secret. I haven't told anyone here. Not a soul."

"I won't say a word." Flushing, I directed my attention away from him. "Neither will Skye. Right, Skye?"

Skye shrugged, disinterest in the whole matter etched upon his face, besides disgust.

"Are we leaving now?" James asked.

"You don't have…" As I began to ask, sorrow tipped his smile. Of course not. Neither of us had come here with anything. Neither of us had anything to pack. Holding his hand, I nodded. "Yes, we're leaving now. Skye, are you coming?" I didn't know where we were going, but I wasn't going to force him away from his home. Even if I'd never seen him leave my side for more than a few spare minutes ever since we found each other.

Wordlessly, he sat on my shoulder and folded his arms. My stomach swirled, thankful he was going to stay with me as everything in my world uprooted yet again. In a matter of hours, I'd learned the truth about James, the horrible truth. My eyes swept the scene, and my lips pressed together. Yet I loved him.

∾

Stumps crumbled. Sticks turned to black bits.

I loved him.

Remnants of pixie floss hung across the dilapidated remains of houses like spiderweb. Nothing moved. Nothing breathed. But our hearts beat together, and our hands clasped each other.

I loved him.

Tears in my eyes, I faced him, floating to meet his lips with mine. The touch was cold at first, hesitant, but it melted. It melted and was molten. A heat I'd never known bonded us together. I disappeared into it, for in that place so shrouded by mistakes and death, magic lived on.

I didn't know how to tell him. How could I possibly? Resting a hand against my stomach, I stared at the door. Beyond it, the waterfall rushed, sending glittering light over our home. After weeks, perhaps months, maybe years of exploring Neverland and leaving dozens of half-homes all over, we had settled here in a magical grove filled with pixies.

What would James say?

My breath held when the door creaked open. James saw me and frowned. "What is it?"

"What? What do you mean?" My eyes widened.

He quirked a brow at me and pursed his lips. "The last time you stood there waiting for me to get back from hunting, you'd set the kitchen on fire." He strode in with a bundle of fish and glanced at the peaceful kitchen, sniffing for the remains of some misadventure.

I gnawed my lip, swallowed, and shifted.

Skye chimed impatiently, buzzing between us and making full-body gestures at my stomach.

James's eyes dropped to my middle. "You've...gained weight?" He eased completely, smiling as he went to the

236

kitchen and delivered his catch to the washbasin. "Is that what you're worried about? I hadn't really noticed."

"James!" The man didn't so much as look up. "I'm pregnant. It hasn't even been long enough to show. Have I gained weight?"

He froze, every muscle in his body tightening. Shock overtook his face, and he blinked at the wall above the basin. "You're what?"

Nerves knotted in my belly. "I know we haven't really talked about having kids. I still feel like a kid myself but—"

He met me in two strides, looping his arm under my rump and lifting my body against him. "You're having a baby?" He cupped my cheek, his eyes sparkling. "Really? I know you tease me. Your pranks never grow old, but really?"

Tears burst to my eyes, and I nodded.

"I'm going to be a father?"

"And I, a mother."

For the second time in my life, I saw James Darling cry. The moment of joy lost itself shortly after. His brows crashed low, and he looked at my stomach, tension filtering into the small spaces between us. "You can't give birth here."

I looked around. Though modest, we had created a comfortable home, but he had a point. I knew very little about delivering a baby, and I supposed he knew about the same. "I left the natives so suddenly, but I could return to them, explain, and they could help."

James shook his head. "If you have our child here, Neverland's time will move for them like it does for the natives. We would outlive our baby." Memories darkened his face. "I've seen it happen before, and I'll be damned if it happens to us."

My heart twisted, my hand closing around my dress. "What do we do?"

"You can still fly." His gaze flicked to Skye, and hatred I hadn't seen in so long curled his lip. "Find Pan. Follow him out of this cursed place."

~

Night cooled the air as I watched Peter's silhouette cross the silver moon. My heart pounded; it had been so long since I'd seen the other world. Hundreds of horrible memories twisted in my skull.

What if I made it, but no one in the war-strewn land would help me? What if I made it, but I couldn't get back to James? What if I didn't make it at all?

Skye murmured softly by my ear, yanking my attention from Peter. His deep blue eyes delved into me, as though he could hear my every thought. So much calm existed in his stern expression.

"You're right," I whispered. "I trust you, and I trust myself."

Together, we followed Peter straight into the sky. My head lightened when I felt as though I was about to touch the stars. Closing my eyes, I shook the sensation off, then squinted ahead again. The floating isles I had seen from the beach so long ago lay before me as they always had.

Hung above the ocean, basking in the moonlight, spattered with stars and speckled with magic, the untouchable land bustled with a quiet nightlife I hadn't expected to see.

"People live here?" I asked the air.

"Sure." Peter's voice made me leap in the sky and spin around. He leaned against the wind, his arms folded. "When the filthy pirates burned down so much of the pixie forest, Neverland wept, crying parts of itself away as a haven apart from itself. Loads of pixies came first, shortly after I'd found Tink. Then I helped the native children who could fly reach its safety. We didn't know how far the pirates would go, and everyone wanted to make sure their families, the future, would be safe."

Though I hadn't seen Peter since that day on the pirate ship when everything changed, he didn't look a second changed. Though, now, his eyes were solemn.

"They were all young. None of them remember Neverland, their parents, any of it. My stories are fairytales to them, and perhaps that's for the best. They've lived in peace off Neverland and away from the rest of this world." He shifted his attention off the islands and smiled at me. "Nice to meet you. I'm Peter." Extending a hand, he sniffed. "Awfully strange to see an adult up here. Why were you following me?"

"I…" Blinking at his hand, I tried to gather my thoughts. What he'd said had been so…sad, yet it was over now, like he'd torn out the page carrying such heavy thoughts and tossed it into the sea. "You don't remember me?"

Skye chimed, and Peter's lips pursed. He pulled his hand back, lifted his green hat off his head, and ruffled his bright hair in the moments his pixie rushed out from underneath his cap. "You don't say?"

Skye chimed some more, glancing at Peter's pixie. She tilted her head, an eyebrow quirked, then fixed her gaze on me, and tinkled.

"I'm sorry, I don't understand pixie," I stammered.

"She says you look like you're about to pop." Peter's brows lowered with an odd mixture of suspicion and concern. "Did you eat a watermelon?"

I didn't need to understand pixie to pick up the

239

dryness in Skye's tone as he seemingly relayed the reason behind my ample middle. It had been several months since I'd found out before we'd caught sight of Peter. A couple weeks since he'd decided to leave Neverland after visiting. I didn't know quite how long I had left before I would pop, but surely any day now. The only time I felt some semblance of comfort was when I was in flight. Otherwise, I was quite the beached whale.

"We need to get you to Skyla." Peter took my hand, and I jerked at his touch. He blinked at me, nothing but innocent confusion in his eyes.

Skye landed on my wrist, speaking in chiming reprimands.

"He's right. I'm only trying to help."

"And if I were a pirate?" I blurted, unsure where the words had come from, why I would give him a reason to leave me and my child when I desperately needed his help. I couldn't risk losing it. But I couldn't stop my question. "If I were a pirate, would you still help me?"

Laughing, he snatched my hand again and pulled me toward Skyla. "Nonsense. Pirates can't fly."

∾

"If you go back to Neverland, you'll be stuck with a month-old baby forever." Peter stopped me before my feet left the ground. Hugging my little boy against my chest, I turned to face him. He leaned against the tree he and his Lost Boys had built into a house for me. "Some of us can hear his sleepless night in Aire. I'm not sure why you'd want to prolong this time."

Silent, I stared at him. He had been nothing but a considerate, if prideful, child during my time here. Never once did he forget to check on me. He spared nothing to make me comfortable. So why had he turned James away in his time of need? "I'll be back. It's just that..."

"His father hasn't met him yet." Peter stiffened, age showing only through the tension suddenly in the air. "Tink told me you fell in love with the captain who burned her forest."

A shiver ran over my skin, but I raised my head. "How does she know?"

The boy's brown eyes landed on Skye, who hadn't left my baby's side for even a second. The pixie glanced up, but paid my shocked expression little mind. "Word travels fast between pixies," Peter said.

"He's different." I bit my tongue. That wasn't true. It just seemed the right thing to say. The truth was he hadn't changed. He was still the same man who cared for his home and would do anything for it; he was still the same man Peter had refused to help when he was desperate to return home. I clung to my boy, my sweet boy with James's face and my eyes, and unleashed the question that had been plaguing me since I left Neverland. "Why didn't you help James? Why did you cut off his hand?"

"James?"

"Hook. Captain James D. Hook." I forced my breath calm. "Why didn't you help my husband when all he wanted was to go home?"

"I'm sorry." He didn't meet my eyes, but his brow furrowed like he was searching for something, anything, a foothold or a scrap of sense. "I don't remember. I do know that the pirates have tortured so much that I care about. When I close my eyes some nights, I see blood. When there's a breath of silence, I hear screams. So when the silence passes and I open my eyes again, I forget. I forget, so I can remember what's important." He nodded at the bundle pressed close to my heart. "Be careful with him. *I may not remember, but I know I can fly.*"

"What does that matter?" I asked, breathless. My heart ached with cold from his words, and I didn't know what to think. I had gotten nowhere closer to learning the reason.

"You can only fly with a very special kind of belief. The kind children naturally have before they're too tall. And you can't trust a pirate."

I let my feet leave the ground. "I believe in love."

His lips curved in a smile, but it didn't reach his eyes. His eyes, in that moment, were chillingly ancient. "If you never forget that, Wendy, you'll always be able to fly. But it would do people like us good to remember that love is a powerful weapon, and it doesn't discriminate whose hands it falls into."

He left me with those words and the horrible sensation there was nothing I could do to stop such a weapon if it were wielded in the name of evil.

21ST NOVEMBER

"**B**ay!" I sighed, swiping hair out of my face. Neverland wasn't a safe place to wander around, especially as a child. The ground groaned, and I sidestepped a chasm when it split open across the land. Black water churned through the valley, and I shook my head. Skye was with him, I knew that much—the pixie had never left his side since the second he was born—and I'd never met a more responsible pixie, but still.

"He has an adventurer's heart." James's fingers skimmed my hand. "There's nothing wrong with that."

"He's only seven." My lips pursed, but I caved at the mischief lighting James's eyes. They whispered of the little terror he had been when he was Bay's age. Slipping into his arms, I closed my eyes, content.

His thumb pressed against my cheek. "You look older, Wendy," he murmured, his finger running over the lines near my eyes.

"Older by about seven years, I'd say." Cupping his hand, I met his gaze, but it brewed with something dark, and a shiver cut down my spine. I knew every time I came home from Skyla, I had aged some, but it was only until Bay could make the trip himself and decide whether or not he wanted to. James knew that. I tugged on his beard and smirked. "Besides, you look older too, what with this forest on your face."

His brows lowered, and he sniffed. "It makes me look fatherly."

"It makes you look like a sailor. A fisherman, maybe."

His lips parted to say something more, but Bay's head dropped in between us. Since he had been born, his eyes had lightened into something hazel, wide, bright. Those beautiful little eyes stared at us both now, his hair hanging free as he spun upside down in the air.

"Skye said I shouldn't interrupt." His young voice held no hint of his true age, but his eyes always spoke the truth. "I didn't listen."

"Why you little rascal." James caught him, spun him, and tickled him into submission, all to the tune of the rushing river fault. Laughter filled the woods, even Skye chiming along with us.

～

"I don't like it," James said from the couch.

I looked at him from in the kitchen and found his arms firmly folded against his chest. We had discussed this. "It's good for him to play with other children and *have friends while he's in Neverland. I let you bring him to visit your old crewmates. The natives were very welcoming, and they don't know the truth. Even if they did, Bay's a child."*

"He's named after the Pirate Bay itself, Wendy!" Standing, he strode toward me.

I continued chopping wild onions. "He's a child. They aren't going to hurt an eleven-year-old boy even if his father was a pirate."

"Is. I can't be forgiven for what I did." Torment tightened the muscles in his face, and his mustache twitched. He clutched his hook. "It will mark me for all eternity. He made sure of that."

I set my knife down. "James…"

"And you!" He threw his hand up in my direction. "Isn't eleven old enough to make the trip alone? Time keeps slipping away from us. I—" Nostrils flaring, he turned away.

I had made friends in Skyla. Initially, I planned to make the trip with Bay until he was thirteen, but then my life changed; I had two: one in Neverland and one in Skyla. Pressing my lips together, I set a hand on his back. "Actually, I was thinking…maybe we could find a way to make the trip together, the three of us? Pixie dust works on pixie wood. If we could—"

He spun, a wild craze coating his face. Between his mustache and his beard, his lips curled.

The door slammed open, jerking us both out of the conversation. Bay stood there, smirking. Held proudly in both hands was a sheet of leather all tattooed with the visage of a ship. Finding us both in the kitchen, he floated over, presenting what he had made. "They're teaching me how to tattoo, so I can be good enough to do Tiger Lily's mark when she grows up." Gloating darkened his hazel eyes. "I made the Jolly Roger, Dad. And look, there's you and Uncle Smee on the deck."

"Well, isn't that just wonderful," James spat. "I'm sure they adored seeing that."

"James Darling," I warned.

He shook his head, ruffled Bay's hair, and sighed. "Sorry. It's well-done."

"Not really. All the pressures are different, so it isn't very smooth. If this had been a person—" He laughed. "—ouch."

James was already heading for our bedroom before our son had finished speaking, and my heart sank.

"Is everything okay?" Bay's eyes peered between his retreating father and me, concern muddling his expression. Just a moment ago, he had been a true, proud eleven-year-old, but now, my baby was once again bearing the mark of his unusual upbringing. A young man hovered before me, already over twenty.

"Some days are brighter than others," I said. "We sometimes have to wait out the darkness."

Skye mumbled something on Bay's shoulder, glancing at me, then back down at the floor.

Bay's feet touched the hardwood. "He says I'm old enough to know the truth."

Bitterness stung my throat when I swallowed, but I pushed the taste aside and shook my head, holding my hand out for Skye. He jumped onto my fingers, and I lifted him close. "That isn't for any of us to decide," I told him sternly. "Please. You know that."

A child may have complained when Skye nodded, agreeing, but Bay didn't.

～

Fire scorched the night, gleaming in erratic wisps. My heart pounded the second I opened my eyes on the scene. Neverland burned. Bay's hand left mine before I had time to register what had happened.

"Bay! No!"

He and Skye zipped through the sky, toward the still-lit embers dancing in the wind. I followed.

"Tiger Lily?" he shouted when he landed on black earth. Wind whistled and howled around us. "Chief!"

My nose caught the scent before my eyes noticed the remains, blood and bone, charred flesh and muscle. I threw myself before Bay's face, but he had already gone unnaturally still. "We have to leave this place, now," I said, rushed, holding his body near.

The flight home, I was numb.

"You shaved?" I blinked through my starting tears. I had wanted nothing more than to rush into James's arms and cry about the horror I had witnessed, but something was wrong. I felt it the second I stepped into our home.

James had shaved his beard, leaving only his mustache behind. With the change, he wore leather, leather I hadn't seen since we'd left the burnt pixie forest and started a new life. Anger marred his beautiful face. But it wasn't beautiful anymore, I realized.

It was cruel.

"It's all gone," he hissed, stepping toward Bay and me. "Everything."

Choked, I whispered, "I saw."

He cupped my cheek, but the motion wasn't gentle. A tear traced down my face, but he didn't wipe it away. He had honed in on the corners of my eyes, where thin wrinkles spiderwebbed my skin. "Peter is gone. There's no hope for us now."

"Wh-at?" My arms hung limp at my sides; my body

tremored.

"Out of all of them, he got away." James sneered, his fingers tightening around my cheek until I could feel bruising against my bones. "He refused me again. He left me no choice. All I wanted was his secret. Why could he travel back and forth without aging? Why did you have to? You were slipping away from me; what choice did I have!"

Insanity sparked in him, and my breath grew short. "James," I croaked, "please. Tell me you didn't. You didn't do that. You didn't make that horror."

Jaw tight, he harshly stroked my cheek, hissing, "What choice did I have? Time was taking you away from me."

I stepped back, bumping into Bay, and looked down at him. His wide eyes stared at his father, unblinking, but thin streams trailed down his round cheeks.

"Bay." Hook reached for him, but he lifted off the ground, floating back. Panic erupted in Hook's black eyes, looking at me. "Wendy."

Bay took my hand, squeezing and pulling me back.

"I did this for us, Wendy! So that we could have hope!"

I couldn't move. Only Bay's hand and Skye's dust pulled me back. "We had hope." My throat was raw. I had believed in him so completely. I had ignored all the signs. "Now, it's gone."

~

Years in Skyla passed in a blur. My health declined.

"She can barely stand, Father!" Bay, nearly eighteen, yelled. The pirates laughed. I leaned against a house, feeling Neverland against my skin. It eased some of the pain, but nothing could reach into my heart and cool

248

the torture of seeing Hook with his laughing crew that mocked my son's desperation.

My James was gone entirely. I ached, everywhere.

"Please!" Bay's fists closed, shaking. "There has to be a cure! Surely here. Help me find it!"

Somewhere deep within me, I still hoped. I hoped as the man I still loved refused to meet my eye and refused to help me. I hoped as Bay helped me hobble out of the town, north of the Whispering Meadow, and out of the empire Hook had made in my absence. I hoped until my eyes closed, and everything went black.

22ND NOVEMBER

Ascream caught in my throat. *My* throat. Lyric. Lyric. I was Lyric. My vision blurred on the scene around me, and I scrambled away from the woman in the glass coffin surrounded by flowers. Gasping pants filled my lungs while images still charged through my head.

I couldn't breathe. I could, but I couldn't. With every inhale, magic rushed through my lungs, with every exhale, it freed me some. A cool wind slapped my cheeks, and I shook. Where was I again? How long had I been inside the woman's head?

No. Not *the woman*. I knew her name now. Wendy. Bay's mother. Hook's wife.

I scooted farther away from her glass coffin, flashes of the burnt natives prickling behind my eyes. Black flesh bubbling like charred meat. Gaping faces and melted skin. Bones stacked high before they had been pecked clean. The scent of it all scathed my nose, and I screamed, curling tight into a ball I swore I would never leave.

Claws dug into my shoulders, swiftly eliminating that plan. I threw myself out of their hold and lay sprawled upon the grass, eyes wide, burning with tears. Darkness coiled around me, around the area. It was night. *When had it become night?*

"Easy, child," the siren before me murmured, her sisters stepping out from behind her wings on either side.

"What have you done to me?" *Not me.* I shook my head to clear it of the fog. "Wendy. What have you done to Wendy?"

The youngest siren folded her clawed fingers before her. "We have spared her. Our Bay brought her to us many years ago, and we stopped her time completely to remove her pain. Only the Fountain of Youth can save her now."

The middle siren spoke, "Only you can save her now."

"What?" My throat hurt, like I had personally gulped the cinders from that night when everything changed in Wendy's world forever. "Why didn't Peter help Hook? Why couldn't Peter have just helped him?"

Sorrow laced the women's eyes, and they peered at one another. "My dear, that is in the past. There is nothing that can be done about it now."

"But I can know the truth now. Why didn't my father help Bay's?"

"Peter does nothing without reason. He sees more clearly than anyone we have ever met. He knows the

252

best of people and the worst. Had he been able to help, he would have provided a strong man eternity and power enough to control that eternity. James Hook was raised to be a weapon in a military force."

The youngest's teeth bared. "He lacks discretion and kindness outside of his interests. The lives he sacrificed to meet his end pile high, as you have seen in both past and present now."

"Whether he could have changed in his soul, we do not know and can no longer tell. All we know is that twice he did not, and the Fountain is not a magic that gives more than it takes."

"You said 'had he been able to.' Why wouldn't Peter have been able to?" My fingers felt numb with cold, though the air around me seemed warm enough. I rubbed the stiffness from them and tried to control my swirling thoughts. They remained garbled, lost as Wendy's mind melded with my own.

"You know as well as we how his memory acts. By this point, Neverland has ceased to exist. By that point, he had well forgotten the Fountain."

"We must warn you." The eldest raised her head, her dark curls spilling down her back.

"Any who drink from the Fountain as Peter has will bear both its blessings and its curses. His body and mind continuously restore themselves, leaving only echoes of what he comes to know. He has trained himself to work with the power, forgetting much of his own will, but the echoes..." She closed her eyes, covered her mouth full of fangs.

"The echoes haunt him."

"We sirens are blessed with seeing the future and the past. Our present is a blur and we have no connection to it. Otherwise we would have met you sooner and warned you."

"You see the future?" A chill made gooseflesh rise on my arms. "Couldn't you have found me easily then? Waited for me somewhere?"

"Without a present point to determine an anchor in time, it is very difficult to accomplish such a task and see what has happened versus what will as well as where we stand in it all." Their eyes closed as one, their faces washed in an eerie night glow.

I swallowed, then my heart thudded, Wendy's memories parting long enough for mine to burst through. "Where's Whisper?"

They didn't open their eyes. "We left her with the children when last we saw her."

"She does so love the children." The youngest smiled her horrible smile, and my blood ran cold.

Stumbling to my feet, I swayed. Claws dug into my arm, forcing me to steady.

"Careful, little one. You've been under a spell for days now." The harsh touch turned almost motherly when the woman cupped my cheek. "We don't mean you any harm, and she is safe."

I believed that, but... "I need to see her. I need to save Bay. We need to save Tiger Lily. Wendy. Skyla." My vision blurred, tears stinging my eyes. "Why didn't he tell me the truth? Why didn't Tiger Lily? I've been so in the dark about so many important things. Am I not worth an explanation?" The realization of something hit me, and my mouth went dry. "You said Peter does nothing without reason. Why did he keep me trapped on Skyla when I've always wanted to explore the world? Is it still at war like in Wendy's memories? Has Peter lied to me my whole life?"

"No, child. Breathe. Doubts can consume you here;

do not let them."

Breathing seemed impossible right now.

"The world has been at peace since your birth, but now you are of age, so war is returning." An odd weight settled those words on my chest, making it even harder to breathe.

"Why do you say that like I have anything to do with it?" A cold breeze touched my hair and cheeks.

Her golden eyes softened. "Because, you have everything to do with it. Magic runs through your veins, powerful magic. Magic of the gods. Unwielded, it allowed peace. Now it returns to your hands, so you must use it to wield peace yourself along with your siblings who were given to the other kingdoms. Once this battle with Hook comes to an end, you must seek out your eleven brothers and sisters from the other kingdoms and save the rest of the world alongside them, else you will never have the chance to come to know it." Those chilling eyes gleamed with light. Her sisters laid their hands on her shoulders, and all their eyes took on the same ghastly glow. They looked past me, past the space before them. "We see your mother, a goddess. Ages have gone by. But we see her and you and Peter. The night is young, the victory, too, when she delivered you to him."

"Stop it." I stepped back, but the glass coffin rested behind me, keeping me from wanting to get any closer. "I'm nothing special. Definitely not the child of a goddess. And siblings? I don't have any blood family, surely not eleven brothers and sisters. Who even has that many kids?"

As one, they blinked and returned to the moment. "You have so little belief in yourself, Lyric. Is it so hard to see how you are a part of a much larger story? Does it not bother you that your entire life has been spent looking up to others? Peter, your friend, the pixies."

"What are you talking about? I mean, the pixies are incredible, and Whisper is so strong. And Peter? Peter is Peter. He's defeated monsters, gone everywhere, done everything. He built an entire country then saved it!"

"With your help."

The very idea was ludicrous. "No, I was a baby. I couldn't have done anything."

"We do not mean then."

The wind hushed, sucked from the space in a single breath. *They see the future.* My head shook, unwilling to believe any of it. "Where's Whisper? All I care about is saving my friends and my home."

"And yet you are destined to save the world."

Anger spiked in my chest. "I don't want to hear any more of this! If the world needs saving, Peter and the rest of my so-called family can do it."

The youngest one's lips tipped down. "He is not as infallible as you might think."

My teeth gritted. "Where. Is. Whisper?"

She sighed, extending a long-nailed finger. "Follow the lark. But remember: you are more than you have allowed yourself to believe. You were not unwanted; you were needed elsewhere."

"And we wish you well until we meet again."

Though gently spoken from maws filled with prickling teeth, the words became more foreboding than anything else. I didn't want to think I would meet these sirens again, even if they weren't monstrous creatures. I wondered briefly if they knew the stories Bay told behind their back using their name. It got very little thought in my scrambled mind. Sitting in the gnarled branches of the surrounding trees, a single brown lark hopped away. My legs wobbled as I crossed to the slim opening. It hardly looked like an opening at all, and I had to squeeze my way out of the copse to reach dark woods. Packed close, trees blanketed everything, and a slice of fear trickled down my back.

Though physically feeling better than I had since I'd stepped foot in this cursed place, mentally, I was drained beyond compare. I trudged after the lark, finding Whisper the only thing I allowed to remain on my mind.

I needed her sense, her upbeat attitude; I needed her to tell me that, whatever happened, we were still in this together. I trusted her with my life, and I knew only she could help pull my pieces back together, return me to 'Lyric.'

At this moment, what I needed more than anything was my friend.

Her laughter met my ears first, and I stiffened, remembering the changelings and the games they played until I caught a glimpse of her. She sat in the center of a minute clearing, her arms stretched like a princess. A hundred or more birds perched around her, chirping merrily.

Moonlight and starlight—or even just her own light—illuminated the scene, her smile, her peace in the midst of so much wrong.

When I blinked, tears cascaded down my cheeks, and I didn't think twice before shattering the image completely. Barreling toward her, I careened through the birds, sending them screaming to the trees.

Her wide eyes looked up a second before I threw my arms around her and fell to my knees at her side.

"Lyric!" She laughed. "There you are! I was getting worried, but the sirens said what they had to show you was complicated and unavoidable. What's all this?"

"I love you." I gasped lungfuls of air, but it wasn't enough to quell the panic in my mind or the pictures of destruction still running through my skull. Heartbreak lingered, and I didn't know if it was mine or Wendy's.

"I love you too, Lyly." She ran her fingers over my hair. "Are you okay? I know...a lot happened. And the sirens said what they had to show you wouldn't be easy."

It hadn't been. What they had to tell me wasn't either, but I didn't really believe them. How could I? If I were a demigod or had some awesome magical heritage, wouldn't I know? Have an inkling of an idea? Or was I just that oblivious? And if I had blood family, why hadn't they tried to find me?

"Lyly, are you okay?" she asked when I still hadn't replied.

I squeezed her. "I don't know what to do or think."

"What happened?"

What hadn't happened? Piece by piece in the darkness, I relayed every detail I dared. The love. The betrayal. Peter's involvement in Skyla's birth. The unbelievable knowledge about mine. The apparent future I was meant to protect with siblings I didn't know. Overwhelmed and tired, I slipped into the ending, but it felt more like an unwelcome beginning.

"So..." she began, clasping my hand tight. We lay in the clearing, staring through the gaps in the trees. If I imagined hard enough, we were back home on a night like any other when Peter was somewhere else in the world, and I was in her backyard, watching the stars fall from the sky. "You're supposed to save the world from Hook and the enchantress, and let's face it, anyone else that woman has gathered to her side."

"That's what they told me."

"Well, demigod or not, I think you could save the world. You can fly. Hit a target from a mile away. And not to mention, you've been talking with pixies. Hardly anyone can do that."

"You know three people who can do that."

She pouted, crushing my hand for a moment. "Hush. I'm lucky to know incredible people. I'm just saying whether they are telling you the truth or not, you can do it. And if something like that needs to be done, shouldn't you?"

Her point made moral sense, but not logical. If I tried to do something like that, I was going to get more people killed than saved. "I just want to make sure the people I care about are safe. Then I want to go home. Maybe I'm not cut out for the adventures I've always dreamed about. Peter made them sound so simple, but the truth is...they're hard. You lose people. You see things you wish you hadn't. And the valiant battles between good and evil? They're painful. So painful. And hard." My eyes closed, and I rested my arm across my forehead. "So very hard."

Whisper kept silent for several long moments, then she let a rush of breath fan past her lips. "I guess I hoped you wouldn't ever realize that, Lyly."

"I'm scared." I could only imagine what was happening in the rest of the world. I didn't want to imagine what was happening with Bay. I had seen first-hand how his father could take what seemed like a perfect life and destroy it, abandon those he professed to care most about in their time of desperation. I wanted him to be okay. I needed him to be.

"What happens now?" Whisper asked.

I wanted to go to sleep. Take a long nap and wake up in my room, listening to my weird little family debate over what game they would play next. But I couldn't. My weird little family probably didn't even remember me now.

Through the fear and painful memories, resolve flickered. It was weak, but it existed in me. In Peter's stories, when he crafted a scene where all hope was lost, what did I always ask?

"What happened next?"

And what did he always say?

His dramatic expression flipped on its head in my mind, going from wounded to daring. *"What happened next? Well..."* A gleam shot through his eyes, like it always did. *"I held onto the most important thing I had, and I never gave up."*

The most important thing he had. *Faith. Trust. Belief.*

Maybe things weren't as theatrical and wonderful as he'd made them seem in his stories, but those ideals had been my world for over eighteen years now; they had gotten me through everything so far. With that same childish belief that good would triumph, that efforts would be rewarded, that I would win if I never gave up, we had a chance.

"We're going to save Bay and Tiger Lily if Hook didn't actually free her, which I wouldn't hold my breath about. Then we're going to save Skyla and Wendy." It felt like a lot. It was. But I took a deep breath and swallowed my apprehension, holding how Peter would handle this in my mind because I knew I couldn't do it alone. "To save Bay's mother, we need the Fountain. It's a wealth of power, so maybe we can give it to my siblings to help them save the world, assuming I am a useless demigod, and they exist."

"Why are we assuming you're useless?" I could hear the smile in her voice.

"Because I haven't done anything special my entire life."

"Hardly true." That voice wasn't Whisper's.

I jerked upright, my eyes wide and searching.

Barely visible in the darkness, Skye hovered alone a few feet away, his arms folded and his head raised. "You really think freak wind just happens to follow you around for no reason? You made an entire tornado in front of Hook mere days ago." I stared at him. He lifted a brow. "Please tell me you can still understand me. It would make my life much easier."

Bay was alone. My heart dropped into my toes. *Bay was alone.*

"What are you doing here?" I choked on the words.

He frowned. "Hardly a warm welcome."

"Is Bay okay?" Whisper asked, glancing between us. Sticks and leaves stuck in her curly blond hair when she sat up, but she ignored them.

"He's...in a pirate town with his father, the worst pirate Neverland has ever known, and we've had some really bad ones. So 'okay' needs some specification. He's alive, last I saw."

My gut tightened. "What do you mean 'last you saw?'"

"I'm accounting for travel time. You're a ways north of Pirate Bay, and Hook's blade can be swift and unpredictable."

I covered my mouth, my hands going clammy. "Why did you leave him alone?"

"He said you'd need me more than him right now. I was inclined to agree, and after listening to that conversation, I'd say we were right." His face twisted into something nasty—for a pixie—and he sneered. "I don't care how unspecial you think you are, Lyric.

You smell like magic, so *wake up*. If we're going to save Bay and everything else on your pretty list, we'll need all hands on deck—including, if not specifically, your magic ones." He huffed. "Am I clear?"

Dumbly, I looked down at my hands. "But I—"

"*Am I clear?*"

"No." I stood. "Frankly, nothing has been clear for a while now. You said I smell like magic, so you knew. You knew, so Bay more-than-likely also knew. Yet another thing neither of you told me."

"Like you haven't kept secrets from us."

"Is now really the time to fight?" Whisper remained seated on the ground, watching, but the line between her brows deepened.

"No," Skye sighed, "it's not." Worry tightened his little body when he looked away.

Whisper stood, brushing off her clothes, then she clapped her hands. "Okay. We need to get some sleep. We all seem exhausted, and we won't do much good while exhausted." Her smile didn't quite reach her eyes, and I knew why: neither of us wanted to sleep right now, but we needed to. Everything in Wendy's memories had drained me beyond a point of usefulness. None of us could afford to be sluggish if we had to take on Hook in the morning, or in the next few days, depending on how far away we were from him.

Reluctant as I was to return to the place with Wendy's body, Skye convinced us it was the only safe place in the area, so we slipped back into the cluster of grass and stopped.

The sirens stood in the space as though they hadn't moved since I'd left. Their eyes clung to us when we stepped into the clearing, and eerie smiles curled their lips. "Skye." The youngest's eyes glimmered, and her arms opened.

The pixie zipped to her, hugging her cheek, and she laughed, cupping her hands around him. "I am glad this future is now. I have missed you."

"How is she?" he asked, his voice small and hardly heard at a distance.

"As she has been and will continue to be until the future."

The younger sirens turned with him. He hovered above Wendy's glass coffin, and I remembered in flashes that he had been her friend before Bay's. How desperate would I be if Whisper were in that case, forever frozen? Eyes closed. A tiny, eternal smile pulling her lips into an instant of peace. An instant that didn't end. An instant that was years of torture for me.

It sickened my gut, steeling my resolve to fix it.

"You are welcome to stay here again this night." The eldest siren folded her hands. "We have provided food to last you through the journey ahead." She nodded toward some branches protruding from the wall of trees around us. My bag hung there, innocently, and my hands felt my waist for it. With everything else, I guess I hadn't realized it was missing. "We have a final warning. When you have secured Bay, go directly to Nixie Cove. If you do not, you will not succeed." Her eyes rested on Whisper, unmoving, until she nodded.

Together, they left, and we settled down to what I suspected would be a restless night.

I was right. Staring at the thick branches above, unable to locate even a sliver of sky, I found nothing but convoluted thoughts to consume my mind. Skye had mentioned the tornado of wind back at the bay. That was me?

It couldn't have been.

I'd thought it was the sirens. At the moment, I hadn't paid it much mind at all.

"Lyly." Whisper's voice was soft beneath the chirping sounds of insects. "Are you awake?"

"Yeah."

She turned on her side to face me, curling one arm beneath her head. "Why do you think they said that?"

My brow furrowed. "What?"

"They said when we had Bay, we had to go directly to Nixie Cove. Wouldn't that be our plan anyway?" She swallowed, and even in the dim light, worry pinched her expression. "Do you think..."

I was already shaking my head and gripping the painted feathers on my arm. "No. No. We won't leave anyone behind, especially not Tiger Lily. She's been a mother to us both for too long."

Whisper forced a laugh, but the tension made it come out garbled. "For too long? Try our whole lives."

"Exactly. Way too long." Rolling on my side, I faced her and smiled. Some of the worry marring her face drifted away, and she reached for my hand. Our fingers linked.

"I've always been jealous of you, you know," she murmured.

My brows shot high. "Of me?" She couldn't be talking about my newfound heritage and possible abilities that I could in no way control. What was there to have *always* been jealous about concerning me?

"You can still fly." Her eyes shifted away. "I thought it was unfair; it wasn't just to spare your feelings when I didn't tell you I couldn't anymore. I was ashamed of growing up while you refused to. But you've grown so much since you left Peter and came here. And instead of losing anything, you've gained the ability to talk to pixies. I've wanted that kind of magic ever since I was born." She huffed playfully to lighten the moment, but I knew she had kept this secret so close for a reason. "And now you're a demigod. So that's nice."

I didn't know exactly how to reply. It seemed everyone had kept something important from me. Though maybe this didn't seem as important as being the daughter of a goddess or the son of my father's worst enemy, it was important to her. And I'd never had a clue. "I don't actually know why I can still fly or talk to pixies. I didn't do anything that I can think of."

"Isn't that all the better then? It's annoying when pretty people know it. You're flawlessly brilliant."

Even lying on the grass with twigs sticking out of her hair, she was still the prettiest person I knew. I smirked. "Look at you, a butterfly calling the moth special."

"Do you even *know* how cool moths are compared to mediocre butterflies? You are absolutely a moth in my book." Her hand squeezed mine, and I laughed. A useless fuzzy little moth, that was a good image for me.

"I believe you can learn to fly again." Grinning, I pressed my forehead against hers. "If I'm going to try to learn completely new magic, you can remember what you forgot."

"But that's not how it works. Once you don't believe you can, you're never able to again."

"That's the kind of thinking that will make sure it's impossible," Skye mumbled.

Both our eyes went wide, and Whisper shot up to look at him in his little bed of moss. "How long have you been listening to our very private conversation?"

"Please. Like I'd be able to sleep tonight either."

Whisper looked at me. I scrubbed a hand down my face. "Since the beginning. Without discretion."

"There was discretion. I waited this long to chime in."

Whisper shook her head, smiling. "Well, he says it's impossible, right?"

"Just because it's never happened doesn't mean it's impossible. I'm worried about her mindset, though." Arms linked behind his head, he shot her a glare.

I rolled my eyes. "He says he believes in you, but you have to believe in the pixies."

"Is that all there is to it?" Whisper murmured.

"Oddly,"—Skye peered at me, a brow raised—"yeah. Easier said than done, though."

Whisper flopped back into the grass and pursed her lips. "Okay. If I'm going to try relearning how to fly, you're going to embrace your inner moth. Is that a deal?"

"How does one embrace their 'inner moth' exactly? Should I begin drinking nectar?"

"Please. Most moths don't eat as adults because they don't have mouths." A tiny sigh escaped her lips as her eyes went all dreamy. "Adam taught me that. Goodness, I miss him."

"She's telling me to starve, Skye."

His chiming laughter filled the space, ringing out through the packed treetops. It eased the pain and loss that lingered in the area, and with it and Whisper at my side, I felt as though maybe I could embrace my own magic—if it did really exist. "It's a deal," I said, closing my eyes.

Soon after, we all finally succumbed to sleep.

266

23RD NOVEMBER

I felt stupid. I didn't look stupid, hopefully, but I felt stupid. We had been following Skye through the woods all day. As we walked, I continued to imagine magic running through my veins, overflowing out my fingers, and entering the world at my whim.

Nothing happened. The breeze surrounding me felt as normal as the mucky bog we trekked through felt gross. I scrunched my nose when an unwelcome scent greeted my senses. How had such a beautiful grove dropped into such thick woods before diving into this disgusting place?

Whisper kept her head high, but her lips stayed pursed as she picked her way through the moist land. Her eyes shifted to every shadow, every vine, as though she were waiting for something to grab her.

I couldn't blame her. I was just as suspicious, and my hand kept checking my empty sheath for a weapon. It dawned on me a little late that we didn't have one.

When she gasped, I whirled, hand on my empty sheath. "What is it?"

"A moth!" Her wide eyes were pinned on a furry green creature resting on the dark brown wood of a tree. Its wings opened and closed, displaying magnificent red eyespots.

My stomach twisted. The thing was the size of my hand.

"Do you know what kind it is?" I asked, hoping too much disgust hadn't made its way into my tone.

"It's a nosferatu. Don't get too close." Skye landed on my shoulder and held onto my hair to stabilize himself.

"Nosferatu? What?" I glanced at him.

"It drinks blood." His face contorted, though he looked less unsettled by that fact than I was.

I didn't hold any disgust back this time. "Hold on, Whisper. Don't get close to that thing. Apparently, it's one that eats people."

Horror transformed her entire face, and she reeled back, mouth agape. "*You're kidding.* Neverland has ruined *moths*?"

"I didn't say it ate people. It's just uncomfortable, and unpleasant," Skye protested.

"Yep. Come on. Let's get out of here." I ignored Skye's waning look. Something about the moth was creeping me out. "How much longer until we can walk without worrying about stepping ankle-deep in a puddle?"

"Depends on how fast you walk," Skye snipped, fluttering off my shoulder.

I watched him until he spun around and shot us both an "are you coming or not" look.

Picking up the pace again, I tiptoed through the myre, Whisper at my side. An ungodly amount of mud clung to my boots, and every step suctioned me to the ground.

"I hate this." Whisper glared at the ground, slopping along. "Remind me not to build a summer house here."

"If you need me to remind you about that, I don't know whose memory I need to worry about more, yours or Peter's." Neither of us smiled. My stomach ached, but the silent consensus was that we weren't going to eat until we could breathe without gagging. Whatever was rotting around here, the air bore the tale of it with a vengeance.

Something cracked behind us, and I twisted to see what sorry animal lived here. My heart stopped when I peered into distant giant eyes. Clinging between two sparse trees a stone's throw away, was a mammoth green moth. Its proboscis lowered into the mud like a giant straw into dung.

"What is it?" Whisper turned, freezing beside me. "Nope. Nope, nope, nope."

"Skye," my voice wavered, but he flitted right to my side.

"Okay, so that could probably eat a person." He twirled, narrowing his eyes. "You're bait, Lyric. Whisper's with me."

"What?" I squeaked.

He drenched my limbs in dust the second the moth twice my size peered up at us. Its proboscis inched out of the mud, curling slowly. "And fly!"

The creature lunged. Whisper shrieked, running after Skye when he tugged on her shirt. I barely escaped one long, furry leg as I zipped into the air.

"Lyly!" Whisper's voice carried, pitching with terror.

"What are you doing?"

"Keep going!" I yelled, my heart thundering and my blood boiling in my ears. "I'll catch up!" No sooner had I said that than one of the moth's legs thrashed into my side, slapping me across the bog and into the mud. Thankfully, the soft ground pillowed my fall, but the grime covering me made my skin crawl.

The moth scuttled through the weeping trees, and I scrambled out of the way, launching myself into the air. The flurry of weightlessness didn't take hold, and I plummeted back into a splatter of mud.

What?

The creature's wings hummed. I dodged behind a tree when it jumped. Furry legs crunched wood, and all I could do now was run. Dodging through the densest parts of the swampland I could find, I managed to stay out of its grasp. Its wings caught on branches, fraying the edges and leaving glimmers of scales in our wake.

What now? What now? What now? echoed in my head to the beat of an erratic drum—possibly my heart. The mud had washed my dust away. I couldn't fly, and every step was like running through sap.

No weapon. No dust.

Every inhale smelled like rotten eggs, and every exhale sawed out of my chest like I'd held it captive for too long. Somehow in all of Whisper's rambles about moths, she had neglected to provide any information about surviving an attack.

My foot caught on a root, and I slammed into broken branches and twigs. Rocks bit into my skin, drawing blood. The moth crushed its weight over my back. Turning my head, I witnessed the slow descent of its proboscis.

Screams caught in my throat. All air ripped from my

lungs when it laid itself over me. Its furry body leeched damp heat through my muddy clothes. It writhed, settling in for its meal.

Two lives flashed before my eyes: Wendy's and my own. Both tragedies if it ended like this. Mud pressed against my mouth as I sank into the wet earth.

Grappling for anything I could use as a weapon, my fingers locked around a stone. Blindly, I smashed the blunt object behind me, gasping when it connected with flesh and some weight lifted. I rolled, coming face to face with the monstrosity.

Pouring every ounce of strength I had left into the action, I slammed the rock against the moth's eye. The membrane burst, and its wings pounded, sending it backward. The creature didn't make a sound past its humming wings as it flailed, and I didn't wait for it to gather itself.

Drawing myself out of the mud, I turned and ran.

The ground beneath my feet hardened until the slapping of boots against mud gradually changed into the thunder of boots against solid ground. I panted, looking over my shoulder through the darkness every few seconds as though the beast would be back, blood oozing from its face, and hungry for revenge. The bright green never appeared in the drab woods.

"Whisper!" I cried. "Skye!" Silence responded. *Was I going the right way?* Before I could decide what to do if I couldn't find them, Skye's form glittered through the trees.

His eyes widened. "What in the name of the airwoman did you do? Have a wrestling match?"

"I won, thank you." I grimaced, wiping my face. Caked mud covered every inch of my skin, and I didn't want to think what the gritty taste in my mouth was.

Whisper broke from the foliage and fell forward, bracing herself against her knees. When she finally caught her breath, she looked up at me, and her mouth gaped. "Oh, Lyric! Are you okay?"

I was itchy, uncomfortable, and the horrid smell encompassed me like a wet rag. Forcing down bile, I nodded. "I lived."

"Did you use your powers?" Skye asked.

"No, as a matter of fact, they didn't even cross my mind." Flicking mud off my bag, I frowned and hoped the worst was on the outside, and our food was unscathed. I stopped, looking at Skye. "Is that why you left me like that? You wanted me to use powers I have no idea how to control?" My voice rose. "I could have died!"

He held up his hands, blue eyes wide. "It was an afterthought, I promise."

Huffing, I glared, then looked away. "Fine. Sorry."

"Did its legs touch you?" Whisper lifted my pinky between two fingers to raise my arm. "Normal moths have hair on their legs that can irritate the skin. I can only imagine what that..." Her lips pursed. "Never mind. I don't have to imagine."

I followed her gaze to my side where my shirt had been shredded straight through my vest. Mud and red coated my skin, and purple darkened whatever I could see. I shivered.

"That needs to be cleaned, and we need to rest if we're going to have any chance of rescuing Bay." Skye winced, staring off in the distance. My thoughts wandered to the same place. We couldn't afford any setbacks. Bay needed us. Skye shook his head, nodding off-course. "There's a native settlement in that direction. It's tiny compared to the others, but it will have a water source and a change of clothes."

The thought of a bath was almost too much, but my head shook. "I'll be fine for a day; we can eat and rest up ahead."

"No, we won't."

"What's he saying?" Whisper folded her arms. "If he thinks that we're going to continue without cleaning that—"

"He's thinking just the opposite. But Bay—"

Whisper set her hands on her hips and stared down her nose at me. "Bay can and will handle himself for the extra hour or so it takes to make sure you aren't going to get an infection or some magical Neverland disease."

Skye nodded, though I could see the reluctance on his face. "Bay told me specifically to make sure you would be okay." When his gaze shifted away, my heart thudded.

"He told you to take us back to Skyla, didn't he?" With all that happened during the encounter with Hook, I hadn't seen it, but thinking back, it was so clear. Bay had said goodbye. "Didn't he?" I repeated, sterner.

"None of us would have been happy with that." The statement held no bitterness, no ire. We both knew it was true. Skye hadn't guided us to this point against our will. I'd mentioned saving Bay before he'd even said a word; it had never been—even for a second—an option to overlook.

"Okay." I hoped to heaven Bay hadn't given up and taunted Hook into doing something irreversible. "Clean up. Get back on track. When will we make it there?" My side stung, but I gritted my teeth against the pain. By now, I was used to Neverland's attacks.

"Tomorrow afternoon. No later, if nothing else goes wrong."

Nodding, I turned to Whisper. "Tomorrow afternoon."

She peered up at the sky and squinted. The cheerful blue mocked what had just happened, the near-death I'd just experienced, and a breath fanned past her lips. "Okay, let's get going."

24TH NOVEMBER

We had planned our rescue mission from outskirts of the woods until sunset had poured over the bay, painting it in shades of blood and orange. Beneath the bandages Whisper had wrapped around my waist, the cuts burned, making me disinclined to move, but on the surface, I appeared ready to fight.

Worn and long-forgotten clothes from one of Hook's other victims caressed my skin, providing me with even more reasons to battle with everything I had. His reign had tormented too many for too long, and it was time to end it.

"The whole town will be looking for you two," Skye murmured near my ear. He hadn't left my shoulder since we'd broken from the trees and seen the bay at a distance. "We'll have to keep to the shadows and ease our way to Hook's castle. I really don't know how we're going to pull this off."

I looked at him when he scrubbed a hand down his face. I'd never known any of the pixies to be quite as expressive as him. Tinkerbell was flighty, vain, and the tiniest bit motherly when she felt like it. The ancient, magical creatures seemed more like glorified children than anything else. No childishness crossed Skye's eyes, only worry, pain, and fear.

"Maybe I can remember how to fly?" Whisper asked, determination lighting a fire in her gaze. "If I can fly, we'll have a better chance."

Skye wordlessly lifted off my shoulder and flew several circles around her head. Dust settled in her hair, glimmering against the blond locks. She took a breath, closed her eyes, and...nothing.

"There's a good chance we'll be able to find a sword along the way." Skye returned to the matter at hand without missing a beat. "Drunk pirates tend to lose those things right before they lose their heads."

Whisper's face fell, and she turned inward. Her small voice stung almost as bad as my cut. "What's he saying?"

"You're relying on the wrong thing." I took her hand, feeling some of Skye's dust had touched my hair and neck. It wasn't much, but it would be just enough for a second. "You can't do it if you just rely on yourself. You have to believe in it, let it carry you." My feet left the ground; hers remained planted firmly in place.

"I hardly know him. How am I supposed to do that?" Her fingers nearly slipped out of mine, so I held tighter. "I've seen you go too high and fall before, Lyly. What if—"

"I may have fallen before, but I've never hit the ground. No matter what, even though they are so *pissed* with me, a pixie always catches me." I shrugged a shoulder. "They're pixies, Whisper. They love children and games and laughing. They don't like to see pain or fear."

"We're darling incarnate." Skye's wry smile caught my eye, and I sighed.

"If you don't believe in him, believe in me."

Her gaze dropped to our hands, then she let out a deep breath. Tension tightened the lines between her brows, and I wanted to tell her she was concentrating too hard. Flight was effortless; it had to be, but she was trying so hard, and I didn't want to interrupt.

Ripping her hand out of mine, she shook her head. "I'm sorry. I can't." She didn't meet my gaze as she turned her back on me. Her shoulders, always pulled back, caved in on herself. "I just can't."

My feet returned to the ground, and I bit my cheek, my heart sinking. "It's okay," I said, but it didn't feel okay. "We'll get through this, and, hey, Bay's been flying a lot longer than I have. Maybe he can help."

Without a word, she nodded, and we turned to face the endless sea.

"Let me go!" I spat, my heart stampeding. We hadn't even made it into the town before pirates surrounded us. Skye hid in my bag, so they hadn't seen him yet, but that didn't change the fact that a tiny pixie could do very little to help us.

The man holding Whisper yelped when her heel swung back into his shin, but the victory ended in her scream as he caught her by the hair and tugged her head down. "Sit still, you little bitch," he hissed.

"Where are you taking us?" She gritted her teeth

against the pain, fury clear on her face even in the darkness. Torches flickering in the lanes did very little to illuminate the roads as they took us through one alley after another.

I could hardly count them. There may have been ten men, twenty? We hadn't stood a chance.

"Cap'n Hook is busy. His order of magic came in, so where should we take 'em until he gets back?"

The man holding me shrugged, his hold never loosening even with the action. "Might as well throw them in with the other brat. I doubt they'll be able to get up to much trouble, all things considered."

The laughter that followed made me pale. *What had they done to Bay?*

Glancing at Whisper's face in the dimness, I saw she had a very different thought. Her wide eyes glassed like tears were about to fall, and her lips parted, mouthing a single word to no one in particular. *Mom.*

I didn't want to know, but I would very soon. My stomach lurched with every step that brought us down winding stairs into the maws of a dungeon. It smelled no better than the bogs we'd only just escaped the night before, but the hints of iron cutting through the musk were what terrified me more than anything else.

The creak of an old metal door broke my thoughts, then pain erupted on my side, splitting my scars anew as a pirate threw me into the cage. Warm blood gushed, and I curled in on myself while Whisper crashed in beside me. She didn't allow pain a second to hold her as she scrambled back to her feet and hissed at the men, teeth bared and feral.

The gate closed, their sneers and laughter drifting away. Whisper whirled to my side once the noise had faded out of earshot. "Lyly," her hands hovered near me, "can you breathe?"

Every inhale was a shot to the gut. It felt as though my flesh had been ripped open, torn further than before like cloth. Lip quivering against my will, I nodded. She clasped my outstretched hand, squeezing it to help me balance the pain, then her head whipped in all directions, searching for her mom in the shadows. With every second, her expression dropped deeper into hopelessness.

"Skye," I choked, trying to move my body in a way that would allow my bag more mobility. I thanked the airwoman I hadn't landed on it, but surely he'd been jostled inside. Whisper helped me open the flap, and the little pixie zipped out, paying us no mind at all.

"Bay." The soft word made my heart skip a beat. I followed Skye's trail to a crumpled figure in the corner and crushed Whisper's hand. In the bare light from a single torch outside the cell, I could see swollen flesh and battered, purple skin. One eye was swollen shut; the other hadn't opened, despite all the noise the pirates had made when they'd thrown us in here.

For a second, I thought he was dead; we were too late. All the pain in my gut vanished. I pulled myself up, desperate to reach him and discover the truth.

"Lyly!" Whisper tried to stabilize me, but I broke from her hands and made it to Bay's side. Things were so much worse up close. My breath entered and left me in erratic gasps as I scanned his torn skin and clothes. Blood painted his open shirt, and the massacre continued down his chest. Dozens of thin lashes bloomed with beads of red like he'd been whipped just minutes ago.

Tears sprung to my eyes. "Bay..." Shaking, my hand reached for him, but my gaze dropped when his chest stuttered with an inhale.

"Is he..." Whisper didn't finish the question.

"He's alive," I choked on the words, closing my eyes and trapping the tears waiting to fall. "He's alive."

"What have they done to him..." Skye's fists clenched as he landed on Bay's shoulder and examined his swollen eye. One of his lips was split, and a stray hair was caught in the blood. Gently, I pushed it back over his ear and stopped when gold gleamed in the firelight.

An earring, like those so many of the pirates had, protruded from his lobe. The metal was stained with dried blood, rust, and grime. How could they? *How dare they?* Wind rushed down the line of cells, swirling the fire and feeding it into a blaze. My hands shook. My side stung.

Dust fled the wind, the all-consuming air, but rocks fled it too. It only stopped when Whisper squeaked. "Careful!"

The wind died, and I looked at her. She sat curled behind me, covering her face, and a rock skidded to a stop behind her. When she met my gaze, a laugh bubbled out of her.

"I didn't mean to," I stammered, dropping my attention to my hands. "I..."

"You can't control it, but dang if you don't have it, Lyly!" She attempted to tame her hair, but our journey plus the wind just now made such a thing no less than impossible. I didn't even want to know what my hair looked like. "We may just have a chance."

I looked back at Bay. "Not if he doesn't wake up. Not if he can't walk."

"He'll be fine," Skye said, planting himself on Bay's shoulder. "He's come out of worse."

I looked him over, from every cut to every oozing

wound, and the thought of that made me sick. The sickness tightened in my stomach, pulling on my own superficial injuries, so I set a hand against them and adjusted myself near his side. As carefully as I could manage, I removed the earring marking him as a pirate and thrust it away.

There was no hope of my falling asleep in this dungeon with the smell of blood so thick in the air. I tried desperately to pull a clean breeze into the room, but no matter how hard I tried, nothing happened. A great help powers were when you had no control over them...

We had decided to wait until Bay woke up, getting some rest ourselves in the meantime before we attempted escape, but only Whisper and Skye seemed to have managed in the "rest" department. I couldn't stop blaming myself. If only he hadn't sacrificed himself for us. If only he hadn't taken me to Pirate Bay at all. If only he'd open his eyes.

I traced his jaw with my fingers, focusing on a dark bruise. What father could do this to their child? What person could do this to anyone? I had seen Hook in love. I had seen him in pain, anguish even. How could he find it in himself, knowing that pain, to bring anything like it upon others? Upon his own flesh and blood?

My soul ached for Wendy.

Bay's face twitched, his brow deepening, and my heart rate picked up. His groan barely made a sound as he shifted his weight. Just as soft, a stream of curses befitting his heritage tumbled past his lips in a fluidly skillful manner that made me blush. Unsure what to do, I waited for him to crack open his good eye. When he did, he saw me. I waited for him to respond, yell, say everything he'd gone through meant nothing now that I was here, but he barely acknowledged my presence, simply mumbling, "Great."

"I'm sorry?" I meant the apology; I hadn't intended for it to come out as a question.

"Still dreaming," he grumbled, "which means this pain is a hell of a lot worse than it already feels."

I wasn't sure how to reply to that. I was flattered he thought I looked like a vision from his dreams—because I knew that a scullery-maid-who-had-been-working-in-a-coal-mine was a more appropriate description.

"Can't you give me a break?" He coughed, and his whole being winced with regret at the action. Despite that, he continued, "I'd expected nightmares, or my mother, to haunt me, but you won't leave me alone." He narrowed his good eye at me in accusation. "Is this how bad it's gonna be missing you, Wind Song?" He lifted his arm, cupping my cheek, and my breath held completely. So completely that the wind in the whole room stilled. Even the fire didn't so much as flicker. "We've only known each other for a few weeks. You'd think I'd be able to let this shit go."

"I know I wouldn't be able to," I whispered.

He smiled, his thumb running over my cheek. "If I had half a mind right now, I'd tell you I loved you, but I can barely feel half my body."

My eyes widened, and my lips parted. No words escaped them. In my chest, my heart erupted, pounding in my ears, and I knew hot red covered my cheeks.

Bay's smirk widened as if he'd noticed. "Maybe I won't wake up from this one. If I can stay here with you, I think I'd like to."

Stay here with me. In pain, in a dingy cell. And yet it was worth it because I was with him? I shook my head. He was delirious, beaten within an inch of his life. And I was tired—clearly. There were a hundred more important things to dwell on right now. "Bay,"—I sterned my voice, hoping I'd tossed away the enchantment he had over me—"this isn't a dream. We have to get out of here. Right now, Hook is gone. We need to leave before he comes back." My eyes dropped to his chest, and I pulled them away before they could linger. "Do you think you can walk?"

He blinked dumbly, his smile fading, and I thought surely now he'd yell if he had the energy to do so. He tapped my cheek twice, dropped his hand, and looked away. "Are you serious?"

"Yes?" I gnawed my cheek.

"So, I lived. That's always a nice surprise." He looked himself over, disgust curling his split lip. "Okay, that's less nice. But living. Love when I live."

"Are you...okay?" I don't know why I asked. Physically, definitely not. Mentally, he'd just said he'd loved me, so also no.

"Just fine. Where's Skye? I can't walk. Might have a broken rib, but I'll be damned if I can't fly. Literally. We're damned if I can't fly." Though said in Bay's usual lighthearted manner, the weight of those words settled in my gut. As if aware, he glanced at me, the brow above his swollen eye jumping. "Don't look so worried, Wind Song. I've never not been able to fly."

There were a million things to worry about right now. Even if he could walk, we were still in a cell. Who knew how many pirates were waiting at the mouth of this dungeon to catch us if we managed to get that far. No sign of Tiger Lily either. Maybe before everything had happened, Hook kept his word and released her?

I could only hope.

Whisper shifted, squinting, then she gasped. "He's awake. Thank the airwoman." Easing into an upright position, she stretched, her back popping audibly. "Ugh. I don't want a summer home here either."

Skye stirred shortly after Whisper, blinking drearily as he floated off the ground. Sleep left him the second he saw Bay, and he darted in to hug his cheek.

Bay hissed as the tiny body collided with his bruises, but he didn't complain. "I thought I said, very clearly, 'make sure they make it back home'?"

"What good does being on Skyla do if the world is ending?" Skye grumbled.

"We weren't going to leave you." I held his gaze. "That would never have been an option." *And*, I wanted to add, *you could have told me the truth. I would have helped you.* But I left those words unsaid.

"So," Whisper broke the moment, "how do we get out of here? And find my mom? And get to Nixie Cove?"

"One thing at a time," Bay started. His mouth closed halfway through what he was saying, and I raised a brow. His attention fell to the ground, as though he were searching for something, then he looked into the cell next to ours. "Well, one less thing at a time. Your mom is probably searching for you in Neverland by now. We'll have to find her once we get out of here."

Whisper sighed with relief, her eyes sparkling. "Thank you, Bay." She looked him over. "For everything you did to make sure she was freed."

He stiffened. "Don't thank me. I haven't done anything for you. Really."

Most people may have been hurt by such words, but Whisper only smirked, sending me a wink. "Well, then."

"How are we going to get out of here?" I asked, pushing aside my friend's comments. We weren't in any position to be distracted by red faces and pounding hearts.

"Easy. I'll smash the lock with the rock that nearly smashed me, then when we get up the stairs, you can blow everyone out of the way. We'll make a mad dash, get to the cove, save the world, and go home in time for my moth prince and me to have a charming honeymoon."

Bay glanced between us. "I guess you know about your magic stuff now?"

"There is no magic stuff," I frowned. *So he had known. And no one thought to tell me.* "If there is, I can't do anything with it, so there isn't."

"You knew she was a demigod?" Whisper's eyes widened.

Shock twisted Bay's already mangled face. "A demigod? What? No. I figured she had magical heritage, probably a sylph."

"Surprise! It was a goddess." Whisper giggled. "Maybe the airwoman herself. I'm going to start saying, 'Oh, my Lyric' from now on."

"Please don't." I pulled my legs against my chest and held a hand at my wounds. "We need a better plan. We can't rely on me."

Bay stretched his left arm, and I noticed he hadn't moved his right one since he'd woken up. "In that case, we may just have to pull a Peter."

"What's that mean?" I asked.

Silently, Skye pinned his arms at his sides, and twirled into the air, imitating Peter's crow. He smirked at Bay, then all three of us ended up heavily dusted. Bay floated to his feet, not quite landing on them.

"When we get the signal, we have to move. The second we're in the air, they won't be able to get us."

"One problem." Whisper raised one hand and bit her lip.

"Right." Bay pointed at her. "Right. Okay..."

"Could we pull a moth?" Skye grinned at me.

My nose scrunched when Bay quirked a brow in my direction. "A moth?"

"We'd be the diversion, so Whisper can get away under their noses." I rubbed my side and sighed. "It went passably well last time."

"Diversions, we can do, right, Skye?"

"I'll rally the forces. Give me an hour." He fluttered toward the iron bars, then turned and pointed at me. "Don't lose your dust this time. And, Bay, save yours."

Obediently, Bay settled back against the wall and raised his good hand. "Fine, fine. As for you." His expression darkened. "Don't get caught."

Waiting was torture. Sitting cross-legged, I watched my knee bounce. Bay relaxed against the back wall, his skin shimmering with dust and bruises. How much pain was he in? He seemed so at peace in the face of so much danger. "How often does this happen?" I asked.

"What do you mean?" He didn't open his eyes.

"She means you're sitting there like it's an average day in Neverland." Whisper glanced down the quiet dungeon hall. "Which isn't actually hard to believe."

"I don't feel well enough to panic." His chest moved slowly, each breath a tedious effort.

"What if Hook gets back before Skye can make it?" Whisper turned toward the stairs that led out of this place. "What if Skye didn't make it at all?"

"Then we're doomed." Bay didn't bother with sugar-coating, though he didn't appear ruffled by the notion.

I frowned. "He'll make it. We only have to worry about whether or not we will."

"I'm certain I can break the lock. This place doesn't look like it's been used for years. It's practically falling

286

apart on its own." Her nose wrinkled. "Not that I'm complaining."

She was right. The whole place was old, musty, and vacant. Perhaps the last part was the only real indication it hadn't been used in a while. Old and musty were nearly requirements for a dungeon, but empty was not.

"No Lost Boys and no natives. In a lawless land, who are the only people worth throwing in jail?"

Looking at Bay, I knew the answer. *People you wanted to make pay*, To *torture*.

Bay took a deeper breath, letting it out slowly. "Anyway, they're all gone now."

What would Neverland have looked like now had the pirates not taken over completely? Would the terrain still be as treacherous? Or would the people living here have known how to navigate it in a way that tamed the wonderland to their will?

Shouts sounded above, feet stampeding. Bay smirked, lifting off the ground. His hazel eyes opened, and they sparked with determination. Distantly, crows sounded, overlapping. They repeated, louder.

"At the ready, men," Bay said, not unlike Peter would have. The mix of nostalgia and his infectious spirit made my racing heart believe we had a chance.

I nodded at Whisper, and she lifted the rock. The lock trapping us here came undone with her second hit, and she tossed the screeching door open. Grinning, she dropped the rock, but before it could hit the ground, Bay snatched it with his left hand and tossed it up, gliding through the air on his back. "Waste not, want not."

Adrenaline pounded through my veins as I floated. "What exactly is Skye doing up there?" It sounded like an army had come to our defense.

"He called in a couple favors from a couple friends. We should really get moving." Bay wore his pain well as he slipped out of the cage, but something about the form of his flight wasn't right. Instead of his body moving with the air, he skimmed through it, rigid. To watch it felt wrong.

The sooner this was behind us, the better.

Snatching my own rock off the ground, I nodded at Whisper. "Make sure the way is clear and keep to the shadows."

"If you need help, we have your back," Bay added.

Her gaze clung to our elevated feet for a brief moment, then she smiled; it didn't reach her eyes. "Got it."

We began our ascent. The noises got louder. Yells and chiming laughter mixed with familiar crows as we flew out of the dungeon into a mad fog of pixies and pirates.

"Well," Bay said, diving into the air above the pirates and dropping his rock on one of their heads, "this will do nicely." He plucked a floating sword out of some pixies' hands, examined the blade, then looked at me. "Want one?"

The mindless scramble around me, the endless noise, the pain in my side, and yet I laughed. "A dagger if you can," I replied, slipping to the side when a pirate lunged for me.

"You heard the lady." He motioned extravagantly toward the pixies, several of them giggling and saluting before rushing off. His bruised face didn't look any less handsome from this angle, or maybe it was his spirit I found myself attracted to. Whatever it was, my mind wandered during the fray to his earlier words. *If I had half a mind right now, I'd tell you I loved you.* Only Whisper had ever told me she loved me before. It was a statement unbefitting of Peter, though I liked to think he showed it sometimes, and Tiger Lily said a good number of things with her eyes instead of her mouth.

I dodged out of the way of someone's blade, glancing behind me to see if Whisper had made it out. She was nowhere to be seen, so I had to hope she was well on her way.

We'd make sure we got the best of these scallywags, then we'd meet up, and the adventure would continue. In the rush, I almost forgot all the bad things. Following Bay's lead, I twirled and dove and danced. The pixies snagged me a dagger, and it joined the ballet of singing metal.

"You appear in your element." Bay sidled up beside me, deflecting a jab.

I glanced at him, and the thrill of everything dimmed. Sweat drenched his brow, and his blood-matted hair stuck to his face. With every attack, vibrations ran through his broken body, accentuating every shred of pain.

"I think it's time for both of us to immerse ourselves in the elements." I motioned with my eyes to the cloudy sky. He caught what I meant and tucked his sword in his belt before snatching my arm and pulling me out of reach. Daggers came flying, but when I saw them and gasped, a strong wind plowed them off track.

When we were high enough that fog consumed us, Bay released me, stuck his fingers in his mouth, and unleashed a shrill whistle. Shortly after, Skye popped into our cloud, arms folded and frowning. "I am not a dog," he stated before providing Bay a fresh coat of dust. During the battle, the pixies had each taken their turn showering us, so I wondered why Skye felt the need to reinforce what was already so thick on Bay's skin. The instinct to leave a scent felt very dog-like, and my lips fought against the smile the thought brought on. Skye's brow furrowed when his attention fell on my goofy face. "I've got eyes on Whisper, and she hasn't been followed, but she is stumbling through a Neverland forest at night, so we don't have time to waste."

Keeping high in the cover of fog, we darted for the forest, dropping in where a tree's branches met us in the sky. I peered through the shadows, hovering above the leaves and sticks until a mass of curly foliage shifted behind a bush. My nerves settled instantly.

"You made it," I breathed. "We all made it."

She jumped, turned, then peered above the bush at us, sighing at last. A small smile curved her lips. "Well, what took you both so long? I've been waiting here for *hours.*"

"We were having too good a time." My eyes rolled. "And it was ten minutes at most."

Bay set a hand against my shoulder. "While your reunion is adorable, we actually need to keep moving. Hook's away getting the supplies he needs to invade Skyla, which means every pirate down there knows they are dead if he comes home to find us gone."

"Right. You already freed his bait. I don't want to be anywhere near him when he finds out you escaped too." Whisper looked behind her and stilled. I followed her gaze to find flickering lights blinking on past the boundaries of the trees. Torches. The search parties were already on the move.

"They're expert trackers, have to be to survive here." Bay's eyes narrowed. "Skye, you go with Wind Song and Whisper. I'll loop back after creating a couple false trails."

Skye's wings ruffled, but I spoke up first. "We're not

splitting up. You can't even move your right arm right now. We'll have a better chance if we're together."

He threw a look through the trees at the approaching lights. "I'd argue, but we don't have time for that." Running his gaze over the ground, he nodded at a broken log. "How good is Whispering Meadow's balance?"

"This is the dumbest smart thing I have ever done." Whisper stared at the glowing log beneath her feet and clung to my arm while I flew beside her, guiding her after Bay and Skye. The log floated just above the ground, barely high enough to keep her from touching it and leaving a trail. "I kind of wish I didn't have to do it for hours, though."

"*She's* complaining?" Skye spun around her feet, dashed over my head, then returned to collapse on Bay's shoulder.

"We're almost there." Bay's voice was deep with the same exhaustion that I felt in my bones, and I hadn't been beaten nearly to death. "The Nixies guard their home, and they are terrifying creatures. We'll be safe within the bounds of the cove."

"Sorry. Are they terrifying or not?" Whisper's brow jumped, and her lips pursed as I moved her around a tree, ducking us beneath low-hanging branches.

"Same kind of terrifying as the sirens."

"Speaking of the sirens." Whisper's voice took on an air that made it clear if she could have, she would have folded her arms. "They saved our lives, gave us vital information and food, and have kept your mother safe for years. Why in the world were you running from them?"

Bay didn't reply immediately, and when he did, his answer was less than ideal. "Because they're nosy." Pausing, he turned with a frown. "*Speaking of,* what vital information are you talking about?"

"Oh, I don't know. Lyric's a demigod and the entire story of what happened between Hook and your mother." Whisper shifted, and I grappled for her, wondering if, at this point, the flying log method was really necessary.

Bay stared at us aghast. "They showed you that?"

"Well, they showed Lyric. I got the lovely abridged version."

"*Why* would they need to show you that?" He continued flying backwards before we caught up to him completely.

Truthfully, I didn't know exactly. Aside from fulfilling my curiosity, why had they thought I'd need to know what happened in a past they'd told me I couldn't change? "Sorry," I found myself saying, "I didn't really have a choice in the matter, but I didn't mean to invade your privacy or personal life."

"She told me you were an adorable kid. Where did all the pudge in your cheeks go?" Whisper's teasing had lost its filter, and I had half a mind to drop her on her ass when my cheeks flared red.

Skye scoffed. "Please, Bay's cuter now than he was as a brat, wouldn't you agree?" The pixie's smug little expression met my eye, and I was only spared by the fact Bay whirled around, mumbling reprimands.

Minutes passed, and the forest changed—entirely. I didn't even know when it happened. One moment, faded browns and greens surrounded us, then the next, blue and silver washed over trees heavy with blooms instead of leaves. Ponds, clear and sparkling, dabbled water pockets throughout the sparse trees.

I glanced over my shoulder, but it was too late. We were in the center of it.

And before us, a golden temple shot into the sky, the

relic pulsing with magic. Shivers cut down my spine as I watched a hundred eyes snap open in the ponds. Yellow, blue, and glowing, they watched us from within scaly faces.

One of the creatures rose out of the water, her arms opened wide. "Welcome." Her voice shimmered. "We have been waiting for you."

GODDESS

OF AIR

25TH NOVEMBER

Sunlight touched my cheeks, waking me from my bed of moss. I blinked, unable to remember when I'd fallen asleep. Last night was fuzzy. I recalled reaching the Nixies and greeting their leader before they led us to the pile of moss I now rested on. An eerie song filled the air.

I felt as rested as I had when I'd woken in the sirens' garden, and I lifted my arm to find the bandages, and my wounds were gone. Whatever laced the air around creatures like the Nixies and the sirens had healed me again, fortunately. I would need my strength, and so would Bay.

Sitting up, I peered around. The glimmering pools of water remained where they had been, every weeping tree's branches skimming the reflective surfaces in a light breeze. Calm as it seemed, something ominous lurked. My heart thumped.

Bay and Whisper. They weren't in sight.

"Worry not." A voice rose from one puddle orifice, and a Nixie followed, the same from the night before, I think. But it was difficult to tell. They all looked so similar with large, regal foreheads, scaly green and blue skin, and glowing eyes. "Your friends have gone on ahead."

Ahead? Ahead where?

Nerves bundled in my stomach as I glanced at the golden temple. In the sunlight, it looked even more imposing. At night, gleaming with silver and swallowed by darkness, it hadn't appeared quite as large. Now, just looking at it directly was blinding.

"Why didn't they wait for me?" I asked, throat tight.

"It would not have mattered. They must face their nightmares alone for now, though only you must succeed alone."

"Wow. Thanks," Skye droned, and I jumped, finding him hovering beside the Nixie, arms folded. She looked at him, meeting his nasty frown. "Am I or am I not going with her?"

The Nixie's lips pursed, and some spattering of knowledge flashed through her eyes before she smiled. It was a moist, dreadful thing. "Yes, well. You will see what I mean."

He flinched, flitting to my side and standing on my shoulder. "I'm not sure we want to..."

Her laughter was like a bubbling brook, soft and cheerful, but a film closed over her eyes when she blinked, and a chill shot down my spine. "I agree with Skye."

"You have done this before." She tilted her head, and

her wet hair slapped against her cheek like seaweed. "These temples were erected by the first natives with a magic more powerful than what this world or yours remember. The souls of any who have stepped foot within linger in fractals, ready to test the next guest. You will face your own mind in a quest each of you must overcome if you are to make it out alive with the answers you seek."

"It relies on all of us?" Air stuck in my chest.

"Yes," she said, "but mostly you, Lyric."

"No pressure," Skye mumbled.

I was feeling all the pressure. I was a demigod who didn't know how to use my powers, tasked with saving my home and then the world. And I was staring at a quest that my friends had already started and could perish from unless I somehow passed.

Why couldn't they have waited? We could have talked about this more, maybe found a way around taking more chances with our lives. I shook my head. No, I had to stay strong. The Nixies had protected us through the night and healed me. The woman before me, though unsettling in appearance, didn't appear unsettled by the fact that Hook and whoever else the Enchantress had gathered to her side would have fewer people to stand in their way if we failed. If I trusted these powerful creatures and they trusted me, could I trust that meant everything would be all right?

"Don't overthink it, child." Her brows knitted delicately, and for the moment, she appeared less monstrous. "You may enter the temple when you are ready, but realize the longer you wait, the longer your friends must face their demons."

She had said nothing about demons. Skye stiffened, shifting uncomfortably. We looked at each other, and worry darkened his blue gaze, but he didn't press me. He only nodded, offering his support.

I leaned on that, took a deep breath, and nodded, standing. "Let's get this over with..."

"You mean to say you are ready?"

"As I'll ever be..."

She laughed again, but this time other voices joined in her mirth. They pooled together until the sound was akin to the rush of a waterfall. "That is simply not true, but you are on your way. You have all you need, and that will be enough." She extended a webbed hand toward the temple entrance, and I squinted against the sun at the pit of darkness she expected me to enter.

It was not a gradual descent into the pitch. I stepped forward, stopping before the wall, and lifted my hand. It disappeared into the blackness, and my breath held. The second I entered fully, I wouldn't be able to turn back.

"We've done this before," Skye murmured near my ear, but his hold on my hair tightened.

"You have to promise not to leave me like last time."

He stayed silent a moment, and my heart pounded with every second he delayed. At last, he whispered, "If the Nixies are hinting at what I suspect, I don't believe I'll have a choice. However, for as long as I can, I'll stay with you."

That was as good as I was going to get. Glancing back at the Nixies one last time, I met the woman's glowing eyes, shoved down a shiver, and stepped into the temple. A blinding light consumed me whole.

Night curled around me in an unusual way. Like I

was a part of it. I stood firmly, but my feet were not visibly on the ground. I checked for Skye and found him still perched on my shoulder. His tiny presence calmed me enough to take in the rest of the dream-like surroundings.

Home. It was home. Peter's tree stretched before me in the forest, the same limbs and plateau I had grown up in yawning into the sky. Pixies darted around like they didn't see me at all, like this was a normal night for them. I swallowed, waiting for the twist, the moment when everything changed, the moment when what I loved disappeared before me, and then an impossible task presented itself.

That hadn't happened in the first temple. But that temple hadn't ripped me away into a vision the second I stepped inside either.

Everything stopped. The pixies halted as one and peered at each other with wide eyes. Their voices were questioning, but my ears only picked up bells. "Do you understand them?" I asked Skye.

"Understand who?" His brows lowered.

"The—" My heart skipped. A baby. The soft wails of a child cut through the trees, and from the corner of my eye, a form appeared garbed in a cloak. My heart rate picked up when I caught a snatch of orange hair peeking out of the bundle in the woman's arms. Me. That was me. And if that was me, and this was here, then...

Desperate for a glance of my mother, I tried to fight through whatever held my feet on a solid plane, but my body remained suspended in the air, feet firmly planted against the barrier.

"Lyric,"—Skye's voice pitched—"what is it? What's going on?"

"It's my mother and me and my home. You can't see it?"

"I'm seeing something completely different," he replied but didn't elaborate. Only a touch of anxiety tainted his tone, but he gripped my hair tighter, and his heels pressed into my shoulder.

Any question I was going to ask Skye died when the woman lifted her hand and knocked on the tree. Every second waiting was torture. This was the moment she left me, abandoned me, decided I wasn't worth keeping, and that a twelve-year-old would be good enough to raise me.

Who was she? How dare she?

Peter peeked out of the secret entrance and lifted a brow. His eyes narrowed, and something inaudible mumbled past his lips.

I hoped, and I prayed that the woman would hesitate, kiss my cheek, show that she didn't want to give me up, but when Peter stopped speaking, she held me away from her body without reservation. He floated over me, disgust scrunching his nose. The woman, my mother, said something, and his eyes widened. His head shook. He reeled back.

By now, the other lost boys were fighting at the secret entrance for a glimpse of what was going on. My eyes were filled with tears.

Peter looked horrified when the woman urged him to take me. His head shook again, and his arms folded. Tinkerbell zipped out of his hat, hovered over me, and then laughed, disregarding me. Both of them nodded their dismissal and turned to leave.

A tear fell, a sob wracking my chest, and I covered my mouth.

"Hey, Lyric, what's going on over there?" Skye asked.

This had to be a lie, I reasoned. Peter *had* taken me. This was just a matter of the temple getting into my head. Nothing more. Peter would walk away here, and I'd have to confirm it was a lie. What a simple, insipid little test. "I'm fine," I choked. "It's stupid. Are you okay?"

"Well enough," he mumbled, and even I could hear the lie amidst my clogged head, but neither of us addressed it further.

I waited for the scene to end. It didn't. Peter's retreat stopped, and he looked over his shoulder, listening to unheard words my mother spoke. His eyes narrowed, but he faced her again, peering at me. I continued to cry, both presently and in the scene.

Peter stuck his finger in his ear and toyed with whatever she had said. When she offered me to him again, he sighed, glanced at the Lost Boys, then took me into his arms. A tiny frown marred his lips, and he held me like I was something filthy, but my gold-rimmed eyes opened, the deep brown meeting his, and the expression drifted away into something of surprise.

Baby me sniffed, and my wails ceased when Peter poked my forehead.

A deep sigh filled his chest like I was a burden he couldn't care less about, but he said some final thing to my mother, then turned back toward home. She turned away as well, and I watched her, waiting.

She didn't so much as slouch.

The scene dropped out of my sight, and I blinked at a long cave tunnel lined with glowing moss. At least, it looked like moss, but it breathed. The whole of the stretching path before me swelled and deflated with breaths like I was standing within a living creature, and panic filled my chest.

Peter hadn't wanted me.

The thought entered my mind when the creature surrounding me inhaled. It left with my shuddering exhale. My lips trembled as they parted.

Peter hadn't wanted me.

He had taken me, but he hadn't wanted me either. Only whatever my mother had told him convinced him I was worth the trouble.

"Skye?" I choked, squeezing my eyes shut.

"Yeah...?" Torment filled his soft voice, but he was here; he was still here.

"What do you see now?"

It took him a second, but he mumbled, "Creepy cave."

"Glowing, mossy walls?"

He half-scoffed. "That's not moss, but sure."

"Well, at least we're in the same place now," I snapped, not needing the reaffirmation that the walls were indeed not harmless moss. "I just saw my mother abandon me with an unwilling Peter. So that's nice."

"Peter's twelve, Lyric. He's stuck in an eternal cootie phase. Of course, he wasn't thrilled to be handed a baby girl, but the point stands that he kept you when he could have given you to any number of people on Skyla." He tugged on my hair, and I winced. "Don't let this place get in your head, Daughter of Pan."

Daughter of Pan. I hadn't heard that for so long.

He's right. Peter kept me. *Because of what my mother told him that made him take me?* I opened my eyes and glared at the tunnel. I would have shaken my head if it wouldn't have sent Skye flying. *Skye was right*, I confirmed again, harsher. *Besides, it doesn't matter now; Peter's forgotten you.* The new thought sliced a deeper gash, and I swallowed, blurting, "What did you see, Skye?"

"Bay."

The vague answer led to a rush of annoyed thoughts. Just as well since they pushed out the darker ones.

"Let's get moving," he said.

"We're going deeper into this thing?" I tensed, eyeing the monster.

He sighed. "What else can we do?"

I glanced behind me, immediately wishing I hadn't. At my back, the moss closed off wherever we'd come from, and it was closer than I'd ever want to be to the breathing walls. At least, solid ground rested beneath my feet, but when I blinked, it turned neon in a flash, softening like flesh. I blinked again, and it returned to stone. "I don't like this. What the hell is this?" I wrapped my arms around my chest and stepped forward to move away from the back wall.

"You can't trust anything in here, Lyric. Remember that."

That's right. Thank goodness he was here with me. I don't know how I'd be able to do this on my own. Taking a deep breath, I walked forward, grounding myself in the light weight on my shoulder.

Of course. The grim thoughts bubbled to the forefront of my mind. *The Nixies knew you wouldn't be able to handle this alone.*

"Airwoman," I breathed, talking myself through it, "the voices are incessant."

He hummed in agreement, and I gnawed my lip, glancing at him. His eyes were dull, and his lips rested in a firm line. Worry ate away at my gut.

"More specifically, what did you see?" I asked.

His gaze found mine for a moment, then it drifted away. "I saw what they did to him. That's all."

The pirates. Bay's torture. Sickness tightened my stomach. "What angle are the voices taking with that?" Somewhere in my heart, I knew I shouldn't pry, but talking kept my mind off my own demons. At least, until my thoughts wandered. *Demons. That's what the Nixie said Whisper and Bay were facing. Demons just like this. And I had to save them somehow. I didn't even know if I could save myself.*

"They're saying I wasn't there for him. They're blaming you for that, trying to make me leave you alone in this. But I won't." His brows furrowed, and I didn't mind the pull on my hair. "Sure, I wasn't there for him then because he told me to make sure you were safe, but I could have refused. More than that, I don't have to take responsibility for what *they* did. I know the real enemy. I can't be turned against myself or my friends." He offered me a weak smile that was the strongest thing I knew in that moment. "Pixies are pretty loyal little assholes, aren't we?"

Despite myself and my terrifying surroundings, I smiled back at him, my soul feeling a little lighter. "They sure are."

The second the last word left my mouth, he disappeared.

My soul jerked out of my skin. "Skye?" I called into the darkness. Nothing responded.

You're alone.

The walls breathed. I stood in the belly of some magical beast, alone. Alone with my thoughts. They screamed in my head, reminding me how little I had accomplished in my life, how everything up until this point had been wasted time. There wasn't a single thing worth mentioning.

I was utterly worthless.

Just a sad little girl who wanted to explore the world, a sad little girl who had nearly died dozens of times on her first adventure.

No wonder Peter didn't let you leave Skyla. He knew better than to send you to your death.

"Shut up," I hissed, moving forward. The ground jerked beneath me, and a lump caught in my throat. The ground was the same living substance as the walls. "This isn't real." Skye had said so. I believed in him. *This wasn't real.*

This is magic. Anything is possible. Even if it isn't "real," it can definitely still kill you.

The words in my head were far more potent than the ones I forced past my lips. This place had taken my final lifeline away. And the Nixies had known. I couldn't trust my thoughts. I couldn't trust myself at all.

"But what if," I murmured, forcing myself to stumble over the rocking terrain, "they aren't your thoughts. What if something else is in your head, and it's not you."

"On the contrary," the collection of voices I faintly remembered from the last temple brushed past my ear like a soft breeze. They collected into a glowing form, then they took my shape. "I am you."

The temple beast took a deep breath, and wind howled through the expanding walls.

"These thoughts are bred from your mind. At one point or another, they've belonged to you. Aren't they pitiful? And aren't you?" The glowing reflection sneered and looked away like I disgusted her. And didn't I? Myself, I mean. Didn't I disgust myself?

According to the sirens, I was some great piece in a bigger plan, but I couldn't even find it in myself to embrace the idea of that.

"How do you expect to believe in yourself when no one else does? Your oldest friend," my reflection winced and looked truly pained, "Whisper...she didn't even believe in you enough to fly. And Bay? He sent a pixie to babysit you the second you were separated."

The walls closed in, tighter than they were before. I could hardly breathe.

Was Skye still here, just invisible? Was he watching me crumble? Was he regretting believing in me to save him and Bay and Whisper?

Picturing his frustration frustrated me, and my fists clenched. "I said, shut up!"

"Pathetic."

"That isn't shutting up." I gritted my teeth and glared at myself. She looked more like me now. Orange bled into her hair, and brown swirled in her eyes. Her despondent eyes. Another monstrous inhale. Another whip of air. My hair flew before my face, and I realized that hers was a dirtier shade. Her eyes were a duller mud.

She was every mediocre idea I had of myself. No gold touched her irises because I didn't believe I was special like that. Her hair was thin and bland because I didn't believe I had any right to stand out, to look even a fraction like Peter. Unwanted, she slouched.

I hated her.

The walls constricted further, but only I seemed to notice.

"Might as well end up swallowed here," I spat. My other looked at me, and I narrowed my eyes at her. "Is that it? I thought it. I said it. But I don't believe it. I *can't*. My friends need me."

"Since when have our friends ever needed us?"

"No," I growled, and the creature froze, the mossy

walls still for the moment. "*My* friends. The Nixie said they would need me, so I'm not going to let this be where my adventure ends."

"Must you always rely on someone else?"

I unfolded my arms and took a step toward her. "So what if I rely on others?"

"It's pathetic."

"No, it's not." Those words resonated in my heart, resounded in my head, and I felt them swell in my chest. "It's strength. The ability to believe in others isn't easy. It's so much safer to build walls and stay inside them. I may be wrong about someone. I may trust something that I shouldn't. I've done that countless times since coming to Neverland. When you rely on someone, you allow them access to your foundation. They may rip the ground out from under you." I thought of Bay, Hook's son. "They may not be who you thought they were at all."

"It's stupid then," she hissed.

I smirked. "Yeah? So?"

She didn't miss a beat. "You're an idiot."

Scoffing, I lifted my chin and said, "I prefer 'pretty loyal little asshole.'"

The form's features broke, shattering my likeness and morphing into something else. "Can you do nothing on your own?" it shrieked. "Can you not even find your own words to say?"

The fleshy walls snapped to life, roiling, and the ground beneath my feet jerked with them. I lost my footing and fell. My stomach lurched. Air whipped against my face as I plummeted into a pit of darkness. Untouched by whatever gravity yanked me, the form remained standing before me, unmoved, a howling wraith of a creature.

I grasped at thin air, finding nothing to hold onto. There was nothing. All around us, pitch black, and yet I could see myself and the figure clearly. None of this was real. But again, it was magic. And magic could kill.

"No one is here to save you!" the figure screamed, a harsh wind scratching through its throat.

I squeezed my eyes shut, hoping the jumping feeling in my stomach would vanish if I blocked the sight. It didn't. It continued to accelerate, leaving my gut behind. If only Skye were here. I could fly if he were here.

I can fly even if he isn't.

The thought came unbidden, and I wondered if it was me or some force in this place. Who here would encourage me when so far everything had tried to break me down? I swallowed, but a thought hit me.

Even if we were separated, I wasn't in here alone. I was never alone. If I was going to believe in Skye, in Whisper, in Bay, in everyone, then maybe I should start listening to what they had to say.

Whisper said I could save the world.

Skye said I could create tornados.

Bay said he loved me.

I swallowed, tears burning in my eyes and dashing away in the torrent of wind as I fell. "You're wrong!" I yelled. "Everyone is here to save me. Everyone I've believed in, relied on, trusted, they live in me. Maybe I'm not strong enough to believe in myself effortlessly like Whisper and Bay can. Maybe I have to find a convoluted way to do it. But maybe, just maybe, that's okay." I flattened myself against the wind, slowing my descent. "This is who I am." I threw out one arm. "And I am loved." I threw out the other. "And I am enough."

My body became what it was fighting against. Lighter than air. No dust on my skin. I flew. It may have been a magic-induced dream, but I decided not to believe that thought. This was within me. It was natural, like flying always had been. It was real. Something powerful skated beneath my skin, making me aware of every breeze, every breath. The blackness surrounding me and the form before me weren't real at all.

Air was. It was everywhere. And I felt it in every empty space. Exhaling, I caught sensations of solid walls, chambers, long halls. Inhaling, I recognized a gentle breath nearby. Skye hadn't gone anywhere after all.

I looked over the amalgamation before me as it shuffled through a dozen forms, grasping the fragments of past souls who had dared to step foot here. Whisper and Bay blinked by before it was me again. But the not-quite-me. Dull hair. Bland eyes. Weak and afraid.

I floated in the black space, staring at her. There were so many flaws. So many doubts. But that didn't make her worthless. That didn't make me worthless.

"I accept you," I said. "We are enough."

When I blinked again, the blackness had disappeared. Before me, was a temple chamber outlined with eerie blue torches. I looked down to find my feet above the ground and grinned. I lifted one leg, then the other, and pressed my lips together to hold back my smile. A tingle of pixie dust wasn't anywhere to be found. This was *me*.

All those years I'd spent collecting something I already had within me... If only I'd known sooner. The feather marks on my arm burned with purpose. They *were* from my wings; I had always been able to fly.

Skye groaned, and I found him hovering beside me, his face twisted with twinges of discomfort. He blinked out of something unseen and set a hand against his face. "Why do these places have to hate people...?" His eyes widened after he squinted at my dangling feet. "What the... But I haven't..."

I landed softly. "I think I figured some part of this demigod thing out."

He blew a laugh out his nose. "Atta girl. So we can get the hell through this now?" He returned to my shoulder, sitting this time and rubbing his temple.

"As quickly as possible." I lifted off the ground, skimming forward down the tunnel path, embracing the sensation of magic-fueled weightlessness. "Have I ever told you that you curse an awful lot for 'darling incarnate'?"

He scoffed. "Who says darling incarnate doesn't curse?"

After several minutes—or hours—of flying, the scene before me changed in a blink. I was somewhere else. Somewhere I hadn't ever been before. My brows furrowed, and I put up my guard, keeping from touching anything.

"Are you with me?" I asked Skye.

"Yep." He glanced over the flowering fields with similar apprehension. It was so bright. I knew we had to have walked into either Whisper's or Bay's nightmare, but whose nightmare would be so...

A swarm of brilliantly colored butterflies filled the air as a girl ran through the flowers. Her dark skin and bouncing hair told me exactly who it was, but she was far younger than she had been for a long time, and only panic filled her eyes.

"No!" she screeched.

My immediate instinct was to make sure nothing chased her, but Skye tugged on my hair and pointed the other direction. Walking away, but somehow moving faster than she could run, was her father. Tears streamed down her cheeks, her little arm outstretched.

She tripped, smashing face-first into the plants. She curled in on herself there and didn't bother to get up.

I blinked, and the whole scene rewound.

Butterflies burst off every painted petal. "Papa!" She fell, sobbing.

And again.

Butterflies. "Please!" She collapsed. Her tiny arms covered her head, and wracking breaths filled her chest. I had never seen her like this concerning her father. By the time I found out what had happened, she only smiled sadly and said that sometimes that was how the tide was: giving and taking without emotion.

My heart ached for the little girl lying in the grass, and determination lit a fire in my stomach. I had to break the cycle. This time when the world reset, I floated to the spot where she always tripped. She ran toward me, staring directly through me, her plea on her lips. "Don't leave!" Her foot snagged on something invisible, but this time, I caught her.

The pleasant meadow broke with an ear-splitting crash. Stone walls replaced the flowers, the blue sky, and the hundreds of butterflies. We stood in a tiny, towering room of thick grey, only the ceiling open to display a starry night. Whisper, her correct age now, sobbed, gasped, and realized things had changed.

Darting away from me, she took in her surroundings, then steeled, wiping her cheeks. They were splotched beneath her red eyes. "I'm sick and tired of this," she hissed. "Let me out of here already."

I opened my mouth to tell her that's exactly what I planned to do, though I wasn't exactly sure how, but her voice replied behind me, "No. This is where we're safe."

I turned, coming face-to-face with a pristine Whisper. A cold, hardness held her brown eyes in a state of unshakeable charm. The real Whisper huffed, folding her arms and facing the wall, trying to find a place to grasp; the fake Whisper took the moment her back was turned to glare at me.

Whisper grumbled, "I'm not safe in here. I have to get through this, find the answers we need about the Fountain, and get back to Lyric."

"Lyric?" her other questioned, her voice lilting with humor. "Sweet, sweet, little Lyly? She's practically helpless without you, isn't she?"

"Hush your ugly face," Whisper snapped, but my heart had already clenched. Were those her real inner thoughts? Was that how this worked?

"What an,"the other chuckled—"interesting insult to choose, all things considered."

Damn. I swallowed, watching the other Whisper sashay to her side and drape herself against the wall. *Whisper's inner voice was sassy as shit.*

"Back to Lyly," the other glanced my way, "you really have to protect her, don't you?"

"Of course! I mean, she is younger than me." Whisper gripped the stone, and I realized her fingers were bloody.

"Yes, well, not by too much, though you'd think there were eons between you."

Whisper planted her feet against the wall, managing to hold on. "So she's a little immature. Like I'm any different; all I want to do is marry my 'moth prince,' whom I call 'moth prince.'"

"At least, you know better when it comes to important things." The other checked her prim nails. "I mean, she knew that Bay kid a week before running off with him to airwoman knew where. He's Hook's son. He might be using us to get to the Fountain. Pirates are conniving like Mom has said. I wouldn't put any faith in a single one of them."

Whisper sucked in a breath as her grip faltered, and she skidded back to the ground. "Listen," she spat, "you aren't going to get in my head about my friends. Lyric is Lyric. I love her to death, no matter what you say."

"I never said we didn't love her. Just that sometimes she can be a bit of an ignorant child."

Whisper bared her teeth and growled. "She fell in *love*. That's a thing that happens, and it can be blinding."

Her other set a finger against her cheek and pursed her lips. "Yes, right, you never would have been pushed off Skyla at your birthday party had you not been blinded by your own little *love*."

Whisper's chest pumped. "There, see? Who saved me then? Lyric and Bay."

"And if they hadn't?" Her other's delicate brows dipped. "We can't let our guard down like that in case they decide not to next time; there can't be a next time. We already know that the people we're supposed to trust the most fall through when it matters the most."

"Can I hit you?" Whisper raised her fist. "Are you real enough to hit? I'm not normally an aggressive person, but I feel like I'm allowed to give myself a beating when I'm talking crap."

"Is that really what she thinks of us?" I asked, my throat tight. How exactly was I supposed to step in? She couldn't see me.

"Maybe they are things she's thought of, but that doesn't mean that they resonate as truth." Skye looked at me. "This place preys on our cracks. Whatever it can use, it will. Sometimes passing thoughts appear when we don't want them to. Recognizing the lies is important

313

to overcoming them."

My resolve hardened. "How do I reach her?"

Her other tittered. "Should we go back to our memories? Which time someone has failed us is our favorite?"

"I don't want to hear it. I don't want to see it. And I *definitely* don't want to relive any more of it. I don't care if it's dangerous out there. I know it's dangerous out there."

Her other threw out her hands. "Then why are you trying to leave? I'm trying to keep you safe."

"I'm strong enough to keep myself safe!" Whisper yelled, facing herself, tears gathering in her eyes. "I'll get out of this by myself and deal with whatever happens because of that choice by myself as well."

"You don't have to deal with anything by yourself!" I blurted.

"Lyric—" Skye started, but I stepped in front of Whisper, ignoring him.

She stared through me, but I didn't care. Maybe if I spoke enough, she'd be able to hear me. "All these years, we've been by each other. And sure, maybe I've failed you a lot, maybe I'm not as mature or smart or confident, but no matter what, we've promised. Again and again. *We will never be apart.*"

Whisper blinked, two crystal tears slipping down her cheeks. Surprise touched her expression, and she lifted a hand to her face.

"Lyric's going to save the world. She's destined to." Her other exhaled, bored. "After that, she'll be strong enough to go on the adventures she's always dreamed of. You'll become a memory in her life just like you've become one in your father's." She flicked her gaze up, smiling brightly. "A pleasant memory, of course. We're

314

wonderful."

"Lyric is going to save the world," Whisper said. "I believe that. I believe in her."

Her other unleashed a booming laugh. "Oh, really? No, you don't! You can't even trust that she'll make it back from her little Skyla adventures when you've asked her to help you plan something!"

"That makes me horrible then, not her!"

Her other's smile was nasty and cruel. "I never said she was horrible."

Whisper swallowed and turned back to the wall. She lifted her bloody hands. "Just go away. You're annoying me."

"I am you." Her other sighed, leaning against the wall.

"No, she's not." I reached for Whisper, but she stepped away from me, searching the fortress for another handhold. My fists clenched. "How am I supposed to do this if she can't hear me or see me?"

A scraping noise made me jump away from the walls. They inched closer together, and my stomach flipped. The other Whisper smiled calmly and continued to check her nails.

"Not again," Whisper murmured, swallowing. Fear filled her eyes, and she gnawed her cheek, controlling her breaths as she placed her hands on the grey stone and tried to lift herself once more. Her moccasins skidded, and she couldn't catch herself this time, falling flat on her rump. Wincing, she held her bleeding hands against her chest.

"Maybe you don't want to leave after all."

Whisper sneered at herself, but she remained seated on the ground, cradling her bloody palms close to her body.

"She's not going to do this alone." I looked at the walls, then lifted my hands. Something hit me, and my eyes widened. Air surrounded us. I could find myself as a part of it. I floated off the ground, and a buzz of magic lit beneath my skin. Holding onto that sensation, I wrapped my hands around the wind and sent it sailing toward Whisper.

Her hair whipped across her face and over her shoulders. She turned her head and tried to tame her locks, but she still didn't see me.

"Maybe you can lift her out of this place?" Skye mused.

"My thoughts exactly." I took a deeper breath and let it out as I clenched my fists.

The wind harshened, creating an updraft that tore at her clothes. Panic filled her gaze, and she scrambled away from the gusts. "What is this? What are you playing at now?"

Her other merely shrugged.

I cut the wind off and drew back, shaking my head. "I don't have that much control, and I won't risk hurting her."

"Don't doubt yourself now." Skye flitted off my shoulder. "The only way we reach Bay is if we figure this out."

I pressed my lips together and lifted my hands again before promptly dropping them. "No. This can't be right. It's all a test, and this isn't my test; it's hers. Before, in the other temple, the only way I got through was when I decided I would trust myself over what that thing told me. This time, I had to accept myself and believe in my own power." Realization hit me hard and cold. My feet touched the ground again. "Neverland. It's your home, the birthplace of pixies, creatures of belief. Everything here tests belief. The changelings and pirates try to shake your trust. The sirens and Nixies don't appear safe to trust, but you have to believe in them because they hold the secrets." I recalled Peter and Wendy. A child and a bright-eyed dreamer. All the pirates. Why did pirates end up in this place? Because they dreamed of something more? Because they believed in impossible things like treasure and ruling the seas? Because, at heart, they were confident explorers who believed in themselves? They believed in themselves to the point of destruction. Peter and Wendy believed in everything. "Only children and dreamers can find and master Neverland because children and dreamers have something in common. They either violently trust others or themselves. Whisper has never had a problem trusting herself." I looked at Skye. "She needs to trust us."

Skye's face twisted, and he threw up his arms. "How? She can't see us!"

I flicked my wrist, calling a swirl of wind to spin around her, teasing her hair upward. "Maybe not. But our efforts aren't completely invisible. In the end, this is her test."

Whisper narrowed her gaze at the sky, searching for something, some answer to my breeze, and I nodded at Skye. He huffed, skeptical, but circled above Whisper, showering her in dust. She blinked furiously when it fell into her eyes and tried to rub it away.

I caught her hands before she could.

"I love you." I smiled. "You know that. You don't have to do this alone."

Skye returned to my shoulder as I lifted off the ground, still holding her hands, whether she could feel my touch or not.

"It won't work." Her other slinked off the wall, and Whisper's gaze shot up to it. "You know that. You can't fly on your own."

"You're not alone." I squeezed her hands.

Whisper's fists clenched as she met her other's eyes. "What makes you think I'm alone?"

The woman who wasn't quite Whisper smirked. "Look around. It would take an awful lot of belief to assume otherwise."

The creature's words pounded into my skull, and I whipped my gaze to her. She winked, and everything changed in that moment. *These beings weren't our enemy.* They were us. Us and those before us. Neverland's spirit. *They wanted us to succeed.* I called on the air around us, curling it in a hug that pulled Whisper off the ground for the first second.

"I believe Lyric's right here then!" Whisper laughed. "We have never been apart." Tears pooled in her eyes, and she extended her pinky, bowing her head forward. I linked my finger around hers, noting the moment when my wind ceased, and she remained airborne beside me.

"Well, I'll be damned," Skye murmured, his blue eyes wide.

"More darling language?" I snickered.

He grumbled, "It happens when I'm stressed."

By all appearances, we rose out of the fortress, though when I checked the air, we hadn't moved but a foot off the ground. As Whisper's other disappeared below us in the vision, I watched her shift forms. For a split second, it was Bay. Then in the last instant before the vision disappeared, Peter grinned up at me, folded his arms, and nodded me onward.

My eyes closed; emotion choked me.

Whisper's gasp yanked me from the moment, and her

arms crushed me against her body. "Oh, my airwoman! You were here!" She looked down and squealed. "And I'm *flying!*" Her gaze went huge. "And that was you making freak wind!" Excitement bubbled around her, something physical in the air, until her smile fell away, a little at a time. "How long have you been listening to... everything?"

My head shook even as my chest pinched. "It doesn't matter. Trust me, I said far worse things about myself."

"I believe that." Her attention drifted down the hall lit with blue flame. It seemed to go on for an eternity, and both directions looked identical. "I suppose we have to find Bay next...?"

I nodded.

She winced, gnawing her lip. "If I'm honest, I don't trust him." She looked at Skye, and her brow furrowed. "I don't actually trust you either. I'm a thousand percent sure I'm only flying because of Lyly right now."

"It's nice that you're bringing down your walls, but do you really have to insult me to my face like that?" Skye rolled his eyes, hardly sounding perturbed.

Whisper smiled. "Yep, still can't understand him."

"The Nixies implied we all made it out together, and besides," I pursed my lips and met her gaze, "Bay isn't like his father."

I wonder about that.

The words slithered into my head, chilling my blood, and in the next instant, Whisper and Skye were gone. The scene had changed completely, and I was alone on the edge of something...something terrifying and magical.

It was a grove. And there was a fountain.

26TH NOVEMBER

Light gleamed off the pool of water, winking into my eyes, and I had to squint to make out the rivulets shooting from the center in rainbow arcs. Trees curled their bows over the fountain, blocking out a would-be sky with foliage and dangling moss.

So enclosed, I wondered where the light came from, but I didn't have much time to find it.

"Wind Song." The words came breathless behind me, and I turned to face Bay. "You're here."

He strode to me, cupped my cheek, and kissed me. Any relief at seeing him vanished in that moment. My heart thundered within my chest, and creatures exploded in my stomach. Heat bloomed on my cheeks, and where his hand found my waist, his touch scathed me. When he pulled away, I was almost too shocked to notice how tired he looked or how battered he was.

Blood smudged his cheeks and his hands and his clothes. My heart rate picked up. "Are you okay?"

"I'm fine." He smiled, glancing over my shoulder at the glimmering water. "I can't believe all this time it's been here. I waited for you; I thought we should do this together."

Magic pulsed in the air, and my brows bent. This couldn't be the real Fountain; the water of the real Fountain was gold. I peered around for Bay's other, but no one else stood in the grove. Unrest made me tense. "What happened? What have I missed?" Something was wrong because something had to be wrong. That was the point of a trial.

"A skirmish or two. It's fine. I knew there'd be trouble." He shrugged easily despite the blood all over him. I examined him closer, and my stomach went sick. *He wasn't injured.*

It wasn't his blood.

"Bay..." My throat closed, and my gaze fell on his sheath. It was hooked on his belt, and blood dripped through the laced leather. "What did you do?"

He quirked a brow at me, then looked himself over. "Oh. Right." He ruffled his hair, having the nerve to appear embarrassed. "Yeah, I know it looks bad, but none of it is real. The temple guardians aren't real. I've done this before; we both have, remember?" He touched my hand with his bloody fingers, but I didn't feel the stickiness, and none left a trail. "See?"

"You killed your other...?"

"If you'd met him, you'd have killed him too." Bay laughed, but there was something deeper in the sound, and it died far too quickly. His shadowed eyes recalled whatever dark words had been said, or maybe they still spilled into his skull. He shook either or both free. "I knew you'd make it. Should we wait for Whispering Meadow?"

Whisper had vanished along with Skye. My chest was panicking right now, but I checked the air for them. No breath disrupted the space, though, as I'd guessed, we were in a room. This wasn't real. "Whisper and Skye aren't in the temple anymore."

His brows rose. "Really? I suppose it decided only we would take care of this, then." He faced the fountain and sighed. "Look at it. Isn't it perfect? All this time, and now, finally, I have what I need to save my mother." His hand found mine, and my heart leaped when he smiled at me. It was purely joyful. How was I supposed to tell him it was all a lie? That we still had work to do?

What was the test? How was I supposed to help?

My gaze shifted over the edges, searching for any shadows, any hints of danger, but my eyes continued to be drawn back to the blazing water. Bay pulled me along with his stride, approaching the glittering pool, and my anxiety raced. I clutched his hand and shook my head. "It's not real, Bay. I don't think we should go near it."

"Don't be silly." Anger sparked in his eyes, and his hand gripped mine tighter. "Do you know how hard I've fought to get here? It has to be real. Why bother protecting something fake?"

"Believe me, Bay. It isn't real. We have to figure out the trial, then we'll be able to find where the real Fountain is."

His hand slipped out of mine, and he narrowed his eyes. "Of course," he said darkly, "it's all been too simple. You aren't real either, are you?"

I stepped back when his fingers found the hilt of his

blade. "Bay..." The gleam in his eye. I had seen it before. On Hook's face. When I was Wendy. "No," I breathed, and my exhale shook.

"Prove it. Don't stand in my way. If it's not real, we have nothing to lose." He faced the pond. "But if it is..." His head dropped, and he scrubbed a hand over his face, leaving a trail of blood that he ignored. "You're a demigod, Wind Song. I don't know how a goddess's ancient blood permeates you. What if time takes me away from you?" He turned to me, lifting his tortured gaze. "I love you. If you care for me even a fraction of how much I care for you, I don't want to slip away. I refuse to leave you alone like my mother left me."

You were slipping away. Time was taking you away from me.

What choice did I have!

"You don't have to do this," I choked. Hook's face overlapped Bay's, and I stepped back, terrified of how realistic it looked. The temple was toying with my vision again. I knew that, but the meaning behind it sank deep into my soul. "You don't have to choose this."

He sighed, a joking, pained smile lifting his lips. "Is that how you're going to reject me then? By implying you'd like to watch me die?"

Airwoman. Would that really happen? Tears sprang to my eyes, but the sirens had warned me not to let him drink from the Fountain. They had told me why Peter was the way he was. I couldn't bear to watch Bay— or anyone else I loved—die, but we didn't know what any of our futures held, and watching him become like Peter...wouldn't that hurt far worse?

"I see," he murmured after I hadn't replied. Turning, he stepped toward the fountain.

I jerked after him, catching his wrist. "Don't!" This

was why the sirens showed me his parents' past. They were warning me that history would repeat itself. I couldn't lose him like this. I didn't want to watch him die. I didn't want to live forever. I wanted to go on adventures with him. Grow old together. Watch our kids raise their kids. "Don't do this. This is *exactly* what your father did. I don't want to see this again. Please, Bay!"

He whirled on me, sneering. "So you are just another part of this damn temple. I should have known they'd use you against me as well." His blade flew for my throat, and I slammed my eyes shut, knowing that sharp weapon was real.

Cold metal didn't reach me.

A force burst to life between Bay and me, wrenching my hand off his. When I dared to open my eyes, his other stood between us, but unlike Whisper's and mine, his other was a precise copy. "Stop," his other said, nothing wavering in his voice. "We love her. I won't let you hurt her." One of the being's hands squeezed mine while the other held Bay's sword, refusing to let it move. Its gaze narrowed as Bay wrestled with his weapon. "Bay Darling," he said after a moment. "You have failed."

The world washed black.

"It's okay." Bay's voice called me from the darkness, and blue lights lit in the tunnel. I peered around us, then at our joined hands. He wasn't the real Bay. He wasn't there at all. Though his chest rose and fell with breath, the air around him remained undisturbed.

His expression gentled, and he repeated, "It's okay."

"It's not," I choked. "It's really not. This place brings out the deepest parts of people. *That* was Bay? I don't want to believe that!"

Bay's other cupped my cheek, offering me a half-smile. It looked so real, and I had to remind myself I had already passed my test, and this amalgamation wasn't my enemy. I squeezed his hand for strength, and it kissed my forehead. "It has been so long since I've felt this way. You and your friends have brought me fresh love." His smile became too gentle. "Thank you for it. I've already released the pixie and Whispering Meadow. I will show you where the Fountain is, then I will send you back to your friends."

"What about Bay?"

Sorrow touched the being's eyes. His hazel eyes. Bay's hazel eyes flecked with gold. "He failed. Most violently. Only the pirates who dare to enter a temple decide to cut their way through us. He has displayed greed and hatred. We cannot free him again."

"Again?" My breath caught. The last temple. He said he'd done this before.

His other nodded. "We knew you'd need him to survive this far, but now, you have Whispering Meadow and your own strength. We allowed him another chance for your sake, but we cannot risk another Peter, a cruel Peter." The being morphed, and fiery hair burned on his head. He grinned, the likeness cutting me to my core. "I was special. All of Neverland knew it. I was special, like you, Lyric. We can hear the pixies. We are fearless."

"Bay can hear the pixies! And I'm not fearless! I'm actually terrified right now. You can't keep him." Panic swelled in my voice, but the being didn't appear troubled by it.

"To be fearless isn't to be without fear."

"I'm certain that is *exactly* what it is," I hissed, still clutching Peter's hand like a lifeline. To hear his voice and see him like this, after so long, when I knew he'd likely already dismissed me from his mind. This might be the last time. That also terrified me.

"To be fearless is to not let fear hold you back. You have come this far."

"By relying on others."

Peter's brows lowered. "We have been through this; you are enough."

"Don't take him from me. I love him." The words left my throat raw, and I closed my eyes. "I love him. Give him another chance."

"We know we love him." My voice. My eyes snapped open, and my other stood there, holding my own hand, torment reflecting in my own eyes. "But another chance would be too great a risk."

"He isn't his father."

"He followed the exact path his father did. For greed, masked by love, he justified horrible things."

"He knew it wasn't real. That's the only reason he did what he did. If he..." A thought occurred to me, and I raised my head, staring my other directly in the eye. "How much control do you have over the mind of someone in your walls?"

Her head tilted, and she was Whisper's cocky other. She smiled. "These minds are ours. We do not take them because we are built from love. From the first, we were erected as a sanctuary of belief and love." Her eyes widened, and I felt fingers caressing my thoughts. "And if he fails this?"

"I will stay with him here until he succeeds."

Her head reeled back. "You can't change someone, and you don't have time to wait for him to choose to change himself."

"Then, if he fails, change time in this place. I'm not leaving without him."

Whisper's eyes narrowed, and she lifted a perfectly

manicured hand. "I won't accept that." Her grin bared. "Fine. I will paint this picture you have in your mind, but you may not help him, and if he fails...I will take the memory of him from you. Your destiny is too important to be held here. How strong is your belief now?"

I trembled but took a breath. I believed in Bay. He wasn't his father. If he thought it was real, he wouldn't carve his way through in the name of his greed. "Strong enough."

Whisper sighed, smiling kindly, almost like my real friend would. "See, Lyly? This is fearless."

With those words, she, and the tunnel, disappeared, replaced by a cavern with a single entrance. Behind me, a dry fountain sat in the center of the plateau. Light rained through cracks in the ceiling. I stood before the tiered fountain, no longer myself.

Dark skin encased my small body, white robes hung to my bare feet. I felt my hair and found it silver. Something weighed against my back, and I looked over my shoulder to see wings. I was a young siren. And I was not alone in my head.

We have been here before you, child.

Or perhaps after.

Time is as it must be, confusing.

"You knew," I whispered, keeping my gaze on the only entrance, waiting for Bay.

We have always known.

And that's why they warned me.

"Finally," Bay's voice reached me from the entrance. "We finally made it, Skye."

"Let's get this over with." Skye zipped in before Bay, met my gaze, nodded, and zipped back to his side beyond where I could see. "Lyric and Whisper are counting on us to bring the power of the fountain back to them in

Skyla *before* Hook attacks."

"We won't fail them. Or Mom." Bay appeared at the entrance, awe in his eyes. "I've never felt magic like this before. We're here."

"Welcome," I said, raising my arms. My voice throbbed with the voices of those before me, and my heart raced in my chest. "Welcome, Bay Darling."

His brows rose when he met my gaze, and he looked me over, glancing behind me at the empty fountain.

"I have been waiting for you." Though I couldn't see my smile, I knew it was as chilling as the sirens'. "My sisters have guided you to this moment. We are sorry to keep you from this for so long, but for the sake of the world..."

His lips parted. "You... You don't mean they've known all this time where the Fountain was?"

I closed my eyes. "We see everything. The war. The pain. The suffering. The answer."

"I don't understand. Why keep this from me? I've been looking for years! My mother—"

I raised my hand, cringing internally when I saw the pain in his eyes. "The price of this power is one of blood and sacrifice, our Bay. It appears only for a short time after that price is met. Only now, when you must use it to save the world, may we allow you access."

"Blood and sacrifice?" He approached me, crouching to my height. "What do you mean?"

My gentle Bay. "I have known my fate from the moment I was born. Please, don't worry. You must take this power with you and for yourself, or everyone will perish."

Horror filled his eyes, but he didn't move away. "You aren't saying..."

"I am."

He shook his head, rising. "No. Peter Pan wouldn't have done this. You can't be telling me the truth."

Wendy's memories of the world in her time flooded me, and I saw the words to say. "Peter Pan did what he had to in ages past, in a time when war also brewed over the land. We needed him to be our hero then. Now it is your turn."

"Lyric won't be able to fend off the pirates for long unless we do something. She needs the fountain's magic." Skye's fists clenched. "Would any sacrifice work?"

"Any precious life," I said, repeating what the voices echoed for me to say.

Skye pressed a hand against his chest and looked at Bay. "Then let me."

"No," Bay growled. "What do you think I'm going to do without you? I can't fly without you. I wouldn't even be able to get the water to her."

There were other pixies still on Neverland. My brows furrowed, and I almost spoke, but Skye's own voice murmured in my skull, *Bay can't fly using any dust. Only mine. He only trusts me.*

Bay winced, pacing and running his fingers through his hair. His short braid came undone, and he cursed as the tie fell, before glancing at me again.

I smiled, though my heart hammered. "It is all right. I am a small price to pay for the world. I have already seen what I may miss."

"That doesn't matter," he spat. Anger boiled in his expression. "Your sisters, your family, how can I possibly take you from them? I know what that does to someone."

"But Lyric—" Skye began.

Bay snatched a dagger off his belt and flipped it in

330

his hand. "Yeah. I know. She needs this."

"What are you—" I bit my tongue when the voices hissed at me. A siren would have no question.

Bay didn't seem to notice as he positioned the blade at his chest. "Make sure it gets to both her and my mother, Skye." His gaze flicked to me. "Tell your sisters thanks for everything."

Panic welled in my heart as he closed his eyes and—

All breath left my body when everything disappeared except for Bay. Frozen in place, he stood, his empty hands positioned before his chest. The spirit of the temple stood before him, its faces shifting constantly. "So," they said, "this is the path he has found." A sigh breathed through them, and they turned, smiling at me.

I looked myself over and found I had returned to normal. Steeling myself, I met its gaze. "He passed. I told you."

"Yes, he is capable. But such dramatics don't surround the real Fountain. It is only hidden. When found, he must not drink it. Hook, once, was like Bay. The years on Neverland have made him what he is now. Bay's core is still good, but his father's blood runs through him. He would not wear the time well either."

"What are you saying?" The words burned in my mouth.

"Some die heroes. Others become villains."

"Bay's not like that!"

The being approached and cupped my cheek. It sent a chill through me. "Your belief is a virtue; it may just be enough. Peter was young; he avoided the venomous effects of the Fountain when he took it in ignorance because he was innocent. The true terror of everlasting life through the Fountain is that the power eats away at you, again and again. What it would leave behind for those out of their innocence is nothing short of monstrous. We would all be like that."

"I won't let him drink it then." I swallowed.

"You must be certain." They nodded. "The Fountain rests on Skyla, just beneath your nose. You will not need its power. Allow Bay only what he requires for his mother, then destroy it."

"How?" I asked.

"All wind that rises must fall." They lifted their hand, and a vial appeared as they morphed into the eldest siren. The gentle woman's voice did not match her grave expression. "This. Only this. You must be certain." She clamped it against my palm, and I looked over her shoulder at Bay.

He remained frozen, his eyes closed and his hands at his chest. "How do I explain what happened here?"

"You will not have to." She released the vial and flicked her wrist. Bay vanished. "He failed. He will not remember anything past that. It has been important for him to know his failure and you to know his redemption."

The being morphed again, this time into the youngest sister. She smiled. "Protect our Bay. Good luck."

When I blinked, I stood at the temple exit. The Nixies turned as one to face me from their puddles, their eyes all aglow in the night, and my stomach clenched. Darkness swallowed the cove in evening. *How long had we been in there...?*

"Lyly!" Whisper came from the air, slamming into me with a hug that nearly knocked me back into the temple. Involuntarily, I called a rush of air to me, pushing me back to safety. It didn't get past her, and she gasped. "Did you just freak wind?"

Outside the temple, it felt more real. I lifted off the

ground, effortlessly, without dust, and grinned. "I think I did."

"Ah! This is incredible!" She laughed, squeezing me. "Did you get the location?" No joy touched that voice.

My heart skipped, and I looked at Bay. Skye hovered near him, his eyes downcast until he glanced at Whisper. Silently, the pixie provided her fresh dust, then returned dutifully to Bay's side. Shadows bled in the corners of Bay's usually bright eyes, and I winced, nodding. "I have an idea where the Fountain is, but we can only take this much." Lifting the vial still in my hand, I held Bay's gaze. "It's just enough for Wendy. No more. No less. Then we have to destroy it."

"What?" His brows shot high, and I was glad he appeared surprised more than angry. "Won't you need its power to save the world?"

I shook my head. "Worse things will happen if we don't do as the temple spirits said. Promise me, you three." I divided my attention between Bay, Skye, and Whisper, only so it wouldn't seem like I was calling him out.

Confusion muddled Whisper's face. "Of course. I don't have any use for the Fountain anyway. I'd rather not Peter-ify myself, thank you."

Some stray thought flickered in Bay's gaze, but he ran his fingers through his loose hair and nodded. "If that's what you were told..."

"It was." I landed, suddenly exhausted, and slipped the vial into my satchel. The bed of moss we had slept on the night before called to me, and I offered Whisper half a smile before I passed Bay, heading for it. "I think we should rest now. Tomorrow, we meet up with Tiger Lily, then we're heading home."

27TH NOVEMBER

"Wind Song." My heart responded immediately when Bay's voice hit me, but I didn't face him. The sun rose above the trees in the cove, showering me in a golden light. A soft breeze touched my skin, and I breathed it in.

Ocean brine.

A hint of magic.

Bay floated to my side, concern filling his eyes. His lips parted, but he looked away before words came out. "I'm sorry."

Heat crept up my neck. "For what?"

"I failed in the temple. That..." He rubbed his jaw. "It was really you in there, wasn't it? I almost—"

"It's all right." I laced my fingers together and tried to remember he had passed in the end. It wasn't easier.

All I could see was a dagger plunging for his heart. "There's no way you could have known for sure."

"Still, I was so blinded by what I wanted. I thought it made so much sense. The only places in Neverland I haven't picked apart are the temples. For the longest time, I've had a hunch that the Fountain was in one, but I grew up surrounded by lore of how dangerous they were. I was too scared to enter."

"Until you met Peter's daughter and thought if Neverland loved him so much, you'd be safe if you brought her along." The clearer things became with him, the less I wanted to know. There were so many lies and plots. Why couldn't we have just stayed in his treehouse, talking about silly adventures?

"I'm sorry. My mom, she..." His voice cracked, and I glanced at him. He had brought a leg to his chest. His hair fell like a curtain over his face, blocking it from view. "She's the only family I have left other than Skye. You know what happened."

"I know a lot." A lot more than I wanted to. "And I understand. You were desperate."

"Yeah." He exhaled, and the air from his breath shook. "For the longest time, I've been living for her. Now, she's not all I have anymore. I used to only be able to see my life up until the point she woke up. Now, I can imagine something after that." He didn't look at me. "I meant what I said in the temple, and what I did."

The kiss. How had I forgotten? But then that was a silly question. It had happened right before he tried to kill me, which happened right before he tried to kill himself.

My fingers brushed my lips, and the heat at my neck crawled across my cheeks. "I like you, Bay. But..."

His fist clenched. "I never should have faced the test

like I did. I was just so blinded by my preconceived notion the Fountain was within reach. I shouldn't have kissed you either. I don't regret it, but I wasn't in my right mind. I just... What they showed me... What I told myself... I've spent so many years hating my father for what he's done, worrying that I'm exactly like him. It was too much. So much that I caved and did exactly what he would have." A gentle breeze caressed his cheek, pulling his hair away from a face awash in torment. The torment eased with surprise, and he glanced at me.

My lips pressed together. "Sorry. I didn't mean to do that. I couldn't help it."

He smiled, though pain still rested in his eyes. "You're amazing, Wind Song, and I hope you know that I'm glad you found my treehouse."

A laugh escaped me. "That seems a world away."

"It is." Voice soft, his murmur drifted through the weeping trees around us and toward a horizon I couldn't make out past them.

I swallowed, feeling a lump form in my throat. Why did it have to hurt like this? I didn't know what I was supposed to do. Yesterday was a whirlwind, and now I stood on the brink of a war? A war where Skyla was only the beginning. What if I failed?

I couldn't afford to fail.

Bay tucked my hair behind my ear and smiled, half-shrugging when I looked back at him. "I couldn't help myself."

He hovered, inches away, and my heart ached. My fingers begged to touch him. Before I knew it, they had. They slipped through his hair, hesitating only when I recalled what had happened to his hair tie, the moment it had fallen in the temple.

"What's wrong?" he asked, his voice little more than

a whisper.

What was wrong? This? He was Hook's son. He had proven himself better than his pirate father in the end, but the spirit had assured me darkness remained a seed within him. I shouldn't— I shouldn't, and yet...I wanted to believe. Mouth dry, I said, "I'm scared."

He swallowed, his body going rigid. "Of me?"

"No." My hand slid out of his hair and found his chest. His heart beat, racing mine. I wasn't scared of him, and maybe that scared me a little bit too. I believed in him like Wendy had once believed in Hook, and now look where she was... I was terrified of being wrong because I desperately wanted this. "You're almost out of dust, Star Boy."

He traced the feathers running down my arm. "A pity, some of us don't have wings."

In that moment, everything was him. My breath stilted, and I fought the pounding beats of my heart that brought me closer and closer to an edge I couldn't return from. Did it matter if I fell? I had never been afraid of falling, even before I knew I could fly without pixie dust.

My hand clamped in his shirt and yanked, drawing his lips to mine. He kissed me, and I melted into his arms. *Please don't be wrong.* I clutched him tight, unwilling to let go. He was air. He was ocean. He was endless.

When we parted, we didn't separate. I rested my head against his shoulder, still clutching his shirt, allowing his scent to hold me along with his arms. He squeezed me close, as desperate as he had been in his kitchen so many days ago when I'd first called him my friend. He was more than that now, though I wasn't exactly sure when it had happened. "I love you, too," I said.

His breath shuddered, and his lips touched my neck as he buried his face against my shoulder. In his embrace, it was easy to hope. It was easy to believe. This couldn't be wrong; it couldn't fall apart. A cold sort of determination took refuge in my chest.

As long as I could, I wouldn't let it.

Bidding the Nixie Cove goodbye, we picked our way silently through the treetops, deciding that flying on a clear day would only allow the pirates to know where we were if they searched, and if we took the land route, they could be lying in wait.

Somewhere in the middle, then, Whisper had said, landing on a branch and setting her hands at her hips. I'm not sure she'd left the air since she regained her ability to fly.

Skye made himself busy flitting between the two of them, and exhaustion filled him every time he collapsed on Bay's shoulder, face down against the clothes.

"Are you okay?" Bay murmured, but I heard him. He poked Skye's cheek.

The tiny creature mumbled against the cloth, "Of course, I love being hunted by pirates and having to monitor two people so they don't fall out of trees. Can someone please tell her that the dust is for if she needs it and not for doing tricks?"

Whisper skipped from one branch to the next, hardly touching even the sturdiest limbs. Her face was so bright. Bay saw it too, and he pouted. "But she looks so happy."

"I see how it is." Skye pushed himself up, fluttering indignantly. "You'd rather let your girlfriend's friend be happy than let your pixie rest. How the loyalty has shifted. I trusted you."

Bay caught my eye then, and I looked away like I

339

hadn't been watching the whole exchange. I had no helpful input to provide. I hadn't so much as touched a branch for the last ten minutes.

Bay floated to me, drifting at my side, and Skye groaned, falling face-first against his shoulder again. Bay's hand skimmed mine, inciting butterflies in my stomach. "Being nosy again, Wind Song?"

My cheeks flushed.

"What do you propose we do to fix this problem?" he asked.

I glanced at Whisper, who cheerfully tapped her way over the awkward terrain, oblivious. It was nice to see her so at peace after so many days of seeing restrained tension in her limbs. "She should have her own pixie."

Skye scoffed, glaring at me. "*Pardon?* People don't just 'have' pixies. We only cling to people who can understand us."

"Wendy couldn't understand you."

He rolled his eyes. "No, duh. I was never meant to be 'hers.'"

My brows rose. From even before Bay was born, Skye knew? Or had he been told? Who knew what the sirens manipulated. One problem at a time, I supposed. "Then where's my pixie?"

"Maybe none of them like you because you think we're something to be owned?"

Bay snickered, glancing away.

I narrowed my eyes at him and addressed Skye. "You know that's not what I mean. And what use would I actually have to 'own' a pixie now?"

"Um. Your friend." He rolled his eyes. "Or have we forgotten what we were talking about."

"Sometimes, you're unbearable." I huffed.

He gave me a tight smile, flitted back over to Whisper, and replenished her dust before I could get another word in.

340

But he definitely was a loyal little asshole.

Shaking my head, I smiled. Bay's fingers brushed mine again, then slipped around them. I looked at our joined hands before meeting his gaze quizzically.

He shrugged. "The pixie has spoken. You're my girlfriend now."

"Is that how relationships work?" I couldn't hold back my smile or blush.

His brows shot high, and a flush coated his cheeks as he glanced away. "Don't look at me. I wouldn't know either. Remember, you're the first girl I ever went to a party with. The closest thing I've had to a girlfriend before that was a girl who was a friend, and also that one's mother, so..." He pointed at Whisper, who had stopped up ahead and was hyper-focused on our joined hands. A wide smile consumed her face.

"Oh, great. She's noticed." I bit back my smile. "Play it cool."

"Have I missed something, Lyly?" she asked when we reached her.

"Of course, you have," Skye snipped, throwing up his hands and collapsing on Bay's head. "You've been high on pixie dust ever since you left that damn temple. It's a wonder you aren't hallucinating!"

"Translation?" Whisper's brow quirked.

Bay and I looked at each other, then he said, "He's kind of worn out and would appreciate you using your dust sparingly."

The innocent darling breathed curses into Bay's hair.

Whisper wasn't having the diversion. She waggled a finger between us. "What happened here."

"He kissed me," I answered.

Bay countered, "And then she kissed me."

"And we got a pixie's blessing."

"So here we are."

Whisper pressed her fingers against her lips, squealed, then jumped us both with a hug. "It happened! I thought it would happen, but now that it's happened, it's so much more than I'd hoped! The children of sworn enemies... A demigod and a pirate. Star-crossed love."

"Fitting, isn't it, Star Boy?" I smiled, but Bay's grin had fallen into something softer.

"I'm not really a pirate. More of an explorer or adventure seeker."

Or a Lost Boy. In that moment, something in his eyes reminded me of the Lost Boys. I had once asked Peter where they had come from. He said he didn't quite remember. All he knew was that, at one point or another, they had gotten lost and decided it was better to be lost together.

My hand squeezed his. "Bay was raised beside your mother for a time, Whisper."

She turned, looking at the sky. The sun reclined on the horizon, not quite painting it in shades of dusk. "Speaking of my mother, we should almost be at our camp."

Nixies around the meadow. "Maybe thirty minutes more?"

Bay tensed. "Should we stop for dinner first?"

"We can have dinner together. We'll probably need it before we head back to Skyla. We shouldn't waste time." Whisper held her arms out, balancing as she walked across a branch. "I'm kind of worried about what they did to her. When you saw her, did she look okay?" Worry pitched in her tone, though she tried to hide it well.

He was crushing my fingers now, but his expression

remained calm and distant. "I said before, they have a certain respect for each other. I don't think Hook would hurt my childhood friend."

"It didn't stop him from killing all her people." Whisper moved on before we had a chance to say anything in response. What could we say anyway? She was right.

It was easy to see what she had told herself in the temple clung. Hopefully, that would pass when we were all safe again.

I started to follow her, but Bay held me back. "Wind Song," he whispered, his voice raw.

"What is it?"

Skye jolted up suddenly, spun to face Whisper, and groaned. Darting, he showered her in a fresh coat of dust, leaving us alone.

My chest tightened, making it hard to breathe. "What's wrong?"

"I don't actually know, for sure, whether or not Hook released Tiger Lily."

Ice washed over my skin. "What?"

"I never saw her," he confessed.

A sinking sensation overcame me, sending my heart to my toes. I could only repeat stupidly, "What?"

"If she isn't where Whisper thinks she would be, then—"

I stared at him, my eyes wide, my heart still, dread filling every inch of my body. Mouth dry, my mind grasped for what exactly he was telling me. He had lied to us. And if she wasn't safe... "Then Hook still has her and could be in Skyla right now, with enchantress magic and a hostage." I choked, tearing my hand out of his and floating back. I covered my mouth, trying to control my suddenly panicked breaths. "Why are you only telling me this now?"

"Skye told me what the sirens said. We didn't have time to make sure she was okay. I trust they wouldn't have said what they did unless she would be safe, but we couldn't take any chances." He held his hands out, pleading, but I could hardly look at him.

I shook my head in disbelief. "How could you?"

His jaw tightened. "We couldn't risk failing. The sirens said—clearly, which is rare—if we didn't go directly to the Nixie Cove, we wouldn't succeed."

Anger exploded in my skull, hot and red. I glanced at Whisper, who danced onward with Skye, likely believing we were back here having a "moment" that she shouldn't disturb. Even when she didn't trust him, she wouldn't interrupt if it made me happy. *Airwoman.* How could I have been so stupid? Hook could already be in Skyla; he could have already confronted Peter, failed to get what he wanted, and killed her. Leaning forward, I hissed, "You better hope Tiger Lily is at their camp, Bay. In fact, you better pray."

With that, I flew to my friend, ignored my cracking heart, and left him behind.

The silence did not bode well. With darkness rising over the meager, deserted camp, everything appeared eerie and forsaken. I held my breath, praying to the airwoman, to whatever deity had birthed me, that Tiger Lily would appear.

An untouched fire pit rested beside a simple lean-to, any past ashes already stolen by the wind. Tucked in a corner of the forest with high brush, footsteps would hardly be noticeable, but something would have been disturbed had anyone been here in the past few days.

"Maybe they found her again?" Bay's voice had the decency to be choked.

Whisper stood beside me, staring blankly at the tiny

camp. "She should be here. She said if we got separated, we'd meet back here..."

"Whisper..." I reached for her.

She shook my hand off her shoulder. "No! I trusted your trust in him, but my mother isn't here! We shouldn't have left the bay without her!"

"No, we shouldn't have." I faced Bay, bitterness on my tongue.

He started, "The sirens said—"

"I don't care!" A torrent of wind ripped through the space, and the lean-to collapsed. "Why didn't you tell us the truth sooner than now? If we had known, we could have left for Skyla yesterday! Every day we wait, we don't know what's happening over there; we don't know if—"

"Hook could have released her." He swept back his hair and had the gall to defend himself. "I just wasn't sure."

A sour laugh sputtered out of my mouth. "Really? You weren't *sure*? You know your father, Bay. The man had you tortured and thrown in a cell for lying to him, and that's just his most recent crime."

He winced, distress in his eyes. "I didn't know. I only did what I thought was best for us."

My chest hurt. Something stung in my heart. The scene before me twisted, and I was Wendy, staring at Hook. He smelled mostly of ash, but beneath that was a far worse scent: the tang of blood. "You did what was best for yourself," I whispered. "If you had done what was best for us, once we were safe, days ago, you wouldn't have hidden the truth. You knew lying to us was wrong."

"I knew you'd want to go back." He swiped his hair away from his eyes again. "We couldn't afford to go back. We couldn't afford to be captured. The second my father came back, he would have killed you, Wind Song! You're most useful to them dead. I did what was best to save you."

Because he didn't believe I could save myself? My heart cracked; I swallowed the bitterness and didn't let any welling tears fall. "I thought you were better than him." The image of him sacrificing himself in the temple came to mind, but beside it, the thought of Tiger Lily already out of reach burned. So what if he was willing to sacrifice himself for his goals? It was clear he was also willing to sacrifice others. "You're exactly like your father. If you had just..." *Told me the truth, ages ago, all of it. But again and again, he hadn't.* I was foolish. Belief and trust and faith and dust could be magic, but it didn't just magically change people. Each person had to choose to do that themselves.

I turned my back on him. "Come on, Whisper. Let's go home. We'll find Tiger Lily, I promise."

The wounded look in her eyes didn't hurt half as much as the doubt. She had only just begun to believe in me, and now, thanks to Bay, all I could see on her face was pain and question.

Taking a shaky breath, I lifted my pinky. "I promise."

She glanced at Bay then at my hand. Biting her lip, she nodded, linking her finger with mine.

I clung to the action whether she felt it in her heart or not. Without looking back, I asked, "Skye, did you know the truth?"

A moment passed, and I already knew the answer. *Of course.* He knew Hook as well as his son, they shared everything, and the damn creature was exactly as he'd said: loyal. "I'm sorry," he replied, voice meek.

"I guess this is where we part ways." I blinked,

and tears traced down my cheeks, but I refused to acknowledge the dampness.

Whisper's lips parted. "How will I..." She stopped, realizing. Already, even with dust, how could she possibly trust it enough to get home?

"Wind Song, please," Bay started, touching me.

A rush of air slammed into his chest, throwing him back. He crashed into a tree and winced, sliding down the bark to land on his ass in the foliage, but I had seen the moment his feet left the ground. If I could do that, I could get Whisper safely home.

"Good eve, Star Boy," I murmured. Supporting Whisper around the waist, I exhaled, peering through the canopy at the sky. Star-speckled as it was, I pinpointed home. My feet left the ground right as Bay gathered his bearings.

"Please!" He shouted over the wind building around us. "I went about it wrong, but I didn't mean— If I had known—"

Whatever else he said was lost in the gusts.

Exhaustion ached in my limbs by the time I landed with Whisper in Skyla. She released a held breath, but that was all. We both looked around. No signs of a war had touched Aire. Everything, for the most part, was quiet. Normal.

"They haven't come yet?" I took a step, but my head spun.

"Lyly!" Whisper caught me before my face landed in the dirt. "Are you okay?"

"I'm not used to my power, I guess." Or my trust had shaken. I had been so wrong. How was I supposed to keep things from falling apart when they already had? "Flying is one thing, but flying and using the wind to carry someone..." I tried to shake off the nausea, but it didn't want to go anywhere.

Whisper scanned the empty market streets. Each stall had a brightly colored cloth hanging over the entry. Any scents of baked goods or warm food had long since dispersed, and now only dust swirled down the paths. "Since it doesn't seem like the pirates are here yet, let's get back to my house so you can rest for a bit."

I leaned on her, taking slow breaths and not bothering to soften my words. "Your house isn't here anymore." Neither of us had a home to go back to right now.

"Oh. Right." Her lips pressed tight, and I closed my eyes to avoid seeing the sorrow in her gaze. She gasped. "Moth prince! Adam lives by himself in the woods where the moths and silkworms breed. It's closer anyway, just past the goat stables."

No wonder she hadn't seemed worried about him. The island that housed a majority of the animals was at the opposite end of the disaster. "Will he be okay with us appearing in the middle of the night?"

"He's an introverted young man. I doubt he'll mind two pretty damsels on his doorstep, one of whom is very, very into him. If he does, I think he'll get over it." She began dragging me in that direction, murmuring, "Besides, what choice do we have? Hook's on his way, and you can barely walk."

I shuffled along with her as best I could. Crossing the swaying bridge, we found ourselves bombarded with the soft bleats of goats and sheep. A single shepherd lay snoozing at the pen exit, his staff laid against his side. Other than him, the few homes tucked among the fairy oaks were dark and hushed, void of life.

We continued through the spattered woods gleaming with silver dust until they thickened, and a simple cottage covered with vines and huge white flowers appeared. Whisper breathed a little sigh. Obscured by the trees as this place was—and not in the habit of stalking poor, innocent, young boys—I'd never seen where our prestigious Silk Moth Babysitter lived. It looked plucked straight from a fairytale. Huge moths with forest green wings the size of my hand dallied from one flower to the next to rest and seek mates.

"Isn't this enchanting?" she whispered like she was sharing a secret and didn't want Adam to hear. "I'm going to live here one day."

"It fits you perfectly," I whispered back, and she smiled. Airwoman, it was good to see her smile even if nerves still wound tight in her limbs.

She knocked on the door and waited, fidgeting slightly. A look of sheer terror overcame her, and her hand rushed to her tangled, unwashed hair, but it was too late. The door eased open a crack before swinging the full way.

"Whisper!" Adam's wide blue eyes clung directly to her, ignoring me like I didn't exist. "You...you're okay?" He swallowed and shook his head, scrubbing a hand over his short, dark hair. "I've gotta be dreaming. I saw...I saw your name on the list of people we lost in the attack."

She blushed, holding her gaze on the ground. "It's a long story."

He looked at his bare chest and turned an impossible shade of red that stood out even on his brown skin. "I—I'm so sorry. I wasn't expecting—" He glanced at me as though seeing me for the first time.

I lifted my hand in a pitiful greeting.

His brows lowered, and he looked past us, scanning the bloom-invested area. "Is everything okay?"

Whisper's smile wobbled. "Not really. Can we come

in?"

He nodded without hesitation and stepped aside. Whisper helped me into the modest living room strewn with crocheted blankets and embroidered pillows. I landed on top of a pillow boasting the same kind of moth that lingered outside and reclined gratefully into the couch.

Adam sat across from us in a loveseat, moving aside a most recent embroidery project that made my brows furrow. He wasn't what I'd call a small guy or the type to live in this pastel-washed place.

"You live here alone?" I blurted.

Whisper jabbed me with her elbow. He laughed, smiling kindly. "It's okay. Yes, I do. My friends like to call my home, 'Grandma's Cottage.'"

I swept my eyes over the room again, rested on Whisper's tiny frown, and mumbled, "Really? That's odd. No idea why."

She shook her head and sighed, pushing my comments aside. "We need a favor. The pirates that attacked us several weeks ago aren't finished."

Adam's smile dropped away, and he cupped a hand against his mouth, leaning forward, pensive. "I know. There have been more sightings. As we've worked to rebuild, we've also been preparing for the worst. We know they have magic. Any time Peter and the Lost Boys get close to one, they use a spell and vanish."

Whisper's wide eyes turned on me. "What are they doing? You don't think..."

"Probably." I nodded. "They don't play fair. They are going to get all the information they can about where they'll be fighting and what they'll be up against." Thing was, Skyla didn't have a formal military or army or fighting force. We merely had our location that kept us separate from the world and a handful of children who practiced with wooden swords as it crossed their fancy. Something told me that this time, a group of pre-teens wasn't going to cut it.

The same thoughts rolled through Whisper's eyes like a storm, and she looked at Adam, biting her lip. "My mother comes from a magical place called Neverland. That's where she took me when our home fell. That's where Lyric and I have been. Now, she's been captured by Hook, and we know he plans to attack."

"Hook?" Adam breathed, straightening in his chair. "But that... He's always been just another one of Peter's fairytales, the villain behind his trophy pirate ship."

"The pirate ship is Peter's trophy for defeating Hook." I swallowed rising bile. "But I guess he didn't defeat Hook quite as well as he thought."

Adam's calm never broke, but he mussed his short hair and breathed deeply, pinning Whisper with his gaze. "You said you needed a favor? How can I help? Anything you need, anything at all..."

Her cheeks darkened as her eyes ran over him. "Just a place to stay for tonight. Lyric's exhausted, which is something of another story. In simple terms, she's our only hope of defeating Hook again, and then she's a piece of a much larger picture. Our world is in trouble."

"I apparently have eleven siblings that our goddess mother abandoned in each kingdom to protect from villains just like Hook. As we come into our magic, it no longer is a barrier over our homes." I didn't let the shock on Adam's face faze me. "I'm supposed to find them and save the world after I destroy a magical relic and after I save Skyla."

His mouth opened and closed twice before he managed, "Sounds...simple enough." He shook his head, moving forward in the conversation. "Of course you both can stay here. I'm sorry I don't have much space, but you're welcome to the couch, and then Whisper can have my bed in the back room." He glanced at her, linking his fingers between his knees. "If you'd like?"

Whisper murmured, "Where are you going to sleep?"

He chuckled. "If I can sleep after this information, right here. I expect, instead, to finish that, though." Gesturing at the half-complete embroidery circle, he shrugged. His smile softened, and there was love in it as he traced patterns on the rug with his toe. "I'm really glad you're okay, Whisper. I didn't know what to think when I saw your name with the...missing. After what happened at your birthday party, I thought that would be enough excitement for a while." His clasped hands tightened, and his lips pursed, emotion clogged in his throat as he repeated, "I'm just really glad you're okay."

Whisper sat still beside me, watching him as her eyes glassed. Sighing, I jabbed her with my elbow and motioned with my eyes for her to get her pretty little ass over there. She looked at me like I had grown two heads.

Adam cleared his throat, and the moment was gone. "I don't mind you both staying here, of course, but why didn't you go to Peter? Is the secret of his home that strict?"

My heart sank. "Not really. Not right now, anyway. Just..." My voice faded, and I took a breath. "Well, you know Peter. Everyone knows Peter. I've been gone for a while. I don't think he—" My throat closed, and I closed my eyes to avoid unleashing tears. Today had been hard enough without dwelling on this.

Whisper slipped her hand around mine and squeezed

the same moment Adam said, "Oh. Right. His memory." He took a breath, then added, "I'm so sorry," like he was wishing me his condolences. Adam stood, delicately setting the matter aside. "If either of you would like something to eat, or a shower, or just anything, you're welcome to it. I can make tea?"

I'd seen why Whisper liked him before, but he was absolutely a prince, an angel. An angel with a four-pack. Airwoman, there was nothing bad to say about him. Except that he made me think about my demon.

Whisper kissed my hand before releasing it and standing to meet him in the middle of the room. "A shower and tea sound incredible."

Every muscle in his body relaxed, and he brushed her tangled, curly hair away from her forehead before bending to peck it. He whispered something to her that I couldn't make out, but whatever secret it was, she turned a deeper shade of cherry red.

Without missing a beat, Adam met my eyes. "Tea?"

I wordlessly nodded and hoped that it, plus a night of rest, would prepare me for tomorrow. Whatever Bay had done, Wendy didn't deserve her fate. I still had the vial that held the precise amount to heal her, and I still needed to find the Fountain so I could destroy it. If possible, before Hook had any chance of finding it as well.

28TH NOVEMBER

"Lyric!"

I gasped awake, staring blearily up at a face too close to mine to make out. I slashed my arm out, grabbing the air around me like a cloak and throwing it over the person. They moved effortlessly out of the way, but something broke across the room.

Scrambling for purchase, I blinked against the darkness, glanced at the chair where Adam had been when I drifted off, then swallowed when I found him missing.

The shadowy form hovering in the room was too small to be Bay.

"Shout in her face again. That worked so well the first time," a high-pitched voice I didn't recognize snipped. A pixie zipped to me, tilting her head. "It's just us," she said gently.

"Tinkerbell?" I blurted, squinting at the boy behind her. *Peter*. Was I dreaming?

Tinkerbell buzzed right back to him and sat on the rim of his hat. "I think she's okay."

"Where have you been?" Peter demanded, throwing his arms out. "Do you know how hectic it has been around here since you left?"

I stared at him, mute. It made no sense for him to be here. How would he have known I was here?

"Well?" he prompted, his voice pitching higher.

"Neverland," I replied in disbelief. If this were real, Adam would be seated in his chair like he was when I'd fallen asleep, and Whisper would have heard us by now.

Almost on cue, the door to the back room creaked, and light flooded the space. I squinted through it as Peter whirled on Adam and Whisper.

Adam stood protectively before her, holding an oil lamp, but there was a significant amount of murder in her tired gaze as well. At least, until she saw Peter.

"What are you doing here?" Her eyes went wide.

Peter folded his arms. "Doesn't matter. What are you doing here?" He dismissed them both and directed that question at me, frowning. "There are pirates *everywhere*, and I haven't been able to find you for weeks. Why didn't you come home?"

I swallowed, my heart rate picking up. "I," I began, my eyes filling with tears, "I didn't think you'd remember me."

His arms loosened, and his shoulders drooped for half a second. Hurt flickered through his gaze, but he shook it off. "Stupid."

"It's a valid point," Tinkerbell chimed mercilessly,

kicking her legs through his hair.

Peter ignored her. "Well, I do remember you, so come home. We're on the edge of a war, and it's not just here either. This whole world is falling apart."

"I know that. I'm supposed to fix it." Though *how exactly* was another topic.

"Fix it?" He blinked at me, incredulous. "I don't think so. You're going to stay safe and let me handle this. It isn't the first time I've had to deal with pirates."

After everything, he thought I was just going to sit by and let him fight this battle alone? I rose off the couch, folding my arms as I faced him in the air. "It isn't exactly my first time dealing with them now, either."

"Lyric," he warned.

"No. I don't want to hear it. You've kept me on these islands for my entire life. And, sure, maybe when I left, I wasn't in the best mindset, but even then, I survived. And not only did I survive, I survived a place that's more dangerous than anywhere I've ever heard of. I came out of it all stronger." My fists clenched. "Skyla is my home. I'm going to stand beside you and defend it."

"This isn't an adventure!" he yelled. "This is war! And I'm—" His voice cracked. "I'm not going to lose you to it."

"For the love of the stars," Tinkerbell sighed dramatically, "Peter, she's two feet off the ground without pixie dust. I think she's learned a lot on her adventure. We've always known this day was coming. Or at least I have. Did you forget?"

He glared upwards, but didn't reply to her.

"What does she mean you've always known this day was coming?"

The annoyance on their faces disappeared. Peter's arms dropped by his sides, and his eyes went huge.

Whisper coughed, sidling up to me and wrapping her arms around my shoulders. "Yeah, she also understands pixies now. So maybe it's time to stop treating her like a child?"

Tinkerbell's breath seemed to hold, then she murmured, "So you really have been to Neverland, and it decided to grant you our tongue."

"I have. And we know that Hook is coming to try and take Skyla. And we know that he's not alone; he has magic, an enchantress backing him up."

Whisper nodded. "And also, he has my mother hostage."

Peter's concern was blank, but Tinkerbell's eyes shone with something deeper, and she whispered, "Hook is back, and he has Tiger Lily?"

Sunlight gleamed through the window, catching on Adam standing patiently in the hall. Dawn meant we hopefully had another day before Hook could reach us. I landed with my feet on the floor and found my bag where I'd discarded it beside the couch the night before. It had definitely seen better days, but it would still carry food for the trip to the Fountain. Other than that, my spyglass and pan flute were all that had survived Neverland. I hesitated before picking it up. "We have to find and destroy the Fountain of Youth before Hook even has a chance to reach it. He wants to use the magic for himself and in whatever plot the enchantress has set him on."

Tinkerbell flitted off Peter's hat and waved her hands before my bag, blocking me from grabbing it. "You know about the Fountain?"

"Yes. Do you know where it is?"

Her gaze dropped, and she landed on the flap of my satchel. "I vaguely remember."

"Home, right?"

She straightened, holding herself in a hug. Her huge eyes met mine, and she swallowed, nodding.

"No way." Whisper threw her hair back and blew out a breath. "All this time, the Fountain has been in your home?"

"Hidden under it." I snatched my bag strap, and Tinkerbell moved out of the way so I could pull it around my shoulders. My eyes caught on the feathers marking my arm, and I clenched my jaw. Exhaustion punctuated my movements, but I would have to accept the fact I hadn't had much sleep. "Right under my nose, just like the temple spirit said."

"Forgotten in time by the only one who had ever been allowed to find it." Tinkerbell exhaled, looking at Peter. "It was ages ago, back when Skyla had first appeared in this world as a refuge for those fleeing Neverland's tyrants."

"How do the other Lost Boys share his eternity if only he found it so long ago?"

Sadness made Tinkerbell settle back into the dip of Peter's hat, her legs pulled tight against her chest. "After the first war with Hook, Peter took a blood oath, promising to protect the Lost Boys who survived; unknowingly, he bound them to the power running through his veins."

Peter scratched his head, peering at us all like we were talking in another language. At least, he understood both of us, though. Whisper tugged on my sleeve, a brow quirked in question.

"They shared blood," I said.

"Oath blood," Peter added, and something lit in his eyes, but it was gone in the next second. He pumped his chest. "None of whatever you're talking about matters.

If pirates are on their way, we need to secure Skyla. And that means getting you home."

I frowned. "How did you even know I was here?"

His expression didn't change as he tried to push me toward the door. "Doesn't matter."

"You don't remember, do you?" Whisper accused.

Peter glared at her, but that was exactly it.

I looked directly at Tinkerbell, even though she had sunk deep into the groove of Peter's hat, hiding everything but her leaf-clad feet from view. "Someone told us. The other boy who also glitters with pixie dust."

Bay.

He had followed us? He was here?

My heart wouldn't settle from the moment it knew Bay had followed us back to Skyla. I floated in a daze toward home, ignoring all Peter's complaints about "strangers discovering the base" even as he led us there. Whisper ignored him too, guiding me along behind her like a balloon. Periodically, she shot me a worried glance, but I tried to smile and reassure her when I noticed.

He was here, in the shadows. He knew where our home was. Had telling Peter where I was been to distract him? Had Bay figured out where the Fountain was, even though I'd never said anything specific about its location?

Worry ate away at my gut, and I tried to temper it. Bay was still Bay. Even if what he'd done concerning Tiger Lily was unforgivable, he wasn't the kind of person who would...go behind our backs and burn down an entire civilization of people, right? I had seen in his second temple test that he had boundaries.

I squeezed Whisper's hand and hoped. He had proven himself to be like his father in too many ways. My heart still wanted to believe in him, but I couldn't afford misplaced trust in these dire moments before what could be the devastation of the entire world.

Peter grumbled the entire way down the tunnel into the base, swiping the furs aside. Whisper followed. I followed behind her, spotting the Lost Boys at the table, their hands filled with food. They peered at one another, then back at Whisper, but no recognition touched their gazes.

"Ah..." Slightly began, "Who're these girls, Peter?"

A part of me chipped away. Peter had remembered, but they hadn't? I looked between the Twins, but they shifted their gaze to one another, exchanging shrugs. Tootles' brows were lowered with concentration, but nothing sparked, and for some reason, that made him deflate in sorrow. One by one, each turned away to wait for Peter's answer.

"What do you mean? It's Lyric," Peter snapped, finding his chair and plopping into it.

"Lyric?" Nibs scrubbed the edge of an empty bowl against his head. "Is that a new friend of yours?"

Peter sighed, waving a hand at them, and a sliver of brokenness splintered over his face. He wiped it away when he looked at Whisper and I. "Your room is untouched, and there should be enough food in the stores."

Swallowing the lump burning in my throat, I nodded and crossed to the door.

"Her room?" Chubs and some others chorused behind me.

"I always wondered why we had that."

Someone said with a scrunched nose, "So girly."

My stomach tightened, but I pushed into my space and let the familiar glowing mirabel, bed, and random bits and bobs calm me. They did a poor job.

"It's just like I would have imagined!" Whisper laughed, though the sound was strained. She lifted a hand-made arrow off a dresser and twirled the shaft between her fingers. "I can't believe it took this long for me to finally see your home."

I couldn't believe it took me this long to really see how fractured my family was. What did the world look like through their eyes, when everything was new and remade and the games they played again and again were always the same but never recalled? I didn't know how often the Fountain's magic reset them, but it was clear only Peter knew how to tamper with it.

And he fought. He fought to keep me.

A sob swallowed me up, and I gasped, leaning against the dirt wall and covering my face with my hands.

Whisper set the arrow down and was at my side in an instant. "Hey," she said softly, "it's okay. Let it out."

Tears poured down my cheeks, and strangled breaths left my chest. I hadn't cried like this since that night I thought I'd lost her. Now, she held me, letting me muffle my pain against Adam's shirt, the one he gave her after she showered with his soap; she smelled like a stranger, and that made my sobs worse.

I stayed in her arms for several long minutes. Eventually, the tears dried, but the ache in my chest remained. "Let's find that accursed Fountain and get rid of it," I whispered. I took a few spare moments to change out of the clothes I had borrowed from a native camp in Neverland. Promising to avenge them once and for all, I pulled on my own familiar shirt and pants.

Whisper scratched her moccasin against the corner of my rug. "You said the Fountain was under your home. How do we get under this?" She looked at the hard dirt floor, and her nose pinched. "Do we just dig?"

A flutter zipped into the room, and Tinkerbell swept her gaze over me before tilting her head. Some emotion filled her eyes, but neither her voice nor her countenance conveyed it. "I can lead you to the entrance. The Fountain itself is under our home, but you can't reach it by digging." She flew within an inch of my face and narrowed her eyes. "But before I take you to one of the most powerful relics in the world, how do you plan to destroy it exactly?"

I scrubbed my cheek, taking deep breaths, then muttered, "I don't know. The spirit of the temple—"

"The temple?" she chimed.

"In Neverland."

Her eyes widened, and she jerked back. "You've spoken to the spirit of Neverland? You survived those tests?"

Dumbly, I nodded.

"What did she say?" Her words came airy and breathless, reverent, and her hands clasped in prayer.

"'All wind that rises must fall.' I don't know what it means. I just assume it has something to do with my powers." I wiped my hands on my shirt and offered Whisper a weak smile. It was all I could manage. "Tink's going to take us to the Fountain."

Tinkerbell shook her head. "No, no. I'm going to lead you to the entrance, but I'm not going there again. That magic is a drug. If Neverland trusts you to handle it, then I will too, but I can't go back. I just can't."

"What did she say?" Whisper asked.

"She's leading us to the start, but we have to make it from there on our own." Biting my lip, I clenched a fist around my bag strap.

Tinkerbell raised her head, eyeing Whisper haughtily. "Does your friend have what it takes to make it out of there, Lyric? If Neverland entrusted you with this, I'm sure you'll be fine, but..."

"Whisper made it through the temple's tests, as well." I frowned.

Tinkerbell zipped to my ear, brushing my hair aside and whispering like someone else in the room could understand her. "But, she can't even fly."

I swatted at her. "Yes, she can."

"Oh, really?" Tinkerbell's brows shot up, but her expression remained indignant. She fluttered over Whisper, then pulled back and crossed her arms as pixie dust rained into my friend's light curls.

Whisper looked at me, shaking her head. "Oh, no. No, I don't think— Not after..."

"You said it before, even if I didn't realize it then. You weren't flying because you trusted Skye." I held out my hand. "You never trusted them, and you were right. I should have listened closer to what you were telling yourself in the temple, but why could you fly?"

She looked at my hand, her brows knitted. I floated off the ground, and realization overcame her. "I trusted you wouldn't let me fall." Clasping my hand, she grinned, throwing a sassy look at Tinkerbell before curtseying into the air. "Guess both our heads were a little jumbled after all that, but yes, little miss priss, I can fly."

"Hmm," Tinkerbell tittered, "interesting. I've never seen someone regain their ability to fly."

"Maybe she never lost it. Maybe she just needed to remember that she wasn't afraid of falling because there was still someone who wouldn't let her, no matter what."

Tinkerbell shrugged. "Well, nothing regarding Neverland is straightforward or makes sense, and we—

the pixies—were birthed there, so naturally, our magic reacts in questionable ways. One thing is clear, you both were accepted. And if Mother accepts you, so will I." Her eyes darted, and she huffed. "Come, I'm sure we don't have much time."

I landed as soon as Tinkerbell zipped out of the room. Whisper landed beside me, skeptical. "You're still not feeling well, are you?"

"Barely any sleep after flying us both between entire worlds? No wonder I'm not in my best shape." I sighed, squeezing her hand. "We'll get through this. After all," I straightened, fluttering my lashes, "we have been treated to mythical moth prince tea. Don't you dare think I didn't notice you both coming out of the bedroom an hour ago."

She flushed. "There was a lot on your mind. Of course, you didn't notice."

"His hair was all ruffled, and I'm certain the dark promise in your gaze was a reaction to interruption, not threat."

She snatched her hand out of mine to press against her breast. "My my, Lyly. How soon we forget. It was you who told me to tempt him. But don't we have more important things to dwell on, aside from my dreams coming true in the moments before the world could very well cease to exist as we know it?"

"Yes,"—Tinkerbell zipped back into the room, her hands on her hips—"we do. Now hurry up!"

Whisper glanced at me, then at Tinkerbell's trail as she left once more. "I almost understood that one." She chuckled, touching my shoulder. "Are you okay?"

I peered at the mostly closed door, hearing the Lost Boys murmuring beyond it, and took a deep breath before nodding. "I'm trying to be. Peter remembers.

Relationships can be rebuilt. We just have to make sure there's a place to rebuild."

"Let's do just that."

I thought I'd explored every nook and cranny on two Skyla islands: the mainland and home. Turns out, I had missed a hidden cavern nestled a ways past Peter's tree. Beyond the pond where we always played while I was growing up, within the cleft of a sheer rock wall covered in brambles, there lay a single section of vines that clung to nothing but air. The opening was little more than two feet across at its base, and we would have to crawl through there since it only narrowed into a crack at the top.

"Be careful," Tinkerbell said, giving my cheek a quick hug. "The closer you get to the magic, the stronger its allure. You'll find reasons you need it, but nothing is worth that power." Her eyes flicked to Whisper, and she pressed her lips together. "Be each other's strength."

"How did you overcome it?" I asked.

She puffed her chest and folded her arms like I had insulted her. "I have no use for such a thing when I'm beside Peter. A pixie's life is extended through belief. As long as he believes in me, I will remain. And I will protect. And I will love." Her cheeks tinted crimson, but she nodded before saying more, and she was gone.

Whisper nudged aside the brambles and looked at the small space we'd have to squeeze through with pursed lips before judging her midsection and bosom with an exaggerated sigh. "Any final wisdom from her ladyship?"

"We have to be one another's strength to make it through this." I crouched, squinting into the dark. It lightened toward the end of what I could see, the same flowers that grew on my ceiling blooming along the walls. "Also, I think she's in love with Peter, which is just weird on a million levels. I'm sharing so I don't have to suffer that knowledge alone."

Whisper's nose scrunched. "Okay, I'm more than happy to face certain doom to get that picture out of my mind. Are you ready?"

"As I'll ever be."

Together, we slipped into the coolness of the cave. A tingle ran down my spine, and the hair on my arms raised the second I was immersed in the space. Whisper met my gaze, took a deep breath, and tugged Adam's shirt sleeves over her hands.

We moved on. I waited for something to take over, for some sense of magic to overwhelm me and steal my thoughts away, but minutes passed, drifting into an hour, and only the flowered walls met my view. The tunnel wound like a snake, twisting and coiling, sometimes inclining and sometimes declining.

"Are we actually getting any closer?" Whisper asked after any initial fear or resolution had worn off.

"I can't tell," I replied, exhaling. I checked the air to see where we stood and what we might be looking forward to. There were only two streams of wind flow, a massive, rushing one before us, and a quiet, seeping one behind us. But there were two touches of something more back there too, something irregular.

I froze.

"What is it?" Whisper asked.

I swallowed, gripping my bag until my knuckles went white. "He's here." He'd followed us. But, of course, he had. We already knew he'd come with us to Skyla, and finding the Fountain had been his sole purpose all along. My empty sheath weighed more on my thigh than it did when it was full, and my fingers found it with a level of dread. Even if I had my knife, could I fight Bay with it?

Perhaps the real question was: would he fight me with the knives I knew he had?

The thought broke my heart.

When the path jackknifed, creating a bend where we wouldn't be seen, Whisper and I stopped, waiting. Sure enough, after several minutes, Bay drifted around the corner silently, spotted us, and went still. Our eyes locked, and my chest pinched. Before I could say anything, he raised his hands and blurted, "You can't destroy the Fountain until I save my mother. That's the only reason I'm here."

Whisper snarled, "Oh, so now you're interested in saving mothers, huh?"

True remorse seemed to flicker through his gaze when he looked at her, but he shook his head and pinned his eyes back on me. "Please. Try to believe me. This is all I've lived for since I lost her. It's only Skye and I. Any friends I had are more than twice my age now or no longer have any qualms about beating me to a pulp."

I wanted to believe him. Believing in the people I cared about came so easily to me, but he'd abandoned Tiger Lily and didn't tell us. Worse, he led us to believe she was okay, knowing his own lie.

Whisper gripped my hand. "We don't believe liars."

"Wind Song," he begged, disregarding her completely.

I dropped my gaze. "We are going to save your mother, Bay. I still have the vial, and I will make sure the water gets to her."

"But—"

"No buts," I snapped, glaring. Releasing Whisper's hand, I took a deep breath and raised my head. "We can collect water just as well as you can. Unlike some of us, we aren't in the habit of ignoring people our friends care about."

"Maybe try trusting in us for a change." Whisper tossed back her hair and huffed. "If it bites you in the rear, you deserved it."

Skye clenched his fists and fluttered before Bay. "These walls are lined with the same magic that courses through the temples in Neverland."

"He's right. The further you go, the stronger the magic gets. It's safer toge—" Bay pleaded, hands outstretched.

"Thank you." Whisper scoffed. "We already know that."

"Tinkerbell told us what to expect." I held his gaze, though the desperation in it burned in my gut. "We have each other; we know we can count on each other."

He deflated, hearing what I hadn't said. He'd proven that we couldn't count on him. He couldn't be trusted.

"I'll know if you follow us," I said. "So don't."

Lamely, he nodded, looked at the cave wall, and floated to it, sliding to the ground. "I'll be here then." He drew his legs up and clasped his hands between his knees, no longer daring to glance at us. "Good luck."

Before I was sure I had done the right thing, Whisper grabbed my arm and pulled me along with her. When I peered over my shoulder, Bay's head was in his hands, and his whole body shook with tears.

It didn't take long after we left Bay to come upon the Fountain. It was unlike anything I'd ever seen, and neither of the temple visions had done it justice. The mirabel clinging to the cracks in the ceiling tripled in mass, boasting luminous blooms twice the size of my head. The blossoms flooded the space with light, revealing a pit that led into churning waves.

That pit stood between us and the Fountain. It sprayed gold, glittering water over the edges of several wide bowls. Intricate designs depicting a history I hardly knew decorated the pearl dishes. Just the sight of it all left me breathless.

Whisper touched my shoulder, her eyes pinned on the magnificent structure. "Can you believe it? All this time, right beneath our feet." Her voice drifted off, and I checked to make sure she was still with me. Nothing glassed her eyes when I met them, and I exhaled with relief.

A distinct tang of magic vibrated in the wind, skating down my throat when I parted my lips. "It's beautiful."

Moments passed, each of us staring and waiting.

"Do you feel any different?" Whisper asked finally.

My head shook. "No, you? Any urge to join the forever-twelve cult?"

"Pardon you. I'd be forever nineteen. And I think I'll pass." Holding my wrist, she leaned to look into the swirling ocean. "The only way across is over. How are you feeling?"

An ache spread through my chest before dipping into my stomach. "Still incapable. I'm not sure I'm willing to take the risk. If I drop you..." Bitterness overwhelmed the taste of magic on the back of my tongue. "I'm not willing to take that chance."

Her brows furrowed. "What are you saying?"

I sifted through my bag, drawing out the vial and clasping it in my hand. "The faster I get over there and back here, the better. It should only take a moment."

"And if something goes wrong?" Lips pursed, she narrowed her eyes. "You're also supposed to destroy that, remember? How are you going to manage *that* quickly?"

Sensing skepticism, I smiled. "I can see you're getting defensive, but trust me. I've lived with the forever-twelve cult. There is no way I'm joining it at any age." I lifted off the ground, but she didn't release my wrist.

"Be careful. If something starts to go wrong, you come right back, and we'll figure things out from there."

I nodded. Dread showered me, cold and murky, but I didn't let it show. She let me go, and I faced the magical pool of golden ichor. Crossing over the pit of waves and secrets, I felt a hot pour of the spirit's words come to the forefront of my mind.

All wind that rises must fall.

Was I supposed to somehow push the Fountain into that pit, into the ocean?

I landed on the other side, and sweat coated my skin. Doubts bombarded me. If I couldn't even fly Whisper here, how was I supposed to—

"Are you still okay?" Whisper yelled.

My mouth was dry; my palms were clammy. "I'm fine!" I called back, not looking at her. "I think I need to get this thing in that thing."

"In the hole?" Surprise coated her tone, but when she spoke again, it had mellowed. "That makes sense. Do you think you can use your wind to get it there?"

No. "I'll try."

First things first, I tried to shake off the overpowering sensations burrowing into my skin. With every step closer, it seemed impossible. It was so strong. And I wasn't. No wonder Peter could do so many insane things. And I couldn't. He had drunk this stuff. And I hadn't.

My hand shook as I uncorked the vial and hovered the glass above the pool of water. A gentle mist fell before my eyes, the closer my fingers got to the liquid.

To fill the vial, I would need to touch it. Touch the magic that had enough strength to provide people eternal life.

"Still okay?" Whisper's words were nearly lost beneath the sound of water.

I swallowed. I wasn't. I wasn't okay at all. So what if I believed in myself a little more now than I did before my adventure in Neverland? I still had to face a pirate that not even Peter had been able to get rid of.

I wasn't strong enough.

"Lyric?" Whisper's voice pitched.

I closed my eyes and filled the vial. Magic touched my fingers, permeated my flesh. It flooded my veins. If I wasn't strong enough, this would be. It had to be. Too much relied on me when I couldn't even rely on myself.

"Lyric!" Whisper yelled. "Lyric! No!"

Her scream filled my head the second I brought the vial to my lips. My fingers trembled, and I blinked, but it wasn't enough to draw me out of the haze. *I needed this.* If I didn't have this power, then I wouldn't be able to save Whisper, or Peter, or anyone on Skyla. This wasn't just a battle for Skyla, either. After this, should I succeed against Hook, I had to help save the world.

Squeezing my eyes shut, I—

"Nope." The firm word was said directly into my ear. A strong chest hit my back, and someone's hands gripped mine, stopping me from throwing the water down my throat. The person wrestled the cork out of my grasp and secured the vial before meeting my gaze. Hazel eyes.

Bay. *He wasn't supposed to be here.* They had warned me to make sure he didn't drink from the Fountain. It...didn't look like he was drinking? Brows drawn, he stared at me. My vision blurred, but I felt his lips against my cheek, and his exhale shook. "Let's get

372

you out of here."

Everything went dark.

29TH NOVEMBER

Comfortable heat. Security. The gentle scent of ocean brine and magic. I breathed it in, drifting softly back into my dreams. Someone jostled my body, and that jerked me fully awake. My eyes snapped open, and hair brushed my cheek.

"Careful!" Whisper snapped. "You're going to drop her."

Bay hitched me up again. "Well, I don't see you offering to carry her."

"Give her here." Whisper shot him a tight-lipped smile and opened her arms.

"I knew we shouldn't have slept back there. First rule of life: don't sleep in a magic-tainted cave." Bay shook his head, and his loose hair tickled my cheek.

"It's made you delusional."

"What else were we supposed to do? We'd been walking all day; she had fainted." She folded her arms. "I'm well-rested. I can carry my friend now."

"You really can't," Skye muttered. "You're like half her size, and while she's asleep, she isn't aware enough to even unknowingly make herself lighter."

"Excuse me? What did he say?" she demanded.

"You've already got your shoulders full with Skye." Bay sighed, adjusting his hold on my thighs again.

It was in that exact instant I realized he was holding me by my thighs and keeping my chest pressed against his shoulder blades. I floundered, flailing backwards.

"H-hey!" he stammered, grappling for purchase, but I tumbled out of his grasp, managing to perform a backflip midair before finding the ground with my feet. Bay blinked at me, looking me over. "I guess you're awake now?"

"Lyly! You're okay!" Whisper pounced, wrapping her arms around me in a full swing that made Skye retreat off her shoulder.

Memories flooded back, and I swallowed bile, the sensations of fog in my mind not fully abated. Lifting a hand, I jabbed a finger at Bay. "You followed us! We told you not to, but you did! We asked you to trust us, but you didn't. You didn't trust me! Again!"

"*What*?" He balked, an injured expression melding with exasperation. "I heard Whispering Meadow scream and came to the rescue. I'm your knight in shining armor."

"You didn't trust us!" I swayed into Whisper, and she held me up, grunting under my weight.

He folded his arms, ignoring how tipsy I was. "I did. I sat still, and I waited, and I developed a nervous habit

376

of bouncing my leg, and then I heard a scream and thought maybe it was code for, 'something is wrong; send help.'"

I blinked at him, and my arm lowered.

"If you're speechless, may I suggest 'Thank you'?" Skye frowned at me, his tiny arms folded as he landed on Bay's shoulder.

Bay shook his head and dragged his fingers through his hair. "Actually, I'd be happy if you consider it the beginning of an apology. I want to help make things right because you were right. I was selfish. Just like my father, I convinced myself I meant well, but I didn't want to risk forfeiting the Fountain or getting what I needed for my mother, even if it meant sacrificing yours..." He winced, moving his gaze to Whisper. "Not even. She isn't just your mother; she was my friend. And I threw that away."

Remorse touched his lips, plucking the strings of my heart. Swallowing, I murmured, "You didn't take any of the water?"

"Just the vial."

"Didn't you hear the temptations?" Even now, doubts floated in my ears, beckoning me to turn back. If Whisper weren't holding me upright, I didn't know if I'd obey them or not.

He shrugged, scuffing his hair a final time and dropping his arm. "Sure. But I was a bit too worried about you to listen to them. They promised useless things anyway." A secret hid beneath the pain in his smile, and I wanted to know what it was, but I couldn't find the words to ask.

"You two can talk after we confirm my mother is safe. Before then, you're still on probation, and I refuse to give Lyric my blessing. That is to say, I'm still not convinced you won't hurt her like your father hurt Wendy."

His fists clenched, and his gaze blackened, but he steadied his breaths and turned on his heel. "Fine. That's fair. If I can prove it to you, then maybe I'll be able to prove it to myself, too. And if I can prove it to myself, maybe I'll finally be free of his shadow."

I reached for him, clutching his shirt.

He jerked away before looking over his shoulder. His eyes widened, then softened. "How are you feeling?"

"Awake." And very, very reluctant to be.

"It's a start." His feet left the ground, and he focused on the path ahead. "We've been in here for a day and a half. Magic stretches the tunnel, making it difficult to get in or out, but we should be getting close. The flowers are thinning."

I squinted at the ceiling. He was right. I hadn't even noticed.

"Do you think you can walk?" Whisper asked.

"Maybe?" Leaning off her support, I found my balance, and my head settled some. "Yeah. I'm all right." I wiped my forehead, but it was dry. Why did I feel so hot? "I didn't drink any of that stuff, right?"

Whisper paled, looking at Bay.

He shook his head. "No, I made it in time."

A wash of ice hit me. "I never destroyed it. We have to go back. I'm supposed to destroy it."

"There is no way we're going back there." Whisper folded her arms and glared at me.

I turned, starting back. "But I promised."

Bay landed in front of me, arms folded. His mouth opened, but he never got a chance to speak. Reverberating thuds vibrated down the walls, hammering into my skull, and shaking the Fountain's grip free at last.

Clarity shot through my veins like adrenaline.

"The warning gong..." Whisper's hair rose on her arms. "That has to mean they're here. This is it."

"We don't have a second to waste." Bay nodded at Skye, and he doused Whisper in fresh dust before stopping in front of me. I was already off the ground. Panic, determination, and fear wound so tight in my stomach, I could hardly catch a breath. Bay grabbed my arm before I had the chance to move. "Here," he said, offering me one of his knives. "You're not going up there defenseless."

I looked at the gleaming metal. It shone blue in the flower light. Wind touched my skin, and I held onto it, curling it around all of us. I wasn't defenseless, but I wouldn't turn down a weapon. "Thank you." Taking it, I delivered the blade to my sheath. It didn't fit quite right, but that mattered little.

"This is it," I echoed. A hypnotic whisper touched my thoughts, calling me back to the Fountain, claiming I had to destroy it, but I didn't have time to dwell on the alluring voice. I would destroy it. But that would have to wait.

We crawled out of the cave into the blaring notes of the gong. Night surrounded us, and I paled, seeing that the purple hint of twilight still cradled the sky. We had been trapped in there far longer than we'd thought.

The pirates came under the guise of night. But, of course, they did. If they came from the sky using some sort of magic to fly, they had to. My heart pounded in my chest, and my breaths wouldn't settle. *This was it.* The battle. The one I had failed to prevent. Things had gotten so out of hand since I left for Neverland.

Mouth dry, I soared above the trees, Whisper and Bay at my sides. Ships. Not one. Not two. Dozens.

Dozens of ships speckled the sky, glowing like stars with the magic that held them afloat. I shuffled through my bag and drew out my spyglass. Peering through it, I went deathly still.

Tiger Lily stood beside Hook at the helm of the largest sloop. His metal hand stroked her cheek.

"What do you see?" Whisper choked, clutching my sleeve.

"Tiger Lily is okay. She's alive, and she doesn't look hurt."

"Oh, thank the airwoman," she breathed, and some tension around Bay eased as well.

I looked at him, pinpointing Skye on his shoulder. "We'll need all hands on deck. Even the small ones."

He nodded stiffly. "I'm running on empty, and Bay's low on dust; don't let him fall. I'll be back."

Habitually, Bay began braiding his hair, freezing when he seemed to remember he didn't have anything to hold it back.

"What is it?" Whisper asked.

"I lost my tie somewhere a few days ago." His lips pursed. "I can't fight well if it's loose."

"Don't you have a backup?" Whisper sneered.

Bay scoffed. "I'm not a girl."

Rolling my eyes, I grounded myself in their banter. "Use a reed or vine."

"Or hack it off." Whisper folded her arms.

"Don't you dare." I scowled at him. "Use a reed or a vine, and please, both of you."—I took a shaking breath— "we need to be on the same team here." Lowering my spyglass, I bagged it and brushed the handle of the dagger Bay had given me. "This is war."

"We'll never make it against those numbers. We need to somehow get an advantage." Whisper's brow furrowed, stiffness in her form. Something lit in her eyes. "Our pirate ship. It still has ammo inside. If I can get the cannons to work, maybe we can at least take out some of the ships?"

"Perfect. Gather the people who aren't trained to fight and head there. Tiger Lily is front and center, so watch where you aim, and watch your dust or replenish." The idea of her being inside a pirate ship, safely away from the thick of the battle, settled my nerves, but the idea of her leaving me in this moment made my heart jump erratically. "Be careful."

"Look who's talking." She threw her arms around me and squeezed. "I will never abandon you."

"We will never be apart," I murmured.

With those words, she zipped away, landing and running through the trees until I couldn't see her anymore.

Anxiety fought for a hold on me, but I couldn't let it take over. I believed in myself. If I didn't, I wouldn't be flying right now. "We need to meet up with Peter."

"Unless I'm mistaken, he's way ahead of you." Bay pointed at a streak of orange and green. I squinted, making out Peter hovering before the armada. He glowed, a different shade than the ships, but he was little more than a speck against the pale blue, ever-darkening sky; they were foreboding suns.

My heart jerked, and I was flying toward him before I could think, Bay hot on my heels.

"Wind Song!" he shouted, and I whirled in time to see him drop.

My stomach fled, and I shot after him, reaching for the wind to grasp his body and carry him safely to the ground. When he had landed, I hit the earth, panting. "Are you okay?" I stammered. "I'm so sorry. I didn't think you were that low on dust, and I was focused on—"

A cannon fired; my lungs tightened. Any words I was saying deserted my mind and my mouth.

"It's okay." Bay held my shoulders, and worry swam in his eyes, but he found half a smile to offer me. "I already fell for you once."

I stared at him, ignoring the flush running over my cheeks. *Everything could go wrong.* Another cannon fired. *I could lose it all.* Wincing, I linked my hand around the back of his neck and pulled his lips to mine. Tears pooled in my eyes as I kissed him quick. "Wait for Skye," I said, pulling away. "And don't do anything stupid."

I turned, but he caught my wrist. "Like running into battle alone?"

"I'm not alone. I never have been. Even when I thought my mother had abandoned me here, people surrounded me and gave me a home. My strength comes from each and every one of you. Each breath alone may not be much, but together, they create a storm." I held his gaze and hoped he didn't see the way terror consumed me.

Whether he did or not, his grip loosened. "I believe in you, Wind Song. But that doesn't mean I'm not scared of losing you."

I was scared of losing everything, and I didn't have time to waste. The second he released me, I left, pushing myself to meet Peter in the air.

Head raised, arms folded, cannons blasting behind us toward the ships, Peter barely glanced my way.

"How can you not remember me?" Hook sputtered, his face red with rage. He had dragged Tiger Lily to the front of the ship, and both of them were pressed tight against the deck rail.

Peter shrugged. "Maybe you just weren't entirely too memorable?"

Tinkerbell laughed, the chiming sounds too merry for the moment.

"You!" Hook spat, lifting his metal hand off Tiger Lily to jab toward me as though just noticing I had appeared. "You remember me, don't you?"

Peter looked at me then, raising a brow.

I caught the unspoken glimpse of mischief in his eye and tilted my head. The bundled nerves in my stomach settled, if a little. "Not sure? You have one of those faces. I think I've seen it before, maybe? But then again, maybe not."

Hook blustered, slashing his arm outwards, accidentally smashing his hook into Smee's face. The stout man collapsed, but his captain couldn't care less. "What madness are you spouting, girl? You were with my son just days ago!"

"Son?" Peter's brows lifted. He floated to my back, all gloat and pride as he presented me. "Hey, that's neat! This is my daughter. Where's your kid?"

Hook snapped. My heart soared with strength and confidence.

"Attack!" Hook yelled.

I didn't need a command. Both Peter and I rose through the night sky, our arms bent at our waists. Our crow rang above the cannon fire, the shouts, the buzz of pixie wings. Everything in that moment was adrenaline, excitement, assurance. There's no way we could lose.

Out of nowhere, the Lost Boys swooped in, diving for Tiger Lily. Their whoops and wallops overlaid the pirates' yells. Cannons went off from Hook's ships, targeting Aire. I felt the wind breathe through me, swirl around me, and I sent the lead balls tumbling right back.

Hook screeched, jumping away from Tiger Lily as one ball crashed through the deck right next to him.

"You missed, Lyric!" Peter teased.

I smirked, brushing away the sweat beading on my forehead; moving lead wasn't exactly the easiest thing in the world, but I had done it. "I'd like to see you do better!"

He flourished a bow. "My pleasure." Drawing his knife, he waggled his brows and zoomed toward Hook.

"Bring her ashore!" Hook hollered, catching Peter out of the corner of his eye. He drew his sword the moment Peter landed on the cannonball protruding from the deck. The pirate crew circled the orange-haired boy, but Hook sneered. "This one's mine."

"Hmm." Peter twirled his blade. "Bold words for a codfish."

The pirate's eyes alighted, teeth baring in a foul grin beneath his waxed mustache. Blades sang in battle, and I turned my attention to Tiger Lily. The Lost Boys had her. She was safe. But the ships were landing quickly, and there were still at least half a dozen to worry about. Whisper had done well, sending so many to the hungry ocean, but I supposed it was my turn. Landing in the clearing just before a break in the trees led to the city, I formulated a plan.

Pixies rushed from the woods and every island all around us, screaming their battle cries.

Skyla's people shouted and raised crude weapons above their heads. As the pirates dismounted, Skyla met them with fury and force.

This was *our* home. Hook had already stolen

Neverland from us, taken Tiger Lily's family and culture, but her people remained here. My people remained here. We remained. And we weren't leaving any time soon.

My fingers brushed Bay's dagger, and my heart wanted to find him in the chaos, but Hook's ship hit the ground, plowing through trees and brush to skid to a stop before me. Atop it, Peter and Hook were locked in an ageless battle that had seen itself play out through generations.

Inhaling, I lifted my arms, fingers splayed. *Wings.* I pictured great feathered wings behind me, gathering the forces of air to my side. The smooth breeze thickened, pooling into a rushing fall. I careened it toward the ship, smashing into the bow with all the force of a hurricane. The wood creaked and groaned. The sails filled. The sloop bounced.

Concentration beaded on my brow, and panting breaths filled me.

"Blast!" Hook yelled, parrying one of Peter's blows and refinding his footing. "You're free to kill," he snapped at his crew.

The men chuckled as they threw themselves overboard. Their boots thumped into the dirt, and I narrowed my gaze at them, but I didn't let up. One way or another, I was getting this ship off my homeland.

"Need a hand?" Bay passed me, flashing me a smile, and lifting his cutlass. When I brightened, he winked, then dashed at my attackers.

Skye zipped off his shoulder and landed on mine. "Whatever is making those things fly, it isn't pixie dust. We can break the spell of the ones still airborne. Can you handle whatever lands?"

I threw a blast of wind toward a pirate, closing in on

Bay's back and flung him off the island. "I think I can." Sweat plastered my hair to my cheeks, but I wasn't going to back down.

"I know you can." He nodded and was gone, calling an army of pixies to him with a shrill whistle. They dashed for the few ships still in the sky, firing cannonballs at Skyla.

I forced all the power I could manage into the gusts filling Hook's sloop's sails, and the ship hopped. Unwilling to relinquish the moment it was off-ground, I poured everything I had into billowing it over the edge.

Pirates tumbled off in the moments before the spell shattered, and the sloop plummeted.

Hook and Peter made it to land, Peter bowing toward me but never losing his stance with the captain. Exhaustion played behind my eyes, but I managed a weak smile amid the budding headache. My focus fell on Bay next. He parried blows from three men, falling back with every hit. Ruthless, they attacked without form, intent on slashing their foe to bits by brute strength alone.

I took his side, drawing my knife. "Hi."

"Hey." His gaze found me for half a second; it was all the time we could spare on each other, but the way his smile brightened stuck with me as I sloppily diverted blow after blow. My arms rattled, and the impacts didn't help my blooming headache. Thankfully, our skills in close combat seemed equal. Unfortunately, they had strength I didn't.

I tried to power my attacks with wind, but the gales deflated. Heaving breaths tore through my lungs. I was spent.

Were we any closer to victory?

We had to be. Cannon fire had died. The final ships

in the air had just met a watery grave. We were winning. *We were winning.* Soon, this battle would be over. Soon, we could go back home. We had already lost so much to these pirates, in the distant past and not one month ago.

Hope gave me a final rush of energy, and I managed to distract our combatants long enough for Bay to serve two a lethal blow. The final man watched his companions fall and ran before Bay had the chance to lay the final attack.

"All right?" he asked me, pressing his back to mine and heaving a breath.

"All right," I confirmed, zoning out of the close combat and back into the full picture. People on both sides dropped like moths. My vision skewed, but I shook my head and pulled myself back together.

"You've lost your touch, Pan!" Hook's voice sounded above the ringing metal and my ringing head. "I'll give you one last chance. Tell me where the Fountain is!"

"Why would a codfish want to live in a Fountain?" Peter jested, but the strain in his voice was terrifying. Blood, golden as the sun at midday, streamed down his leg.

30TH NOVEMBER

My gut flopped over, and horror struck my chest. My body moved before I could breathe. Disgust, hatred, fury, it all corrupted Hook's face as he dealt a single, powerful blow. "Fine!" he spat, spittle spraying from his lips. "To hell with you!"

Peter's dagger flew out of his hand with pristine clarity, landing upright in the scarred ground feet away. Golden blood painted Hook's blade as it impaled him. He plucked the weapon from Peter's body fluidly.

Peter, my father, my family, gaped, falling to the cold ground. Tinkerbell's scream shattered the silence ringing in my head as I reached him moments too late.

His lips parted, he stared upwards, unfocused. I

lifted him into my lap, feeling the rush of blood pour over my skin, hot and wet. "No," I breathed. I blinked fast to keep tears from blurring my vision.

I couldn't— This couldn't— No. *No.*

Hey, Lyric. His voice filled my head, a memory from long ago playing before my eyes. *You don't ever have to be afraid. You know that, don't you?* I had just woken from a nightmare. Curled in the bows of our tree, I sat with my face buried in a blanket, feeling helpless. Concerned pixies had filled the air, and I had peeked out at them, up at Peter. He had been so big once, and I'd never stopped feeling quite so small. *You're the Daughter of Pan. We're the same, you and I. No matter what, we have faith, and we trust, and we believe.*

His green eyes dulled, but they found me. A tear splashed against his cheek. His lips curved in the final moment, peace overcoming him. When his breath left him, it was not an ultimate battle. He released it like he'd held it for far too long. The sensation of air leaving him filled me, and I screamed, clutching his limp body against my chest. One by one around me, the same sensation repeated, echoing. *Slightly. Nibs. Tootles. Chubs. The Twins.*

All at once, their breaths found each other, left together.

I screamed my throat raw. Bay yelled for me, but his voice was garbled. His form stood above us, fighting Hook away from my father and I. Everything hurt. Everything was gone.

I curled over Peter, listening to Tinkerbell's shrieking sobs mirror my own and grow weaker. This couldn't be happening. It had to be a nightmare. It wasn't. I knew it wasn't. And yet it had to be.

Pain knotted in my chest, fighting for an escape. A

bundle of nerves tightened in my back, winding and winding. Something within me burst.

"What on god's earth!" Hook's voice reached my scrambled mind.

My shirt's fabric tore, and my scream silenced as pain held me in its claws; my lips remained parted, gaping. I clutched Peter as something huge and powerful ripped from my body and flapped. *Flapped.* Power surged in my veins, fueled with a distinct thirst for blood. Panting breaths filled me. Rage left me in tides.

Wings. Real, distinct, feathered wings pounded behind me, lifting me to my feet and away from Peter's corpse. Red blanketed my eyes as I pinpointed Hook stumbling away from Bay. Golden blood still stained his cutlass, and I flicked my gaze from it to his wide eyes.

"You," I hissed, splaying my black wings fully. "What have you done?"

Men rushed at me in an effort to protect their captain, but I didn't have to move a muscle. I stalked forward, and a whirlwind surrounded my body, shredding their skin and tossing them away like trash. I shook. Every part of me shook. The air around me trembled, and a horrible thought overcame me.

What if there *wasn't* air around him?

Lifting my hand, I clenched a fist around the air in Hook's very lungs. I watched as his mouth fell open, and his cutlass stained with Peter's blood dropped to the damp earth. He grasped at his neck. I sucked oxygen from the cells in his body, one at a time. His lips flapped, exactly like a codfish.

He lifted a wobbling hand, plunging it into his coat pocket. Removing a small metal box, he pressed the single, centered button on it.

Explosions ricocheted around me, shaking the ground beneath my feet. I lost hold of my magic, and air pooled back over him. He gasped, sputtering. I spun, spreading my wings to stabilize myself. Blasts of light hit nearly every pixie oak I could see, splitting the trunks.

All of the mainland, all of Aire, and every island connected to it by a bridge fell.

The explosions continued on, and I watched the other large islands fall as we dropped out of the sky.

"If I'm not mistaken," Hook coughed, rubbing his throat, "not all of you can fly."

I growled at him; how dare he? The ground ripped out from under me, and I didn't have time to give him another damn. He was right. All around me, my people were heading toward their deaths. My wings pumped, carrying me over the plummeting islands. I located the nearest path off, then I dove over the edge.

Wind howled, obeying my will as I lifted my straining arms. I molded the air into a cushion beneath each falling island. My vision spotted, and I gasped as they continued to career toward the rocking blue waters. I couldn't carry them all. I had to let one go. Swallowing, tears hot on my cheeks, I forfeited the one least likely to have anyone on it right now. My home. Peter's secret hideout. Pouring my energy into making sure the islands with people reached the ocean gently enough to survive, I watched the only world I'd ever known smash into the waves. A glimmering water leaked from beneath the rubble, then dispersed, lost forever in the sea.

All wind that rises must fall.

This had been the plan all along.

He is not as infallible as you might think.

They had known from the start.

This was my nightmare and Peter's long-awaited peace. His war, his time, had passed. His spirit had finally found freedom. No matter how it broke my heart.

I limped, my wings dragging across the ground as I took gasping breaths and stumbled over the battered land, searching for Tinkerbell and Peter. Any pirates had since fled, leaving only the carnage of the war behind.

Blood stained my dragging feathers. Mud matted them down. How could I even begin to care when golden ichor still stuck to my pants? A splash of orange coated with dust gleaming silver in the moonlight caught my eyes, and I swallowed, stopping where I was on the mangled battlefield. People and pixies surrounded him, sobs carrying on the still breeze.

Against his chest, I could just make out a tiny, unmoving form pressed to his unbeating heart. Not a single muscle twitched. I didn't need to check for breath to know Tinkerbell had joined him. I was alone.

Lifting my face to the sky, I bit back the tears pooling in my eyes. I was alone. Utterly alone. Abandoned in a way I couldn't fight. In one I couldn't reason with.

"Wind Song?" Bay's soft voice couldn't draw me from the grief, but I forced myself to find him. He stood several paces away, hesitating, clutching his left hand.

My brows furrowed, and my chest squeezed when I noticed the cloth clamped against his wrist. "W-hat?"

His gaze fell to the same place, and he winced. "I guess you missed that part. Needless to say, I don't think my father forgives me for lying to him."

"He cut off your...your hand?" I choked.

"Jealous that I had two, clearly."

I couldn't take it. Any of it. Wails poured out of my chest, and my wings wrapped around me, hiding me secure from the world. I didn't want anything to do with it anymore. This wasn't right. This wasn't right at all. This couldn't be how adventures ended. We had lost too much. So many people. Peter. *Peter.*

"Hey," Bay whispered, pushing through my fortification with little effort. He kept firm pressure on his wrist but bent to catch my gaze. It was too watery to make out much of anything past the concern in his eyes. "It's okay."

"Nothing's okay!" I spat, gasping air.

His lips parted, but he swallowed, thinking better of whatever he was going to say. "Okay..." he said at last. "Things aren't okay." He pressed his forehead against mine and closed his eyes. "I'm so, so sorry."

I wrapped my arms around him and fell apart. He murmured kind nonsense in my ear and stayed close, promising that's what he would always do. As long as I wanted him, he wouldn't go anywhere.

At that moment, what I wanted was out of reach.

The sun rose on a bleak day over a broken land. I clung to Bay's side as Tiger Lily bound his hand after having seared the wound closed. Her eyes were glassy with tears. Everyone's eyes were. Peter had simply always been there for all of us. Just as he was, eternally.

And now that constant, childish joy and comfort were gone.

The last of the Lost Boys were gone.

Tinkerbell was gone.

My home, gone.

I could do nothing but sit by Bay's makeshift bedside in one of the makeshift homes and curl my wings tight around myself so as not to take up too much room in the cramped space. Whisper sat beside me, similarly coiled, and despite her eternal curiosity, she hadn't

394

said a word about my wings since she'd found me on the field. Her fingers were locked around mine.

"It's a good thing, I'm right-handed." Bay examined his bandaged wrist, no humor touching his voice or expression.

Skye sat on his shoulder, mimicking the tone that had consumed all of Skyla. "Didn't look enough like your father before, I guess?"

"He looks nothing like his father." I crushed Whisper's hand in mine. "Not even a little bit."

Skye glanced at me, then lowered his gaze. "You're right. Sorry."

"I can't believe that bastard got away." Whisper released a pent-up breath. "He can't just get away with this."

"He won't." Bile stung in the back of my throat, making it impossible to swallow yet another lump forming there. "I still have to find my siblings and fix that."

Worry tinted Tiger Lily's gaze. "Great power like this can consume you; it is no different than how the Fountain's power fed on Peter all these years. If you let it take control, it will destroy who you are. You must be careful."

I knew that. I had already nearly fallen into the heady rush of this ability. I had nearly sucked a man's life from him, one cell at a time. No matter what Hook had done, that was cruel. That wasn't who I was, and I would never do it again, not like that.

"If you notice any complications, let me know." Tiger Lily smiled weakly, resting a hand on Bay's shoulder. "I wish we could have met again under brighter times, Bay."

"So do I." He dropped his gaze.

"Thank you for helping him," Skye murmured.

She nodded. "Of course."

My eyes widened briefly, but I wasn't even surprised she could understand the pixies. She had once been Neverland's princess. My heart twisted, and guilt soured the taste in my mouth. Tiger Lily had lived through so much worse than this. Her whole world had crumbled numerous times. And yet, she still found the strength to smile, to raise a child like Whisper, to foster a child like me.

Emotion choked me again, so I released Whisper's hand and stood. "Bay, can we go home? Please?"

His brows lowered with confusion.

"It's still there. In the sky even. I'm tired. I just want to go home, please." My lips trembled, and I couldn't hold back the tears that found their way down my cheeks.

Bay looked at Tiger Lily, standing beside me when she nodded. "Yeah, of course."

I hugged Whisper, who confirmed that she'd be with Adam in his fairytale house in the woods if I needed her. Then I flew beside Bay back up to the Skyla I knew, away from the Skyla that had water to lap its shores instead of air. We tucked ourselves into the woods, silently making our way to his treehouse, where this horrible adventure seemed to have begun in blissful moments of peace.

I held my arms around my waist, walking beside him and watching him float along like he hadn't just lost a hand. Skye dipped in and out of the trees. And for that moment, save for the bandage around his wrist, things were okay.

"Does it hurt?" I asked.

"Like a bitch." He smiled.

I found no strength to return the gesture.

Slowly but surely, his treehouse came into view, still nestled high in the bows of pixie oaks. My heart pinched when I saw it, and I stopped short in the miniature clearing. Bay darted for the balcony, landing at the rail and peering down at me. "Hello," he said. My stomach heated at the look in his eye. "To whom do I owe the pleasure of such a late and unexpected visit?"

My skin tingled, and my lips parted. Mouth dry, I answered, "The Daughter of Pan."

His hair glimmered gold in the afternoon light. Loose, it rested around his shoulders, kissing his cheeks in the sweet breeze. My wings took me to him, but I stopped in the air on the other side of his balcony and hovered there, unmoving.

He ran his gaze over me. "I suppose those are just decoration, huh, Wind Song?"

I squeezed my arm, where the feathers he'd tattooed lingered. "These had to come from somewhere."

"Guess they did." He pinned a stray strand of my orange hair behind my ear, brushing my cheek with his fingers. "I'm not sure why you're here. You know all my secrets now."

My head shook. "Not all of them."

"Really?" He searched the canopy. "Which one are you missing?"

It took me a second to remember. "What did the Fountain promise you if you drank from it?"

Surprise widened his hazel eyes. He rubbed his jaw. "Well, an eternity with you." His voice softened. "But I wasn't sure if you'd want that, and I wasn't willing to risk my rocky present with you on it. I'm...really sorry about what I did."

The world stilled around us. My heart ached to hold

him; my mind ached to forget the entire day. What if we could just be, for this moment, and ignore the ones that had led to it? "Stupid..." I whispered, fighting more tears. Moving forward, I kissed him, melting into the heat of his touch, the softness of his lips, and the warmth of the instant where nothing was wrong. If I could, I would have stayed there forever. But I couldn't. Tomorrow, I had to leave. Tomorrow, I'd set out on an adventure alone, an adventure I knew wouldn't be like the magical stories Peter had told me. Tomorrow, I'd remember adventures weren't always about meeting new friends and seeing new places.

But tonight... Tonight, Bay drew me into his home and called it mine. He curled up with me in his arms and talked like adventures were still wonderful. He murmured about pixies and flying and sirens with golden eyes. He pet my wings, a stupid smile on his face every time my breath held at his touch. He reminded me love hadn't vanished from my life.

We talked.

He helped me laugh, just enough.

And I, maybe a little bit right before falling asleep, believed I'd like to be a part of a future with him.

1ST DECEMBER

"I thought I might find you here." Bay's voice startled me, and I looked over my shoulder, parting my wings to see him past the dark feathers. He landed in the rubble, peering at the collapsed trees and neglected pixies' homes. Before me, almost intact, was the large pixie oak with the flattened space at the top. Memories lived in that space, and they hurt. So much.

"Whisper is nagging me about finding you and making sure you're properly packed. I think she's worried about you heading off on your own." He slid his gaze over my body and the cropped shirt displaying my back, allowing my wings freedom to move. He pursed his lips. "Now, I know you'll be fine, but I'm not thrilled you exist half-naked now. Who knows what exotic guys you'll meet out there?"

"More 'exotic' than someone from Neverland?" I asked.

He shrugged. "Technically native to Skyla."

Skye groaned on his shoulder, rolling his eyes. "If this is going to get flirty, I'm going to leave like I did last night."

My cheeks heated.

"Nothing happened last night," Bay protested, glaring at Skye.

"Ahuh." The pixie rolled his eyes.

"Her feathers were caught on her shirt. I had to be a gentleman and help!"

Skye snickered. "Which was so graceful with your little stub hand, I'm sure."

"Oh, absolutely." Bay looked at me, smiling when he saw my lips had curved up slightly. "What was I saying again?"

I met him, brushing a straying strand of hair over his ear. "Whisper's going to kill you."

"Right. Because she's worried. And I'm not." He rubbed his neck, and his smile faltered a bit as he dropped his gaze to the ground. "But are you?"

"A little."

"Because off the coast, it's going to be really cold, and your back is wide open to any sneaky cold fronts who want to weasel their way into somewhere they shouldn't be?" He quirked a serious brow, and I chuckled. It was a half-hearted laugh, but his eyes softened in response, none-the-less.

"I'm pretty sure I can manipulate the air around me and create a bubble of heat. Also, wings." They were a portable, fluffable blanket. As we'd found out last night.

His smile turned sly, as though he was remembering

400

the same thing. "Whisper is really going to kill me if we don't get moving."

I looked back at the distressed state of my former home and gripped my satchel. I had so little left of Peter now. Hook had stolen my knife, which I would get back soon, but aside from that, it was just memories and my pan flute. I slipped my fingers into my bag and touched the wooden instrument. "Tell her I'll be there in a moment."

"Okay." He lifted into the air, pausing before going too far. "I love you."

Tears pooled with those words. He'd said them to me so many times last night, but they never lost their force. Taking a deep breath, I whispered, "I love you, too."

Silently, he returned to the now-grounded Aire, and I drew out my pan flute.

The warm notes filled the breeze, and I let tears rush down my cheeks as I played homage to Peter Pan. His name would forever be legend. I would never forget him. With every passing generation, I would teach them all the things he had taught me. Belief is never weakness. Hope is never foolish. Love is never wrong.

Even if all such things could be twisted and tainted, faith and trust were gifts worth giving. In the right hands, and with the right magic, they would almost always let you fly.

"You're only bringing one change of clothes?" Whisper folded her arms and peered at me. "Are you only going to be gone for a day?"

"I can only hold one change in my bag. Besides, food is more important."

Adam stood beside Whisper, doing his best to remain behind her wrath. Worry coursed through her gaze, spinning in it like a hurricane. "You better not trust every stranger you meet."

"Yeah, I don't need another boyfriend."

Bay snickered, a giant moth perched on his finger. "I second that sentiment."

Whisper shot daggers at him. "You better be on your best behavior while she's gone. I still haven't decided whether or not I'm going to forgive you."

"Come now. I thought the plan was we'd have sass-castic babies together." He delivered the moth to a flower and drifted over to us lazily. "Is now a good time to tell you Tiger Lily invited me over for dinner? I'm going to be helping reconstruct Skyla, starting with your mom's house. I take atonement very seriously, and we really need to catch up." He was lying upside down in the air, grinning ear to ear.

"Skye, you may want to move. I'm about to punch the pixie dust off his smug little face." Whisper shook a fist.

Skye wordlessly bowed and flitted to my shoulder, gesturing for Whisper to proceed. Bay mumbled something about traitorous swine. My heart squeezed. I didn't want to leave this behind.

Taking a shaky breath, and remembering one final thing I had to take care of before I left, I reached into my bag and drew out the vial of Fountain water. It gleamed in the sunlight, and I bit my lip.

Everyone focused on it, but I faced Bay. "Here. For Wendy."

His brows furrowed, and he shook his head. "Keep it. I'll wait until you're back safe, then we can both greet my mom together. She's better than my dad." He drifted right side up, raised a hand, and crossed his heart with his wrist. "Promise."

"But..." I looked at the vial. "This is what you've been

searching for, for years."

"Yeah. Pretty great incentive for you to come back as quickly as you can after saving the world. I know there's a great big wonderful playground of adventures out there, but you're not allowed to forget to pick me up before going on them."

"The boy's got a point." Whisper folded her arms. "Even if we're going to be apart for a little bit, you aren't allowed to abandon me. We're going to have our adventures like we always planned."

"But it's all we'll ever have." I asked, "What if I lose it?"

Bay and Whisper both cupped a hand over the water. "Don't."

I glanced at Adam, who smiled and shrugged. "Sounds like solid advice, but I'm just the fourth wing in your little trio."

Skye coughed, loudly.

"A fifth wing, then." Whisper chuckled, kissing his cheek. Sighing, a touch of sadness polluted her smile. She raised a pinky. "I'm going to miss you."

"I'll be back soon." *I hoped.* Linking my finger with hers, I exhaled. Her forehead met mine, and I whispered, "Even now, we will never be apart." Not in spirit. Not ever.

She smiled, but her voice wobbled with emotion. "I'll be right here when you get back."

When we finally pulled apart, Bay asked, "May I fly you to the shore?"

Nodding, I hugged Whisper goodbye and set out with Bay across the sky, toward The Vale's borders; they seemed so much closer now.

"Are you sure you don't want the Fountain water for your mom now?" I asked when we had gone a little ways. "I trust you with it."

"I know. Thank you." He lifted his bandaged wrist and pressed his lips together. "But I still feel like I need to fix things. Tiger Lily was okay in the end, but that doesn't change what I did, the chance I took. I'm going to make sure Skyla's rebuild has at least a dent in it while you're gone. I'm going to make sure Tiger Lily is taken care of, and her daughter knows I'm sorry. Then, when you're back, and I feel I can stand before my mom as a son she can be proud of, I'll wake her with you."

My chest swelled, and I reached for his hand. "Have I told you that I've forgiven you yet? Everything was okay in the end, and you came through in the moments when it mattered the most."

He squeezed my fingers. "You forgive too easily, Wind Song, just like my mom. I'm not going to put my sins behind me as easily as my dad did. I want to be better than him for you."

Airwoman, I loved him. I stopped in the sky and pulled him closer to me, wrapping my wings around his body. Skye zipped out of the cocoon the second before I kissed Bay. "I'm glad you fell out of the sky for me, Star Boy," I murmured against his lips.

He circled his arms around me, not hiding his injury like his father always had a habit of doing. They both knew where they had lost their hands. One deserved the burden of shame and guilt; the other didn't have that weight to bear. He whispered, "Come back to me safely, Wind Song."

We parted ways after that, my heart full and beating soundly with a mix of anxiety and faith. I could handle anything that stood in my way if I knew it stood between me and getting back to Bay and Whisper, Skye and Tiger Lily, Skyla and Neverland.

I perhaps wasn't prepared for the group of people I saw on The Vale's beach shortly after I left the air above Skyla. They were all around my age, and—worse—magic clung to them so strongly I could feel it like a magnet, tugging me their way.

One of the girls, a dark-haired woman with striking blue eyes, pointed at me, waving me down. I tucked my wings and landed a short distance from them.

Neither of us needed to ask who the other was even though none of us looked particularly alike. A ring of gold circled all of our irises. My breath held, and I didn't know where to begin. All I knew was that this was the beginning......of the end.

MEET THE TEAM

The Kingdom of Fairytales Series was a team effort.
Below are the people that made it possible:

EQP Management: Rhi Parkes & J.A. Armitage

Our authors: J.A. Armitage, Audrey Rich, B. Kristin
McMichael, Emma Savant, Jennifer Ellision, Scarlett
Kol, Rose Castro, Margo Ryerkerk, Zara Quentin,
Laura Greenwood and Anne Stryker.

Our Editor
Rose Lipscomb

Our Beta Team
Nadine Peterse-Vrijhof
Diane Major
Kalli Bunch
Stephanie Woodwood

Our Proof Reader
Tina Merritt

And to all the wonderful people who loved the world
we created and reviewed our stories.
Thank you

READING ORDER

SEASON THIRTEEN
URBIS
Kingdom of Royalty
Kingdom of Power
Kingdom of Fairytales
Kingdom of Ever After

BOXSETS
AZIA
BLAISE
CASTIEL
DEON
ELIANA
FALLON
GAIA
HALIA
IVY
JAKON
KELIS
LYRIC
URBIS

Printed in the USA
CPSIA information can be obtained
at www.ICGtesting.com
LVHW041025191123
764352LV00032B/240/J